LIGHT

OF

THE

FIRE

LIGHT
OF
THE
FIRE

A NOVEL

SARAHLYN BRUCK

Text copyright © 2024 by Sarahlyn Bruck
All rights reserved.

Published by Lake Union Publishing, Seattle

www.apub.com

Amazon, the Amazon logo, and Lake Union Publishing are trademarks of Amazon.com, Inc., or its affiliates.

ISBN-13: 9781662513299 (paperback)
ISBN-13: 9781662513305 (digital)

Cover design by Adrienne Krogh
Cover image: © Shelley A Richmond / ArcAngel; © NewAge03,
© Photography-by-Stretch, © Roxana Bashyrova / Shutterstock

Printed in the United States of America

To Virginia: You are my nutmeg, my step-over, my fake-out, my rainbow, and I am forever awed and inspired by you. Love you, kid.

PROLOGUE

Fillmore High School, Twenty Years Ago

The first explosion caught them both by surprise. The girls' nervous giggles had masked the warning that hissed from behind the last row of lockers as they bolted out of the boys' locker room and toward the gym.

The boom reverberated from the adjacent locker room and blasted through the open double doors, sending the girls tumbling onto the polished wooden floor of the gym.

Dazed, Beth found herself lying on her side, her head spinning. She pushed her long hair from her face and tried to get her bearings. Just a few feet away, Ally rose slowly and propped herself up on her elbow. She swatted at Beth, mouthing something. Beth grimaced and shook her head. Her ears were screaming; she couldn't hear a word Ally was trying to say.

Ally glanced back at the gaping doors, and Beth followed her gaze. A sudden orange glow burned from deep within the locker room, followed by another, smaller blast, which blew heat and black smoke through the doorway. Ally ducked. Her eyes watered, and she pulled the neck of her sweatshirt up to shield her nose and mouth. Beth felt like she was trapped in a ringing bubble of hurt. Sweat trickled down her back as she gingerly rose to her knees. Suddenly, the immediate danger they were in dawned on both of them. The girls' eyes met, and together, they understood one thing—they must get outside before the entire structure burned to the ground.

Run.

Ally grabbed her backpack as they scrambled to their feet and sprinted toward the nearest exit. When they reached the door, Beth turned her head. Flames had reached the gym and wholly consumed the janitor's closet—no doubt aided by the cocktail of cleaning chemicals stored in there—and now were eating away the eighty-year-old wood floor, licking up the art deco windows, and approaching the New Deal–era mural that spanned the entire north wall. Nearly a century of school sporting events, dances, graduations, assemblies, and rallies erased by one prank by two stupid teenage girls.

Ally yanked Beth through the exterior doorway to the athletic field, where a rush of cool nighttime air hit their faces. Beth's ears crackled to life again, the high-pitched ringing now relegated to background—but still present—noise.

Coughing and sputtering, the girls reached the track and football field and looked behind them at the burning structure. Beth watched in horror as the flames consumed the building. Heat pierced the crisp fall air, warming her face even from this distance. The wails of sirens from afar got louder as they closed in and mirrored her own rising panic. Bedroom lights flickered on in the surrounding neighborhood. The girls shared a knowing glance: they needed to get out of there. Tears wet Beth's cheeks as she and Ally disappeared into the darkness.

PART I: SPRING 2019

CHAPTER 1

BETH

Beth stirred. She felt an urge to run, to get away, but her limbs wouldn't listen. A heavy dread pinned her body down, forcing her back into a past she only wanted to escape.

Wait. She *had* escaped. Twenty years ago.

Beth forced her eyes open, but they refused to focus. It was no longer dark—in fact, the bright light made it impossible for her to see—and the sirens were closer now. Her heart started to pound.

A figure loomed over her.

"Look who's awake," a male voice said. "Just relax. You got a bump on the head."

Beth at once realized the sirens weren't coming from arriving fire trucks, but from the ambulance she was riding in. The light went out again.

A nurse at the hospital would later tell her she'd looked around, seemed to register where she was, and burst into tears.

Beth was glad her memory of that initial awakening was too foggy because even in that semiconscious moment, stuck in some fuzzy time warp, she must have known on some level what this trip to the hospital meant. In the coming days—weeks?—she could expect the return of pounding headaches, the inability to look at a screen or read a book for any amount of time, maybe a decrease in focus. Beth had returned to where she was a year ago—off the starting roster and back on the injured list with weeks, if not months, of rehab ahead of her.

So when her eyes fluttered open for a second time at the hospital, it was almost as though she knew where she was already. The familiar firmness of the mattress, scratchy sheets, thin blanket, beeping monitors, and odor of antiseptic combined with urine and warmed-over cafeteria food all clued her in before she opened her eyes.

She looked to her right—at least she was propped up and her bed located near a window. The sun was starting its dip toward the horizon, and all she could see outside were the long shadows of the light poles that lined the top floor of the parking garage below. How long had she been out?

A woman in teal scrubs walked in and smiled at her as Beth shifted her focus from the window.

"I see you're up again." She walked over to a computer station mounted on the wall and moved the mouse to awaken the monitor. She glanced over at Beth. "You must be thirsty. Let's get you some water and go from there, OK? I know the doctor is anxious to talk with you about your concussion."

Up, again? *Concussion?* Beth ran her tongue along the roof of her mouth. She was, indeed, thirsty.

The nurse filled a tiny plastic cup with water at the sink and set it on the tray attached to the hospital bed. Beth grasped the cup and drank the water in two swallows. She cleared her throat.

"You had quite a wallop to the head," the nurse said, approaching the left side of the bed. "Can you please face the window?"

Beth turned her head again, and the nurse lightly touched her temple with the tips of her fingers. Beth winced.

"It's going to be black and blue for a while. Swollen too." She shook her head and removed her hand. "No wonder they brought you in here."

Beth touched her temple. A raised bump the size of half a golf ball stretched the skin. She wiggled her toes under the sheet. Other than that bump, though, she felt fine. Maybe a bit slow. Foggy. She needed to move. Show this woman just how fine she was.

Beth swung her legs over the side of the bed. She could get her own water.

The nurse stopped her. "Uh, where do you think you're going?"

Beth raised her cup. "I'm still thirsty."

"Of course," the nurse said, taking the cup. "I'll get it for you. You're not going anywhere until you've been seen by the doctor. And you've got a lot of pain medication running through your system. I don't want you knocking yourself out again."

As she rested against the pillows, a familiar wave of helpless frustration filled Beth's chest. She couldn't believe she was back in a hospital bed, with another concussion, being treated like a baby—starting over, when she'd worked her butt off to get back on that field. She wasn't a baby. She was a warrior.

The nurse refilled her cup and set it on the tray. Beth gulped the water down.

"Just go slowly," the nurse said. "You don't want it coming back up."

All of a sudden, Beth realized how parched she was, like she could drink an entire gallon of water if the nurse let her. Which she wouldn't. When she placed the cup back onto the tray, she noticed her phone and picked it up.

She clicked on the screen. April 5, 4:22 p.m.

Four hours ago, she'd been having another pretty remarkable early-season comeback game. Planning her triumphant season and return to the national soccer stage. And now she was alone in a hospital, beat up with yet another concussion.

Beth pressed the home button on her phone and saw she'd missed twenty-seven phone calls. *Twenty-seven?*

She clicked to check who'd called. With her seasonal soccer schedule and the likelihood of having to relocate at a moment's notice, Beth didn't have many close friends outside the professional sports world. No boyfriend. But she wouldn't have been surprised if her coach or her assistant or even a couple of her teammates had reached out. Or her dad.

Oh my God, Dad. Beth saw he'd called eight times in rapid succession, in the span of two minutes during game time. Then he called ten minutes later. And after that, he tried again. And then it'd been on and off for the last three-plus hours. What the hell was she going to tell him?

At that moment, the doctor walked in. He was short and slender, with a smooth light-brown complexion and a thick shock of iron-gray hair that didn't match his youthful appearance. He offered Beth his hand.

"My name is Dr. Bakir, and I'm a neurotrauma specialist. I've already had a conversation with your coach. I understand you were seen by Dr. Kate O'Callahan down at the University of Chicago for your previous injury? She's excellent. She's sending over your file and films." He bent toward the computer monitor and took out a pair of reading glasses to study her chart on the screen. Beth thought the combination of his hair and the glasses made him look like a youth playing dress-up as "wizened elder."

"What did Michelle say?" It irked Beth that her coach had spoken with the doctor before she could. Always meddling. This was *her* head, not her coach's. Beth must have been completely out of it. After her second concussion, she'd been so confused, she couldn't hold a conversation for a full twenty-four hours. Even now, that whole period was a blur.

Dr. Bakir took off his glasses and peered at her. His eyes were kind. She braced for news she didn't want to hear. "Your coach mentioned you'd just recovered after a bad hit—about a year, year and a half ago?"

Beth nodded. "It was my first month back." Tears stung her eyes, which she had not expected. She dabbed them with the sleeve of her uniform shirt, noticing for the first time she was still wearing her grass-stained goalie jersey, padded shorts, and socks.

Way to rub it in, universe.

"I'm going to order an MRI to rule out a contusion. But due to your history and the length of recovery time from your previous injury—" Dr. Bakir took a seat on the wheeled stool beside the bed. His head was almost parallel with Beth's. "You're not going to like this."

Beth's stomach dropped. "What?"

"I'm recommending you retire permanently from playing soccer."

Her heart shrank to the size of a pea.

Beth shook her head. Not possible. She still had years to play. There were too many things left to achieve. She hadn't made it onto the cover of *Sports Illustrated* or had the chance to attend the ESPYs. She'd planned on being the starting goalkeeper for the US Women's National Team—*would* be, if she could just get the tryout—for the next World Cup, like she had for the last one. Sure, all these were long shots, but still. She wasn't even forty yet. He wasn't allowed to tell her when it was over. Only she could do that.

Beth looked up at the nurse for support, but she wasn't even paying attention. She was reading monitors and typing notes into Beth's chart.

"Please . . . don't." She desperately searched her foggy brain for the words to stop this man from forcing her into early retirement. "I can come back. I've done it before. I'll come back stronger than ever. I just need time."

Dr. Bakir's kind eyes were now tinged with pity, which made her feel even worse.

"Beth," he said, his voice soothing, "this has nothing to do with your fitness or determination or work ethic, OK? There's no question that you've contributed enormously as an athlete and teammate. But, as a medical professional, I cannot condone your return to the field, even after a complete recovery. Any high-impact sport is simply too dangerous. You've had three concussions, two very serious ones in a short window of time. I know I don't need to tell you that repetitive head injuries put you at risk for permanent brain damage, erratic emotional symptoms, memory loss, and CTE. Not to mention you're at a greater risk for another concussion."

It was almost a carbon copy of the speech Dr. O'Callahan had given her just over a year ago, except she'd reluctantly allowed Beth to return. As long as she was careful. As long as she didn't take any big risks.

"But I'm not done." Tears were streaming down Beth's face now. "You can't tell me what to do," she said, her chin quivering.

"I'm sorry, but this is nonnegotiable. You are free to see another physician for a second opinion. In fact, I highly recommend it." Dr. Bakir stood. "But this is what I'm recommending to your coach. I'm so sorry, Beth."

When the doctor and nurse had cleared the room, Beth stared out the window.

She knew the hospital would release her the following day as long as she didn't pass out or throw up or give them the wrong answer to questions such as "Who is the current president?" and "What day of the week is it?"

And then what? She closed her eyes and sank back into her pillow. The league would have to take Dr. Bakir's advice seriously. What message would it send if they allowed her back on the field? Beth knew then that once her contract was up in October, that was it. No more professional soccer for her. Not in the US, anyway.

Her phone buzzed. Dad again. She longed to hear his voice, to feel assured she wasn't alone. And he needed to hear hers, to know that she was OK. That she was going to be just fine. He didn't need to learn about the concussion, the forced retirement. Not yet. She couldn't bear that now. That was a conversation for another time.

She wiped her eyes and straightened up as much as she could. She clicked to answer the call, bracing herself for the questions she knew he'd ask that she didn't have the courage to answer.

"Hey, Dad."

CHAPTER 2

ALLY

The white plastic stick appeared harmless, innocent. No bigger or heavier than an oral thermometer or a retractable ballpoint pen. It couldn't do any real damage, right? But in just a few minutes, it would hold enough power to shape Allison Katz's future. It was a fortune teller. *Her* fortune teller.

Ally rested the stick on top of a tissue on the bathroom sink, a few inches away from the chipped "#1 Soccer Mom" mug that served as her and Noah's toothbrush holder. She lowered herself onto the edge of the tub and started the timer on her running watch. In five minutes she would know if the cramping, sore breasts, exhaustion—and oh yeah, going almost two months with no period—meant something.

Ally hoped not. She and Noah hadn't even been dating a year, only since late last May, at the end of the school year. They'd always been careful, using condoms at first; and after he'd moved in three months ago and things had started looking more permanent, she'd decided to go back on the pill.

Maybe she hadn't yet acclimated to the regular dose of hormones. Maybe she hadn't quite gotten into the habit of taking a pill at the same time every morning and had skipped a day here and there. Maybe, at thirty-seven, her body had decided this was her last shot at another baby.

Ally shook her head. She already had two kids. Two *teenagers*. Why would her body betray her like this? She didn't need a baby. Both her girls would be out of the house and off to college within four years. She loved them more than anything, but she was ready for the next phase. Empty nest. Home free.

She scowled at the stick, which lay passively on the Kleenex, then rose from the tub to get a peek at the results window. Nothing. One minute had ticked by. Four left. She sat back down and folded her arms tight across her chest.

She'd worked too hard to return to the days of diapers and spit-up and sleepless nights. It was like stepping backward to her twenty-year-old self, the clueless girl who'd allowed herself to quit everything that meant something—soccer, college, Beth. Her future. All for what? She'd been so desperate to distance herself from her old self that she'd hitched herself to Rob Katz—God, they were young—and a ready-made fantasy of playing house. She'd learned real quick that when you had a baby, you had no time for fantasies. There was no "playing" house. After Morgan was born, she and Rob soon discovered neither one of them was who they'd been in college. And now Rob lived across town with Jules, his new wife, and their toddler—Morgan and Emily's half brother.

Ally couldn't afford another child. And it wasn't all about the money. She didn't have the time to breastfeed and change diapers and stay up half the night soothing. Maybe more, she didn't have the *will* to do this all over again, make more sacrifices than she'd already made.

She felt a little stupid for not having had the "kid talk" with Noah to find out his stance on more children. But wasn't it obvious? She had two teenagers. She was done. And Noah had managed to make it to his early forties without reproducing, so why would he want to start a family now? Plus, he'd always said he thought of his students like his kids. They filled that void—if there was a void. All signs pointed to no kids.

Well.

Ally heard the sound of the front door opening and slamming shut. A pair of legs bounded up the stairs.

"Mom?"

Emily.

"I'm in the bathroom," Ally called. Her voice echoed in the tiled space, sounding louder than she'd intended. School must have let out already. She looked at her watch, which still had two minutes counting down. She regretted leaving her phone downstairs on the kitchen table. Now she couldn't even pass the time scrolling through Instagram or *Inquirer* articles.

Footsteps neared the bathroom door and then paused. Ally almost expected her daughter to just let herself in like she had when she was little, when there was no such thing as privacy. A closed bathroom door meant absolutely nothing to a four-year-old. Or, apparently, to a fourteen-year-old who could still interrupt, even if she no longer barged in.

"What are you doing?" Emily said through the door.

Ally frowned. *About to find out if you're going to be a big sister when you start your sophomore year.*

"What do you think I'm doing?"

Pause.

"I need a ride."

Ally pressed her forehead to her hands. "Can we please talk about this in a minute?"

"Heather's waiting for me downtown. How much longer are you going to be in there?"

Ally could tell her precisely how much longer she was "going to be in there."

"Emily, I will talk to you when I get out," she said, her voice clipped. "Please wait for me downstairs or in your room or just somewhere else." She glanced at the mug. Not exactly a "#1 Mom" kind of tone. A pang of guilt reverberated through her, but sometimes talking with Emily *was* like dealing with a four-year-old.

A heavy sigh emanated from the other side of the door, and footsteps receded down the hall.

Did she really want to put herself through eighteen more years of this? She'd given up college, her youth, her twenties—willingly, happily for sure, but God, did she look forward to leaving behind this life of constant sacrifice. She'd miss the girls desperately when they moved out, but she knew she'd be ready for the empty-nest phase. After all, putting things behind her was what she did best.

Her watch buzzed. Five minutes had passed. She got up from the tub, feeling woozy as she went to the sink.

In the span of minutes, two fuchsia lines had appeared on the results strip.

Ally checked the box and then the test. Maybe she was just seeing double.

Or maybe she was pregnant.

CHAPTER 3

JORDAN

Jordan Miller leaned the headboard of his father's bed frame against the far wall of the bedroom and congratulated himself for having the foresight to tape the baggie with the bed's hardware to the back of the cheap particleboard—otherwise he would have wasted the entire afternoon searching for these tiny necessities. He mopped his brow with a bandanna and stuffed it into his back pocket.

Other than the bed, the mattress, and a battered chest of drawers, the room was bare. His father could have easily moved into one of Springtime Center's furnished rooms—and Jordan could have donated or dumped much of this stuff and been done with it—but the nurse in the dementia unit said having familiar things around him would help ease the transition to the facility and make it less unsettling.

Frightening, Jordan had thought at the time, just one week ago. "Unsettling" was such an understatement for patients suffering from early-onset Alzheimer's.

Oleks, the sole owner and operator of Buddy with a Truck Moving Company, walked in, a small bookcase in one of his meaty hands.

"Where do you want this?" he said. He hadn't even broken a sweat.

Jordan gestured toward an open wall. "There's fine."

He set the bookcase down and wiped his hands on his jeans. "The kitchen and living room are just about done," he said. "And the other bedroom?"

"He's getting a roommate," Jordan said. "We can leave it alone."

Oleks fixed his eyes on the bed frame. "I can set that up for you before I head out."

Jordan nodded in response and carried a box labeled "Books" over to the bookcase, where he ripped off the tape.

He could have completed this move by himself. His sister, Tara, busy with a toddler and pregnant with her second kid, didn't need to make the three-and-a-half-hour drive from Connecticut to pack boxes for a father she no longer knew and no longer had the desire to know. And Jordan wouldn't have needed to hire help if he'd allowed more time.

But he'd wanted to get this over with as soon as possible—one day to pack and move the stuff. He didn't want to give the dingy studio apartment his dad had been living in for the last fifteen years the chance to permanently imprint into his brain. Didn't want to know the details of the life his father had led since abandoning his family and sinking back into addiction.

Though he'd learned his dad had pulled himself out of it—returned to meetings and had been working the night shift cleaning at a warehouse distribution center in Trenton for the last five years. His dad's sponsor had shared this with Jordan a little over a week ago, which was little more than he'd heard about his father in almost twenty years. He'd tracked Jordan down and reached him through his office phone at the *Baltimore Sun*, where he worked as a reporter.

Jordan's attitude toward his father had thawed a little further just that morning when he was packing up his meager belongings in the little apartment and spied the old framed Sears photograph propped up on the windowsill beside his dad's reading chair. Jordan picked up the photo and gazed at his family's frozen smiles.

His parents and he and his younger sister—just ten and seven years old at the time—had all dressed in their church clothes on a Saturday morning to take a family photo at the Sears studio in Moorestown, where his mom was able to use her employee discount. It was the only formal photo of the four of them together. The photographer had arranged his dad, sister, and him around their mom, who was seated on a wooden stool in the center in front of a cloudy taupe backdrop.

Jordan remembered feeling hot in his sweater-vest, standing behind his beaming mother and fighting to stay "still like a statue," as the photographer had directed, his hand resting stiffly on his mom's right shoulder. Tara was to her left and his dad stood behind her. Once satisfied with the arrangement, the photographer adjusted the lighting and snapped seemingly dozens of photos. Before Jordan's growing impatience could get him into trouble, the whole thing was over and, until now, forgotten about. Now here it all was, right down to them filing out of the studio and celebrating with Tex-Mex combo plates at the Chi-Chi's near where they'd parked the car in the mall's lot.

Peering into the smiling faces of the early 1990s version of his family, Jordan thought that might have been the start of the happiest streak they'd had together. His dad had quit drinking six months before, and soon after, he'd landed a full-time job as a custodian at the high school, a steady position with decent pay and good benefits. They'd found a three-bedroom twin just on the outskirts of downtown Fillmore, where he finally didn't have to share a bedroom with his sister. His mom didn't have to work as many hours, so she was home when he and Tara returned from school every day and could help them with homework. In another life, his mom would have made a great teacher. And they'd started eating dinner together as a family. They were finally getting by.

Jordan's heart ached seeing that smiling, sober version of his dad. Ached, then flashed into anger at the thought of his betrayal of them all those years later, during Jordan's senior year of high school, when the world collapsed around him after the fire. His father had messed up, but

17

instead of leaning into his family, he splintered it. Chose drinking over a stable life. Chose the bottle over his wife, daughter, and son. Again.

So it wasn't hard for Jordan to reject his father after he got sober fifteen years later—for good this time, his father said—and plodded through those twelve steps all over again. But here was the catch: Jordan didn't have to accept his apology. By then he was a bona fide adult and could make his own choices. He was still too raw. There were no "amends" for destroying one's family. For leaving when your daughter is still in high school and your son just starting college, figuring out what it is to be a man in the world. The only thing that felt good in that moment was ripping up his dad's pathetic letter into tiny pieces and throwing them into the garbage.

And now he had to find out his father had kept that photo. Not only had he kept it, but he'd *displayed* it someplace he could see it every day. Jordan's heart ached thinking about why he'd do that to himself. The picture served as a constant reminder of what he once had. Of what he'd lost. Of what he'd run from. And, it turned out, what he'd missed. Maybe. Was it some sad need to hang on to something he'd thrown away so long ago? Or was it a genuine sense of connection he'd never let go of?

Jordan had wrapped the photo in newspaper and placed it into a box. A weight settled into his chest, and for the first time, he wondered what else he could have gotten wrong about his father.

And in the course of just a few hours, the Trenton apartment stood empty and Oleks had trucked all his father's belongings to the dementia wing of the Springtime Center Senior Community in Fillmore. Jordan glanced at his phone. Soon, his dad would be heading back for a rest before dinner. The staff had kept him busy for the bulk of the day so Jordan and the mover could set up the space.

While Oleks assembled the bed, Jordan opened the box. The framed photo sat right on top of a couple dozen paperbacks. He took it out and shook his head. There was no escaping it. He placed it on top of the bookcase and unloaded the books to the shelves. Oleks heaved the mattress on top of the box spring.

They were almost done. Jordan knew he would spend the next hour or so hanging his father's clothes in the closet and stacking plates and cups in the kitchen cupboards, but this was it. After twenty years, his dad was back. Back in his life. Back in Fillmore, where he'd spent many of his happiest years.

Well, until the fire.

Oleks walked over, and Jordan placed his hand on his back pocket, checking to make sure the wad of twenties was still there.

"Is that your family?" Oleks gestured to the photo propped on the bookcase.

Jordan nodded. That family seemed entirely removed from him now.

Oleks leaned in to take a closer look. He pointed to Jordan's dad. "That's your father?"

Jordan nodded again. "He should be returning any minute. Sorry it's taken so long." He reached for the cash in his pocket. "I hope this will more than cover the day."

Oleks ignored him, scrutinizing the picture. "I know him."

Jordan frowned. "I don't think so. He hasn't lived here in twenty years."

"Yes, I know him," Oleks insisted, tapping the glass. "He was accused of the gym fire at the high school, yes?"

Jordan blinked, not sure he'd heard him right.

"He was the janitor. I remember."

Jordan took a closer look at his mover. He was burly and appeared to be in his midforties, a few inches shorter than Jordan, but compact and strong. He looked like an ex-athlete with a few years and a couple of extra pounds on him.

Jordan reconsidered whether agreeing to move his dad back to Fillmore was such a good idea.

Oleks shrugged. "I've lived in Fillmore for most of my life. Everybody remembers the fire." He scratched his chin. "But I remember him from before too. I went to Fillmore High. Class of '94." He smiled at the memory. "I got in so much trouble back then, and for detention each afternoon, my punishment was picking up trash. I got to know your dad a little bit. He was a good guy. So patient with me. I hated school but didn't mind those afternoons." Oleks shook his head. "But that fire, man. The town didn't waste any time throwing the book at him."

Jordan's throat felt thick. Suddenly, he wanted nothing more than for this guy to take his nostalgia for his father and go. Jordan thrust over the lump of bills.

"Thank you for your time," he said stiffly.

Oleks pocketed the cash and peered intently at Jordan.

"I never thought your father got a fair shake, is what I'm saying," he said. "The whole thing was rushed. And your poor dad, I remember the pictures in the local paper of him at the hearing. Of course he took responsibility for that fire—he was a good man, and what choice did he have?"

Jordan remembered. Neither his dad nor his public defender had put up much of a fight. To Jordan, giving up like that was equivalent to admitting his guilt. Jordan, along with everyone else in town, turned his back on him after that disaster of a trial.

"But the thing is, the city never figured out what started the fire," Oleks said. "Your dad took the blame, which was good enough for them. And that allowed the entire town just to move on. Except him."

It was true. At the time, his dad had jury-rigged the gas line's automatic turnoff to the gym to regulate the temperature of the locker rooms. He had no idea that this "fix" would provide the perfect environment for a violent explosion. And of course the investigation easily uncovered the fact that his father had lied on his job application. He wasn't certified to be fooling with any of the HVAC equipment. So his father shouldered the burden of that fire alone and pleaded guilty to criminal negligence.

But no one knew what sparked it. It could have been anything.

Oleks offered Jordan a sad smile.

"I hope your dad finds peace here."

To his own surprise, Jordan did too. He hoped his dad could let go of his past.

But after the mover left, Jordan couldn't help but think—what if he was right? What if there was more to the story about that fire than what the town had reported?

CHAPTER 4

ALLY

Ally could keep a secret. She and Beth had done it for almost twenty years. But it took energy to claim it wasn't inside her, that it wasn't still some small part of her. For the most part, she could believe she was a different person than she'd been back in high school.

She *was* a different person. And secrets had no place in her life right now.

So Ally decided she needed to tell Noah about this pregnancy right away. The sooner the better. Get it out in the open so she wouldn't have to be alone, harboring this dark slice of information by herself. Part of what made it easier this time was her certainty that his reaction would match her own and they could move forward. Together. Still, her stomach fluttered in anticipation.

After Emily had retreated to her room, Ally placed the pregnancy test and box back into the paper bag, submerged it deep into the bathroom trash, and then took the trash bag to the containers outside. She then walked back into the house and asked Emily if she was ready to be dropped off in town. A perfect excuse to get out of the house and reach Noah as soon as she could.

When Ally pulled into the visitor's spot at the high school lot after delivering Emily, she put her car in park and took a moment to collect her thoughts. After all these years, this school still made her armpits damp. And it wasn't just because of the fire. It was those three boys. Still.

She hated herself a little bit for letting her memories of them get to her even now, all these years later. She could still hear their taunts, and her face burned at the memory of them passing around doctored pictures of her and Beth superimposed on lewd images to the entire school their junior year. She could still feel the gut punch on game days when the boys did everything they could to make Beth and Ally—the only girls on the boys' team—look bad on the field, like they didn't belong. The simple act of showing up to school every day not knowing what lay ahead often felt like a monumental act of nerve. When she and Beth would complain to the coach, they were met with some version of gaslighting. *Boys will be boys. Just joking around. Don't take it personally. Tough it out.*

Back in high school, Beth had claimed the bullying fueled her, made her more determined to win, to crush them. Not Ally, though she tried not to let on. Inside she found it crush*ing*. Little had she and Beth known what lay in store for them.

Ally took three slow, calming breaths and checked her reflection in the rearview mirror. A slightly clammy sheen colored her face, and pink had risen to her cheeks. How quickly her anxiety could make its unwelcome return. She steeled herself—remembering she was no longer that insecure teenager, but a grown-up with a mission—and then opened the car door and let herself out.

The parking lot was empty except for one other vehicle parked in the spot marked "Reserved for FHS Principal." Noah usually stayed an hour or two after the final bell to catch up on phone calls and emails at the end of the day. Judy, the secretary, would have gone home, and the school was mostly a ghost town, save for a few kids staying behind for sports or clubs or detention. At least she could count on the quiet and privacy of Noah's office.

She knew it would be the only place where they could talk alone, without intrusion. As anxious as she was to share the news of her pregnancy with him, she didn't see any reason to let anyone else in on what could be a little blip in their lives. No way was she going to tell Morgan and Emily that she was one or two months pregnant, especially if there was a very real possibility—no, probability—she was going to end it. They'd just gotten accustomed to having another person around in the house—Noah had moved in over the winter holiday break—so presenting this development to the girls seemed like courting possible opinions she didn't want or need. Or more likely, the girls would fail to keep quiet about it and word would spread all over school and their small town. No, a short-lived pregnancy was no one's business but hers and Noah's.

Ally was certain she and Noah would agree—now was not the time to bring a baby into the world. Still, as she let herself into the school building, she'd replaced her teenage angst with adult jitters. Ally's heartbeat quickened, and sweat formed around her hairline.

She rapped on the doorframe of Noah's office. The office was lit by a single desk lamp, and Noah sat in front of his computer monitor, with his head resting in his palm, earbuds in his ears, scowling at the screen. He looked up. His face broke into a grin when he saw her, and he plucked out the AirPods.

"Hey, kid," he said, straightening in his chair. "To what do I owe this pleasure?"

Ally smiled at the slight formality, a bit of a throwback to when she was merely a parent of a teenager and he a history teacher holding conferences to discuss Morgan's progress. How quickly things had changed. In the past year, Noah had been promoted to both principal and live-in boyfriend.

But now was not the time to flirt. Or talk him into treating her to happy hour at Zeke's before heading home for the night.

She sat in the chair across from his desk, a chair typically reserved for students who were in the hot seat. All of a sudden, Ally realized *she* was in the hot seat. Her pulse spiked.

Noah's grin faded, and he tipped his head. He looked concerned. "You OK? You look a little . . . pale."

Ally gripped the arms of her chair and gave a shaky laugh. "I'm fine. I just wanted to talk, that's all."

"OK, you had me worried," he said, leaning back. "I was just about ready to close up shop. What's up?"

She looked down at her knees, noticing for the first time that one was bouncing. She placed her hand on it and looked up at Noah.

"I'm pregnant."

Confusion clouded his face. "What?"

"I know. I can't believe it either," she said, careful to keep her voice controlled.

"This is wild." He dragged his hand down his cheek. "You're pregnant? But you're on the pill."

"I'm in complete shock too." Ally's shoulders relaxed a little, relieved. They were together on this. "But I missed my period and took one of those home pregnancy tests, and it came back positive." She shook her head. "I just . . . I didn't want to put off telling you."

Noah rose from his chair and walked around his desk. He grasped both of Ally's hands and gently lifted her from the chair. He embraced her.

As Noah closed his arms around her, Ally blinked, not sure how to process this.

"You have made me the happiest person on the planet." His voice cracked.

Tears of Noah's joy dampened the shoulder of her shirt.

He's happy?

She hadn't thought he'd be angry. Hadn't thought he'd blame her for not being as consistent with the pill as she was supposed to be, especially those first couple of months. But *happy*?

Ally gently pulled away from Noah's embrace. He wiped his eyes, but he continued to radiate joy.

She sighed. "I didn't think you'd be happy about this news."

He laughed. "How could I not be? Sure, it's unexpected, but I'm thrilled."

"What?" Ally's eyebrows pressed together. "How did I not know this about you?"

"Well, we haven't really talked about it yet. I mean, we haven't been together that long." He laughed again. "But honestly, I guess I didn't know I wanted a kid of my own until just this moment. If you had asked me yesterday whether I wanted to have kids, I would have said I'm OK not being a dad. I'm forty-two—not exactly over the hill, but not a kid either. I've had a few long-term relationships that didn't pan out." He touched Ally's cheek. "When I found you, I was just happy we clicked. I've been staggering around feeling so incredibly lucky, you know?"

Ally nodded. She did know. She felt like she'd won the lottery with Noah.

"And now, this. It's like icing. Incredible icing." He shook his head, grinning. "'Icing' isn't right. This baby is a happy, wonderful accident, and I trust happy accidents. I've always been pretty 'go with the flow.' I welcome change and think we'd make a great team raising this baby."

The idea of bringing up a child with Noah seemed so foreign to Ally, so far from the future she had envisioned with him, that she couldn't even picture it. Her brain couldn't move on from enticing visions of sleeping in on Saturdays, late dinners for two, and nonchaotic weekday mornings.

"It's early," Ally said. "Anything can happen."

Noah lowered his chin. "I do know that. And whatever happens, happens."

"Let's—" Ally couldn't believe what she was about to say, but her brain felt fuzzy and she needed more time to think. To think without Noah standing in front of her, looking so damned happy. "Let's keep this to ourselves for now. Couples don't usually make the announcement until the twelve-week mark."

Noah took her hands in his. His eyes danced.

"Agreed. We'll be cautiously optimistic." He paused, cocked his head, and sucked in a breath. "Let's get married."

Ally's eyes widened. She thought her heart might beat its way out of her chest.

"Whatever happens with this baby," he said, "I don't want to ever be apart from you. Together we're a family, no matter what." Noah lowered himself onto one knee. "So, will you marry me?"

She touched her fingertips to her lips. Her goofy, boyish boyfriend, impulsive and brilliant and hilarious, was kneeling in front of her, her left hand in his. Nothing about this meeting had gone the way she'd planned. But she couldn't think of a future—any future, baby or not—without Noah. At the same time, she could see her freedom slipping away.

Ally forced a smile.

"Yes."

CHAPTER 5

BETH

Beth closed the lid of her coffee maker and pressed the "On" button. The hospital had released her the previous day, and between the trauma to her body and the medication Dr. Bakir had prescribed, she'd slept late, for her—just past 10:00 a.m.

She was out of the habit of sleeping in. It felt weird now to have coffee and breakfast hours past eight, the time her coach asked the team to get the morning meal out of the way so it wouldn't interfere with training.

At the hospital, slumber had come in fits and starts, the combination of her medications and head injury and nurses checking in on her every hour, ruining any chance for a good night's sleep. Drained and exhausted when she arrived in her small apartment, she fell asleep as soon as her head hit the pillow.

Overnight, the sky had opened up and dumped a foot of wet, late-season snow, and she was initially grateful she didn't have to be anywhere urgently. From the view of her kitchen, on the second floor of an institutional-looking, yellow-brick apartment building in Bucktown, fat flakes continued to fall, filling up the patio below. A depressing view for a depressing early-spring day, when the entire city of Chicago was ready to ditch their winter coats and boots for shorts and sandals. Even the ginormous bouquet of flowers sent to her by the league and sitting on her kitchen table by the window couldn't cheer up this view.

As her coffee dripped into the carafe, force of habit propelled her to wander over to her refrigerator to check on her game schedule. Fastened under a magnet in the shape of the Golden Gate Bridge, the printout read that the team did, in fact, have another home game scheduled for Sunday, which was today.

Well, that *game's gonna get canceled.*

Not that it mattered. She wasn't playing anymore this season. Or maybe ever.

Beth slid the schedule from under the magnet. This piece of paper represented all she had going on in her life. Her whole being revolved around those games, and for almost two decades, she'd shaped her life to fit around very similar schedules—at the expense of friends, family, marriage, kids. Heck, Beth couldn't even get serious about hobbies. Staying focused and mentally and physically strong for the pitch had dictated how she approached everything.

On this one sheet of paper was an entire season that had held so much promise to her. Just a few days before, she'd seen all those games ahead of her as opportunities not just to win, but to prove herself.

Postcollege, she'd played at the elite levels, but only as a backup keeper, and she hadn't had the chance to distinguish herself. And now that it was finally her turn to wear the captain's band, she kept getting hurt. Forced retirement felt like a cruel joke on a career she'd spent her life building and sacrificing for. And she hadn't even made a proper comeback.

For once, she almost envied her long-lost high school best friend, who'd gotten knocked up at twenty and dropped out of college. Dropped out of *life.*

Beth had felt so angry and hurt and betrayed at the time—as though Ally had reneged on their deal, their shared dream, forcing Beth to pursue soccer to the highest levels alone. Ally had revealed the news to her over Thanksgiving break sophomore year of college, after hardly speaking with her at all since summer. They got into a huge fight.

Beth remembered Ally had talked like this sudden pregnancy—that was sure to derail almost everything in her life—was a *good* thing. That she welcomed it. At the time, Beth thought she was out of her mind. To let her clueless boyfriend, Rob, persuade her to give up on her dream meant she hadn't really wanted it in the first place.

Their friendship ended that Thanksgiving. And though Beth's anger had cooled over time, they hadn't spoken to each other since. She'd heard Ally and Rob were divorced before they both turned thirty. And Beth's dad informed her that Ally had eventually returned to soccer—not as a player, though. She'd started a successful girls' travel league all on her own. Her own daughters played for it, and she was making a living from it as a single mom in their hometown of Fillmore. Witnessing the early interest from families with daughters, neighboring townships started adding girls' programs of their own, and what had previously been a soccer desert for girls now thrived. Ally's success had impressed her father and, quite frankly, Beth too. And during Beth's last visit over the holidays, her dad had given her Ally's phone number and urged her to get back in touch.

"Life is short," he'd said. "I don't know what happened between you two, but whatever it is has gone on long enough. You used to be as close as sisters. You need a friend like her, someone who *knows* you."

Beth didn't have the heart to tell him she had no intention of calling her old best friend. She told herself too much time had passed. What would they even talk about? The window of their friendship had closed long ago.

Yet despite not talking for almost twenty years, Beth figured their shared history meant she really *did* know Ally and doubted anyone else in their hometown could say the same. She didn't mention it at the time, but her dad was right. Beth loved her teammates, and they were all close, especially during the season, when they couldn't escape each other if they tried. But none of them knew Beth to her core like Ally did. So though she didn't think she'd ever call, she'd dutifully taken the slip of paper from her father and punched the digits into her phone, saving the information.

Beth took one last look at the playing schedule and ripped it in half and then stuffed it into her recycling bin. She didn't have any desire to see that schedule again, and she didn't have the strength to watch her teammates move on without her, at least not now.

There was a part of her that hoped she'd eventually change her mind about her team, that she'd feel a little more generosity toward the league in general. But for the time being, it was far too painful to know her teammates would play the game without her and someone else would rise to her position in goal—one she hadn't even had the privilege of playing for more than a handful of games.

The coffee maker beeped three times. She reached for a cup from the cupboard, poured herself some coffee, and sat down at the kitchen table to watch the snow fall from the sky onto the street below.

And what now? Get a real job? What the heck was she even qualified for? She imagined herself bagging groceries or making lattes or waiting on customers at a clothing store. Beth almost laughed out loud at the images. Her chances of getting hired for anything that paid more than minimum wage probably weren't great. Not that she was making much as a professional soccer player, but at least she could pay rent in a major city. Not for long, though. Her contract ended in October. She had less than six months to figure out what to do. And she had to do something. If she couldn't play professionally in the US, she'd have to play elsewhere.

The buzz of her cell phone on the kitchen counter interrupted her thoughts. She rose from the table to glance at the screen. The service station. *Dad.* He'd been checking up on her after finally reaching her that evening in the hospital. They'd talked four separate times yesterday. No one had her back like Dad did. He worried about her, and she sensed he knew she was keeping something from him. That she wasn't being fully honest about her recovery and prognosis. Beth hated lying to him, but he had enough to worry about back home. A Firestone Tires had moved in mere blocks away from his modest service station, which had occupied that sliver of downtown without competition for more than forty years. Already, Firestone had siphoned business away from him with the lure of cheaper prices and weekly specials. Not that he made a fortune pumping gas and fixing brakes and swapping out tires, but it'd been enough for as long as Beth could remember.

"Hi, Dad. What's new?" She tried to make her voice sound buoyant and light, like she didn't have a care in the world instead of being in the midst of a complete and total identity crisis.

"Heya, Beth, it's Bill. Bad news."

Bill?

Bill had been her dad's right-hand man, prime mechanic, and dear friend since the 1980s. Beth couldn't imagine the service station running without him. But she rarely spoke to him on the phone. Usually just a quick "hi" before passing the phone off to her father.

"Oh God, what happened?" Beth said, not sure if she wanted to hear it. An accident? Hopefully her dad still had all his fingers.

"It's your dad. He had a stroke today here at work."

She blinked, not sure if she'd heard him right. She had nothing to say. Her voice had gone into hiding.

"Beth? Are you still there?"

"Uh-huh," she managed to croak.

"We'd just gotten through the morning rush, and all of a sudden your dad couldn't put two thoughts together. His face started drooping on one side, and his legs seemed to stop working. My mom had a stroke, and I was pretty sure that's what happened to your dad."

"Uh-huh," Beth said again. Her mind seemed to be functioning at about thirty seconds behind. She was still trying to grasp that her dad had had a stroke. That he wasn't sitting on his wobbly wooden stool by the cash register chatting up the neighbors. That he was now lying in some hospital bed connected to a bunch of tubes and monitors.

"OK, I know this is a shock, Beth. But I need you to listen. Your dad's in pretty bad shape." At the last sentence, Bill's voice cracked, and she could hear him pause to swallow down the emotion. Bill was her dad's closest friend, almost family. "He's been taken by ambulance to the hospital in Mount Holly. I gotta take care of things here at the station. We have a few appointments for oil changes and a tire rotation. And someone's got to mind the pump. We can't shut down. I couldn't do that to him."

The room closed in around her, and she took a seat at the kitchen table. Her temple began to throb.

"So, how soon do you think you can get here?"

Bill's direct question snapped Beth to attention. How soon? She supposed as soon as she could get a flight. She looked out her window, where the falling snow obstructed her view of the dry cleaner and café across the street.

"I'll try to get out there tonight if I can," she said in one breath. She had a singular purpose now, which was to get to her dad as soon as possible. Her career woes seemed so distant and unimportant. "Tomorrow at the latest."

After they hung up, Beth took her mug of coffee and sat at the small desk in her living room. She knew her doctor would not have approved of her flying so soon after banging her head, but she logged on to her computer anyway and looked up flights; she wasn't surprised to find that both O'Hare and Midway had canceled everything for today. She could be stuck here for at least one day, if not more, depending on when this storm passed. Anything could happen to her dad in that time, which filled her with an overwhelming sense of helplessness.

The snow outside seemed to mute all sounds, and her apartment felt very quiet all of a sudden. The only interruptions she could hear were the soft, slushy noises of the occasional car cautiously making its way down her one-way street.

She could *drive*. She googled how long it would take to get to Fillmore, New Jersey, from Chicago. More than twelve hours, which, if she left now, would get her there in the middle of the night. But she'd be there. She'd drive straight to the hospital.

Beth's chest tightened. She could feel the tears starting to push at the back of her throat and up against her sinuses. She wanted to deny the last two days. Just say no to the past forty-eight hours. In an instant, she could get hurt, her dad could become sick. No warning. Just like that.

She slammed her hands down on the small desk, which made her cup jump, sloshing the coffee and spilling some next to the keyboard. With a swift motion, Beth swiped her hand, sending the mug hurtling into the air and out of the living room, down the hallway that led to her bathroom. The cup fell with a thud, and the handle broke off, skittering even farther down the hall, leaving dark spots across the walls, living room rug, and hardwood floor.

For a moment, she felt more like a petulant child than an adult with responsibilities. But at least she wasn't crying.

She took a breath. She needed to clean up this mess.

And then pack her bag.

CHAPTER 6

JORDAN

The newsroom had quieted Monday after lunch. Jordan had already submitted a story to his editor about the ongoing trial of a disgraced professional baseball player who had evaded paying his taxes, and was now gathering research on a longer feature about Baltimore's labor unions. Jordan found it easy to focus in the open office, and today, he was absorbed in learning about the Baltimore Federation of Labor's beginnings. When Jordan's cell phone buzzed, he almost let it go to voice mail before taking a second glance and recognizing the area code—Fillmore.

Dad.

The affectionate and familiar moniker automatically sprang into his head, as if his father had been the sort of guy who'd been there for his family the whole time, who'd provided support and needed advice, proudly attended his son's graduation from Columbia, and danced with his daughter at her wedding. As if they hadn't been estranged for almost twenty years.

Jordan pursed his lips together before tapping the screen. He lifted his phone to his ear.

"Hello?"

"Hi, this is Mandy Schultz from Springtime. Is this Jordan Miller?"

He clenched his jaw. *Already?* It'd been a mere three days since he'd moved his father into the facility, and already they were calling him?

"Yes, this is Jordan," he said, curbing his clipped tone and trying not to sound as annoyed as he felt. "Everything OK?"

"I didn't want to worry you, but your father went missing this morning."

Jordan felt his face grow hot.

Way to go, Dad. It's not enough to disappear from your family, now you're disappearing from your new care facility? The place that's supposed to keep you safe?

"But I do have good news—he turned up," she continued. "Or someone called to tell us they found him."

"I don't understand . . . he just left?" Jordan was at a loss. "I thought the Center had safety precautions in place to prevent stuff like this from happening."

"Every now and then a patient slips by us. It's rare, but not never, unfortunately. I'm *so* sorry this happened," Mandy said, her tone contrite.

Jordan considered some of the places his dad had been found before—passed out behind Zeke's bar by the dumpsters or sleeping away a hangover and missing his work shift for the umpteenth time. Would his father's dementia rob him of the knowledge that he was also an addict? He could tumble right back into the grips of it, home in on the nearest liquor store or bar. Jordan would need to call his dad's sponsor and ask what to do about dementia patients who are also alcoholics.

"Where was he found?"

"Apparently"—Jordan heard the rustling of papers—"he made his way to your family's old house? Is this your former address?" She read him the location.

Jordan blinked. *Unbelievable.* "Yes," he said. "That's it."

"OK, good," she said. "The family who lives there is very under-standing. They called us after they put two and two together and figured your dad was a Springtime resident. We're ready to go get him right away. We wanted to bring you into the loop first, though."

Jordan's heart broke a tiny bit thinking about his dad. He'd man-aged to escape, and instead of his addict self leading the way, it was his old self—the one who spent possibly the best years of his life in that house—who'd taken over.

"I'll get him."

"Oh, Jordan, you don't have to do that. It's our responsibility. We feel terrible."

"It's OK," Jordan said. Well, "OK" in no way accurately expressed how he felt about his dad escaping Springtime within two days of his arrival there. But he was probably the best person to bring him back. Or maybe he wasn't the *worst* person. "I'll come get him right now. It'll take a couple hours—I'm driving up from Baltimore—but I'd like to pick him up, if it's all the same to you. And the folks who called in about him, of course."

"The family has been very sweet with your dad, but if it's OK with you, I'd like to meet you there. I'll head over in a little bit. I'd just feel better if someone could keep an eye on him. If he becomes agitated, I'll bring him back. Otherwise, we'll wait for you."

Jordan closed his laptop. "Leaving now."

Jordan pulled up to the curb in front of the house on Cherry Street, where he'd spent both the happiest years of his childhood and the worst. The sight of the home after almost twenty years made the breath catch in his throat. It wasn't just his dad who longed for the life they'd had in that house, but Jordan, and likely Tara and their mom too. All of them, missing who they'd been as a family there, until they suddenly weren't that family anymore. That's why he'd held on to his anger at his dad for so long. Even now his pulse spiked at the memory of his father robbing them of what turned out to be a temporary sense of stability.

The house itself didn't look like much from the outside. It was situated in Fillmore's historic district, where all the homes were smaller in scale and set on postage-stamp-size lots, butting against the brick sidewalks. The Millers' old house was an attached colonial painted in white, with a red roof and original black shutters and a small but cozy front porch that was covered and featured enough room for a chair and a side table. Jordan noticed with a pang that later owners had converted the shaded grassy side yard that he and Tara had played on throughout all four seasons—for catching baseballs and passing soccer balls, for snowball fights, for the Slip 'N Slide—into a paved driveway. But the magnolia tree was still there—taller and fuller now, and heavy with spring blossoms.

Mandy emerged through the storm door onto the porch as Jordan got out of his car.

"I saw you pull up," she said, meeting him on the sidewalk. She had a bag slung over her shoulder and was zipping her fleece jacket up over her Springtime polo shirt. She tucked a piece of her silver bob behind her ear.

Jordan raised his eyebrows. "How's he doing?"

"He's OK. Telling stories, talking about the old neighborhood. Entertaining their kid. He's thoroughly charmed the Mateo family." Mandy folded her arms across her chest. "But I think he's tired. I'm glad you're here to take him back."

He nodded slowly, wondering what stories his father had chosen to tell.

"Thanks for keeping an eye out." Jordan eyed the front door, unsure he was prepared to step inside. "I'm relieved he didn't need to be rushed out. So it sounds like he just wanted to . . . reminisce? Remember? I don't know much about dementia or Alzheimer's. Or whatever's happening in his brain."

And I don't know my father anymore either. If I ever did.

Mandy nodded in understanding. "Want me to stay? We could all ride back together, if you'd like some support."

Jordan put his hand up. "No, we'll be all right." He met her earnest blue eyes and wondered how much of her job was devoted to making relatives of Springtime's residents feel better. "But thank you."

She reached to touch her hand to his arm. "It's OK not to know what's happening in his brain. You don't need to. Just being there for him is enough."

When she left, Jordan opened the storm door and paused for a brief second before rapping on the front door. He almost felt bad about taking his father away from this home that he obviously still felt connected to. But he couldn't stay there forever. The Mateos had been more than patient and were probably ready to get him out of their hair.

The door opened to a pretty, plump woman in a tank top and jeans. Tattoos covered her arms and what was visible of her chest. She smiled.

"You must be Jordan," she said, her voice friendly. She held the door for him. "I'm Amy. Come in."

When Jordan stepped inside his childhood home, he was surprised at how little had changed. Sure, the furniture and light fixtures had been swapped out, pictures of the Mateo family and friends adorned the walls and shelves, and the titles in the built-in bookcase were different. But the footprint had remained, from the bay window in the living room to the two pillars that led to the dining room. Jordan knew that beyond lay the kitchen and laundry room. Upstairs were the bedrooms and the lone bathroom. The third floor was a glorified attic, which twenty years ago was Jordan's room. This familiarity reassured him in a small way, a response he also couldn't have predicted.

Jordan edged into the space and noticed his father sitting at the dining room table across from a child of about eight or nine. They each held a fan of playing cards with a pile of pennies between them.

"This is Ethan." Amy gestured toward the pair. "They're playing—"

"Penny poker." A smile escaped his lips. His dad had taught him how to play when he was a kid too. He gave Amy a rueful look. "I hope that's not against house rules."

Amy laughed. "Of course not! They're having a blast." She turned toward him and cocked her head. "It's been so much fun hearing what it was like here all those years ago. I hear your dad was quite the gardener."

It seemed like a hundred years ago, but yes, his dad used to love to garden. Jordan's mind flashed back to the day he and his father had hauled eight heirloom rosebushes he'd purchased from a nursery in central Pennsylvania.

"Are the rosebushes still in the backyard?"

She nodded. "Those roses are hearty," she said. "I don't have a green thumb, but the rosebushes have survived me."

Jordan heard the sound of the back door closing, and soon a man emerged from the kitchen. He was tall and sported a thick beard. He pulled off a pair of gardening gloves and tossed them on the beverage cart in the dining room. Amy narrowed her eyes at him, and he quickly grabbed the gloves and stuffed them into the back pocket of his jeans.

"I'm Jake," he said, extending a hand.

"Jordan."

Jake gave Amy a quick glance. Jordan took the hint and clasped his hands together. "Well, Dad. I think it's time you and I head home."

His father didn't move except to look up at him, unimpressed.

"We *are* home."

Jordan reached to touch his dad's shoulder.

"You have a new home. The Mateo family lives here now." He pressed his lips together, bracing for the worst. He prayed his father wouldn't become obstinate. He hoped his father's behavior wouldn't make this nice family regret hosting him for the past two-plus hours. "And I'm sure they have stuff to do, and we need to get you back for dinner."

"It's OK," Ethan piped up, setting down his cards. He looked up at his mom, who nodded. "You can visit if you want to. I like playing penny poker with you."

Jordan's father leaned in. "I like playing with you too." He stood and started for the kitchen as if to refresh his coffee cup.

"*Dad.*" Jordan gritted his teeth. "We have to leave."

His father's shoulders drooped. As he turned toward him, Jordan saw a resigned lucidity in his father's eyes.

At least he wouldn't have to fight him to get him into his car.

Seat belts buckled, they waved their final goodbyes to the Mateos, who were seeing them off from the sidewalk.

His father was quiet as they started the drive back to Springtime.

The last time Jordan had seen the house was after his mom had been forced to sell and move her and Tara into a one-bedroom apartment on the outskirts of town—she couldn't afford to pay the mortgage on her own after their dad left. The three of them packed all the boxes and furniture into the moving truck and then walked through the house one last time. The sound of their footsteps seemed louder, more pronounced in the empty house. Their voices bounced against the empty walls and bare wood floors, emphasizing the hollow feel. It was one last humiliation their family had endured since the gym fire.

Jordan glanced at his dad, whose eyes had closed. He'd always been on the lean side, but when he was sober—and younger—he was sturdy. No one worked harder than he did as custodian of the high school. However, buckled into the passenger seat, dozing beside him, he looked smaller, fragile now that dementia was ransacking his brain of his memories. His doctors weren't sure how quickly his father's memory would disappear altogether, but the clock was ticking.

As much as that job had meant to his father, after the fire, he took the safest possible route by accepting full responsibility. He didn't fight the accusations, and he got screwed anyway. But did it have to be so? Jordan wondered what had been going through his father's mind at the time. He probably didn't want the trial to capture any more attention than it already had. He didn't want to drag his family down with him. Agreeing so quickly to take the blame surely seemed like the best path forward. Or at least, Jordan imagined that's what he'd been told by his public defender.

But now that Jordan was at last able to look at the whole thing with something that felt like objectivity, there were missing pieces to the puzzle. The biggest piece: What if there was evidence somewhere that proved, beyond dispute, what had sparked that fire—and that maybe it hadn't been totally his dad's fault?

Jordan knew that it was up to him to at least try to fight for his dad. And the time was now, before his dad's memories evaporated completely.

CHAPTER 7

BETH

Beth gripped the steering wheel and squinted through the windshield as the wipers flung wet clumps of snow off the glass in rapid tempo. She'd managed to hold her headache at bay with high doses of ibuprofen, reducing it to a dull throb behind her eyes. Other than the swish-swish of the wipers, the car moved quietly as it sped east along Interstate 90.

What a mess. Judging by the sheer emptiness of the highway, it seemed that most people had exercised the wisdom to stay inside on this craptastic day.

Beth glanced down at the speedometer. Sixty-seven miles per hour. *Too fast.* She eased off the gas pedal. *Better to get there in one piece,* she reminded herself. From the moment he'd taught her to drive, her dad said she had a lead foot.

Beth's chest constricted at the memory, and she let out a deep breath, trying to mute the sick panic that threatened to spill over at the slightest provocation. She couldn't afford to fall apart. Not now. Her dad needed her.

Why couldn't he have had a stroke on a day that wasn't scheduled for an early-spring snowstorm? Or maybe kept himself healthier in the first place by watching his weight, monitoring his sodium intake, and quitting smoking sooner than a mere four years ago? Or maybe gotten himself checked out by a doctor now and then, so she could avoid a thirteen-hour, heart attack–inducing drive through wet snow to the hometown that she'd managed to mostly avoid for the last twenty years?

Beth gritted her teeth. *No.* These were not helpful thoughts. This stroke was not her dad's fault. Or if it was, it didn't matter. It didn't change the fact that he needed her to be there now, because there was no one else *but* her.

She didn't see him nearly enough. Sporadic visits, weekly phone calls, and televised games just didn't cut it. Because of her unwillingness to come home for any length of time, he'd had to be content with seeing her more on cable TV than in person. She knew why she'd stayed away, of course, but here she was, speeding down the highway to get to Fillmore as soon as possible to be with him. Dad trumped the weight of her secrets, of confronting the long-simmering shame she'd buried almost two decades ago.

Like it or not, she was his only person. And he was hers. Always. Without a doubt.

The terror she felt over the gravity of her dad's condition plunged her into a panicky tunnel vision as she drove. Her phone rested in the cup holder, a silent reminder that she hadn't received an update about his condition since Bill's rattled phone call that morning. Was this a good thing? A "no news is good news" that she should be grateful for? What the hell was she expecting? A nurse, on the other end of the line, telling her that her father had made a full recovery—walked out of the hospital on his own and gone straight back to work? "Please," the nurse would say, "turn that car around and drive back to Chicago. He's fine." Relieved, Beth would—for once—do as she was told.

After three hours of silence, crossing the flat farmland of Indiana and now Ohio, relief was the last thing Beth felt. Midafternoon yet eerily dark out, the entire drive gave her nothing but time to become more and more upset. She'd have nine-plus hours more of this. Beth glanced at the phone again and then back at the highway.

The one person she could call was Ally, of all people.

Countless times she'd thought about calling that phone number her dad had pressed into her hand two Christmases ago. But, really, it'd been too long. What on earth would they talk about? They had nothing in common anymore—Ally, a single mom of two girls and a Fillmore townie, who reportedly knew everything and everyone, and Beth, a single, childless professional athlete, who traveled the globe and avoided her hometown as much as possible. But she often wondered about Ally and whether she ever regretted giving up soccer for a shot at normal life.

Beth's thoughts returned—a well-worn path—to the last conversation they'd had, on Thanksgiving Day, their sophomore year in college.

"I took a pregnancy test before we left for break. You're the second person I told. Rob was first, of course," Ally had said. The two girls were in Ally's bedroom with the door closed. Downstairs, Beth's dad chatted with Ally's family over drinks as the Thanksgiving turkey rested. Beth sat on Ally's bed, her back to the wall, and Ally at her desk.

A surge of panicky rage ripped through Beth. She'd hoped the two would get to catch up after a fall of sparse emails and missed phone calls. She'd expected they'd get their friendship back on track. Yes, Ally'd been distracted by her boyfriend of over a year, Rob Katz, but Beth was certain Ally could veer back on course. It wasn't too late.

"You're not"—Beth held her anger in, protecting it like she protected the ball, cradling it in her arms, tight against her chest—"*keeping it, right?*"

At the time, she knew in her bones it was a ridiculous question. Of course Ally wouldn't keep it—she was playing soccer for Caldwell University. She'd have to be a lot more careful if she wanted to continue playing—or even finish college. Hadn't she heard of condoms? Or the pill?

Ally tilted her head and turned up her lips into a soft, knowing smile. "We're keeping it."

Beth almost laughed. The beatific look on Ally's face was so ridiculous—absurd, even—like she was doing an impression of someone far older and wiser than she was. And *we*? So all of a sudden Ally was no longer her own person? Beth didn't appreciate her tone either. Like Ally was . . . above it all.

No way did Beth believe Ally was going through with it. "Are you kidding?"

Ally just shook her head. "I knew you'd say that," she said, her voice calm. "But Rob and I have been dating over a year. And sure, this wasn't planned, but it just feels right, you know?"

That would be no, Beth didn't know. She sat up on the bed. "What about college? Soccer?"

Ally waved this away as if shooing a mosquito. "It's all meaningless. I dislocated my shoulder this season, anyway. That's why I avoided talking to you about the pregnancy—you wouldn't understand. I busted my shoulder and couldn't even play for weeks. And you know what? I didn't really miss it. Not that much."

Beth felt like she'd just taken a punch. Now Ally was keeping things from her? She swallowed the lump that had formed in her throat. "And your degree? Are you going to bail on that too?"

"No, of course not. I'll probably take a semester off, but there's no reason I couldn't go back to school and finish my degree."

Delusional, on top of everything else.

"But it just"—Beth raised her hands as if to help her form the question—"seems so *quick*. You're so young. You have everything ahead of you. Why waste your time on a baby?" A framed photo on Ally's desk caught her eye—the two of them after the district finals win, Beth's arm draped over Ally's shoulder, the two of them grinning widely. It was the same photo the *Times* had used in their piece about the disparity in girls' sports programs from region to region. If it weren't for the media attention that fall, Beth and Ally might not have received their college scholarships, funding they'd fought and lied for.

It baffled Beth that her friend would throw all that away. "Or why *now*? There's so much time for all that. It seems like you're giving up before you even tried."

"Giving up on what? Seems like I'm getting a jump on real life, not some extended adolescence." Ally scowled. "And what do you know? You only focus on soccer. That's fine for you, but I want more."

That's what had hurt the most. That wanting "more" in this moment meant different things to both of them than it had in high school. It's like Beth hadn't even known her best friend anymore.

And she certainly didn't know her now, almost twenty years later. She glanced down at her phone in the cup holder. Calling after all this time . . . Ally probably wouldn't even pick up if Beth's name came up on caller ID. Still, Beth kept looping back to it. After all these years, Ally was the only person she could think of who she could call about her dad. The only one who'd care. And the torture of not knowing about her dad, this sense of helpless ignorance about his condition, overwhelmed her. Tears pooled in Beth's eyes.

Would he be OK? Would he be able to talk? Would he even be . . . alive? After all he'd sacrificed to provide for her in the best way he knew how, the only thing Beth could think of was—what if she arrived too late? What if someone else—anyone else—bore witness to his final moments?

She needed to talk to someone who understood. Understood *her*.

Beth squinted through the windshield and spotted a blurry sign on the right advertising gas stations and fast food one mile ahead. A sign. A *literal* sign.

She could pull over and find that number on her phone.

It couldn't *hurt* to give Ally a call, would it? Ask the person who knew everything and everyone to keep tabs on her dad until she arrived? Beth would do it for her if the circumstances were reversed. In a heartbeat. And Ally had to know someone who worked at the hospital who could give her some information about Beth's dad. If she didn't answer, well, then at least Beth had tried. And if Ally was still mad after all this time? The worst she could say was no. Beth would accept that because she didn't have a choice. And she was desperate.

She nodded to herself and pulled off at the exit.

The wet snow had accumulated on the pavement, and when Beth drove into a near-empty Taco Bell parking lot, it felt like she was driving through a giant slushy. She parked the car but kept the engine running.

Dad had always made it clear how much he loved Ally, how much he loved that his only daughter had found a best friend, and didn't understand why the two girls hadn't remained in touch—which was no doubt why he'd slipped her Ally's number that day. Now, Beth was glad she'd punched it into her contacts, though today was the first time she'd actively entertained the thought of actually calling it. She typed in Ally's name, and sure enough, her phone number appeared. She clicked on the number before she lost her nerve.

The phone rang once, then twice. After the sixth ring, it switched over to voice mail.

"Hi, this is Ally. If you're calling about urgent league business, such as a weather emergency, athlete injury, or a field issue, please reach me at my cell. Otherwise, please leave a message after the beep."

Beth hung up. Her heart pounded.

She hadn't heard Ally's voice in close to two decades. She sounded the same. And not. Maybe more . . . responsible? Was her own voice more responsible sounding now that she was thirty-seven, not twenty?

And the *league*—Beth's dad had filled her in on Ally's girls' league she'd built from scratch when her eldest was skilled enough for a travel team. Beth and Ally didn't get the opportunity to play for an all-girls anything when they were growing up. At the time her dad told her about Ally's new league, Beth felt an immense sense of both pride and envy that Ally had created something so valuable and life changing for those girls. This generation wouldn't have to endure years of humiliation from bullies who felt emasculated by girls who outplayed them.

Beth's phone rang, making her heart leap to her throat. For a split second, her thoughts jumped to the worst possible scenario—the hospital calling to say her father was gone. That she was too late. She willed herself to glance down at her phone and saw that Ally was calling her back. She braced herself.

"Hi, Ally," she said into the receiver, hearing the uncertainty in her voice. "It's Beth."

"Beth, hi." Ally sounded distant. A little cool? "I'm sorry I didn't pick up. I didn't recognize the number."

Beth conjured up how she remembered Ally had looked back when she'd last seen her—short dark hair that she'd cut in a pixie around her heart-shaped face, with liquid brown eyes and high cheekbones that seemed permanently blushed. She was short, much shorter than Beth, certainly, but since Beth was five feet, ten inches (as of the end of middle school), almost every girl was smaller than she was. Physically, though, Ally looked like a soccer player—lean up top and all power in her glutes and legs. Beth had to work to build muscle; otherwise she was just lean. Skinny. Weak. Kind of how she felt now.

"It's OK," Beth said. "It's been a while."

Massive understatement. She thought about the last thing she'd said to Ally—that Ally had given up. Beth swallowed. Maybe she should just get to the point. "This is so awkward. But, I don't know if you've heard—"

"Heard what?" Concern colored Ally's voice.

"My dad. He had a stroke this morning." Beth's voice cracked, but to her surprise, she wasn't embarrassed. Ally must have known how close Beth and her dad still were.

"Oh, gosh. Beth, I'm sorry. I didn't hear anything."

What happened to the one who knew everyone and everything? Beth heard the sound of a door closing.

"Sorry," Ally continued. "I just shut myself in the bathroom. The girls just got back from school, and as usual, it's madness. The bathroom's the only place I can get any peace and quiet."

Beth smiled at the image. Hard to believe, but Ally had a busy family now, and she probably juggled a lot between raising two kids—*teenagers?*—and working and running that soccer league and everything else. Of course the bathroom would serve as a sanctuary. And Beth related: rooming with rowdy teammates on the road, she'd pulled the same move.

"I get it," Beth said. "Should I call a little later? I know you're busy." She stared out at the snow-covered parking lot where an eighteen-wheeler was backing up to a gas pump in the distance. She wondered if she'd be able to summon the courage to call again.

"No, no," Ally said. "After seventeen years, I'm guessing you're not calling just to say hi."

Good point.

"So, what happened?" Ally said. "I see your dad all the time. In fact, I just bought new tires at the station last week. He seemed fine. Normal. Chatty as always."

Beth's cheeks burned. Ally saw more of her dad than his only daughter did. Ally could stop by and say hi anytime she wanted. Of course, Beth's circumstances were entirely of her own making. She took a breath.

"His partner, Bill, called," Beth said. "Said I needed to get home as quickly as possible."

Her heart squeezed. She couldn't get there fast enough.

"But we got a storm overnight," she went on. "Which grounded most flights out of Chicago. So I packed a suitcase and started driving." Beth looked around her ancient Civic with no snow tires and no all-wheel drive, feeling lucky she'd made it this far without incident. "I just headed east not knowing what I'd be coming home to. I don't know what's going on, and it's already making my head spin."

"Where are you?"

"I'm . . ." Beth glanced out her windshield at the Taco Bell obscured by the fading daylight and the dreary, wet snow. Interior lights illuminated the restaurant, drawing attention to its emptiness, its vulnerability. Beth wondered how many of the workers had been told to come in despite the soggy weather. The soggy weather she'd been driving in too. How long had she driven? Three hours? Four? "Somewhere outside of Toledo, I think."

"OK, wow. You've still got a ways to go."

"I know." Beth took a shaky breath. "All I know is he had a stroke and he's at Mount Holly in intensive care. Bill filled me in on what happened after the ambulance took him away, and he made sure the hospital had my contact information. When they called, he'd already had a CAT scan and an MRI, and they gave him something to break up the clot. He's stabilized but not conscious. They put him in an induced coma." A heaviness settled into her chest. "And that's all I know. I haven't heard anything."

"And you've been on the road since."

"Yeah, well." Beth swallowed the emotion threatening to choke her voice. "What else could I do?"

"So listen, Diana Flores—a mom of one of Morgan's teammates—is a nurse at Mount Holly, I think in the ICU. Is it all right if I reach out and see if I can get more information? Like now? While you're still on the way?"

A small eruption of gratitude burst inside Beth. Her instincts hadn't let her down. Sometimes it paid to take a chance even after seventeen years.

"Thank you. I'd really appreciate that."

"Anything. Truly," Ally said. "I'm guessing you don't know how long you'll be in town?"

Beth couldn't decide if she sensed hopefulness in Ally or trepidation.

"No idea," she said. It was the truth. She could be back for a week or two or for months, depending on her dad's condition. Her stomach clenched at the thought. She had no position on the team to return to, so her full-time job for the time being was her dad.

"Look, I hope—"

"I'm sorry I haven't called," Beth blurted. "My dad gave me your number a while ago. I was just too chicken, I guess. Or I thought maybe you wouldn't want to hear from me after all this time. It's wild that it takes my dad having a stroke to get me to reach out, you know?"

Beth heard nothing on the other end and wondered if the line had dropped and she was merely talking to herself.

"You know you can always count on me," Ally said, finally. "You can trust me."

Of course she knew she could trust Ally, but the real question was: Could Ally trust *her*? After all, Beth had gone home many times over the years but had never gotten in touch with Ally, and now here she was, calling her because she felt Ally could do her a favor. That, and they'd burned down the high school gym together and never told anyone. So Beth hesitated, bracing herself for what Ally could bring up next. The sound of her voice alone had already dredged up too many memories, and she found herself too drained to think about anything more than getting to her dad.

"I know that. And I do," Beth said, seizing the opportunity to end the call. She needed to get back on the road. "I'd appreciate it if you'd call me when you find out anything from that nurse you know. I'll be there in, like, nine hours."

A familiar sense of relief flooded over Beth as she disconnected from one of the two ties to her hometown. And joined with that was an equally familiar feeling of guilt. The two people in her life that she had loved the most—her dad and, yes, Ally—were the two people she'd also felt compelled to leave.

Now here she was, hurtling toward them both.

CHAPTER 8

ALLY

Ally flicked on the overhead kitchen light, taking a brief moment to enjoy the early-morning quiet that would soon be replaced by a hurricane of teenage energy as the girls raced to get ready for school. A pot of already-brewed decaf—another new development, *sigh*—indicated the start to her busy day. Theo, their skittish, half-feral cat, scurried to her and wound his way through her legs, signaling breakfast time. She poured herself a cup of coffee, took a sip, and rounded the corner to the laundry room, where she scooped a portion of cat food into Theo's bowl.

One down, two to go.

Back in the kitchen, she opened the refrigerator, pulled out containers of leftover egg noodles, stewed chicken, and salad from the night before, and placed them on the counter. She popped the egg noodles into the microwave first, and then reached for two insulated food jars and two plastic containers from the cabinet.

Ally sat at the kitchen island drinking her coffee while the noodles warmed. Her thoughts returned to Beth's phone call the day before. She couldn't believe they'd talked yesterday; it felt like a strange, incomprehensible dream rather than an actual conversation. Yet they *had* spoken—after a seventeen-year pause—and Beth's dad was in poor shape.

The news of his stroke had rattled her almost as much as it had surely shaken Beth. Ally had known Mr. Snyder (she still had a hard time calling him Ralph) all her life, even before she'd become friends with Beth. For the last four decades, her parents had filled their family van with gas and taken it in for minor things like oil changes, brake replacements, and new tires at his service station right off Main Street.

Mr. Snyder knew everyone, and that had fascinated Ally her entire life.

Unlike Beth, who had always been more focused on soccer than people, it was rare to see Ralph without company. He was known in town as a talker. He'd strike up a conversation with the driver as he filled their gas tank and cleaned the windshield and rear window. He'd chat up a customer as he leaned under the hood of their car checking the fluids. Or he'd be standing outside the garage, smoking a cigarette and talking with Bill, the mechanic, who was swapping worn tires for new ones on a vehicle. There weren't too many people in town who seemed to literally know everyone, but Mr. Snyder was one of them.

When Ally's mom made the rounds every winter dropping off her signature Christmas sugar cookies to teachers, friends, and family, Mr. Snyder's service station was one of her first stops, even after she and Beth stopped talking to each other in college. He got along with young people, too; he'd employed dozens of teenagers over the years to help him out over the busy summer months and provided them their first real work experience.

Despite his perpetual presence at the service station, Ally remembered he'd rarely missed one of her and Beth's home soccer games during high school. Ally's own parents' attendance was spotty at best, but she could count on Ralph. She smiled at the memory. She could always make out his voice cheering loudest for her and Beth when they played. After all they'd gone through, they needed his support—his cheers were a life raft throughout four very challenging seasons. And now that booming voice had been silenced, as he lay unconscious in a hospital bed at Mount Holly.

Ally pressed the button to illuminate her phone, thinking she should text Beth for an update about her dad now that she'd joined him at the hospital overnight, but thought better of it. Too soon in a possibly rekindled . . . what? Friendship? *Well, that's presumptuous.* In any event, it was most likely too early in the day to contact her. With any luck, Beth would be catching up on sleep and didn't need an interruption now—from a friend or former friend—that could wait a couple of hours. Ally curbed her impulse to meddle and set her phone down.

Her younger daughter, Emily, shuffled into the kitchen wearing pajama bottoms, a T-shirt, and slippers. She rubbed her eyes and opened the refrigerator.

Ally watched her fourteen-year-old stare into the cool, open void. She set her coffee on the counter. "You're not dressed?"

"Do we have cereal?"

Ally frowned, annoyed. "Why are you still in your PJs?"

Emily faced her mom and dropped her chin. "Relax, Mom. It takes me, like, twenty-eight seconds to get ready for school."

"Fine," she said, more than prepared to witness Emily dress, brush her teeth, comb her hair, and pack her backpack in under thirty seconds. Ally remembered the days when it could take fifteen minutes for her to just put on her shoes alone. "And, yes, we have cereal."

Emily grabbed the jug of milk and closed the refrigerator as the microwave beeped.

"So my art project's due this morning," she said, grabbing a bowl and the jar of homemade granola from the cupboard. "It's a little awkward carrying it on the bus. Can I get a ride? Pretty please?"

Ally swapped the noodles for the chicken and pressed "Start." She scooped noodles into the insulated food containers as the chicken rotated in the microwave. She looked up to answer Emily just as Morgan entered the kitchen.

Morgan wore a soft cream-colored sweater over track pants and sneakers, and her glossy hair was pulled back into a ponytail. She placed her packed book bag onto the kitchen table and said, more to the entire room than to Emily, "You don't need a ride." She reached for a bowl and sat next to her younger sister at the table. "Mom, it's a poster board, not like a heavy sculpture or anything."

Emily glowered at her. "I *do* need a ride." She gave Ally a pleading look. "It's *super* awkward getting that thing on and off the bus, the bus is disgusting, and if it gets wet, it's ruined." She turned back to Morgan. "*And* it's half my midterm art grade, you moron." She frowned at her cereal bowl, muttering, "God, mind your own business."

Ally twisted the lids onto the food jars and snapped shut the containers of salad. "Can we *please* start the morning without bickering?" A wave of nausea hit her without warning. She closed her eyes and reached her hand out, steadying herself on the counter. She could feel her cheeks flush and beads of perspiration form on her hairline.

"Mom, did you *hear* me?" Emily asked.

"Mom, are you OK?" Morgan asked at the same time.

That's what I get for drinking decaf on an empty stomach. Ally opened her eyes.

"Yes, I'm fine." She refocused on her daughters at the kitchen table. "Once you're done with breakfast, I'll need your lunch bags."

"What about a ride?" Emily's voice sounded hopeful.

Morgan waggled her spoon at her sister. "We can take the bus. Just suck it up."

Emily turned to Morgan, a smile spreading across her face. "What, are you afraid you won't see Benjy Moore on the bus this morning? You two are so cute—listening to music, sharing the same earbuds."

"Shut *up*." Morgan's eyes narrowed, and she pushed out her chair and rose from the table. Ally recognized that look of fury on Morgan's face. It was the same look she'd seen after a player from an opposing team knocked her down or tripped her up on the soccer field. *That* never happened twice.

"Enough, you two. Morgan, go brush your teeth and double-check your soccer bag. Emily, please get dressed. And I'm holding you to that twenty-eight seconds."

"Twenty-eight seconds?" Emily said, scrunching her brow in confusion.

"Never mind. Just both of you, be ready in ten. School's on my way today, so I'll take you." Ally pivoted toward Morgan. "Unless you'd rather take the bus on your own."

Morgan side-eyed Emily, who smirked back. "It's fine. I don't care. I'll just go with you two."

"Great." Ally started rinsing off the breakfast dishes and then remembered. "Pack up your lunches!" she shouted toward the doorway after the girls had escaped the kitchen.

At that moment, Noah narrowly avoided a collision with the teens as he entered the space and made his way over to Ally, touching the small of her back and pecking her on the cheek.

"How are you feeling, kid?" he asked and grabbed a coffee mug from a shelf.

"Why, do I look a little green?" Ally touched her forehead, which still felt clammy.

"You look like you've just been accosted by two squabbling teenagers." He smiled. Noah understood. He always understood, and that was one of the many things she loved about him. Ally smiled back.

"I've got a gazillion things on my plate today—actually, the entire week and next week too. Why do tryouts always have to be so *trying*?"

Noah reached for the coffee decanter and then hesitated. "Is this half caff?"

"Decaf. I thought you'd be on your way to school by now and would grab something on the way."

He set his coffee cup on the counter and faced Ally.

"Any news from your friend?"

For a second, Ally thought Noah was just trying to be clever—the little pea-size thing was certainly making its presence known most mornings—and then realized he was talking about Beth.

She shook her head. "Diana was going to call Beth from the ICU if she heard anything. No one's contacted me."

"It's good you reached out," he said. "You said you and Beth haven't kept in touch, but it says a lot that she called out of the blue."

Haven't kept in touch. As if they'd simply drifted apart like friends do, sometimes. The fact was, all those years ago, when she was first pregnant with Morgan, it was surprisingly easy to let go of their friendship. It was like letting go of the past and giving her permission to build a whole new life. A life that no longer had to include harassment from those boys in high school, or her and Beth's disastrous attempt at retaliation, or giving up on soccer, or a friendship with Beth, who just reminded her of her past.

Noah glanced through the kitchen archway, then stepped closer to her.

"Actually, I wanted to talk to you before I left."

"Yeah?" Ally looked up into his handsome, boyish face and wrapped her arms around his waist. He'd served as the high school's principal since September and taught history for more than fifteen years before that, but even at the age of forty-two, he honestly didn't look too far removed from the high school seniors.

"When do you think we can start telling people about the baby?" Noah's cheeks flushed. "At least, you know, our families or parents? I don't need to shout it from the rooftops—though I think I'd *like* to do that." He cleared his throat. "But even though this was sort of—unplanned, ever since we learned you were pregnant, all I want to do is talk about it."

Ally had hoped that by biding her time during the next few weeks, still early in her pregnancy, she would catch up to Noah's enthusiasm. It didn't help that the timing of her pregnancy corresponded with travel-team tryouts, her busiest and most chaotic part of the year. Well, no, the beginning of fall season was pretty intense too. And their yearly tournament in

November had a thousand moving parts. Was there *any* good time to be pregnant?

Did she even *want* this baby? Noah was already eager to tell the world about it, but she couldn't stop cycling through all the fundamental ways a baby would thwart her empty-nest fantasy and change her life, her work, her freedom, her body.

"I should probably make an appointment with my ob-gyn first. She'll be the next person we discuss it with."

His face broke into a grin. "And then we can tell our parents. And then the girls." He squeezed her hands and appeared ready to give her a twirl around the kitchen. "We can have a party. This is something to celebrate."

"Slow down." She softened her tone. He was *so* happy, so lovable right now, she knew sharing her true feelings about this pregnancy might break his heart. Ally worried her ambivalence would grow and fester as his excitement bloomed. Usually, his enthusiasm was infectious.

But what about me? Where is my choice in the matter?

She didn't ask for this fetus growing inside her. She wished she weren't so ambivalent. She wished she could match Noah's excitement. But the truth was, she was a little mad at the tiny, pea-size thing, expanding in size with each passing day. It was all just going too fast, and she knew all too well how an unplanned pregnancy could derail one's future. Beth had been right about that.

I'll have to start over.

Onesies, Diaper Genies, strollers, spit-up, endless rounds of "Itsy Bitsy Spider" and *Goodnight Moon*, and lack of sleep were part of this future. Would trips to the park and the children's library replace the career she'd spent more than a decade building from scratch? She'd never had to split her focus between a baby and career before—she started the league when Morgan turned seven and Emily was five. But girls were portable. Plenty of working parents figured out how to have a career and raise a baby. She tried to imagine going to field locations, dropping off equipment, and attending games all while balancing a baby at her hip. She couldn't do it.

Ally bit her lip. She was getting ahead of herself. She just needed a bit more time to think. She'd have to let Noah down today, but didn't know how much longer she could reasonably put this decision off.

"I know you're excited, but can it wait until tryouts are over?" Her voice rose almost to a squeak. Ally's gut twisted, and she wasn't sure if it was the little pea having its way with her or her guilt for lying to him.

A flicker of disappointment flashed across his face, but he held her gaze.

"That's weeks away. I feel like it's almost dishonest not to at least tell my parents." He turned away and rubbed the back of his neck. "Every time I talk to my mother, it's like I'm lying to her by not telling her she's going to be a grandma again."

"You know how it's going to go when we make the announcement," Ally said. "As grateful as we'll both be for everyone's enthusiasm, it's a distraction I don't need right now. And you've got a lot now, too, with seniors hearing from colleges and the Spring Fling fundraiser next month, not to mention prom and graduation. Can you imagine your parents? My parents? Once we announce, they're going to want to rope me into baby shower planning."

Ally'd attended all sorts of events leading up to the birth of her friends' babies, but she herself didn't have a shower before the girls were born, and gender-reveal parties—Ally found the concept itself repugnant—weren't even a thing. Her and Rob's parents had chipped in to help out the young, unprepared couple buy big-ticket items like a crib, stroller, car seat, and high chair before Morgan was welcomed into the world. It was hard to believe how much had changed since Ally'd had her girls, well before anyone else her age.

Noah turned to face her. "But what does it matter? It's just one more thing. I can handle it." He leaned in. "So can you. I've never seen you shrink from a challenge."

Even though she knew he was playing to her ego, Ally grinned in spite of herself. Then she had an idea. "What about an engagement party?"

Noah took a step back and cocked his head to the side.

"I'm listening," he said.

"We are early in this pregnancy. *Anything* can happen, OK? I was barely twenty when I had Morgan and not even twenty-three when Emily was born. I don't—" Ally paused, unsure of how to frame what she wanted to say. She needed to temper Noah's expectations but also stall for more time to make her decision about whether or not to stay pregnant. She needed the space to think on her own without Noah's enthusiasm distracting her. Yet. Her dishonesty here was palpable. She felt the heat rising to her cheeks. "There's a reason people don't say anything for at least twelve weeks."

"My sister told my family right away." Noah crossed his arms over his chest. "We're a family that likes to know. And it turned out all right for them."

Ally looked down at the kitchen floor. A crack stretched across the porcelain tile for the length of the kitchen, from the sink to the cabinets. It'd been there when she'd moved in.

"It's not just your family, Noah. We'd have to tell mine too. And the girls. And, well, again: we might as well just tell all of Fillmore after that, because news will spread, whether we like it or not." Ally moved closer to him and looked up into his eyes. "If we lost the pregnancy, just think of how much more painful it would be."

Noah rubbed the back of his neck and let out a long, resigned breath. Without saying a word, Ally knew she'd convinced him. Warmth radiated through her body.

"Just a few more weeks won't hurt," she said. "I have a doctor's appointment scheduled for Monday. We'll know how far along I am then."

"Me. You're asking *me* to wait weeks?" Noah leaned on the counter.

"I believe in you. And in the meantime"—Ally threw her arms around his neck—"we'll celebrate our engagement."

"I guess this means I should buy you a ring or something."

"Or not." Ally realized she really did have a lot to celebrate. She glanced at the tile again. "I think I'd rather save the money to fix this crack in the floor."

"Or for a crib," Noah said.

"Or for a crib," she agreed, feeling a chill for being dishonest with him. Again.

"All right," he said. She looked up into his eyes, which practically twinkled. "An engagement party it is." He leaned in, pulled her toward him, and kissed her. "How lucky am I?"

Ally knew that, in an instant, this happiness could all go away.

She heard the girls thump down the stairwell. "That's my cue," she said, turning to grab a protein bar from the cupboard.

Morgan and Emily scrambled into the kitchen, reusable lunch bags in hand, and placed the containers of food, a plastic fork, and a paper towel into each bag. Emily had changed out of her pajamas into a T-shirt that read "Shad Fest" tucked into ripped jeans, and high-top sneakers. She'd lined her eyes with heavy eyeliner, but otherwise, her face was makeup-free.

Noah smirked. "Late for the bus, I take it?"

Emily looked up at him as she zipped her lunch bag shut. "Mom's taking us. Oh wait—you're still here. We should just go with you."

"I like that idea," Noah said. "And you," he said to Ally, "have a little time for something other than a Clif Bar for breakfast."

"Or," she said, brightening, "I can swing by the hospital on my way to a meeting and check in with Beth."

The girls, loaded down with backpacks and gym bags, looked with expectation at Noah.

"Right," he said, pausing to give Ally a quick peck before they all headed out of the kitchen. "Take care of yourself today."

"Love you guys," Ally called out as the doors closed behind them. And she did. But that didn't stop the hands from her past from closing around her throat.

CHAPTER 9

JORDAN

The sun made an appearance late in the afternoon, and Jordan stood outside in the ShopRite parking lot, leaning against the driver's side door and feeling the warmth of the sun on his face, holding his cell phone up to his ear. His sister had demanded updates about their father's first week in Springtime but insisted she had no interest in helping out.

"There's nothing preventing you from coming down and seeing for yourself," Jordan said.

"You know that's impossible," Tara said.

Jordan knew her making the trek to New Jersey was, in fact, *not* impossible. Her husband would watch the kids. Connecticut wasn't that far a drive; she could have made it a long day trip and been back for dinner. She just didn't want to spend the time on the road, the money on gas, to see her father in person after he'd abandoned the family all those years ago.

But still. She was eager to learn what he was like now.

"He's not—" Jordan stopped himself. He needed to choose his words carefully. Tara had every right to feel the way she felt toward their dad, whether or not he'd changed. In some ways she'd felt even more betrayed, since she was barely in high school when he left. Tara's high school years were marked by financial hardship and trauma that Jordan had happily distanced himself from in college. "Sobriety and Alzheimer's have softened him."

Tara sighed into the receiver.

"Did you tell Mom that he escaped yet?"

"Not yet." Jordan hesitated. Only a couple of weeks ago, he'd held the same reservations as his mother and sister. Those two were a united front, and they often made him feel defensive. "I never saw myself getting involved either. But he's alone and needs help. I couldn't live with myself knowing that he'd wasted away in that studio apartment, or even alone at Springtime."

"I could."

"OK." Jordan shook his head. "I'll stay for the next few days. He's getting a roommate tomorrow, which will be one more new thing." The *Sun* had approved a few personal days at the last minute. Plus, as a journalist, he could take his work with him. Maybe he'd have some time to dig around about the fire. Tara definitely didn't need to know about that.

"Let me know how that goes," Tara said. Jordan thought he sensed her tone lightening. Maybe she did care after all.

Returning to Fillmore, having his dad back in his life—it was messing with his head. All he wanted now was a beer to go with the Chinese takeout he'd planned to pick up on his way to the hotel. When they hung up, he made his way inside the store and to the refrigerated beer section.

If there was any truth to what Oleks said about the fire . . . the trial . . . Jordan needed to know. It was probably nothing. His dad had confessed. End of story. Except it wasn't. It ruined his father. Destroyed his family. Everything in Jordan's life that year blew up, while everyone else in Fillmore got to move on. And he couldn't stop turning it over in his head.

So what *was* the story? Jordan had been fed the same narrative as everyone else. He could start by digging up those old newspaper articles from almost twenty years ago. As a reporter, he had a ton of investigative tools right at his fingertips, but he'd probably start searching the old-fashioned way: Google.

Jordan opened the refrigerator door and slid out a six-pack. As he started walking toward the register, he spotted a familiar face in the produce section. He almost thought he was seeing things.

Beth Snyder.

No, it couldn't be her. She played for the Chicago women's soccer team. Or she did; during the game he'd caught on ESPN last Friday, she collided with the forward from the opposing team and lost consciousness right there on Soldier Field.

He allowed himself to take a longer look at her profile. Her most striking feature was still her height. She'd been an imposing presence even as a teenager. At almost six feet, she'd towered over him in high school—Jordan had matured later and didn't get his height until college—and he'd always been in awe of her. Who wouldn't be? Strong, fast, confident—she had such undeniable talent. Her focus had been so zeroed in on soccer, she had no time for anything else, including boys like Jordan, who'd cultivated a long-standing crush on her all through high school. So much so, he volunteered as the coaches' assistant—basically a glorified ball boy—during soccer season. She'd been his dazzling introduction to what would prove to be his lifelong attraction to ambitious women—women who knew what they wanted and just went for it. And he had his own drive to contend with, which didn't always make for long-lasting relationships.

Beth's honey-colored hair had darkened some since high school and was now a golden brown pulled back into a limp ponytail. She didn't appear to wear any makeup, but she didn't need it. Never did. Her ruddy cheeks gave her face a natural glow.

But Jordan couldn't reconcile her presence in the here and now. The National Women's Soccer League had just started their season. Why was she shopping for vegetables in a Fillmore grocery store? Jordan didn't think she had a twin sister.

She cocked her head so that now she was in full profile. And there it was. Her temple sported an angry purple lump the size of a silver dollar. This was Beth Snyder, all right.

So now what?

Jordan's stomach tightened. He *could* just walk over and say hi instead of staring at her from afar like a stalker. He'd grown up, too, after all. Was no longer the skinny shrimp lugging a giant bag of soccer balls from the gym to the field.

Jordan sucked in a breath, feeling like this was taking a little more courage than the moment warranted, and walked toward her.

"Beth?" he said. "Beth Snyder?"

CHAPTER 10

BETH

Beth had come straight to the ShopRite from the hospital on her way back to her dad's house, eager to pick up something nourishing to consume after a day that had drained the life out of her. The store felt too quiet, too sleepy—like everything about Fillmore, and in stark contrast to any grocery store in her Chicago neighborhood, which bustled at all hours of the day. Even late Saturday afternoons. In the heart of big cities she'd lived in, like Chicago and, before that, Seattle, grocery shopping was both communal and anonymous. Strangers and regulars alike could browse the aisles in relative obscurity. But now, unaccustomed to the vast starkness of her hometown food store on this afternoon, Beth felt exposed and on display as she shopped, often the only person walking through the aisles. She didn't want to be seen. She just wanted to pick up a few things and get out of there.

When she paused too long in front of the organic chicken, a well-meaning store employee behind the meat counter asked if she needed help finding anything.

"No," she said, her automatic response to any question by any stranger. Maybe a city dweller's defense mechanism, but she knew it came off rude in places like Fillmore. She looked up, meeting his eyes. "But thank you. I'm good."

Beth hurried to the fruits and vegetables, stopping at the bagged-salad section. She placed some baby spinach into her basket, knowing if he were home, her dad would never touch the stuff. At least it was a start. Something green in the fridge that wasn't mold.

After her marathon drive Sunday into Monday straight from Chicago to Mount Holly, followed by an exhausting day witnessing her dad in his heartbreaking new state for the first time, and then catching up with her father's health-care providers, all Beth had wanted to do when she arrived at her dad's house late last night was crawl into her old childhood bed.

She'd awoken to a kitchen devoid of any fresh-food options.

As unsurprised by this as she was, Beth swallowed her irritation when she opened the refrigerator to find Styrofoam boxes of rotting leftovers, multiple half-empty and presumably abandoned jars of spaghetti sauce, and an open twelve-pack of Bud, among dozens of saved packets of ketchup and soy sauce stashed in a baggie.

The contents of the freezer provided even more clues to his lifestyle—potato wedges, frozen pizza, ice cream that had been in the freezer so long, protective ice crystals covered the sticky contents. She grimaced and fought the urge to rage against the unhealthy choices he'd made for her entire life that had most likely led to his current critical condition. He'd never taken care of himself. Ever. Always other people—customers, friends, community. Always *her*.

If he'd known she was going to visit, he no doubt would have made an attempt to stock the fridge and pantry with food she was used to eating as a top-level athlete—fruit, vegetables, chicken cutlets, oatmeal, sweet potatoes, nuts. Sometimes, he'd even asked for a list.

Not that it would have been necessary, anyway, she reminded herself. She'd "retired" from her sport, her profession.

Dad doesn't know that.

And now this afternoon, after spending all day again at the hospital, getting a sense of her father's current condition and planning for potential futures—yes, plural—Beth found herself staring bleary eyed at produce, with another headache forming at the edges of her brain. *Just a few things to tide me over.*

"Beth?" An unfamiliar male voice from behind her. "Beth Snyder?"

She should have known she'd never get through ShopRite without running into someone who knew her. *Small-town living.*

Beth turned to find a man a few inches taller than her—and at five feet, ten inches, Beth rarely had to look up to meet a man's gaze—with a sturdy frame, curly brown hair, and dark eyes that, in any other situation, would have made her melt. Even now, she felt her cheeks warm under his gaze, and for a second, she forgot about her father, the ICU, and being stuck in Fillmore. She blinked. His rugged face looked somewhat familiar, but she couldn't place him. Maybe one of the kids her dad employed during the summers?

"Yes?"

In one hand, he held a six-pack of beer. He raised the other to his chest. "It's Jordan Miller. We went to high school together."

Jordan Miller. At once, the name conjured an image of an energetic and tiny kid—even as a senior, he'd looked like he could have been in seventh grade—who made it his business to be everywhere. He volunteered for every committee, edited the school newspaper, and served as the assistant to her high school soccer coaches. Last time she'd seen him was at graduation. She didn't think he'd made it to grad night. His dad also happened to be the school custodian—until the man was fired without warning.

The unwanted recurring memory from high school bloomed in her brain—the explosion, the gym engulfed in flames . . .

Stop it.

She forced a smile.

"Oh wow, Jordy—of course. It's great to see you." Beth blinked again, refocusing her vision and trying to square this tall, strapping, confident guy standing before her with the hyperactive kid who used to haul the practice jerseys and net of soccer balls to and from the field.

She thought again about his dad and his abrupt firing. She and Ally had practically pushed him into his downward spiral. Had it really been twenty years? Guilt clouded her vision, and she fought the urge to abandon her items and make a run for her car.

"Great to see *you*," he said. "How's your head?"

Beth frowned. "My head?"

Jordan gestured toward her temple. "You conked your head, last game I saw."

God, her career-ending concussion had taken a back seat to her dad's health over the last couple of days. Some small kind of twisted mercy, she supposed. She touched her fingers to the lump. The swelling had gone down, but the pain of her fingertips on the injury sparked a mini lightning bolt.

"It's OK." She squinted at him. "You *saw* that game?" The few times Beth had been recognized as a professional soccer player were in airports when she wore her team warm-ups and was surrounded by other teammates wearing the same thing. And even then, virtually no one knew her name or what position she played. Sometimes she'd get asked what sport or team she played for. Most of the time, Beth was happy to be able to live her life in relative anonymity. "Hardly anyone in this country follows women's soccer. Except for the tween girls who play. And maybe their parents."

Jordan laughed. "Well, I guess I'm opening up a whole new category for you."

Beth offered a reluctant chuckle in agreement.

He gave a little shrug. "But how could I not follow the career of the most successful soccer player Fillmore's ever produced?"

She looked down at her feet, her face and ears burning.

"So," he continued. "What are you doing in town? Don't you live in Chicago?"

Her smile faded. "I'm . . ." She trailed off, unsure of what, exactly, she *was* doing. "Waiting," she said. That'd do. "Here for my dad. He's had a stroke."

Worry creased his brow. "Beth, I'm so sorry."

"Thanks." She looked down at her basket. A gloomy reminder that the items were for one person.

And the concern in Jordan's face immediately made her think about *his* father. She couldn't ask what had happened to him. The little she'd learned wasn't good. After high school, she'd heard that his firing and sentence had rendered Mr. Miller unemployable in their small town. Jordan's parents broke up. Her dad had told her that Jordan's mom lost the house, relocated to an apartment in town for a few years, and then eventually moved to Philadelphia so that she could find higher-paying work. Mr. Miller just disappeared. Beth was relieved her soccer schedule had kept her from having to think too hard about rumors from home.

"How long are you in town for?" he asked.

She shrugged. "I have no idea. As long as he needs me, I guess." Beth knew that was the right answer, but saying it aloud drew her chest into a fist so tight, she could hardly draw a breath. The truth was, she wanted—*needed*—to make her escape as soon as she could. The sooner her dad made a miraculous recovery and returned to chatting up his customers at the service station, the better for them both.

The problem was, she had nowhere to go. Back to Chicago? Without soccer, there was nothing left for her there. Could she find another team that would have her? Not in the US after her concussions. With her opportunities drying up, that left her back in Fillmore, New Jersey.

Home.

"He's lucky to have you."

Beth cringed at the praise. Her father's attending physician had just said the exact same thing to her yesterday. *No.* Her dad deserved better than a daughter who was already plotting her escape while he lay in a coma.

She needed to change the subject before Jordan flattered her with any more "good daughter" commentary. "What are you up to these days?" Perfectly reasonable, appropriate question. And she was curious. "You still in town?"

Jordan offered a tight-lipped smile and shook his head. "No, but I didn't go too far. I live in Baltimore now."

"Oh? What are you doing in Fillmore on a Tuesday afternoon?"

"Family stuff." His grip tightened on the six-pack. "Just staying for a few days."

"Oh," Beth said, sensing from his tone there was more to it than what he was saying. "I hope everything's all right."

"Thanks," he said. "I think so."

It's like he was trying to convince himself.

Of course Beth remembered Jordan and his father. She recalled a fuzzy vision of a younger sibling—a sister—who might have been a freshman their senior year.

"You have a younger sister?" she asked, hesitant. She had no business poking around about Jordan's family. The family that she and Ally had inadvertently helped destroy.

He nodded. "Tara. She's got a family of her own up in Connecticut."

Beth realized Jordan probably knew a lot more about her than Beth did about him.

"And you? Do you have a family of your own?"

He offered a slight smile. "No," he said. "No wife. No kids. Like you, my job keeps me pretty busy."

Not anymore.

"What do you do?" Beth asked, now curious.

"I write for the *Baltimore Sun*."

"A reporter?" She gave an uneasy laugh. Reporters and law enforcement always made her feel like she had something to hide. But this time, she *did* have something to hide. Especially from him.

"I can't imagine there'd be anything interesting to write about in Fillmore."

"You'd be surprised at what can happen in these small towns." Jordan shrugged. "I'm not here for work, though."

He left it there.

After one day, the town already felt like it was closing in on her. Her chest tightened. Beth sucked in a breath and looked down at her shopping cart. She exhaled. "I better go. It's been a long couple of days, and I just want to get home."

"Of course. Sorry I've kept you. It's just really good to see you after all this time, you know?" Jordan looked at her with those warm eyes. Dimples creased both scruffy cheeks. "If you have time, it'd be great to catch up—over coffee, or a drink? While I'm in town, you know?"

Catching up with Jordan Miller. As much as Beth approved of how well he'd grown up, meeting with him, dredging up stories from the past, would put her in a very awkward or even dangerous position.

"I can't. I need to be there for my dad," she said. "And when I'm not, I'll need to help Bill with the service station. Until Dad's stable, I can't really make any plans." She allowed herself one last deep dive into those dreamy eyes. How had she not noticed those eyes back in high school?

"I get it," he said. "Maybe I'll see you around, OK?"

As he passed her en route to the checkout line, she made a detour to the wine aisle. She was relieved to be away from him. A thin mist now adhered to her forehead. She wiped it away with the back of her hand, then took out her phone and typed as she walked.

Ally—I just ran into Jordy Miller from hs. We need to talk. Can you come over?

She clicked "Send" just as she found the red wines. She slid a bottle out and felt her phone vibrate in her pocket.

Omg. Meet you at your dad's after work.

Back home for forty-eight hours, and she'd already resumed the habit of turning to her old friend. There was no one else she could talk to about this.

Just like old times.

CHAPTER 11

ALLY

She hadn't stepped inside the front door since college, but almost everything about Ralph Snyder's home had remained the same as it had been for as long as Ally could remember.

The bungalow sat on a small corner lot a few blocks from Fillmore's tiny downtown. Mr. Snyder always walked the short distance to the service station, no matter what the weather threw at him. When they were in high school, Beth told Ally that her parents had bought the house before she was born—their starter home—based on the proximity to his business. After her mother died in a car wreck when Beth was three, the "starter" home became the "forever" home for Beth and her dad, and as far as she knew, he'd never considered relocating.

Ally paused on the sidewalk. A small, tidy lawn divided by a concrete walkway led up to the front porch of the two-story home. Late-afternoon sun bathed the landscape in a golden light—a home encased in glowy nostalgia. Two plastic Adirondack chairs took up one end of the porch and a rusty exercise bicycle the opposite end. Ally surmised all of it had probably remained in the same positions since the Clinton administration. She'd never seen anyone touch the bike, but on warm days, she'd often catch a glimpse of Ralph sitting on his porch, reading the paper or talking to Bill or someone else, while sipping a beer or coffee or a glass of iced tea. It made her sad to think he might never have the opportunity to do that again.

She walked the short path and up the steps to the front door. The door had at one point been closer to a turquoise blue, but after decades of facing the afternoon sun, the paint had faded to a pale mint. Ally had grasped the door's handle to let herself in before she remembered she hadn't done that in almost two decades.

Old habits die hard.

She pressed the chipped doorbell, which delivered a single but loud buzz.

A few seconds later, Ally heard muffled footsteps and a click as the door unlocked. Her nervous stomach clenched, and her mind flipped into hyperdrive.

Ally hadn't seen Beth in person since that Thanksgiving so long ago, and she braced herself for an older version of her former best friend, reminding herself she needed to keep it together and not appear too . . . she wasn't sure. Shocked or surprised weren't really the right emotions, since she'd given in to temptation and googled Beth from time to time over the years. And she'd also caught some of the games on TV during the big tournaments like the World Cup and the Olympics. But seeing her face to face, up close and without makeup and flattering light, would surely be much different from viewing an airbrushed headshot of her on the computer.

This fed into a high-speed accounting of some of the ways she knew her own looks had evolved—she'd added fifteen pounds to her short frame; smile and forehead creases now lined her face; and strands of gray had invaded her otherwise dark hair. (*Not to mention the little, pea-size fetus growing inside you,* she thought, but slammed the door on *that.*) Point was, these days she was far from the cute little spitfire with a pixie hairdo that she'd been in high school and early college. And she was fine with it. Wasn't she? She looked her age—not yet old, but definitely . . . softening.

Beth, though—Beth had spent the last twenty years playing soccer at the highest levels. No kids, no spouse. Obviously, she'd be in phenomenal shape. Worlds better than Ally, who'd birthed two kids and didn't have the time or the access to trainers and nutritionists. *She'll probably look amazing even without the makeup.*

Now, as the footsteps approached the door, Ally steeled herself for how Beth couldn't help but see *her*—a common, ordinary, unspecial soccer mom.

Beth swung open the front door.

If anyone appeared like they'd spent too much time at the hospital, Beth fit the description. *Haggard* was the first word that came to mind when Ally laid eyes on her. It was likely she'd hardly slept in days. Her long hair was pulled back into a messy ponytail, and her bright-green eyes—how could she forget?—were bloodshot, eyelids heavy. She wondered if Beth had thrown on whatever was at the top of her suitcase— faded jeans and a wrinkled T-shirt. And, yes, as expected: no makeup. And was that a bruise on the side of her head? In a word, Beth looked a mess. Ally ached for her, and she abandoned the meaningless comparisons and jealousy.

"Aw, Beth," she said, opening her arms for an embrace.

Beth was a good six inches taller than Ally and had to stoop slightly as they hugged.

When they drew apart, Beth looked down at Ally and gave her a tired grin. "I can't believe you rang the doorbell. I didn't even think it was you—thought it was the mail carrier or something."

Ally laughed. "I almost did waltz right in."

Beth gestured her inside the house. The living room still featured the same overstuffed sectional that was too big for the size of the room, an ancient olive-green shag rug, and outdated lighting and side tables that wouldn't have sold at a secondhand shop. Dusty, feminine curtains hung in the windows. Ally had never asked, but she imagined Beth's mom—so many years younger than they were now!—had chosen window dressings at some point in the late seventies or early eighties before Beth was born.

A heavy wooden shelf that stretched from the floor to the ceiling took over most of the wall on the way to the dining room. Soccer trophies, medals, team photos, and framed certificates of Beth's athletic accomplishments crowded each rack. It was like a shrine that chronicled every achievement from childhood to now.

A much younger Ally was featured in a few of those photos, and she'd shared in a couple of those trophies. Even now, Ally felt a small tug of pride seeing some of her high school exploits on display. Her own parents—both worked full time and were usually too busy to attend her games—had boxed away all her soccer paraphernalia once she moved out of the house, gave up on college, and had babies. It was like all those years she'd devoted to the sport as a player no longer existed.

Ally only recognized one new item in the living room, which was a giant flat-screen TV that dominated an entire end of the room.

She couldn't help it—she smirked.

Beth noticed. "I know. That TV is obnoxious." She motioned for Ally to sit on the couch, where she took in the full spectacle of it. Last time she'd been in this living room, Beth's dad had still owned a tube television. "He got it when he heard the women's league games were going to be broadcast on cable."

Ally melted a little. *Ralph Snyder: the most supportive parent on the planet.*

"How's he doing?" she asked, though she knew—out of the ICU and lying in a hospital bed, sedated in an induced coma.

"The same," Beth said, still standing in front of her father's BarcaLounger.

"I'm sorry." Ally wondered if Beth had thought about what a long road she had ahead of her, if her father survived. Probably.

"I know."

Ally sensed a slight edge to Beth's tone, making it clear she'd received a lot of useless sympathy over the last two days. Or maybe she was just feeling awkward and tired. She was never a people person. Not like Ally was.

Ally raised her hand to her own temple. "That's quite a war wound. From a game?"

Beth gave a quick nod and angled her head away from her, like she was trying to hide the injury. "It's nothing. Just a bruise."

In the awkward silence that followed, Ally looked down at her hands, which were empty. She didn't even bring food. Nothing. She'd done nothing. Nothing but bring up everything painful to her old friend.

"I'm sorry," she said again. "I should have brought something."

Beth waved this away. "I've only been here two days, most of them at the hospital. And you have a life—the girls, the league. Your friend at the hospital—the nurse—told me you've got a new guy."

Ally blinked. Diana always had a bit of a big mouth. Not that the entire town didn't know her relationship status. "Yes. Noah. He's the new principal at the high school. Just started in the fall after teaching for more than a decade."

Beth at last seated herself on the recliner. "At Fillmore? Is that weird?"

Ally paused, not sure if Beth was alluding to twenty years ago or to the fact that her own daughters attended the school. She decided to play it safe and stay in the relative present. At least for the moment.

"It was a little weird with the girls at the beginning, especially since we met because he'd been Morgan's history teacher her junior year." She shrugged. "But not anymore."

"Really?" Beth leaned forward in her chair. She had the same look on her face she'd had as a teenager, when she was about to hear something juicy. "I bet *that* got tongues wagging around here."

It had indeed.

Ally's cheeks grew warm. "Well, you know how it is." Did she, though? It's not like Beth had spent any real time in town recently. "So, speaking of high school, what's this about you running into Jordy Miller?"

When she'd received Beth's text, Ally had tried picturing him and could only envision a short, delicate-looking boy with dark curly hair who'd helped out their high school soccer coaches during practices and games. *The custodian's son.* Ally's stomach churned. For a second, Ally wondered if it was nerves or the faint stirrings of the baby. "He was our age, right? I remember he looked so much younger."

Beth nodded. "He's taller now."

"So where'd you run into him?"

Beth sat back in the chair. "ShopRite."

Ally frowned, trying to conjure up any gossip she might've gleaned about him in the last twenty years. Nothing. "The grocery store? Did he move back or something?" If so, how strange Beth had seen him in the two days she'd been back and not her.

She shook her head. "Definitely not. He lives in Baltimore. He's a reporter for the *Baltimore Sun*."

Crap. Dread flowed through Ally.

She almost didn't want to ask the only question left.

"What's he doing in town, then?"

"He didn't say." Beth absently touched her fingertips to her chin. "'Family stuff' was all he'd let on. But I got the sense there was more to it, you know?"

The sentence hung suspended between them.

"OK, so tell me." Ally wanted to take the full story down, like medicine.

"That's all he said." Beth's face paled as she sank down onto the BarcaLounger. "Which is what worries me."

Clearly Beth hadn't lost her flair for the dramatic.

"Come on," Ally said, pressing herself down into the sofa. "Where's the intrigue? Everybody's got family stuff."

"Yeah, but his family moved *away*," Beth insisted. "You know, after everything."

Ally paused. As far as she knew, that was still true. If any of them had moved back in the last few years, especially either of Jordy's parents, word would have gotten around.

This was ridiculous. What, the *Baltimore Sun* had dispatched Jordan here to tear the lid off the botched investigation into a twenty-year-old gymnasium fire? *Think about it, Beth,* she should be saying. *It just doesn't compute.* But Ally couldn't form the words. Speaking them would bring the whole thing into the open again, even just for the two of them, and that prospect swelled her with the urge to rise from the couch and bolt out the front door. So instead she sat still, her body rigid.

How could Beth dare to bring this up? Hadn't they all moved on? She had.

She'd had to.

As destructive and traumatic as it had been, the fire was ancient news. Construction on the expensive new gym—the "sports complex"—was practically completed. Ally felt almost certain the entire town had put the fire well behind them. Hell, they'd probably forgotten it had ever happened. They certainly would once that new gym opened.

"Sounds like Jordy won't be here long," Ally said at last. "How long did he say?"

Beth took a quick glance at the shelf of trophies, as if gaining strength from her past accomplishments. The bruise reflected the glare from the ceiling light. Ally wondered if that conk on her head had done more damage than Beth let on.

"A few days." Beth rested her chin in her hand. Her forehead relaxed. "But you're right. I'm just tired and jumping to conclusions."

A wave of nausea took hold of Ally for a brief moment. She felt a flash of anger toward this tiny thing growing inside her, which, at any time, anywhere, insisted on reminding her it existed. Her thoughts returned to bolting, but this time to the powder room. She tried willing the nausea away and forced herself to look up at the medals and photos that crowded the shelf—Ralph Snyder's Monument to Beth's Achievements—seeing if she could find strength there too.

Her stomach calmed as she zeroed in on a framed picture that stood out to her as though a spotlight were trained on it. Ally rose from the couch to take a closer look and plucked it off the shelf. Her heart twisted when she saw it was of the newspaper article about the two of them during their senior year. In the photo accompanying the story, Beth and Ally were captured after clinching the district finals, Beth hugging Ally's shoulders. Their faces were pure joy.

Beth stood to take a closer look. "I remember when the guy took that. Just another fun moment, a cherry on top. Little did we know how much mileage we'd get from that story. No way would we have gotten even a sniff from good programs, much less scholarship offers."

"I don't know about that," Ally said, leaning in a little closer. She and Beth beamed in the photograph. They both looked so young, so proud. Ally knew the confidence she'd displayed in the picture was all show. On the inside, she'd been packed to her eyebrows with fear, like she'd known that was as good as it was going to get for her. *Faker.* "You certainly would've gotten offers. I was just along for the ride. We were just always thrown together because we were the only girls on the team."

Beth scowled at her. "We were two of the best players on that team. No one controlled the center like you."

"I don't know about that. But I *do* know that no one scored on you that whole tournament."

"It was a long time ago," Beth said, seeming lost in the memory. "It was about a lot more than just soccer that year."

"Well." Ally didn't have a response. She refused to think about the past, but Beth was right. They'd survived a lot their senior year. That photo represented a life she'd long ago given up. "We played hard." Ally looked up at Beth. "And then you left. Ditched me."

Beth flashed a mock glare at her. "Uh, college. Scholarship. Soccer." She crossed her arms on her chest. "What you mean is that you left *me*." Beth's voice had gone quiet. "Left me for Rob, and babies. Your 'new life.'"

"Soccer wasn't everything," Ally said brightly, though in fact it was exactly what she'd told herself at the time. And it turned out, she'd been right. Mostly. Now, Ally strained to keep it light between her and Beth, tossing it off as a simple statement of fact about a time they'd both left way, way behind. But a whirling stew of jealousy and resentment and God only knew what else had begun to bubble in her chest.

"It was everything to me," Beth said, her tone matter of fact. "*Is.*"

Ally tried to turn down the heat inside her. Willed herself to take a breath. "Well," she said, "maybe slow down while you're here. Let your head heal. Get to know Fillmore again."

Beth shook her head. "I can't."

"Fillmore's changed a lot since you left. It's not the same town it was in high school." Ally returned the framed photo to its place on the shelf. "The boys are grown, for one thing." She shot a glance at Beth, who groaned.

"Are they still around?" Beth's lips formed into a sneer. "Wouldn't mind punching them each in the face. Wouldn't mind that at all, actually."

"Travis and Evan moved away. Kyle's here, but he's an adult with a job and family. Thankfully, I don't really run into him. I doubt you will either," Ally said. "And the gym—it's being rebuilt."

Beth stared at the photo a moment longer. "What should we do about Jordan Miller?"

"I don't know." And Ally didn't. What *could* they do that wouldn't just raise questions? "Probably let it go, right? I mean, really. For you, focus on your dad instead of worrying too much about something that's nothing."

Beth nodded, though Ally could see there was a lot going on behind her eyes.

"Hey, look, your dad's prognosis is going to change day to day. I can help you research his options when you're ready." Ally wanted to help and knew that if soccer really was everything to Beth, she'd probably find untangling the complicated mess of medical insurance overwhelming and confusing. And Ally needed Beth to stay in the present and not dwell. *Certainly not fly off into something that would only blow up in our faces.*

That stopped her. *Not the best phrase, Ally.*

"Let me look into his insurance benefits. I know my way around benefits thanks to running a league with a dozen employees on my payroll, OK?"

"Thanks." Beth gave Ally a wan smile. "I would appreciate that, actually."

Ally felt a flush of joy that Beth was letting her help her out. She fished her car keys from her jacket pocket. She'd never even taken the coat off.

"With any luck, Noah's making dinner right now." She paused. The house felt so quiet, so empty without Mr. Snyder. Ally could hear the kitchen wall clock ticking two rooms over. "You want to come over? You could stay as long or as short as you like."

Beth reached over and embraced Ally. "Thank you." Her voice was muffled by Ally's coat. Ally wasn't sure if Beth had started to tear up. This was the Beth Ally remembered—tough on the outside but always a softy at her core. "I'm going to cook a little something and then go straight to sleep. I have to be up early anyway to see Dad."

When they parted, Ally noticed that Beth's eyes were a bit damp. Beth opened the front door for her.

"I know it's useless, but try not to worry too much," Ally said. "You can lean on me."

As she walked back to her car, she had a feeling Beth might just take her up on her offer. She hoped so.

CHAPTER 12

BETH

Beth wiped her eyes with the back of her hand. Crying again. It's like she'd turned into a different person. She barely recognized this weepy, sentimental, and frightened version of herself. As though Fillmore had sapped all the fight out of her.

Through her front window, she watched Ally's car roar to life and then disappear into the evening.

Alone again.

She walked back to the multitiered shelf and studied it. The shelf had always been a place for memories. With her father around, she'd never had a chance to really take a good look at its contents without his commentary, but now she had the opportunity to see what he'd included, what mattered most to him.

Her soccer hadn't always come first. When she was young, he'd crammed it with pictures of her grandparents on both sides, of her mom, and of the three of them in those rare family photos. After her mom had died and she'd started to play the game more seriously, the shift began. Gradually, he swapped the old images with new, and over time, the shelf morphed into a space dedicated to Beth's soccer career.

Still, Ally was one of the most featured faces aside from her own.

Her dad wasn't like other soccer dads. Maybe it was because he was a single father. Losing her mother so early meant most of Beth's "memories" of her came from pictures and the stories her dad told her. He'd had to do the work of two parents, and he'd done the best he could.

Or maybe it was because she was the only child. Outside of running the service station, her dad's focus and attention were channeled to her. She didn't always appreciate the attention, but he was there whether she liked it or not.

Or maybe it was her preternatural athletic talent. No one was prouder of her than her dad. The part that delighted him to no end was that her physical strength, confidence, and drive didn't come from him, but from her mother—as if an important and vital piece of her mom had gone on living within Beth. He did whatever it took to stoke that flame.

So as Beth accumulated the accolades and visible forms of achievement, her dad quietly relegated the wedding pictures and family photos to other, less visible parts of the house.

How sport had shaped Beth also ended up defining her dad and how he presented himself to the world. Or at least to Fillmore, which was world enough for him. Her journey as an athlete had become his story too.

Beth hadn't considered how that story would end, never imagining the choice to end it wouldn't originate from her.

She hated herself for thinking that if the stroke did him in, at least he'd be saved from learning she'd been prematurely retired from her sport. *Their* sport.

Beth reached for the framed *Times* article and studied it. Ally was right—they were two of the best players on that championship team and deserved a lot more than a human-interest article spotlighting the ongoing disparity in girls' and women's sports, decades after the passage of Title IX. But the joy on Beth's face masked the guilt she'd spent a lifetime running from. They'd both made irreversible choices that year that had forever changed them.

Well, she couldn't speak for Ally, who seemed to be doing just fine. Maybe only Beth had been irrevocably changed.

And Jordan Miller's father. And Jordy.

Out of everything on that shelf, the *Times* article from her senior year of high school might have held the most meaning. That moment had launched her entire trajectory. It represented all that she'd traded to excel in this sport that she'd fought to play her entire life. And it didn't come without consequences.

Not just for her and Ally. Not just for the high school and township that lost a beloved landmark.

It was supposed to be a joke. A prank to get back at Kyle, Evan, and Travis—the teammates who'd gone out of their way to make Beth and Ally's time on the Fillmore High School soccer team a daily nightmare. Beth and Ally didn't mean to burn the gym to the ground. It was a prank meant as payback for the years of harassment they'd endured. Or according to the boys, the "jokes" and "pranks" they'd "played" on them.

Beth returned the photo to the shelf. Jordan Miller was back. Ally seemed so certain she was worrying over nothing. After all, in twenty years, no one had found any evidence that linked her and Ally to that fire. No one else but she and Ally had any reason to think about it now—except for Jordan Miller. And his family.

God, it always came back to the Millers.

And now, most pointedly, to Jordy. Those bewitching eyes of his. Maybe Ally was right and she should steer clear of him. She was glad she hadn't told her that Jordy had asked her to meet up. Almost sounded like a date.

She thought about uncorking the wine she'd bought earlier, pouring herself a glass, and attempting to settle in for the night. A restlessness stirred in her, though, an uneasiness that made her press the pause button. This house was crammed full of reminders of her past. It was stifling. She wanted . . . out. Even if it was just temporary.

Beth opened the coat closet, grabbed her jacket and keys, and walked out the front door.

The temperature hadn't risen above fifty degrees, not unusual for April. Beth hugged her insulated coat to herself as she fast walked the three blocks to Zeke's Bar and Grill, the only tavern in town.

She prepared herself for who she might run into there—Bill, possibly. Her dad used to drink with him now and again after closing the station for the evening. Maybe an old high school acquaintance. Maybe Kyle. She didn't know how she felt about that—but she certainly wasn't going to let the prospect of bumping into one of their old tormentors deter her from doing whatever the hell she wanted to do. Facing him down might even be just what the doctor ordered.

Easy, she cautioned herself. *Take a breath.* From what Ally had told her, Kyle had mellowed into just another functional townie adult. Everybody got to be an idiot in high school, didn't they?

She certainly hoped so.

In any event, it was just as likely she'd run into exactly no one. Hopefully no one. Maybe she could blend in, pretend she was invisible like she did at airports and hotel bars and restaurants, and enjoy the hum of conversation around her without having to actively participate.

Beth pushed open the door to Zeke's and let herself in. Zeke's had been a staple of Fillmore long before she was born. It might have been around even longer than her dad's service station, which he'd bought when the previous owner retired. As the main eating-and-drinking spot in town, Zeke's had been serving Fillmore residents since the 1960s. She'd come here with her dad all the time when she was a kid. Much less often in the last twenty years—maybe only twice since college. But not much had changed. The bar itself took over much of the entire wall on the right side of the room. A few raised tables and barstools dotted the area near the bar, but lower two- and four-top tables took up most of the floor space. Booths hugged the edges of the room.

The happy hour crowd seemed to be dwindling, with people gathering purses and buttoning up coats, freeing most of the tables now set for casual dinner service.

Beth easily found an open seat at the end of the bar, with a two-stool buffer between her and the nearest humans—a pale young man with red hair and a sparse beard, and an older African American woman, her graying hair pulled back into a low bun, both of them dressed in postal service uniforms. The pair talked and laughed, nursing what looked to be bourbon or whiskey in weighty lowball glasses.

As she unzipped her jacket, Beth admired the addition of white string lights positioned above and around a large mirror that illuminated the wide selection of spirits, wine, mixers, and beers on tap. She felt a warmth from the place that she hadn't experienced anywhere in a long time.

At the far end of the bar, the bartender backed out of swinging double doors carrying two plates of hamburgers and fries and placed them in front of the postal workers, who each nodded their approval. He slid a towel from his shoulder and wiped his hands as he made his way toward Beth. She thought he looked familiar, but how she might know him was blank. He smiled at her in recognition as he drew close.

"Beth Snyder." He slid a cardboard coaster in front of her. "When did you get into town?"

"Two days ago," she said, still trying to place him. "Um, I'm sorry. I'm terrible with names."

"Mike Row. I was starting keeper when you began playing varsity. You were my backup."

"No kidding?" She could see him now. The closely cropped Afro from high school was now fashioned into locs that fell past his broad shoulders. And his powerful frame had softened a bit with age, but his smile and eyes seemed locked in time. Fillmore was truly the smallest world. A freshman when he was a junior, Beth hadn't thought Mike had even known she existed. "How long have you been tending bar?"

He paused, squinting at the ceiling. "Gosh, almost eleven years, now. I also have my own personal-training business." He shrugged. "Gotta pay the bills, right?"

"Right." Beth nodded. "Do you still play?"

Mike shook his head. "Gave it up. My knees couldn't take it anymore. It's why I got into training. I know so many people we went to high school with who have back problems, knee problems, ankle problems. Age, right?"

"Right," she said again.

He straightened, as if remembering he had a job to do. "So what can I get you?"

Something to sip slowly, so she could put off going home for a while. "Bourbon on the rocks."

In an instant, he'd scooped a few ice cubes and poured a generous amount of bourbon into a tumbler.

"On the house," he said, setting it atop the coaster. "So what brings you back to Fillmore? A game? You play for Chicago, right?"

She almost didn't think she heard right. Someone in Fillmore other than her father—and Jordan Miller—kept up with women's soccer.

She shook her head and took a deep sip from her glass. The alcohol warmed her insides and provided a thin barrier to her reality. "My dad. He had a stroke."

"No, really?" His eyes widened. "He was just here last week. Ordered the Wednesday lunch special. Aw, I'm sorry. How's he doing?"

"Not great." Beth knew she'd have to rehash the news of her dad over and over for the foreseeable future, and so far, over the last two days it hadn't gotten any easier with repetition. There would be no escape. That was Fillmore.

Mike nodded like he understood. That made her feel a little better. "You got anyone to help give you a break?"

"It's just me," she said, chewing the inside of her cheek. "And Bill at the station. And a whole team of medical professionals. They're doing all the heavy lifting. I'm basically just waiting around for news." She met his eyes. "Which is why I'm here. I can't sit around. I'm no good at it."

"Uh-huh. I hear that." Mike paused and leaned into the bar, propping his head in his hand. His gaze seemed unfocused, as if he were no longer in the bar but somewhere else. "Twenty years. My God."

Beth took another sip of her drink. Seemed she couldn't avoid memory lane no matter where she went.

"They're building a new gym," he said. "Did you know?"

No avoiding the gym either. She nodded. "I heard it's being rebuilt, but that's all I know."

"A huge facility—I hear they're calling it a 'sports complex,' not just a gym," Mike said. "And it'll be for everyone, not just the high school. Hoping I can use it for my clients."

Beth sat up, intrigued. "Is it in the same spot?"

"Yeah. Right by the field." He shook his head. "I have such a clear picture of it before it all burned. The wood floors, the team banners hanging on the walls. That huge mural—painted by someone famous. Or famous adjacent. One of Diego Rivera's protégés from Russia or Poland or something." Mike's eyes lit up. "And all those rusted-out lockers in the locker room. I even remember the *smell*—like metal and sweat and damp all at once, right?"

Beth remembered too. Their coach had held all team meetings, after each practice and home game, in the boys' locker room, even with the lone girls on the team—her and Ally—present. No one seemed to notice at the time how uncomfortable those meetings had made Beth and Ally feel.

Mike's eyes shifted to the door. Beth followed his gaze and saw Jordan Miller let himself in and make his way toward the bar.

"Well, look at this," Mike said as Jordan approached. "It's like a mini reunion."

Beth's stomach gave an involuntary flutter at the sight of him.

He offered them both a quizzical look.

"Mind if I"—he drew out the sentence, as if unsure he even wanted to ask—"join you?"

Ally's words reverberated in Beth's brain. *Just let it go . . . focus on your dad instead of worrying about something that's nothing.*

"Not at all." She took a long sip from her glass, swallowing Ally's advice along with the bourbon. Sure, Mike had just casually brought up the gym fire. And she'd turned Jordan down for a drink mere hours ago, and here she was—out. But he *had* been clutching a six-pack of beer when she ran into him.

She said, "Finished your beer?"

He shook his head and smiled slyly, as if he'd just been found out. He took a seat on the stool beside her.

"No, actually. Ended up feeling a little cooped up in the hotel. Needed to get out." He turned his attention to Mike, who'd set a coaster in front of him. "Hope I'm not interrupting anything."

Beth's cheeks went warm.

"Just reminiscing," Mike said through a curt smile. Beth hoped that was as far as he'd get about the gym fire. If Ally thought the town had forgotten about that fire, she was sorely mistaken. "What can I get you?"

"I'll have what she's having."

Mike gave him a thumbs-up.

"How's your family stuff going?" she said, trying to keep her voice low. Her face warmed even further as she asked the question.

"Family stuff?" Mike said across the bar. He set a tumbler in front of Jordan. "I thought—" He stopped himself.

Jordan frowned. Beth regretted mentioning it.

"They all moved," Jordan said. "That's right."

"Sorry," Mike said. "Not my business."

Jordan waved him off and relaxed on the stool, a thoughtful look on his face.

What are you thinking about? Beth wanted to ask. *Why are you back in town?*

But she couldn't appear as deeply interested and invested as she was. She needed to shrug it off the way Mike did. Like the subject was just a standard topic of conversation. Like it didn't even matter to her. Like it didn't eat up her insides.

Beth drained her bourbon and started to put on her coat.

"I gotta go," she said. She needed to get out of there before the bourbon had numbed all her good sense and she started asking more questions about the Millers' "family stuff."

Jordan placed his hand lightly on her arm and tilted his head toward her. "Let's talk sometime, OK?" Beth could feel his warm breath on her ear. "When you get another urge to get out of the house, call me." He placed a business card beside her purse.

Beth felt a stirring of both desire and guilt. If he had any clue about who she was and what she'd done, he wouldn't want anything to do with her.

She took the business card and slid it into her jacket pocket.

"OK."

CHAPTER 13

BETH

Beth shut her car door, balancing her purse and a ginormous stainless steel bowl full of salad greens covered in plastic wrap as she carefully turned the key to lock her car door at the end of Ally's driveway, which was already lined with vehicles. *Great, last to arrive.* Her Advil hadn't kicked in as quickly as she'd hoped, and a dull throb lingered at the edges of her skull.

She didn't recognize anyone's car but Ally's and wondered who might be there this afternoon. Certainly Noah and Ally's girls, probably Ally's parents, maybe some close friends. Would Ally's younger brother, Drew, show up? He supposedly lived one town over, so possibly. And what about Noah's family? Did they live nearby? So many in this town just never left. Beth was the odd one. Well, and Jordan.

Her paranoia about Jordan had cooled as soon as she started getting more sleep. After Zeke's, she hadn't run into him anywhere, and she hadn't called the number on the card he gave her. A few days of "family stuff" and she supposed he'd returned to Baltimore, back to his real life.

Real life. Beth longed for some semblance of that for herself. But she felt completely unmoored. In truth, she viewed this casual celebration today as a welcome distraction. A commemoration of Noah and Ally's engagement meant Beth could temporarily suspend all the difficulties she'd yet to work through about her soccer career and, especially, her dad's grim condition.

Over the last two and a half weeks, she'd been knee deep in learning everything she did and didn't want to know about strokes and brain aneurysms, getting her father's affairs in order without a will to guide her (*Thanks, Dad*), and finding out what went into running a small business (a lot, it turned out).

In a word, Beth was spent. Nothing she did seemed to get her any closer to healing her father, getting him on track, and making her escape back to her soccer world. If anything, she was further away from all of it.

Not that she'd just spun her wheels. She'd quietly started working out again on her own. No soccer yet. Who would she train with, anyway? No one at the professional level. Word had gotten around fast in the insular world of US women's soccer that she was out for the season—if not for good. If Beth was going to try out internationally by the end of August, she needed to get back into shape—headaches or no headaches. This small slice of hope fueled her.

And to her utter surprise, she'd also rekindled her friendship with Ally.

If anyone had asked Beth a month ago if she believed she'd be on speaking terms again with her old friend, she'd have said absolutely not. But in truth, Ally had stepped up as a friend, as if she'd been there the entire time—from helping Beth navigate her dad's medical benefits to inviting her over for family meals to lending a shoulder to cry on. And, over numerous cups of coffee, Ally had caught Beth up on her life, too, even if it was just the CliffsNotes version. Beth just wished there was some way she could support Ally like Ally was supporting her.

She stood in front of Ally's home, a two-story colonial at the end of a quiet cul-de-sac. She now knew it was the same house Ally had shared with her ex-husband, Rob, toward the end of their shaky marriage.

They bought it after they moved out of their first, cramped apartment, where they'd lived after her parents' house. Beth could hear the pride in her voice when Ally mentioned she'd figured out a way to buy her share of the house and make the mortgage payments herself—all this after she and Rob had split and she'd started earning an income from her soccer league.

As Beth approached the front door, Morgan emerged carrying a bulging plastic bag. The screen door slapped shut behind her.

"Hey," Morgan called, lifting her chin in greeting without slowing her progress toward the side of the house. Her thick golden hair was pulled back into a saggy ponytail that fell heavily down her back. She made her way to the other side of the garage, swung the bag into a garbage can, and returned in time to join Beth at the top of the driveway. "Mom wasn't sure you'd be able to make it."

Beth grinned. "I wasn't about to miss your mom and Noah's engagement party."

They walked together across the lawn toward the house. When she'd first met Morgan and Emily at their Sunday family dinner two weeks ago, she was struck by Emily's physical resemblance to Ally—small in stature, with rich, dark hair and eyes—and Morgan's emotional resemblance. It was uncanny how Morgan's intensity matched her mom's. But Morgan also carried a certain confidence, a poise that Ally hadn't developed at the same age. Emily, on the other hand, was quieter, cooler, so different from her mom and her sister. Emily's interests lay in her creative projects—which Ally proudly displayed all over her house—and she didn't always seem to care about being the most liked, which Beth appreciated.

Morgan took a breath. "We weren't sure, 'cause of your dad. I miss seeing Mr. Snyder at the station every day on the way home after school."

Beth gave her a fragile smile. "Me too. I'm hoping he'll be out there again soon." She feared the odds of him running the service station again on his own were slim to none at this point.

"How are tryouts?" Beth asked, changing the subject. From what she'd learned from Ally about Morgan's abilities as a forward, she didn't think Morgan would have any trouble making the travel team again. Ally'd bragged that she had a real shot at a scholarship to college the following year, which Beth knew Morgan was hoping for. She and her mom both were.

"They're going good, I think." Morgan opened the front door and let Beth into the entryway. "I think everyone wants to come back and play next year. We have a lot of new girls, though, who are pretty good. We'll see if there's room on the team. Last year our coach had to cut six girls. This year, it's probably going to be more."

Beth knew Ally fretted about making cuts to these travel teams. As the league continued to thrive, the teams became stronger and more competitive. With competition came the cuts. Beth knew it broke Ally's heart to turn away girls who just wanted to play, even if they weren't at the level to get them onto the travel team.

"What happens to the girls who don't make it?"

"Sometimes they try out for other teams," Morgan said. "But now that we have the intramural teams, at least there's a spot for them here in town."

"Really? Your mom started intramural squads too?"

Morgan nodded. "It all just keeps growing."

Ally hadn't mentioned this development. One more thing added to her to-do list. Still, for all that Ally had given up, this life she'd built for herself looked pretty . . . good.

Beth couldn't fathom how she juggled a demanding job along with raising a family as a single mom. Or how any mom did. Beth was sure she'd fail miserably at it. Of course, she'd never put herself in a position to see if she could manage it. But she couldn't even manage a boyfriend and a soccer career, let alone kids. A lot of the professional players were in committed relationships, and a few even had children, but Beth's focus was 100 percent dedicated to the game.

Except, it wasn't anymore.

"How cool," Beth said.

"Yeah, it's all high school–age girls. Every Saturday. Sometimes Mom makes Emily and me help out."

Morgan led Beth back to the kitchen, where her mom, sister, and Ally's mother, Patsy, were all in some kind of motion. Pizza boxes were stacked on the kitchen counter, and foil-covered trays of what were probably rich, bubbling pasta dishes lined the stove top. The room smelled like an Italian restaurant. Emily, who was opening a package of paper napkins, looked up and gave Beth a hang loose sign.

Ally wiped her hands and walked over to Beth. She gave her a quick hug.

"Thanks for coming." She nodded to Beth's salad. "You didn't have to bring anything. Just yourself."

Ally opened the refrigerator and took out bottles of dressing and placed them beside the salad bowl.

"I wanted to. It's sort of nice to make a little something that's not just for me." Even though the salad *was* kind of for her. She'd learned early on in her soccer career that bringing food was a way to ensure she'd have at least something to eat at gatherings. And if she was going to try out for the Australian W-League in August—maybe even fly out for their premier season over the summer—then she needed to keep an eye on what she ate as well as exercise. If she was going to train and get serious about getting back on the pitch, then she needed to curb the pizza and lasagna. "And it's just salad. It's not like I cooked anything complicated. Or cooked, period."

Ally's mom edged away from the kitchen sink and walked over to Beth, then gave her a warm hug, radiating the light, familiar smell of her Sunflowers perfume, her signature scent for as long as she'd known her. It was exactly what Beth needed—to be around a family who knew her as well as she knew herself.

"Oh my dear," Patsy said quietly, into her hair. "I'm so sorry about Ralph. There is no one in town more loved than your father."

Beth was touched by Patsy's words, but knew she wouldn't be able to take it if all anyone wanted to talk about was her father. She'd come to celebrate, to not think about all that, at least for the next couple of hours.

Fortunately, just as they always had, Patsy's emotions could change with the wind. She stepped back to arms' length and gave Beth a little frown. "Are you *still* playing soccer? How's that head of yours?" She shifted Beth's chin and squinted at the bruise. "Well. I see it's still attached to your neck, at least."

Beth laughed uneasily and looked at the floor. She wasn't yet sharing about her unplanned retirement and wasn't about to give up on playing forever. But Patsy wasn't letting her go without a response. She settled for "I'm on leave for now," but even that was enough to lift one of Ally's eyebrows in her periphery. Now she had the full attention of both of them. *What the hell:* "But I plan to make a comeback. Maybe premier or the W-League over the summer. I'll see how it goes and what my neurologist says."

Ally's eyes widened, but Patsy rolled with it. "Well, let us know when we can see you on TV." She turned and gazed at her granddaughters. "We would *all* love to watch you play."

Beth flushed, knowing that probably wouldn't happen again anytime soon. "Sure will."

"Mom, girls, can you please take these pizzas and lasagnas out to the dining room table? And the salad too?" Ally handed stacks of boxes to Emily, and Morgan grabbed the salad bowl, tongs, and bottles of dressing. Patsy lifted a tray of pasta with a pair of oven mitts. They all headed out of the kitchen just as Noah entered carrying a half-filled tumbler. He made his way over to Beth.

"I thought I heard your voice." He gave her a quick peck on the cheek. "So glad you could come."

"Congratulations," Beth said. She'd never seen a happier fiancé than Noah. She glanced over at Ally, whose attention seemed to be focused on gathering plasticware from a gallon-size Ziploc bag and attempting to shoo the cat off the counter.

"Thanks. Wild, isn't it?" Noah shook his head, like he still couldn't believe his luck, and then took a pull from his glass.

Ally walked over and shoved a fistful of plastic forks at him. "Here, hon. Will you put these out?"

"Sure, kid." Noah took the utensils and kissed the top of her head. "I'd do pretty much anything for you."

When he left, Beth and Ally were alone in the kitchen. Ally wrangled the cat out the screen door.

"Oh my God, he is giddy," Beth said, sitting. "Or maybe it's the gin and tonics. Either way, he can't contain himself." She grinned. "It's pretty endearing."

Ally slid the door closed and plopped down at the kitchen table. "I'm exhausted," she said, rubbing her temple. "This week has been murder. But, yeah, Noah's thrilled."

Beth bit her lip. She'd been so consumed with getting a grasp on her dad's affairs as well as her own career woes, she'd neglected to notice that maybe Ally was struggling too.

"And tryouts started this week. Silver Lake field is a swamp again and completely unusable, so I've been scrambling to find another location. Oh, and get this: One of my coaches quit. She got hired at the University of Vermont as the assistant coach for the women's team. I don't blame her for leaving, but good grief, what timing. I wish she didn't have to leave right away. Or go so far away. I need someone now to run the U13 tryouts, and I have a bunch of twelve-year-olds who need a coach. Their parents are going to be furious."

"What are you going to do?"

Ally shrugged. "Probably run those tryouts myself? Maybe step in as coach for a little while? But that means I won't be available to put out the inevitable fires that pop up every day." She counted on her fingers. "Secure another field, probably for the rest of the spring season. Find a coach. Buy more equipment. God. Remind me why I did this again?"

Ally hadn't talked much about feeling this overwhelmed, probably because she'd been so focused on Beth. All Beth had been focused on was herself too. She thought about it—Ally had reared this league for a decade, and it continued to grow into its awkward tween years.

Beth placed a hand over Ally's. "What can I do to help?"

"You can't." Ally offered her a wan smile. "Thank you for offering, but you've got your dad." She shook her head slowly, the smile evaporating. "And you're leaving."

Beth sat back, registering the hurt, the reproach in Ally's tone. "I'm not leaving *now*. I can help." She thought about it. She could run try-outs, at least, and step in as a temporary coach. And she needed something to take her mind off her dad. She couldn't hang out at the hospital twenty-four hours a day.

As she thought some more, Beth felt almost insulted that Ally hadn't thought to just ask her. Who better to coach a bunch of twelve-year-old girls than a professional soccer player? Sure, she hopefully wouldn't be around forever, but for now?

"Let me take that U13 team, at least get it going. I'll run tryouts. If I need to make cuts, I'll run them by you and figure out what to do with the overflow." A surge of excitement energized her. "I can coach the girls until you have more time after tryouts to find someone permanent. I think it's perfect."

Ally drummed her fingers on the table. "I just don't want to be the reason you can't be there for your dad," she said. "He's your priority."

"Oh, he *is* my priority," Beth said. "But even in the unlikely event I get called away at the last minute for something related to Dad, you're still a hundred times better off with me now than worrying about replacing that coach right away. I'm just taking one thing off your plate. Besides, it will get me outside and give me something fun to think about. Tryouts are, when—a few days over the next couple of weeks? And stepping in to coach would be two days of practice and weekend games?" She gave a dismissive wave. "I totally got this."

"And what about the service station?"

"Bill's on top of things. I pop in mornings, but afternoons are slow. He doesn't need me."

"I don't know," Ally said. She winced. "I can't afford another heart-break for this team."

"I won't break their hearts," Beth said, her face serious. "Promise."

Ally's eyes shone. "The girls *would* be thrilled if a professional soccer player was coaching their team," she said. "Thank you. You're saving me, here."

"It'll be fun," Beth said, hoping it would be true. It certainly felt right to her now. "Hungry?"

Ally nodded, and the two walked to the dining room, where Ally's parents and another older pair, probably Noah's parents, all sat around the coffee table, talking and balancing plates of food and drinks. Beth recognized Ally's younger brother, Drew, and the woman standing beside him from some of the framed photographs that crowded Ally's fireplace mantel. They were in conversation with Noah, who looked as if he'd topped off his drink. A small boy dressed in what appeared to be Spider-Man pajamas grasped Drew's fingers with one hand while sucking the thumb of the other. A somewhat bigger boy let himself out to the backyard, where Morgan and Emily sat on swings, tapping their phones. An intimate crowd—warmth flowed through Beth that Ally had thought to include her in it.

Just then, Noah decided to get everyone's attention. The kids all filtered into the room.

"I just—" he said as the conversation died down. "I just wanted to thank everyone for coming out to celebrate our engagement."

Ally walked over and placed her arm around his waist. Beth admired the way she and Noah seemed to fit so perfectly together. She hoped she'd find someone who'd fit her like that someday too. It could happen, right?

"Please join us in a toast," Noah said, raising his near-empty tumbler. "To Ally and her parents, her daughters, her brother and his family, and to my parents and brother and sister, who couldn't make it. I'm thrilled and honored to be joining our families together. And I thank you all for your love and well-wishes."

He looked down at Ally, who beamed up at him. Noah took a sip from his glass.

"And I also wanted to announce that we're expecting!"

As Noah's face flushed with excitement, Beth watched Ally's grow pale. The room erupted with applause.

"This is such great news," Noah's mother said, clasping her hands to her chest.

"Oh my God!" Patsy beamed. "Congratulations, you two!"

Beth tilted her head toward Morgan and Emily, who did not appear as joyful as the others. Morgan caught her eye with a look that read, *Did you know?*

Beth shook her head.

Ally looked away from Noah while keeping her arm wrapped around him, but appearing to fight back emotion. Beth tried to catch her eye, but Ally kept her focus on the floor.

Ally's as surprised by this announcement as her family is. As I am. Why didn't she say anything?

A sheepish look stole over Noah's face, as if he'd just realized he'd spoken a little too soon. He bent toward Ally, who tilted her head up toward him. She swallowed hard and then turned toward her family.

"That's right," she said, forcing a smile. "The baby is due in the fall. We couldn't be more thrilled."

Morgan's eyes widened. Beth could only imagine how betrayed she must have felt in that moment. "Mom," she said, her brows furrowed. "Why didn't you tell us?"

Emily had crossed her arms over her chest.

Ally's smile faltered. "I know, girls. It's still really early in the pregnancy, so I just didn't want to share too soon." Ally frowned, almost to herself. "I should have told you first. I'm sorry."

The girls didn't appear placated.

Beth's phone buzzed in her pocket, and she reached for it. The hospital. Her heart dropped to her feet.

She escaped the happy noise of the living room and made her way to the kitchen as she raised the phone to her ear. "Hello?"

"It's Phyllis from the ICU?" Phyllis always identified herself in the form of a question.

"Hi, Phyllis. What's up?" Beth raised her fingers to her mouth, as if ready to hide the emotion that might escape her lips.

"It's your dad," she said. "He's awake."

CHAPTER 14

ALLY

Ally pushed the purple shopping cart through the wide aisles at the discount department store. At her side with earbuds in, Emily bobbed along to something while her thumbs tapped away at her phone. Ally's eyes fixed on her oblivious daughter. *Multitasking.*

She paused in front of a jeans display and touched Emily's arm to get her attention. Emily removed her earbuds.

"I think you need jeans, right? You've grown out of the ones we bought last fall."

Emily wrinkled her nose. "I don't like the jeans here. I like the ones from the mall."

Ally stifled a sigh. "If you want jeans from the mall, you'll have to purchase them yourself. If you want me to buy your jeans, we're getting them here."

As if to avoid contamination by antifashion, Emily used just the tips of her fingers to pick through the dozens of styles of jeans, most from brands Ally recognized.

"Hmm . . . these are sorta cute," Emily allowed, grasping one of the pairs from a stack and studying the label.

She moved through the section with a little more energy, plucking jeans from piles and on hangers, while Ally waited with the cart.

This is going to be a long afternoon.

Ally cautioned herself to keep her impatience in check. She felt like she'd spent the last twenty-four hours tied up in knots. After everyone had gone home from their engagement party and they'd finished cleaning up, Ally'd snapped at Noah for blabbing their pregnancy news to the entire family. They hadn't even had a chance to tell the girls. Emily seemed to be taking the news in stride, but Ally couldn't shake the hurt that registered on Morgan's face. She felt rightfully betrayed, and Ally knew then she should have included her current living, breathing children, girls who had thoughts and opinions of their own, in her decision about this baby. Of course, by now, the whole town probably knew she was pregnant.

Her heart began to thump in her chest as she watched Emily sort through what had become a growing stack of options. The nausea she'd experienced at the beginning of the first trimester had been replaced by anxiety. Most nights, Ally woke tangled in her sweat-drenched sheets, her heart racing. She feared this baby would be the end of her. Just the act of shopping chipped away at any joy she had left in this life. Before the baby, Ally could see the finish line of these trips to discount clothing stores. Now? She'd have to tack on another eighteen years' worth.

She'd brought up her worries—finally—to Noah later last night. They'd brushed their teeth and were getting ready for bed. Ally had finished rubbing night cream into her face and sat on the edge of their bed. Noah had plucked a book from his nightstand.

"We need to talk about this baby," she said.

He gave her a look of concern and placed the book down.

"Look," he said. "I know. Again, I'm sorry. I just—our families were all there, and the opportunity presented itself." He smiled apologetically. "The G and Ts were doing some of the talking for me. I got carried away."

"You had no business telling them." Ally folded her arms across her chest. "We agreed. I just needed more time."

"More time for what?"

"To . . . *think*," she said, as if it weren't obvious. "To wrap my brain around what we might be getting ourselves into."

"It's a baby. We'll figure it out. You're not alone in this."

"It's not that simple. I've done this already. Twice. I know how much physical and emotional energy it takes to raise a kid. It's exhausting." Ally wiped away the tears that had pooled in her eyes. "I'm getting old. I have a career I'm really proud of. I don't know. I was looking forward to fixing up this house. Taking long vacations with you." She gave him a small, sad smile. "I did not factor in another baby."

Noah frowned. "Wait, so what are you telling me? Are you unsure about this pregnancy?"

Ally sucked in a breath. She *wasn't* sure. She still hadn't caught Noah's enthusiasm for this baby yet. She didn't even think of it as a baby, or even a fetus—she couldn't. It was a clump of cells that would derail the life she had dreamed for herself once she sent the girls off to college. But Noah himself had already delightfully changed her trajectory in some of the best possible ways. A change in plan wasn't always destructive.

"I'm freaking out," she admitted.

"Why didn't you tell me?" he said. "Like, right away?"

She shrugged. "It's my choice." Ally registered how cold that sounded. It *was* her choice. She had every right to make the decision on her own. But she wasn't alone. And she'd also led on her partner, who believed he was going to become a father this fall.

Noah pursed his lips and dropped his head. "Why don't you trust me?"

"I do."

"No, you don't," he said, his tone matter of fact. "You can share your fears with me. That's what I'm here for. I'll have some fears of my own, by the way. And I'll tell you all about those. But also—" He paused. "You can trust that I have your back. I'm not going to leave you to parent a kid on your own. You can still build your soccer league. We can still go on vacation. And I think we could do it together, raising a kid."

When they'd climbed into bed and switched off the lights, it wasn't long before she heard Noah's soft snores beside her. It'd taken much longer before Ally could finally sleep.

◆ ◆ ◆

"I guess these are OK," Emily said, returning. She heaved ten different pairs of jeans into the cart.

"Great," Ally said, feeling something akin to an "I told you so" coming on and fighting it off. "Let's try these on, since I think we're about at the limit. And we're only leaving with three pairs. Max."

"Mom—" Emily stopped in the middle of the aisle, hands on her hips. She looked at her mom as if to make a point, and immediately her resolve softened. "Fine."

Well, that was easy. *Too* easy. Emily must have sensed something from Ally—that pissy energy, no doubt—otherwise she would have just pushed and asked for more.

She steered the cart toward the dressing room, at the far end of the store.

A woman, tween son in tow, also pushing a cart of tube socks and boxer briefs, began angling into Ally's path. From the look on her face, the woman clearly recognized her. It took a second for Ally to recall who she was; being in this environment had thrown her off. *Gloria. From PTA.* Ally remembered she had another son—Jacob—who was a junior, like Morgan. She pasted on a smile as Gloria parked her cart squarely before Ally's.

"Looks like we're both getting in our spring shopping," Ally said, forcing a brightness into her tone.

"It's that time of year," Gloria agreed. She threw her arm around her son's shoulders. "Ezra and I are having a mommy-son day today, aren't we?"

Ezra groaned and hung his head. "Mom, don't."

Gloria laughed. "Well, I guess we're just picking up a few things to tide him over." She eyed the stack of jeans in Ally's cart. "They grow up so fast, don't they?"

"Feels like a blink."

Ally's stomach tightened. *If only.*

Gloria leaned in, lowering her voice. "I heard through the grapevine that you're expecting?"

Great, not even a day later and all of Fillmore knows.

"Are congrats in order?"

Congrats were definitely *not* in order, but she nodded. "We're excited."

Well, one of us is.

"How amazing for you and Noah." Gloria turned to her son. "Emily and Morgan are going to be *very big* sisters."

"I *know*," Ezra said, wriggling out from his mother's arm.

"Mom," Emily said. Ally could tell she was losing patience. Emily tapped the cart. "I can go try these on."

"Sure, honey."

As Emily rolled toward the dressing room, Ally turned to Gloria. "I guess I'll see you at the PTA meeting next month?"

"No," Gloria said. "I mean, *yes.* You *will* see me at the meeting, but aren't you going to the ribbon cutting Friday?"

Ally shook her head. "Ribbon cutting?"

"Oh, you *must* go! It was a last-minute thing—the track coaches coordinated. When the gym was done, it happened to coincide with track season. I think after a decade of fundraising and planning, and two years of building, the school just wanted *something* to mark the occasion." Gloria shrugged. "I only heard about it because Jake's running."

The gym. The one place on earth she least wanted to think about, much less hear mentioned. By *Gloria*. At *Kohl's*.

Ally could manage only a "Huh." Her world had just been squeezed into the space of a marble.

All of a sudden, the department store felt too small, too contained. She needed air.

"Everything OK?" Gloria asked, looking concerned. "Morning sickness?"

Her heart racing, Ally snapped to attention. "I'm fine!" she said, a little too brightly. "I'll see you there."

She made her way to the women's dressing rooms.

"Emily?"

"Over here, Mom."

Ally found the stall—Emily's discarded shoes were visible under the door—and sat on a nearby padded bench.

"Did you know about the ribbon-cutting ceremony for the gym this Friday?" Ally said.

"Yeah," Emily said through the door. "Everybody knows."

"Why didn't you tell me?"

"I don't know. 'Cause it's not a big deal? Besides, Noah would have said something if it was important."

It *was* important.

Ally slipped her phone from her purse. "What time's the ceremony on Friday?"

"After school. Like three o'clock, right before the meet."

She opened her text messages and clicked on Beth's number. She was probably busy. She was neck deep helping with tryouts, navigating the world of Medicare, and visiting her dad, who was awake but couldn't speak.

Ally typed, What are you doing at 3 on Friday? She hesitated, her index finger poised above the "Send" button, knowing this was a big ask. Beth would probably have at least two excuses loaded in the chamber for why she couldn't join her. But Ally didn't think she'd be able to go without her. She couldn't walk through those doors, sit in those stands, walk on those floors without Beth.

Ally's presence would be expected. Beth's wouldn't. By anyone but Ally.

She pressed her fingertip to the screen, the swoosh indicating delivery of her message, and prayed she could convince Beth to come along.

"Mom?" said Emily through the door.

"I'm here."

"It's gonna be weird not being the youngest anymore."

Ally's breath caught in her throat.

"What do you think about that, kiddo?"

"It's good. I think I'm going to like being a big sister."

"Yeah?"

"Yeah."

Ally thought Emily would make a *great* big sister. Morgan already was a great big sister. She let out a sigh. Noah would be a fantastic dad.

Shit. She was having this baby, wasn't she?

Ally's sneakers crunched through the gravel of the new parking lot on the far end of campus as she made her way toward the gym. Although she'd helped plan and raise funds for the gleaming building that stood before her, she'd kept her distance from the burn site, the demolition, the construction, and then the structure itself. The building that housed the main office, classrooms, and library was separate from the gym and athletic field, which made it easy for her to ignore the site as long as she kept her head down.

Fillmore, which had never been a town with an abundance of financial resources, had struggled with poor leadership in the late 1990s and bureaucratic mishandling of public funds. It'd taken two decades for the township to get their shit together—and the money—to replace the high school gym. Over the last twenty years, students played indoor sports like volleyball and basketball across the street in the middle school's multipurpose room. To accommodate PE students and athletes, the high school had made do with two converted portable classrooms that served as changing rooms and bathrooms. But now those were gone, and in their place stood a massive modern gymnasium with two adjoining locker rooms and an indoor pool, which easily spanned twice the size of the old building.

Ally allowed herself to take in the gym. Long before the start of construction, it had been billed as Fillmore High School's sports complex, which would house much more than a basketball court, wooden stands, and locker rooms. As part of the planning committee, Ally agreed to push for a state-of-the-art facility that the entire community could enjoy for decades to come. *Go big or go home,* she'd reasoned, trusting that this giant, shiny new object would help the town forget that the historic gym had burned to the ground. She certainly hoped so.

She steeled herself and opened the metal doors to the large vestibule. The smell of freshly dried paint hit her first, which Ally didn't find unpleasant—certainly an improvement over stale teenage sweat that permeated every gym she'd ever set foot in, and a welcome upgrade from the old building. Her arms prickled at the cold, stark lobby, which featured a speckled ceramic floor and permanent vendor areas that would eventually be open to sell hot dogs, popcorn, and soda to fans. Stairways on both ends of the facility led up to the second level, which she knew from sitting in on countless planning meetings held a dance studio, wrestling area, weight room, and indoor track.

Ally paused before walking through the propped-open doorways to the main gym, unsure she could make herself go any farther. Her face and hands went clammy, and her legs felt like they might collapse. Despite being privy to the planned interior and knowing what the gym would look like on paper, she half expected the old gym to reveal itself to her.

Her brain flashed to the day twenty years ago when Travis had sneaked up silently from behind, grabbed both her wrists, pinned her arms behind her, and dragged her across the polished wood floor to the janitor's closet, where she and Beth were trapped for the entirety of the quarterfinal soccer game. The boys knew that the scouts who'd come to watch the team play that day would never see the girls dominate.

Ally could still feel Travis's hands close around her wrists and jerk them up behind her back, the force of being shoved into the small space that reeked of cleaning fluids, the click of the closed door, and her rage that grew to panic and fear as she and Beth fumbled for the handle and found it locked.

She shook off the memory, stunned that it could come flooding back to her so easily and viscerally after she'd spent so many years pushing it down. Ally reminded herself she wasn't that girl anymore. The boys held no power over her now. She'd spent her entire adult life empowering girls so they wouldn't have to go through what she and Beth had.

As she'd told Beth, neither Travis nor Evan returned to Fillmore after high school. Kyle, who'd held the closet door open so that Travis and Evan could shove Beth and Ally inside, had moved back after college, but she rarely ran into him, and when she did, he'd proved amazingly deft at avoiding eye contact. She knew he had a couple of kids who were many years younger than her girls. His family seemed to travel in different social circles and lived on the opposite side of town. Once, when she and Rob were going over home loan paperwork at the bank, she saw him come inside. As he was making his way to the line to see the teller, she and Kyle locked eyes. His mouth gaped open, and color bloomed in his cheeks. Kyle turned around and left the bank. Other than that, he'd stayed out of her way.

Deciding she had nothing to worry about, Ally stepped over the threshold and into the gleaming space. Relief washed over her, as she could see that of course nothing even remotely resembled what she remembered of the old structure from twenty years ago. Though the beloved mural was long gone, the dreariness of the main gym area was now light and bright and airy. Windows on both sides of the stands let natural sunlight pour into the space, almost enough to illuminate it exclusively. The polished wood floor shone and reflected all the light coming in from the windows and fixtures above. In the middle, right in the spot where future basketball games would tip off, stood a podium, a single folding chair, and two metal stanchions decorated with ceremonial bows holding up a wide red ribbon just waiting to be cut in half.

High school students, teachers, and even members of the community had begun to gather in the home section of the stands. Members of the Fillmore track team, suited up in their uniforms, filtered in from the locker rooms and took their seats together up front. Ally knew that Morgan and Emily weren't part of the crowd today, thanks to after-school soccer tryouts. And Noah hadn't arrived yet, either, but he still had a few minutes. Leading these photo op events was the part of his job as principal that Noah looked forward to the least.

From the gym floor, Ally looked up into the growing crowd and recognized familiar faces from her class of fellow alumni who, like her, had either never moved or had returned after college—people she saw regularly at the grocery store, at holiday parties, and on the soccer field cheering on their offspring. Claire Owens spotted Ally from her seat and waved. She'd inherited the downtown pet store after her parents had retired. Scott Montague—voted Most Popular in the yearbook and now making his living selling real estate—sat one row up. Thankfully, no Kyle.

It still felt strange seeing them here now, so many of them together again in the all-new gym the way they used to be at games and assemblies back in the late 1990s. Before college and jobs and car payments and kids, they were ordinary teenagers most concerned about grades and dating and making the team and getting into college. Or at least Ally was.

She searched the crowd for Beth, who'd texted she was running late. It had taken a lot of convincing to get her to agree to come, and Ally hoped she wouldn't bail on her. She didn't want to try to get through this event without her. Just being here alone now made her a little dizzy again. Maybe it was time to take a seat.

Ally climbed the bleachers to the top row and slid into a seat above the assembled crowd. From her vantage point, she had a clear view of the court and all the activity below. She could feel the excitement radiating. She wondered how many, like her, had arrived with complex feelings about this gym. The mind-boggling amount of time spent to plan the project and raise funds from state grants, a district bond measure, and even local donations and then to finally push through construction brought a mixture of frustration, gratitude, anger, regret, anticipation, envy, and awe all at once. And now, after all this time and effort, the way the high school chose to mark the occasion was with a dinky ribbon-cutting ceremony put on by the track coaches? Seemed terrifically anticlimactic.

The stands continued to fill, but with no sign of Beth.

"Hi, Ally." It was Faith Chen, who'd taken a seat in front of her with what must have been her son—he was the spitting image of her. She'd graduated a year after Ally's class and had gone away to college and returned with a degree in accounting. After earning her CPA, she set up her own business across the street from Mr. Snyder's service station. It struck Ally as strange to see her back in the stands, as if Faith hadn't been doing everyone's taxes for the last decade plus. Sitting behind her in these stands, Ally no longer saw her as the thirty-six-year-old grown-up, but as the girl with the overplucked eyebrows and choker necklace who took pictures for the yearbook.

Ally flashed a quick smile. "Good to see you."

Faith raised her eyebrows. "Quite a change, isn't it?"

Ally nodded. *It certainly is.*

"Seems like the community could do something bigger, more formal, just to mark the occasion, don't you think?" Faith looked around. "This gym is a big deal for us."

Ally nodded. "I was thinking the same thing."

"Mm-hmm. Hey, and the twenty-year anniversary of the fire is coming up this fall," Faith said. "We're due for a celebration, don't you think?"

The tossed-off mention of the fire jolted Ally, but then she found herself considering Faith's casual suggestion.

A celebration? That's actually not a bad idea—out with the old, in with the new.

"Mom, when will this be over?" the boy asked. Faith leaned in and whispered in his ear.

Ally blinked and switched her focus.

The longer they waited, the more her stomach churned. *Where are you, Beth?*

Finally, Beth appeared. Ally didn't recognize her right away, with her hair pulled back into a ponytail and covered by a black baseball hat. Beth was dressed for a workout—zippered jacket over black tights and runners. Ally remembered she was on the schedule today, managing tryouts; she was probably going straight to the soccer field after the ceremony. Ally stood and waved in her direction. Beth looked up and gave her a quick OK signal and climbed the stairs.

"Thanks for saving my seat," she said, sliding in next to Ally. She sensed a similar nervous energy in Beth that had set her thrumming. Or maybe she was projecting.

"Thanks for coming," Ally said. Just having her friend beside her flooded her with relief. "How's your dad?"

Beth shook her head. "He still can't really talk. The doctor says his speech will return, but it'll take time."

"I'm sorry," Ally said and squeezed Beth's arm.

After Beth had rushed from her and Noah's engagement party, Ally hoped that Ralph's awakening would signal the start of an accelerated recovery. That before long, she could expect to see him take his familiar perch back at the service station. Not so. It saddened her that this stroke could rob him of his ability to hold a conversation, which, aside from watching his only daughter play soccer, was one of his true pleasures. "If you need a break from coaching, say the word. I'll figure it out."

Beth's eyes widened. "Oh, please don't. I don't need a break, believe me. I need all the distractions I can get." Beth looked down at her hands and then scanned the crowd below. "Looks like they're running late. Where's Noah?"

"He hates these things, so I'm sure he's just taking his time." One of Noah's favorite parts of his job was greeting students as they entered the school building every day, and then sending everyone off after the final bell. He made a point of knowing everyone's names before the end of September, a personal touch that parents and students appreciated.

Beth pointed to the right of the podium. "There he is."

Noah had entered and was engaged in conversation with the vice principal as he made his way to the podium.

The vice principal fiddled with the mic stand as Noah pulled a folded piece of paper from his pocket.

Noah looked nervous, though probably only to the people who really knew him. Ally knew that the fact that he'd brought a printout meant he was worried he wouldn't remember what he wanted to say, which wasn't going to be much. Maybe she should have been sitting right up front. Or would that have made him more nervous?

Or made *her* more nervous?

Probably her.

She didn't think she could have tolerated sitting so close to where she and Beth had been dragged by those boys to that janitor's closet. Though, really, where *was* the janitor's closet? This shiny new setup was so unlike the old one.

Beth elbowed her.

"Jordan's here." Beth pointed toward the gym floor as a tall, attractive man with curly brown hair slipped in not too far behind Noah and stood to the right of the stands.

Ally's body tensed, and she grabbed Beth's arm. "What's he doing here? I thought he was in town for just a few days. That was weeks ago."

"I don't know," Beth said, patting her hand. "Maybe he's back because he was a student too? Just like the rest of us?"

Ally looked around at the crowd again. It was suddenly less like a reunion and more like an eerie re-creation of their past. With dizzying force, she realized that she and Beth were the only two people in this room who knew exactly how the old gym had been destroyed. Yet here they were, honoring its grand reopening like they were celebrating the launch of a new restaurant or bookstore. Like nothing had ever happened.

What were they thinking?

CHAPTER 15

JORDAN

The vice principal took a seat just as Jordan walked over to Noah. He tapped his shoulder.

"Hi," Jordan said, offering his hand. "Noah Hesse? Jordan Miller. We spoke on the phone?"

Noah accepted the handshake. "Glad you made it, Jordan."

"Thanks for this opportunity to say a few words. I'll keep it short, I promise."

Noah shook his head. "It's no problem. I'll talk for a bit, and then the floor is yours."

Jordan nodded and then sat in a chair in the front row as Noah tapped the mic and unfolded a piece of paper onto the lectern.

Noah looked up into the stands and grinned at the crowd, leaning into the mic. "Thank you for coming." He then felt for the breast pocket of his shirt and pulled out a pair of reading glasses. They looked comically out of place on him.

Noah cleared his throat.

"Almost twenty years ago, Fillmore High School lost what many saw as the heart of the school—the eighty-plus-year-old gymnasium and locker rooms that had served our students for decades. A fire swept through the historic, beloved structure late one Friday night, fall of 1999, and destroyed the entire building."

Jordan remembered exactly where he was that night. He'd arrived home later than usual after snapping photos of the football game for the following week's school newspaper. His sister had a friend over for a sleepover, so he and his mom and dad watched a rented movie over dinner. And then he decided to get a head start on the football game article before going to bed. Totally forgettable evening—except that it was the last normal night in their household. As soon as the fire was put out, his dad became a suspect—the only suspect. And Jordan's world had completely changed.

Noah raised his index finger for effect. "But the high school never lost its soul—its students."

A smattering of applause interrupted his speech, and Noah looked up again in appreciation.

"Over the last two decades, the parents, faculty, alumni, and community have all worked together for this opening day. As we know, it's been a long road—a road we sometimes weren't sure we would see the end of." Appreciative chuckles from the audience. "But we're here. And the gym is beautiful and will serve Fillmore students for another eighty years, if not more."

Noah took off his glasses and placed them back in his pocket.

"So, without further ado," Noah said, lifting up a pair of scissors—ordinary school scissors. "Stella Tripoli is our captain of Fillmore's track team, and it is my pleasure to ask for her to do the honor of cutting the ribbon."

Stella stood and walked to the podium, where Noah passed her the black-handled scissors. She looked over to Noah as if asking for permission. Noah nodded, and she cut the red ribbon in half. The stands erupted in cheers and applause.

As the applause died down, Stella handed the scissors back to Noah and returned to her seat.

"We also have a member of our alumni who'd like to share a few words. Jordan?"

Jordan gave a little nod to Noah and hoped he didn't appear as nervous as he felt. The feeling he was making something out of nothing rose up in him, and he wondered if he should just keep his mouth shut and let the town forget the fire, forget his dad, and be free to celebrate this new gym—or "sports complex," as everyone made a point to remind him. The community had renamed the thing it replaced. Everything around him was urging him to leave this alone. Let it lie in the past.

Except.

In the last two weeks, Jordan had done some cursory research. He checked old newspaper records he'd found online, and there was no mention of what had sparked that fire. Oleks was right: Jordan believed that his dad—a creature of habit who took his job deadly seriously—had locked up the gym and locker rooms that Friday, just as he had every school day for the previous eight years. Then he'd come home to eat take-out pizza and watch *The Wedding Singer* with his family.

Jordan bent toward the microphone. "My name is Jordan Miller. I'm a journalist and member of the class of 2000." His eyes rose to the stands, and he fixed his gaze on the crowd. "The fire happened during my senior year of high school, and in the almost twenty years since, I feel many questions still remain unanswered about its cause."

His heart beat rapid time, but he continued.

"Some of you may remember the man who was charged with criminal negligence—the custodian. Well, that man is my father. After a hurried investigation, he accepted responsibility for the fire, but the accusation haunted him for his whole life. He had a difficult time getting and keeping jobs. After years of sobriety, he started drinking again. And he eventually lost us, his family." Jordan paused and looked down. He was gripping the podium's edge so tightly his knuckles were white. He tried to relax.

"The town was quick to condemn my father for the fire. They needed a scapegoat, and they blamed him."

Jordan felt he saw many in the stands stiffen at this suggestion. And why wouldn't they? Of course they blamed his dad—he'd accepted responsibility, hadn't he?

"If he'd had better representation," he went on, "he might not have been so quick to accept the blame in return for a reduced sentence." Jordan looked out into the crowd. No one said a word. "My dad wasn't perfect. But he was great at his job. He loved working for the high school. This whole thing broke him. Broke his heart."

He stood tall, pushing his shoulders back. "I'm a journalist, and it's my job to ask questions when the story seems incomplete. And I do feel there's got to be something more here. As a son, I need to know if I can clear my father's name. This is why I'm launching my own investigation."

Goose bumps coated his arms.

"But I need your help. If anyone has any information to share about the fire, please find me. Believe me, I'll never tell you any detail is too small or insignificant. I'll be around for the next few minutes and will leave a stack of business cards in the main office. Please call or email me anytime, day or night. Thank you."

Feeling a little wobbly, Jordan sat back down. Noah returned to the podium and leaned into the mic.

"Thank you, Jordan, and thank you again, Stella. And thank you all for coming today. This means a lot to our school community. I invite you all to stay for our first real home track meet of the season. Go Tigers!"

The crowd clapped and began to rise from the stands. Feeling exposed, Jordan rose from his chair. The least he could do was walk over and thank Noah again. Hand over the stack of business cards. And then he'd wait. See if anyone offered a shred of information from that day. Or at least could point him in the direction of information.

The track team exited the gym through the doors leading out to the fields, followed by groups of students and adults, most likely to watch the meet. The day felt like it was made for track and field—the sun burned bright in a cloudless sky, and the temperatures hovered somewhere in the low sixties. As the crowd streamed past, Jordan made his way to Noah.

"Thanks again," he said, handing off the cards. "I can always drop more off if these go."

"We'll see," Noah said. He took a beat. "I don't know if you'd be interested, but . . ."

Jordan's ears perked up.

Noah tilted his head. "But the town archives are stored in the high school library."

"Town archives?" Jordan was definitely interested.

"Yeah, all of the township's surviving historical records and anything of note has been saved in boxes. For a town as old as Fillmore, you can imagine. It's a lot, let's just say." Noah chuckled. "When city hall ran out of room, they moved everything to the library here at school. It's stored where we used to keep the periodicals and things that weren't in circulation. I keep telling myself we'll digitize all this stuff, but it's a pretty daunting task. Not really how I want to spend a summer." Noah shrugged. "Anyway, there are hundreds of boxes."

Jordan's pulse quickened. He'd served as editor for the school newspaper, and now he wondered if any of those old articles would reveal anything. The police had never asked him about all the reporting he and his team had done on the fire his senior year. No surprise, he imagined. The kids and their little school paper. But it had been the biggest news story they'd had to cover, and they'd been all over it. Those archives could be a gold mine.

"Yeah, I'd love to have a look."

Just then, Beth and her old soccer teammate—Ally, was it?—approached. Wearing a baseball hat and leggings, Beth appeared like she was on her way to a workout.

Noah leaned in and kissed Ally's cheek. He slid his arm around her waist. Clearly a couple.

Ally's gaze moved from Noah to Jordan.

"You'd 'love to have a look' at what?" Although her tone was light, Jordan sensed an urgency to her question. Was she always this nosy?

Beth quickly nodded to both Noah and Jordan, barely looking at either one. "Uh, Jordan, I don't know if you remember Ally. She was in our class."

"Of course I remember," Jordan said. "You played on the soccer team, too, right?"

She blushed. "That's right, but not much since high school. Not like Beth."

This time Beth's cheeks reddened.

"Sorry I interrupted," Ally said. "Do you and Noah know each other?"

"No," he said. "I just got in touch. But now it turns out he's got access to some records I'd like to take a look at."

Beth's eyes widened.

"Since the high school's been around so long," Noah said, "we've got records of stuff that date back to the 1920s. It's all here—the main library doesn't have room for it, city hall has no use for any of it. Of course, it just collects dust here."

Beth crossed her arms over her chest. "And you think those records could help you with your . . . What do you call it? Investigation?"

"It's a start," Jordan said. He found Beth fascinating and magnetic, but she also always seemed to put him on the defensive. And she'd never called him. Maybe he should just leave it alone.

Beth glanced at her phone and fished her keys from her jacket pocket. "I've got to run," she said, offering a quick apologetic smile.

Suddenly struck by the fear this might be his last shot with her, Jordan couldn't stop himself. Screw it—let her shoot him down one more time. "Can I walk you out?"

CHAPTER 16

BETH

Beth's cell buzzed twice in her car's cup holder. She was on her way from the high school to the girls' soccer tryouts and would have resisted the impulse to answer the call until her destination anyway, but she knew exactly who it was.

Sure enough, as she pulled into the parking lot by the playing field and turned off the engine, Beth glanced at the message.

Ally.

So?

So.

She wasn't about to spill every last detail of her and Jordan's conversation. That she'd barely paid attention to what he'd said because he'd looked at her with those earnest brown eyes. That when he'd asked if she'd given any thought to having a drink with him, he smiled and she watched as his dimples creased his cheeks. Yes, she'd reminded herself, he was in town investigating *the fire that she and Ally had started*. But if she was truly honest with herself, there was something about that that stirred something inside her now too.

"Hi, Coach!" a piercing young voice said outside her passenger window.

Beth startled and looked up from her phone.

Leah McCreedy waved at her, dressed for tryouts in a T-shirt, shorts, shin guards, and cleats and carrying a bottle of water. She practically vibrated with feverish anticipation.

Beth rolled down her window. She should have known. This kid had been first to arrive all week. Kind of reminded her of herself at twelve.

"Hey, Leah. I'll be there in a sec. Why don't you start warming up?"

Leah nodded. "Coach, can I have a ball? I want to practice my step overs."

Beth had shown the girls how to do this move the day before, to much enthusiasm.

"Sure." Beth pocketed her phone, got out of the car, and popped the trunk. She pulled a ball from the bag and handed it to Leah. "I'll see you out there in a few."

"Thanks!" Leah said and made a beeline for the field.

Tryouts were set to start in ten minutes, and Beth knew she needed to get out there. Her phone buzzed again.

SO????

Fine.

Beth tapped on the message app and started to type.

meeting at Zeke's tonight

Ally's response was swift: WTF

Beth's phone buzzed again, but this time it wasn't a text but a phone call. Ally.

"What are you doing?" she said, barely waiting for Beth to answer.

An SUV entered the parking lot, and Beth watched as three preteen girls popped out from the back seat and ran to join Leah on the field.

"Nothing," Beth said, keeping her voice down. "It's just a drink. Not a big deal."

"Out of all the guys in Fillmore, why do you need to go have 'a drink' with *Jordan Miller?*"

"Please, Ally," Beth said. Her stomach tightened. A few more cars drove into the parking lot, dropping off girls. "Don't ruin this."

"I'm just saying, doesn't it seem a little reckless to be courting the enemy?"

Now who was being dramatic?

"Since when is he the enemy?" Beth said. "I thought he wasn't anyone to worry about."

"I didn't say *date* him. Sheesh. Just—" Ally inhaled. "Leave him alone. And if you see him at the grocery store or the pharmacy or wherever, don't *freak out*, that's all."

Beth clenched her teeth. "Oh, because that's what *I* do—freak out?"

"You always have to take it a step too far, Beth. You can't just be normal and polite to him from time to time, you have to get in his pants."

"Hey! *He* asked *me* out. And since when is having a drink getting in his pants? You are impossible. Truly going off the deep end." Beth rocked back on her heels. "I remember seeing you wear the same pair of unwashed lucky socks for an entire soccer season and eat the same thing for lunch—a peanut butter sandwich—every day for all of high school for luck. But you're being weird. We can't act weird." Beth dragged her hand down her cheek. "Besides, Jordan isn't the enemy. He's a good guy."

"We don't know that." Ally lowered her voice to a whisper. "He's investigating a fire *we* started."

"You know—I can't believe I'm saying this—but you're giving way too much attention to this. He's an old classmate back in town for a little while. So am I. It's not weird to want to hang out. And honestly?" Beth kept an eye on the field. She needed to be out there warming up the team. "If he's looking into the fire, then why not stay close? Maybe he'll tell me about it. Maybe he won't. Maybe it's nothing, Ally. Ever thought of that? Oh, yeah, because that's what you said it was from the start."

Beth blinked. She and Ally hadn't bickered like this since college.

"I think we just need to be cautious," Ally said, her tone dialed back.

Beth followed her lead. "Caution I can do. But I won't overreact. And you shouldn't either. Stressing yourself out can't be good for the baby."

There was a pause on the other end of the line.

"Oh, OK. Thanks for the advice," Ally said. "You don't know anything. You have no right to lecture me about babies."

Beth felt like she'd been punched.

"Wow, Ally."

"I'm sorry," Ally said quickly. "I didn't mean that."

"Right." Beth squinted at the field. Most of the girls were in a circle, passing the ball between themselves. "I'm going now. I have a tryout to run as a favor to my friend, who's acting batshit. I'll see you at Morgan's game tomorrow."

She hung up.

As much as she'd wanted to be right, though, Beth couldn't shake Ally's warning.

Beth thought an hour and a half of wrangling middle schoolers would have been enough to divert her attention. But no. Ally's words of caution still haunted her. What had she been thinking? How could agreeing to a date with Jordan Miller be a good idea?

A wave of doubt moved through her as she thought about Ally second-guessing her decision to reconnect with an old friend—though he wasn't really an old friend. But he wasn't the enemy either. Couldn't he exist somewhere between the two? Jordan was interesting and cute and worth talking to over a drink. One. Drink.

So after practice, when she returned to her dad's house, she decided to go out for a short run, hoping the physical exertion would calm her. It didn't. If anything, it gave her extra time and empty headspace to obsess about the damage she'd done to Jordan and his family.

When she got back from her run, she decided to check in on her dad. The nurse assured her that he was fine. Grumpy, but fine. Beth made a mental note to start looking for long-term care. He'd been cooped up in that hospital for weeks, and the time had come to find him a more permanent home. Her heart twisted—she knew it couldn't be in the house he'd called home for almost forty years.

But still. As she swiped on tinted lip balm and took one last look at herself in the mirror, her worried face stared back at her—and it wasn't all about her father. Would Jordan be able to see right through her? Would he be able to read the creases that now lined her face? She could just admit Ally had a point, text him last minute, and cancel their date. Claim something, *anything*—food poisoning, a bad headache, her dad—and back out.

But what's the fun in that?

Beth never backed down. Her willingness to take risks had led her to places she'd never imagined and had earned her spots on the most competitive women's soccer programs with the most talented players in the world. It'd be hard to find someone who could match her play as a goalkeeper. She'd risked—and sacrificed—the more stable, conventional life of most women her age, including Ally.

Maybe the best thing Beth could do would be to see where a friendship—*maybe more?*—with Jordan could lead. And in the bargain, as she'd told Ally, if she kept him close, she might find out exactly what he already knew about that fire and what, if anything, he'd learned along the way.

And when she did? Beth would be a hero. Ally could finally just relax and let the past stay in the past.

Beth zipped up her jacket, grabbed her key, and closed the door behind her before she lost her nerve.

Zeke's was only a few short blocks away, so she walked toward Fillmore's tiny town center. After a few minutes, she approached a cross-walk and pressed the button for the light. The wind picked up, and she hugged her arms to her chest, waiting for the light to turn green as Main Street crowded with cars that sped past. Traffic slowed and the light changed. Beth crossed the street. Her dad's service station stood to her right in a prominent spot on that block. She hadn't checked in on Bill at all today to see if he needed a hand, but he would have called or texted if he couldn't handle things himself. He didn't seem to need much from her lately. The mouth of the garage was closed, and the neon "Open" sign in the window had been darkened since five o'clock, almost four hours ago.

This town served as a constant reminder of every responsibility she held right now, all of it stuck in her past, as if punishing her for wanting to leave. Probably why Ally's comments today had struck so close to the bone.

Ally didn't know it, but Beth had once gotten pregnant at an incon-venient time too. The big difference was that Beth had lost the baby—she didn't have any choice. Though if the pregnancy had been viable, if she'd gotten to the point where she would have needed to make a decision, she probably would have ended it. Instead, she'd ended it with her boyfriend.

Beth pushed her hands into the pockets of her jacket and picked up her pace. How old would that baby have been by now? Eight? Nine? Would she and Marcus have stayed together if she'd kept it? Probably not. She mostly didn't regret letting go of Marcus, a medical resident with a wicked sense of humor who she'd met after her first concussion during a game on the road. They'd dated on and off long distance for almost two years before she got pregnant. At the time, he'd lived in LA and she in Seattle.

Beth was at the peak of her powers, the height of her game at the time. Nothing could slow her down, though she'd given serious thought to trading it away for a family. When she miscarried between the pregnancy test and her ob-gyn appointment, the relief she felt at the time outweighed the grief over the loss of a chance at a conventional life. She decided to take it as a sign to stay the course and play hard until she couldn't anymore.

Was that now?

The sound of a lively Friday crowd became louder as she approached Zeke's. She'd never spent a lot of time in bars, not only because her profession demanded long stretches of limited alcohol and early bedtimes, but because she personally loathed a noise level that prevented conversation. Yet here she was, about to enter a bar and excited to meet up with Jordan. Beth was doing something she shouldn't after a long time of doing what she should. She wanted to talk to him—to *catch up*, as he'd said that afternoon at ShopRite.

Nerves fluttered in her stomach. They weren't *really* catching up. She didn't know him well—never had. But they were both Fillmore expats, making a brief return to their shared hometown. She could put aside anything else she already knew or thought she knew about him—his profession, his father, the fire. As far as she was concerned, a cute guy had asked her out for a drink. That's how she wanted to approach it. It'd been a long time since anyone had asked her out for anything.

When she made her way inside, the place was hopping, with Mike hustling behind the bar, busy pouring beers and mixing drinks, and too busy to notice her, to her surprised relief. She scanned the space for Jordan.

Beth spied him in a booth on the far end of the restaurant. She smiled as he caught her eye and waved her over.

"Hey there," she said, approaching the dimly lit table. She appreciated the relative quiet of the booth, as if Jordan could read her mind. He put his phone down and rose, motioning for her to sit. Beth's legs felt watery.

"Thanks for meeting me," he said.

Beth took off her jacket and slid in across from Jordan. Maybe it was the lighting or the anticipation of a slight buzz, but Jordan looked even better than he had at the ribbon-cutting ceremony earlier in the day, which seemed like a lifetime ago. Even from across the table, he smelled clean, like he'd made time for a shower and a shave beforehand. And Beth didn't think he'd worn the blazer over his button-down shirt and jeans for the ceremony. *He spruced up.*

A waitress wandered to their table, took their drink orders, and left. Beth leaned into the leather backing, looking around the space.

She shook her head in awe. "Zeke's never seems to change, does it?"

Jordan followed her eyes. "No. Not much in this town does. When was the last time you visited Fillmore?"

Beth thought about it. She'd missed Christmas this year. Had it been over a year?

"Two Christmases ago."

The waitress set two beers onto cardboard coasters in front of them.

"Keep a tab?" she asked Jordan.

He nodded and she walked away.

Beth took a sip from her glass through the froth. She wiped her lip with the tip of her finger. "What about you?"

"Me?" Jordan said.

"When was the last time you visited?"

"Not since my mom and sister moved."

"Seriously?" Beth said, shrinking a little. He'd mentioned he was in town for "family stuff" when they'd run into each other at the grocery store. "Family stuff" seemed to translate to poking around about the fire.

Jordan sipped his beer. "Mom and Tara moved to northeast Philly when I was in college. And you probably heard what happened to my dad."

Beth swallowed. She'd heard rumors at the time about the short trial from her father and that Mr. Miller had accepted responsibility for the fire. Her dad knew most everything that went on in Fillmore. But before today, she had no idea he'd had issues with drinking.

"I didn't really keep up with it much, but yeah." She looked down at her hands. "I'd heard a few things. I'm sorry. I know you said he took getting let go by the school pretty hard."

Jordan nodded slowly. "It's hard to imagine, but that job was his life. He was a custodian, you know? But he felt like an integral part of that school. And he was. We ate in a clean cafeteria because he threw away our trash, scrubbed the tables, and mopped those floors every single day. He cleaned up the teachers' rooms, the bathrooms, the gym. Waxed the hall floors every single Friday after we all left for the weekend." His lips rose into a slight smile at the memory. "He took *pride* in his work. And when he was blamed for that fire, he just—" He paused. A far-off look glazed his eyes. "He snapped. He gave up. Something in him died, I think."

Beth's chest tightened. If this was true, then she was the reason he snapped. She'd destroyed their family, their lives.

Please stop.

"We don't have to talk about it, if you don't want to." The words spilled from her lips.

He met her eyes, and his shoulders relaxed. "It was a long time ago." He took a sip from his glass. "Anyway, I've been back in town these days because my dad's here."

Her throat constricted. "Here?" she managed to croak out.

"Yeah. I just moved him into the dementia wing of Springtime Center a few weeks ago. He's got Alzheimer's."

Beth frowned. "Oh?"

"I know. It's surprising because our relationship wasn't in a good place for so long. After he completed his community service, he basically left us. Left my mom and sister. They had to start over."

A lump formed in the back of Beth's throat. This was so much worse than she'd imagined.

"I'm so sorry," she said, her voice barely audible.

"And then one day, I got a call from his sponsor." He rubbed the back of his neck. "For months, he'd stopped showing up to his AA meetings and he wasn't checking in. His sponsor called me, thinking maybe—after almost five years—he'd started drinking again."

"Had he?"

Jordan shook his head. "I don't think so. But when I went to his apartment, the place was a mess. Piles of newspapers and magazines everywhere. It's like he was organizing his trash. And he was a mess, too—hadn't showered in days, hadn't eaten. He kept talking like he was still in the past, like he still worked for the high school."

Beth's stomach jumped.

"Your poor dad."

"Well . . . ," Jordan started, wearing a pained expression, "I wish he'd been stronger for the family. But seeing him in this state—it was hard not to feel bad for the guy. And remember who he was before the fire. I wondered if he'd been hiding his memory thing for so long that it finally caught up to him." He finished his beer. "Anyway, he loved Fillmore, and I remembered there was a small but nice facility in town that took Medicare."

Springtime. Beth had passed by the place on the way home from the hospital.

"So you've been caring for your dad too," Beth said, her voice quiet.

"Not like you." He smiled at her like she was some kind of saint. "I've been . . . making arrangements, let's say. Just getting him situated in a place where he'll be looked after."

Beth gulped. She wondered if that's exactly what she was doing too. Only her father hadn't abandoned her—Beth was the one who'd left.

She was no saint.

The waitress approached the table again.

"Another round?"

Jordan looked over at Beth and shrugged.

"Sure, why not?" she said.

When the waitress left, Beth picked up her coaster and examined it. YARDS PALE ALE, it read in gold lettering against a charcoal background.

"So how often do you get to see him?"

"Not every day. But over the last few weeks, I've checked in on him pretty often. It's weird seeing him in this new light, where maybe he wasn't to blame for that fire. That maybe his life could have taken a different turn. I just hope I can find out the truth before his mind completely checks out."

A queasy feeling took hold in the pit of her stomach.

Beth knew she needed to make a choice. A large part of her still wanted to believe she was simply having drinks with a nice, attractive guy she was just getting to know better. Why couldn't they chat about the weather? Or about where they'd attended college? Just *catch up*.

But at the same time, she could find out more—what did he know about the fire? What made him decide that now was the time to learn how that fire was started?

Jordan glanced around. Beth followed his eyes. Everyone seemed engrossed in their own conversations. No one paid any attention to them.

"I'm really glad you agreed to meet up." In the glow of the bar's lighting, Jordan's eyes looked like golden amber. "Seeing you after moving my dad in was an unexpected—but nice—surprise."

Beth's cheeks flushed.

"It was a nice surprise for me too," she said, polishing off her beer like it was liquid courage. "So," she began, "how long"—she struggled to get the words out—"have you been thinking about researching the gym fire?"

He sat back in the booth. "Not long. Just since I reconnected with Dad," he admitted.

The waitress appeared, setting two more beers onto the table and clearing away the empty pint glasses.

Jordan, lost in thought, looked down at his hands. "But the more I think about it, it just doesn't make sense. Dad admitted to the police that he'd jury-rigged the gas line's automatic turnoff. But that was because it kept going off on its own, and the locker rooms would get so cold. Do you remember that? They could get freezing sometimes in the winter. Not to mention frozen pipes."

Beth nodded. She did remember. Always either too cold or too hot. She imagined the high school's new sports complex had the ability to calibrate the temperature perfectly to each separate room and its corresponding activity. The custodian could probably set it all from a smartphone.

"Anyway, at the time, I thought Dad took responsibility for the fire too quickly. He felt so guilty, and when he was accused, he just accepted it. His passivity was infuriating. He lost his job, lost his place in the community, and then he lost his family. And eventually he lost himself."

Her dad had filled Beth in as the details from the fire investigation unfolded—the custodian had "fixed" the pilot, despite not knowing how to work on the ancient heating equipment, and also fibbed on his job application about having his HVAC certification. The more evidence the investigation found to pin on the custodian, the more he took responsibility. And at the time, the guiltier Beth had felt. She still felt guilty.

Even though Mr. Miller took the plea deal, the town turned against him. He lost his job, and he couldn't recover.

Beth couldn't get out of there soon enough after high school, while the investigation was still going on.

"But the investigation never turned up what sparked the fire," she said.

Her face felt hot, flushed. She wondered if she might be sweating, but didn't dare touch her hand to her cheek, her neck, not wanting to draw attention to her extreme discomfort. She was grateful for the low lighting. And Jordan seemed so wrapped up in what he was trying to say, he didn't even notice. She took a gulp from her glass.

He shook his head. "No, but I think"—he had a wild look in his eyes—"I found a clue."

Beth's stomach dropped.

"You know what sparked the fire?" Beth held her breath.

"No, nothing like that."

She let out a long, silent sigh.

"But I believe someone was there the night of the fire."

"Not your dad?"

Jordan shook his head again. "Someone else."

"Why do you think so?" she asked with growing horror.

"Because one of the doors to the boys' locker room was hanging open."

Beth let that fact settle in. He was right. No way would Jordan's dad have left that door open. He may have taken a chance and lied about his HVAC certification to secure a job that could support his family, but once he had it, he would never have done anything to risk losing it. As the last one on campus, locking up tight would've been his number one priority.

"How do you know the door was open?"

"Thanks to Google, I saw it in one of the photos used in the trial. Clear as day." He took a sip from his glass and grinned. "And believe me, my dad never failed to button that place up. On his final rounds, he'd close and lock every entry point in every building." No doubt

Jordan himself had witnessed this, following him around the school before leaving for the night. "That was just one Google research session. Once I get a look at those archives in the school library, who knows what I'll find?"

She felt light headed. She'd stayed too long. She never should have ordered that second beer. Sickened, she realized she'd gotten what she'd come for—information.

It seemed impossible he could connect all the dots. But what if he did? Guilt flooded her bloodstream. She hoped he wouldn't put it together. Beth hoped the look on her face wouldn't give her away.

It's just a matter of time before he knows everything.

Her head swimming, she reached for her jacket and purse.

"I'm sorry," she said, fumbling with the zipper on her bag. "I almost forgot—early day tomorrow."

"Oh," Jordan said, a brief flash of chagrin registering on his face. "So soon? I really liked talking to you."

Me too—but it's only a matter of time before you figure me out.

She offered him a tight smile and set a few bills on the table. "I gotta go."

"Can I see you again?" he said, his voice tinged with disappointment.

"I don't know," she said, without meeting his eyes.

On her way back to her father's house, her thin jacket no match for the sudden drop in temperature, Beth walked at a quick pace, eager to get inside the warm safety of her childhood home. There, maybe—finally—she could start planning her escape.

CHAPTER 17

ALLY

Ally stood on the parent side of the soccer field watching Morgan's team get outplayed by the opposing squad. On any normal Saturday, she'd be viewing Morgan and her team play their weekly league game, her heart in her throat. She'd clutch her travel mug close to her chest, fingers wrapped so tight around the mug, they'd almost go translucent.

If anyone had asked her seventeen years ago, she never would have guessed how invested she would be witnessing her daughters play the game she'd loved to play so much. Before kids, she believed nothing could beat the physical and emotional ride of moving the ball in a shared purpose toward the goal. Ally had herself cherished every personal victory, big and small—from a good, clean pass, to a finesse around an opposing player, to the perfectly placed goal that hit the back of the net just so.

It wasn't until she brought four-year-old Morgan to her first pee-wee practice on a warm September Saturday that she realized she'd been wrong. Not only did she get to watch her daughter discovering the game, but she got to experience it right alongside her from the beginning.

From then on, Ally endured the highs and lows and victories and defeats with Morgan, and later with Emily as well. Because she'd played, too, Ally shared a deep connection with her daughters, like an unsevered umbilical cord that kept the three of them tethered together.

Today, though, Ally couldn't keep her mind on the game. She hadn't heard a word from Beth about last night's date with Jordan. What, was she supposed to just wait for Jordan's investigative article in the *Baltimore Sun* to point the finger at Fillmore's own soccer mom and upstanding citizen Allison Katz, who'd been hiding in plain sight all these years?

"Big energy, Blue!" Phil, one of the parents, shouted from the sideline.

Ally glanced at the stopwatch on her phone.

Under ten minutes left and no score. She clicked out of the stopwatch feature and swiped to her text messages. Nothing from Beth yet.

She'd waited all morning for a report and wasn't sure what to make of Beth's silence. Could the date have ended up with the two of them spending the night together? Seemed unlikely, considering Beth had returned to Fillmore to care for her dad, and Ally doubted she'd be up for the distraction. But who knew, right? She'd jumped at the chance for the date; maybe she'd jumped into bed with him too.

Most likely there was nothing to tell. She should calm down. They'd had a drink, talked about the weather, and then left, he back to wherever he was staying and she to her childhood home.

Ally scowled at her silent phone. She clicked into her messages, typed a quick Ahem???, and sent off the text.

On the field, Brittney, the left midfielder, raced to catch up with a through ball. Making herself wide open for the pass, Morgan sprinted up the center with her. But instead of passing, when Brittney got to the ball, she took a shot from out wide, which the goalie punched out. Corner kick.

Should have centered the ball to Morgan. By the look on her face, Morgan felt the same.

"Hey." Beth had sidled up to Ally on the sideline. She heaved a bag of soccer balls and a black duffel bag onto the turf.

Ally's hand rose to her chest. "Jeez. You scared me half to death."

"Sorry." Beth nodded toward the game. "How many goals has Morgan scored?"

Ally frowned. "Funny. It's tied at zero with, like, five minutes left." Ally turned toward Beth and threw up her hands.

"What?"

"Your date?" Ally asked, her voice low. "Did you get my text?"

Beth kept her eyes on the field. "It wasn't a date."

"Fine." Ally sighed. "How was your *drink* with Jordan?"

"Fine."

"Really? That's it?" Ally gave her the side-eye.

Beth shrugged.

Ally had forgotten. Even in high school, Beth held back on juicy details, much to Ally's aggravation.

Brittney placed the ball in the corner, stepped back a few paces, raised her arm, and then ran and kicked the ball. Starting at the eighteen-yard line, Morgan bolted for the goal, clearly hoping to connect with the ball. Poorly aimed, it sailed over the top of the goal and out.

"We'll get it next time!" one of the parents said from the sidelines.

"Nice idea!" another parent called.

"Keep up the pressure!"

"Big energy, Blue!" Phil said again.

From yards away, Ally could see Morgan roll her eyes.

"She's frustrated," Beth said.

Ally nodded. "She's trying to create opportunities out there, but her wings are not up to it today."

Perfectly on cue, Morgan released an exasperated "Not again!" as another teammate, Amanda, lost the ball to a defender.

Beth turned and gave Ally a look.

"Please." Ally waved her off. "She's a leader out there, Beth. Sometimes she's gotta say what they don't always want to hear."

"Really?" Beth crossed her arms and turned back to the game. "Don't they have a coach for that?"

"Wait." Ally tore her attention from the game and gestured to the equipment Beth had dropped at her feet. "*Today's* the first game? Are you done with tryouts already?"

Beth looked at the pile of equipment at her feet. "Scrimmage. We now have enough girls to field two teams. It's nuts. I'm going to have them play each other." She placed the tips of her fingers to her bottom lip and turned toward Ally. "What would you think of *two* teams? There's interest. The ability is all over the place, but the girls want to play. Otherwise, I'll have to make a lot of cuts."

Ally cocked her head. "This is exactly why I set up the intramural league." She pointed toward the field. "I can tell you, if I was assembling this team today, some of these girls would *not* have made the travel team."

Wrinkles formed on Beth's forehead. "I'm not a fan of the negativity on that field. No matter who 'deserves' to be out there or not. They don't all play year round like Morgan."

Beth faced the field again and watched the center midfielder pass the ball too hard to the left wing, who couldn't catch up to it as it rolled out of bounds. She turned back to Ally. "And you know what? Sometimes you have a bad day. Or you learn to play with someone who has less experience. This team can learn how to do that. All without putting down teammates and eye rolling. It's not nice. Do these girls look like they're having fun out there?"

Ally smiled and shook her head. Beth, of all people, should know that soccer wasn't fun all the time. "C'mon. If you can't take a little criticism on the field, then maybe you should play something else. Besides," she said, "once this game is over, these girls are going to move on to the next thing."

Neither team seemed to be having a spectacular day. Ally didn't think she'd seen one decent passing sequence the entire game. She glanced down the line of parents, most scowling at the field, arms crossed over their chests. Ally looked down at her own tightly folded arms and dropped them down to her sides. Heck, maybe the *grown-ups* should move on to the next thing.

"He wants to see me again," Beth said.

Before Ally could react, she caught the end of another failed play. The goalie on the opposing team jogged to fetch the ball that had gone out.

"*God*, Amanda!" Morgan said. She was bent over at the waist, trying to catch her breath. The poor girl looked wrung out.

This game just needs to end.

"Leave me alone," Amanda said. Tears had begun streaming down her face. "You're such a bitch."

Morgan swiveled toward her. "How about you focus on your *game?*"

"Fuck you," Amanda said, her voice infused with hurt and fury. Ally heard Krista's mom suck in a breath.

"That was harsh," one of the parents murmured. Ally pretended not to hear it. The *entire team*, not just Morgan, was letting their frustrations get the better of them.

As the keeper lined up the ball for a goal kick, Amanda turned and stomped off the field. Morgan stood rigid, as did the rest of her team, appearing either shocked or confused. Maybe both.

Ally watched in horror as the girl plunked herself down on the sideline, toward the corner of the field and away from the players, wiping tears from her face with the sleeve of her shirt. In the meantime, the keeper kicked the ball hard down the field where Amanda should have been, and it bounced to their midfielder, who trapped it and passed it to their forward. The fact that the ball was in play didn't seem to register for Morgan's team right away. Ally's eyes widened as she realized what was happening.

"Hey," she yelled toward the field. "Wake up, Blue!"

Ally wondered why the referee hadn't blown the whistle and stopped the game. Profanity alone sometimes warranted a yellow card.

By the time it clicked that the opposing team was gaining on them, it was too late. Morgan's team scrambled to catch the forward, who now had a breakaway. As the forward moved the ball down the field, the goalie readied herself for the shot, finally making the decision to charge the forward, the only way to narrow down the angle.

Ally held her breath, hoping on the surface that the goalkeeper would prevail—like a good team mom would. But deep down she wanted to see the forward pull a rabbit out of her hat. These breakaway opportunities were rare, and she delighted in seeing how players reacted when confronted with such one-on-one pressure.

When she'd played forward in high school and for that short time in college, she'd found herself in similar scenarios—alone with the ball, facing off against a keeper who was just as determined to stop the ball as she was to bury it in the back of the net. Nine out of ten times, anxiety would get the best of her, and she'd panic, shooting either too quickly or right at the goalie, or waiting too long before the keeper would take it away from her.

Once during a league game her sophomore year of college, Ally'd waited so long to shoot, the goalie had pounced on the ball while it was still at her feet. Ally had tripped over the goalie, fallen hard, and dislocated her shoulder. Lesson learned. Once she healed, Ally played a timid game the rest of the season. And then, a month later, she learned she was pregnant with Morgan, and Rob asked her to marry him. With her brain flooded with the "love hormone," oxytocin, soccer quickly became a memory—who wouldn't trade a child's game for true love? Or at least that's what she'd told herself at the time.

But now, Ally couldn't help but grudgingly admire how calm and cool this young forward appeared, easily sliding the ball around the goalie with the outside of her foot and then driving a swift kick to the back of the net. *Goal!* For a split second, Ally was that girl, caught in a triumphant rush. She almost started to clap but stopped herself. God, how would that look, cheering for the opposing team? The forward raised her arms in a V for victory as her teammates rushed toward her for hugs and high fives. A mix of admiration, yearning, and envy stirred inside Ally.

"That was ugly," Beth said, shaking her head.

Morgan's team looked shell shocked as they made their way slowly back into their original lineup. They kicked off the ball, and almost immediately the ref blew the whistle to end the game. After all that, they'd lost.

The parents on the sidelines offered halfhearted claps before folding up their camp chairs and gathering their things. Phil, Amanda's dad, whose enthusiasm usually set the tone for most of the parents, had already jogged over to his daughter and now knelt beside her on the grass. Ally watched as he reached out a tentative hand toward her back. Amanda jerked away.

Both teams formed lines and high-fived each other. Ally could see the fury in Morgan's face all the way from across the field.

Beth smirked, reading her mind. "You're going to have a fun car ride home."

"The ref should have called a time-out when Amanda swore and walked off the field."

"It's not his fault."

Ally looked up at Beth, who, at five feet, ten inches, cast an imposing figure. It was not even noon, and Ally felt small and exhausted. She didn't want a lecture right now about the ref or about this game or about Morgan getting a little snippy. A conversation on the way home about setting a more positive tone as team captain might not be out of the question. But still. She hadn't yet heard details about Beth's date.

"So, Jordan," Ally said. "He wants to see you again. Do you want to see him?"

"I don't know," Beth said, slinging the bag of balls over her shoulder. "Maybe? I like him, and that's the problem."

"Did he say anything?"

Ally glanced across the field. The team was now sprawled out on the bench and grass—Amanda sat on the edge of the group, with her back to the team—while their coach gave them an end-of-game rundown.

"Jordan doesn't think his dad was the last person to leave that day," Beth said, her voice low. "He's found a little on Google, and I imagine he's probably been talking to him, which is probably why he wants access to the files at the high school. I don't know what he thinks he can find, but if he can prove that there could have been an additional person there, he's off to the races."

Her words blew a hole through Ally's stomach. If Jordan discovered his father wasn't responsible, then that meant someone else was. She shuddered just as a wave of nausea overtook her. She grabbed onto Beth's arm for balance.

"You OK?" Beth's eyebrows drew together.

Ally closed her eyes and allowed herself to feel the cool morning air on her damp face. All this—the smell of clipped grass, the sounds of the ref's whistle, the energy of parents clapping and supporting their girls who ran and played together, pushing themselves to be better, be stronger—could go away, just like that. Morgan having a bad game—it might ruin the teen's whole Saturday? So what? What a luxury if that could be Ally's worst problem today. As long as Jordan continued to nose around the high school looking for evidence to *exonerate his father*, she was looking at an anxiety-filled summer.

"Ally?" Beth pressed. "What's going on?"

"Morning sickness," she lied. She opened her eyes and let go, taking a deep breath. "I'm OK."

Beth looked up, gazing at a spot in the distance where a new group of younger players had formed, sitting on the grass, lacing up their cleats. "The girls are starting to arrive. I've gotta go. Are you all right?"

Ally nodded, and Beth heaved the gear onto her shoulder and started lugging it across the fields.

Ally couldn't help but think of how utterly undisturbed Beth was acting. How could she be so serene? Maybe Beth was just calm under fire, while Ally could so easily fall apart. Like always.

Ally needed to focus. Get a handle on what Jordan knew and what he could find out.

◆ ◆ ◆

The next day, Ally drove Noah's car to the high school, parking a few blocks away from campus. The last thing she needed was a neighbor or someone making a casual comment to Noah tomorrow at school about him working on a Sunday. *What?* he'd say, confused. *Saw your car in the parking lot. Burning the candle at both ends, eh?*

Yeah, no.

She was grateful that the hood of her rain jacket obscured her identity without looking too out of place as she approached the school on this damp Sunday afternoon.

The parking lot was empty, and Ally knew she'd have the entire school to herself. But she didn't need the whole school. She just needed access to the files in the library. The ones Noah had promised Jordan access to. The ones that might bring Jordan to the conclusion that his dad wasn't responsible for the fire twenty years ago. She prayed she wasn't too late, and Jordan hadn't already gotten his hands on the files yesterday while she was watching Morgan's soccer game.

Ally's stomach clenched as she walked up to the side entrance, clutching a Fillmore FC duffel bag, crammed with a few more Fillmore FC duffels, and fumbled for the right key. She'd made an excuse to him about the engine light going on in her car so that she could borrow his to make a Target trip—and more importantly, gain access to his keys.

She took one last look around the tennis courts, the garbage bins, the distant sidewalk, a sliver of grass. Empty. Not even a person walking their dog around the neighborhood.

She took a breath and tried each key, going in order, starting from his car key. When she reached the sixth key, the lock clicked and she was able to pull the door open and let herself in. Once the door closed, she used the flashlight on her phone to locate the security system and punched in the code—which Noah had shared with her to pick up an item from his office while he was out of town one weekend at a funeral—and got her bearings. She was at the bottom of the west stairwell. The school had three floors, with four stairwells, one for each side of the building, facing north, south, east, and west. The first floor held the main offices, including those for Noah, the counselors, and the faculty. The lunchroom and library were down the hall, as well as a few computer classrooms. The second and third floors housed most of the classrooms. The documents Noah had given access to Jordan to look over were stored in the library, which was where Ally headed.

Ally hadn't sneaked around this school in almost twenty years, and old feelings rose up in her like graveyard spirits. Part of her wished she'd urged Beth to join her, but most of her was grateful not to involve Beth at all. Ally had found her behavior erratic these last few weeks, since her dad's stroke and dealing with the aftermath.

Ally also wasn't sure what the story was with Beth's status as a professional soccer player. Was she on leave? Had she been let go? Would she retire? Here she was, coaching for Ally's league like she had no life to return to in Chicago. It looked pretty clear she didn't. In fact, the last time Ally had dropped by Beth's house, she spotted a new stack of boxes imprinted with the logo WINDY CITY MOVING.

And then she decided to go on this date with Jordan. For what? Sex? Love? *Please.* How would this diversion possibly benefit her in any way? The only certainty Ally had around Beth was that she'd leave as soon as she could. To be honest, Ally wasn't sure she could trust her.

Today, Ally knew the only one who needed to know what she was up to was Ally herself.

In high school, Beth had been the person she trusted the *most*. As the only two girls on the soccer team, they relied on each other, and by the end of their freshman year, they did everything—played soccer, ate lunch, hung out at each other's houses—together. And those three awful boys picked on them, locked them up—together. At the time, Ally had wished that whole ugly incident would just go away. She wanted to pretend it never happened. Every time she thought about the tiny, dark space they'd been crammed into, the odor of cleaning fluid, those four windowless walls closing in on her, she could feel the panic creep in again. And the tidal wave of rage that accompanied that panic. She couldn't make the mistake of letting either emotion rule her right now, so she pushed the past aside for as long as she could.

Ally tried the handle on the doors to the library, but they were locked. She had to go through Noah's keys again and find the right one before letting herself in to the space. She resisted switching on the lights. For now, there was enough late-afternoon sunlight streaming through the windows for her to find her way to the back room, which stored all the district's archived documents. Ally didn't need a fully lighted library announcing to the surrounding neighborhood that someone was at school on a Sunday afternoon. When she'd let herself into the windowless storage space and closed the door behind her, she flicked on the switch.

The gym and locker rooms had still been open when Beth and Ally had sneaked in all those years ago, but not for long. The Friday-night football game had ended, the stands cleared, fans and players gone, and the parking lots emptied by the time the girls slipped into the deserted boys' locker room, hiding in the last row of lockers. The janitor was the only one who remained on campus, making his final rounds after waxing the floors and locking up the buildings. When they heard the click of the key turning the last lock for the evening and the roar of

Mr. Miller's pickup truck leaving the parking lot outside, they waited an extra fifteen minutes in nervous silence before setting up the stink bombs to go off.

Beth, who'd researched how to make a potent homemade stink bomb from an old chemistry book she'd found in the public library, took three plastic soda bottles out of her backpack, each bottle containing a noxious concoction of what she said was hydrogen sulfide and chlorine dioxide that had been percolating for over a week. They weren't "bombs" at all, Beth had assured her. The only thing that exploded from them was the stink. All they needed to do was open the boys' lockers, uncap the soda bottles, and get out of there before the smell hit them. It might have worked if they'd been able to see what they were doing.

"It's darker than I thought it would be," Beth had said, stifling a nervous giggle.

"Do you think we need a flashlight?" Ally said, performing a quick mental calculation of how much time it'd take to sneak home, grab the flashlight from the junk drawer, and return without anyone noticing. Plus, they'd have to prop the gym door open so they could get back inside. Too risky. Her stomach dropped. Should they put this off?

"We'll be fine," Beth said. Ally liked how soothing her voice sounded. "Travis, Kyle, and Evan's lockers are all in this row. All we need to do is get them open, uncap the bottles, stick one into each, and leave. Monday morning, everything in their lockers will be ruined. With any luck, the entire locker room will stink for a week."

Ally hoped so. She hated this locker room. She hated that she knew this space. This private space reserved for boys. Yet this was where her soccer coach held all the team meetings. This was the setting he'd chosen to announce that Travis, Kyle, and Evan had been suspended from the team for the rest of the season for the "prank" they'd pulled on Beth and Ally. Paltry punishment for locking two human beings in a janitor's closet. She and Beth knew if the boys were going to actually be punished, the girls would have to come up with a "prank" of their own to settle the score.

"OK," she'd said, resigned. "Let's get this over with before the sun gets any lower."

Now, facing the archives, Ally wanted the task of removing these records over with—the sooner the better. With the lights on, her eyes adjusted and took in the space, which was about the size of a classroom. For a long time, this room had stored its immense collection of periodical back issues. She remembered reserving academic journals for her research papers and checking out well-read copies of *Cosmopolitan* from years past. Since her time, the high school had switched to digital subscriptions, and the town decided the back room would be better served as the district's official archive. A wooden table and four chairs stood in the middle of the room. Dozens of rows of metal shelves took over most of the space, each reaching almost to the ceiling and resulting in hundreds of cardboard archive boxes.

Ohmygod. This could take forever. She had thirty, forty minutes, tops, before she needed to be back home. Before Noah wondered why a quick trip to Target was taking so long. Sweat beaded her hairline, and her breathing became shallow. She couldn't panic now. She needed to focus. She needed to get those documents and get the hell out of there before a panic attack or morning sickness got the best of her.

Maybe if Beth and Ally hadn't been in such a hurry that night, the results would have been different. Maybe she wouldn't have felt the need to break in to the school today.

But they'd rushed.

Ally had clipped through the locks on the boys' lockers using the bolt cutter she'd taken from her backyard shed. Her dad wouldn't miss it. And her parents and Beth's dad thought the girls had gone to the movies and would be back for a sleepover at Ally's house afterward. She slipped all three locks into her backpack and opened the lockers, each stuffed with rank gym clothes and soccer cleats. Travis had stashed a shower caddy in there and a bath towel. Evan's locker housed a bottle of Tommy Hilfiger cologne. Ally made a face as the pungent odor from the three lockers hit her.

"Maybe a stink bomb isn't necessary," Ally said, wrinkling her nose and wondering, not for the first time, if this whole scheme was a giant mistake.

"We're sending a message," Beth said, placing a bottle into each boy's locker. "Believe me, from what I read, these are military-grade stink bombs. They will utterly destroy everything in these assholes' lockers." Beth's eyes widened. "Ready?"

Ally nodded. They unscrewed the caps from the plastic bottles, slammed the locker doors shut, and holding their noses, grabbed their backpacks and wove their way through the maze of metal toward the gym. Tears streamed from her eyes; Ally wasn't sure if it was from nerves or because of the noxious fumes from the soda bottles.

A thump came from the back of the locker room. She looked over at Beth, who seemed to have heard it too. Was someone in there? Were they not alone? Their flight instincts kicked in, and Beth and Ally bolted out of the locker room. Just as they'd pushed through the doors to the gym, they'd felt the first explosion.

That same urgency rushed through Ally now, alone in the library. Knowing she had no time to lose, Ally approached one of the shelves, examining the label pasted to the outside of one of the boxes. Her heart sank. Nothing on the label hinted at the contents inside. Instead, each label featured a number that looked like it had been hand printed by someone using a Sharpie.

Ally scanned the labels at eye level: *#145, #146, #147*. She looked up to the next row: *#133, #134, #135*. So at least there was some sense of organization, and the boxes had been placed in numbered order. She pulled #146 from the shelf and carried it to the table.

When she lifted the lid, she found folders crammed with yellowed sheets of paper. She pulled out a folder from the front of the box labeled

A and opened it. Inside, she found report cards for Carey Abrams through John Austen for the 1953–54 school year. The box contained grade records for all students at Fillmore High School for that year, alphabetized by last name. She closed the box and selected the one beside it, #147. *More report cards?*

No, in this box she found hundreds of photos, yearbook proofs, several copies of the *Our Town* program, a French II textbook, a first-place volleyball trophy, and other odds and ends, all dating from the 1953–54 school year. She placed the lid back on the box and slid out the next one, and the next one, before skipping ahead.

In addition to a dizzying number of student records dating back almost one hundred years, the boxes seemed to contain an array of yearbooks, scrapbooks, thousands of copies of the *Tiger Times* newspaper, catalogs, alumni magazines, board reports, home and school notes, diaries of the principals, and old textbooks. She also discovered ragged copies of sports programs, graduation programs and speeches, Hall of Fame posters, ribbons, and student literary magazines. She found thousands of photographs. Ally thought much of the collection could be housed and displayed in a museum, but the township, despite having existed in some form since before the American Revolution, didn't have one.

Surely there would be interest in these items. Fillmore's citizens took pride—a humble pride, but pride nonetheless—in their township. Those who stayed, stayed because they chose to, not because they had to.

She'd been thinking about Faith Chen's gym-dedication idea. Faith was right. The students would love it. The PTA would get on board. Heck, the whole town would probably help throw this party for the new sports complex. The town would finally get closure about the old gym, and in the process she and Beth could finally put the whole thing behind them for good. And if she planned it, she could have access to everything she might need in here to research the celebration, whenever she wanted. No more cloak-and-dagger stuff. For now, though, she just needed to remove anything incriminating before Jordan could get his hands on it.

Ally would have done almost anything to erase the images from that night that haunted her mind. A second explosion had followed the first, and when they'd stumbled out onto the athletic fields and finally the parking lot, Ally and Beth watched in horror as flames licked through the roof and tore into the historic gym. It occurred to her that, aside from the metal lockers, the entire building was probably made of wood, essentially eighty-year-old kindling for a powerful fire that blazed through, engulfing everything in minutes. At the time, Ally couldn't wrap her brain around what had just happened. Did their dumb little prank really start this inferno? It made no sense.

She looked down at her empty hands. Her dad's bolt cutters. She'd left them behind. Her whole body went cold.

"I forgot—" she said, her voice anguished.

Beth glanced at Ally's hands, then up at her. "What? *What?*"

"The bolt cutters."

Beth's eyes widened.

"We have to go back."

Beth looked hard at Ally. "No way. We can't." She gestured to the burning structure. "It's impossible."

Ally covered her mouth with her hands. What had she done?

"We have to go," Beth said, tugging at her shirtsleeve. "We can't just stand here."

Ally scowled and shook her off. "We have to tell someone." She looked around at all the homes surrounding the school. "We can't just walk away."

Beth grabbed her shoulders and turned Ally to face her, her expression serious. "Yes, we can."

In a few agonizing seconds, the cold, clear reality of their future set in. Ally realized this moment could define their entire lives—if they let it. Soccer would become a memory. They could forget scholarships—they wouldn't even need them, because they'd surely be rejected by every college they applied to. Hell, they might even lose the privilege of graduating with their class. Their friends, community, even families would reject them. They might even serve jail time. It felt like her heart was fighting its way out of her chest. What did someone do after she burned down her high school gym? Move out of the country and change her name? How could she make herself just disappear? If she wanted the future she had envisioned, the one she had worked for, her best option would be to distance herself as far from this whole fiery debacle as possible. And pray that those bolt cutters had been destroyed.

Ally heard sirens in the distance. The sounds were getting louder.

"Let's go," she said.

She and Beth jogged away from the school, their backpacks bouncing. By the time they reached her house, Ally knew this was a secret that could never get out.

And so far, it hadn't.

As she removed the lid of yet another archive box, Ally found it: papers labeled 1999–2000—the girls' senior year. She quickly pulled all five boxes and set them on the wooden table. She hoped everything she needed would fit into the bags she'd brought. Ally went through the first box, ruling out grade-related and large items like trophies and yearbooks. She ignored the elementary and middle school items. But when she found a folder of *Tiger Times* newspapers, she discovered most were missing. The October fire was *the* major story all year. She remembered that because during the year, each issue had the potential to trigger a panic attack. She always had Beth scan the articles first to make sure the investigation didn't point to them or their prank. There was never any mention of the missing bolt cutters, to their relief.

As she riffled further through the box, Ally found no school board reports or principal's notes, which the other years' boxes contained. Her stomach dropped. She opened the second box. In it, she could see that even more items were missing. Now frantic, Ally sifted through the third, the fourth, the fifth. She felt dizzy. None of the records were complete. Ally combed through the photographs, none of which featured images linked to the fire or even the gym itself. It's like the whole event had been erased, expunged from the past. Clearly, someone had already arrived before her and removed all possible fire-related material. She was too late.

Jordan.

Heat surged through Ally. Jordan wasn't allowed to just take what he wanted. Those records belonged to the school, to the town. Not to *him.* He no longer belonged to Fillmore. He was an outsider now.

Ally's hands shook as she replaced the lids on the boxes and returned them to their spots on the shelves. Numb, she gathered her empty duffel bags and walked, dazed, toward the door and let herself out.

Jordan had found something that had made him take a huge risk this week—enough to steal. She didn't know what that was, but Ally knew in her gut it was going to be bad.

CHAPTER 18

BETH

Beth had always liked the smell of chlorine. It signified summer, but it also never failed to conjure her strongest memory of her mother—the time when she'd taken pint-size Beth to Mommy-and-Me swim classes at the local YMCA. What little Beth remembered about her mother lingered at the fuzzy edges—a flash of a smile, the scent of her flowery lotion, her pixie haircut, the feel of her warm arms wrapped around her. But at the Y's outdoor pool, Beth remembered everything—probably because repetition had been built into the lessons.

For weeks, they performed the same activities. At the slightest whiff of pool chemicals, Beth was two and a half years old again, coated in sunscreen, her mom already in the water and gently lowering her in from the pool's edge. Mom would hug her close while their bodies got accustomed to the water temperature, and then she'd grasp onto her hands and let Beth float on her tummy, and then on her back, and kick her legs. The group would circle up for songs and exercises. Beth could still hear her mother sing "Itsy Bitsy Spider" and "Row, Row, Row Your Boat" and "Head, Shoulders, Knees, and Toes" while they giggled and splashed. She couldn't possibly discern if her mom had been a good singer, but to her, there was no sweeter sound than her mother's voice. When the lesson ended, Mom would wrap Beth in a large, fluffy towel and kiss the top of her wet head, and hand in hand they'd walk to the locker room to change.

Today, as she and Rachel, the Springtime Center's resident director, rounded the corner to the facility's indoor pool, Beth was almost surprised to see the swimming pool filled with senior citizens, dancing and splashing to "Twist and Shout," rather than parents and toddlers paddling along to "Old MacDonald." Beth blinked, reminding herself that she was here for her dad, not her mother.

"This, obviously, is our pool," Rachel said. A thin cloud of steam hovered over the water. "It's kept at seventy-eight degrees at all times. The seniors seem to like the warmer temperature, and it doesn't slow them down one bit."

Beth turned to watch as the instructor led the seniors through a simple exercise involving a pool noodle and light marching.

"The water-aerobics class is one of our most popular," Rachel continued. "Residents can sign up ahead of time online, and each class usually fills with a waiting list."

Beth nodded her approval, but she knew her dad was a long way from participating in water aerobics. Not that she'd ever seen him in a pool. When her mother died, Beth learned how to swim through group swim lessons taught by certified Red Cross instructors. They were fine. Her dad put her into lots of lessons after her mother died. When she told him she wished he would take her to Mommy-and-Me classes, he said, "It's 'Mommy and Me,' not 'Daddy and Me.'" But even at three and four, Beth had learned to hide her skepticism and disappointment. She'd seen daddies at Mommy and Me. Her daddy was just too sad.

They exited the pool area to a physical-rehabilitation facility and gym area. Easy access to physical therapy, the doctors had advised, would accelerate her father's recovery and enhance his quality of life.

"I know this is important to your dad's care," Rachel noted as Beth scanned the equipment. It didn't look too far off the mark from the gym equipment she and her team used at their practice facility in Chicago. "Springtime offers on-site physical therapy, along with speech therapy and occupational therapy."

Rachel was right—these services put a major check in the pro column for Springtime. Her dad would need all three.

She wondered which services Jordan's dad used, as someone with dementia. She glanced around the room. Pairs of younger and older people utilized a handful of stations. Could one of them be Jordan's dad? The last time she'd seen Mr. Miller had been at the end of her senior year of high school. Would she even recognize him? Would he recognize her? Surely not, right? Why would he? She was just one of thousands of kids who'd gone through that high school. Every summer that a senior class graduated and moved on had to have been an opportunity for Mr. Miller's brain to perform a giant data dump of names and faces of kids he'd probably never see again.

Poor Mr. Miller. If only she could find him and know for certain that he was OK. The morning after meeting for drinks with Jordan, she'd called the Springtime Center to make an appointment for a tour. They could squeeze her in the next day—on a Sunday. Beth didn't mention it to Ally at the game—didn't think this was necessary information, as Ally had become so amped up about anything Jordan related.

Although it wasn't the sole reason she'd decided to take a tour of Springtime, Beth had to admit that locating Mr. Miller certainly played a part in her decision to visit today. She'd hoped to run into him, see that he was happy and well taken care of. She couldn't quite work out the calculus that had brought her to this conclusion, but she'd decided that if a portion of her guilt could be assuaged, it might help her make up her mind about seeing Jordan again.

She tried to imagine his dad featured in each of the photos in the Springtime Center brochure. Maybe he'd be surrounded by new friends, or he'd taken up painting or charcoal drawing or gin rummy or mah-jongg. Would she recognize a grayer, wrinkled Mr. Miller grinning back at her? She didn't know, but found herself desperate to find out.

She couldn't ask Jordan, that was for sure. And her tour guide might find it odd if Beth inquired about a resident she didn't know personally.

Rachel pushed open the door and led Beth down a corridor. As they strolled, they passed residents and what appeared to be visiting family along with men and women dressed in navy-colored scrubs walking up and down the hallway with purpose.

Rachel looked up at Beth. "It's busy this week—several area schools have spring break. I love seeing kids and grandkids visiting the residents. We encourage family to visit just about anytime. We're very child friendly. You have kids?"

Beth shook her head.

Rachel blushed. "I wasn't sure," she said quickly. "Every time I've come to your dad's station to get my oil changed or tires rotated, I see tons of photos and clippings of you up on that corkboard of his."

Beth felt her entire being grow warm. The Corkboard of Pride, she liked to think of it. Another shrine. Her cheerleader of a dad never could restrain himself from finding ways to brag about his daughter, the athlete. The entire town had probably seen that corkboard.

"Well, that's Ralph Snyder for you." Beth hoped she didn't sound dismissive or ungrateful.

Rachel stopped in front of one of the doors and took out a ring of keys. "I think he's going to love it here. He's such a talker. Every time I take my car in, he has a new story about what you've been up to. He's one proud papa." She found the key she wanted but paused, her hand resting on the door handle. She looked right into Beth's eyes, her face serious. "I want you to know, he will be so well taken care of. All of our residents are like family here. And Ralph, who is such a treasure to the Fillmore community—we'll make him feel right at home. I know we'll have a spot for that corkboard here."

The gravitas in Rachel's voice almost made Beth burst into giggles, though she knew enough to hold it in. "Thank you," she said, biting the insides of her cheeks.

Rachel opened the door. Beth stepped into the foyer and took in the sunlit, tastefully staged suite. *Dad* would *like it here.* Beth began to calculate how, exactly, her dad could even begin to afford a place like this.

"Isn't this great? This is our one-bedroom apartment. We do have a couple of two-bedrooms available, if he'd like a little more space," Rachel said, making her way over to the dining area.

Beth glanced around the open living, dining, and kitchen areas. The living and dining rooms featured wall-to-wall carpeting. A recliner and sofa faced a flat-screen television, which stood beside a large glass door that looked out to a small enclosed patio. The galley kitchen was small but functional. Beth figured her dad probably wouldn't use it for more than making himself a sandwich.

All doorways were large enough to fit a wheelchair.

"Do they all have carpet?" Beth wondered if her dad might find it easier to get around on a smoother floor surface.

"I'm so glad you asked," Rachel said. "Many units come with linoleum instead."

Linoleum instead. Because he couldn't walk. He couldn't even use a walker yet. This was her dad's new reality. And it might only get worse.

The realization came crashing down on her like that. A senior community that could accommodate a wheelchair, his walker, his stroke-addled brain. This was his new normal.

Standing in the foyer of this apartment, Beth could envision a future for her dad here. And if they were lucky, he could become one of those smiling seniors in the brochure, paintbrush in hand. Maybe he'd regain his speech enough to chat up the staff and residents and charm anyone else who crossed his path. Maybe he'd enjoy sitting in the garden, soaking up a little sun. Maybe he'd strike up a friendship with Jordan's father. Beth's stomach churned at the thought of the two of them seeking each other out like tray-carrying high school buddies in the cafeteria. And if his new life started someplace like Springtime, then that meant his old life—the house, his beloved service station—that would all end.

And what about her? Where did this leave her? What was *her* new normal? If she closed her eyes, could she envision a future for herself like she envisioned one for her dad?

No. Not anymore.

She had nothing beyond preparing her dad for his new life. She'd always been so sure, so confident that everything would work out somehow. And it always had. But now, as she sat in this staged apartment at the Springtime Center Senior Community, she realized she had nothing. No job. No home. She was all alone.

The thought sent her heart racing, and she reached out for one of the dining room chairs and sank down into it.

Rachel looked over, concern written all over her face. "I know it's hard to process this all now." She shook her head. "It seems like just yesterday your dad replaced the brake pads on my car." She sat beside Beth and folded her hands. "Things happen. Isn't it nice to know places like Springtime can take such good care of our loved ones?"

Beth's chin began to shake, and she covered her mouth with her hand. Hard to believe, but her future was more uncertain than her dad's. In a moment of clarity, she realized she had nothing to return to in Chicago—at this point, she had no income and had already had movers clear out her stuff from her apartment. And she'd probably have to sell her father's house to pay for his new normal.

Rachel rose and reached for a box of Kleenex from the living room side table. She pushed it toward Beth. Beth nodded, grabbing a tissue and dabbing her eyes.

"Thanks." She blew her nose and got up from the table. "I'm sorry. I'm sure you have better things to do than sit here and watch people lose it. I do like this apartment. I think my dad could be happy someplace like this."

"It's an emotional time," Rachel said, offering a soft smile. She held up her index finger. "If you don't mind, I'd love to show you the grounds."

When the tour ended, Rachel led Beth back to the lobby.

"I'm going to leave you with some light reading," Rachel said. "I'm sure we're not the only place on your list, but we hope to be the last."

She disappeared into an office behind the front desk.

Beth looked around. Everything about the community seemed clean, and the staff was warm. Beth thought the place would satisfy her dad's social side. And the residents all seemed occupied with interesting activities, classes, and field trips. A side door off the lobby led to an outdoor patio, which she hadn't noticed before. Beth wandered outside. The trees were heavy with blossoms and the air fragrant with smells of spring.

"Hello, there." The sound of a man's voice came from behind her. The tone sounded familiar.

Beth spun around. Her mouth fell open, and all of a sudden, she was seventeen all over again. Mr. Miller—Jordan's dad, former Fillmore High School custodian, man blamed for the fire that had destroyed the gym and locker rooms twenty years ago—was seated in a deck chair with a well-worn hardbound plant-and-garden guide propped up in his lap and a pencil in hand.

She blinked. It was unmistakably him. The mop of curly hair had thinned and gone from salt and pepper to pure white in the last twenty years. Time had dragged down his face, and the light in his eyes had dimmed, probably due to Alzheimer's. But when she'd turned to face him, he'd smiled. The kindness in his face melted her heart. It was the same kindness he'd shown her and Ally after he'd let them out of the janitor's closet that horrible day.

Beth opened her mouth to speak.

"Oh, there you are," Rachel said, appearing with a Springtime Community folder fat with papers. She handed the folder to Beth. "This is for you to review. Call me if you have any questions."

Beth nodded.

"Let me walk you out," Rachel said, ushering Beth back inside the lobby. Before stepping inside, Beth took one last look at Mr. Miller. He winked at her and then returned his focus to his book, which he stared at with intensity, pencil raised.

No matter where her dad ended up, Beth knew she'd be returning to the Springtime Center very soon.

PART II: SUMMER

CHAPTER 19

JORDAN

Jordan arrived a few minutes early and made his way from the parking lot toward the practice field. Beth didn't notice him approaching right away, and he observed her coaching the girls from the edge of the field as they scrimmaged. Her coaching style was like how she was in life—quietly confident and a bit reserved but with an undeniable intelligence and underlying intensity. For the last two months, Jordan had found himself both drawn to Beth and also kept at a puzzling distance. Yet here he was again—Beth called and asked to meet, and he said yes without hesitation.

From the end of May through the month of June, Jordan had fallen into a sort of routine. He spent weekdays in Baltimore—in his world, his life—most of the hours dominated by his work as a journalist at the *Sun*. Although most people would define the job as one of variety—no two stories were the same—Jordan had learned to lean into the predictability that went with the profession. He always needed to do his share of fact-checking, interviewing, researching, writing, and editing for each story he was involved with. This was the world he'd prepared his entire life for.

Most weekends, however, he shed his Baltimore life and found himself back in Fillmore, where instead of digging up stories on crime, politics, or social interest, he was excavating his past through the evidence he'd found at the high school, but also through a few old acquaintances and his own father.

The more he'd learned about who his father really was as a person, the more he believed he couldn't have been the last one to leave the gym the day of the fire. He just wasn't the careless type—merely a personality trait, unfortunately, and not a fact that could be proved. But Jordan knew in his bones his dad wasn't careless about that job. That job meant everything to him. And it became more and more important for Jordan to prove that to this town before his father completely lost his mind to dementia. He was desperate to give his dad that gift while he could still recognize it.

Beth, as it turned out, remembered the town and the school in similar ways he had, because she'd left, too, and had only recently returned. He knew he could use her simply as a source of information, but he really liked her. She sometimes was guarded around him, as if she didn't quite trust him—but she could also be warm and easy to talk to. They'd met for drinks and coffee a few times. Maybe she was wary of getting to know him, since his future in Fillmore looked about as temporary as hers. Maybe they were better off as friends. But he couldn't resist the desire to spend time with her.

So when she'd asked him to meet for a walk and a quick bite after coaching practice, he'd jumped. He hadn't even asked what it was about, and she hadn't offered. All he wanted was to get closer without scaring her off.

Just then, she placed a whistle to her lips and blew, holding up her hands in a T for time-out. She ran onto the field, pointed to the girl who'd been dribbling the ball and just lost it to a defender. She reset the play, had the defender back up, and motioned where she wanted the girl to send the ball. Beth jogged off the field and blew the whistle once again to start the play. When she turned, she spotted Jordan and waved him over.

The girl with the ball passed it right away to the center midfielder, who sent it to the open left wing. She took a shot on goal, which was caught by the goalkeeper.

"Aren't they great?" Beth said, her eyes shining. "They're getting better and better at creating opportunities out there." She glanced at her watch and blew the whistle once again. "OK, good practice, girls! I'll see you at the same time tomorrow."

The girls sauntered back to the sideline and gathered their gear. Jordan's presence did not go unnoticed, as more than a few players raised their eyebrows and a couple giggled.

"You got a date, Coach?" one of the girls asked.

Beth playfully narrowed her eyes. "Jeez. Can't a girl go for a walk, Leah?"

While the girls guzzled water from their water bottles and gathered their belongings, Beth stacked cones and placed soccer balls into a bag.

"*My dear,*" Jordan said with exaggerated affect as he took the bag and slung it over his shoulder. Beth laughed, and the two walked toward her car. She popped the trunk, and they placed the gear inside.

The girls started to peel away, some on bicycles, some walking, and some in awaiting cars. Jordan liked having this time alone with Beth, just to walk and talk.

To his surprise, Beth grabbed his hand, and they started toward town. His pulse quickened at her touch. Her hand felt cool and dry in his. He looked over and caught her eye, and she blushed, and looked down.

"Hand-holding, eh?" he said. "I didn't know you were the hand-holding type."

Her cheeks reddened. "There's a lot about me you don't know."

The sun had lowered in the sky, taking the intensity of the heat with it. The neighborhood by the practice field was made up of modest one-story homes spaced apart. No fences, just expanses of lawn, with varying levels of upkeep.

"Thanks for meeting me," Beth said, tucking a strand of hair behind her ear.

"I like hanging out with you, so it wasn't a hard decision," Jordan said. "And after two hours in the car and then sitting to catch up on some work, I could use the walk."

Beth grinned and stared off at the uneven sidewalk in front of them. "I'm curious about Springtime. How your dad likes it, how you feel about it."

Jordan took a beat. Since he hadn't spent any time with his father before that fateful day his dad's sponsor had called last spring to check up on him, Jordan couldn't gauge how his quality of life had changed since he'd moved to Springtime. But what he could see was that his dad seemed engaged—often forgetful, but engaged—and, from what he observed, he behaved like a relatively content human being.

"I think he likes it," Jordan said. "Springtime's not fancy, but I don't think that's what he wanted. He wanted more than anything to return to Fillmore, which pretty much narrowed my choices down to one."

Beth nodded. Street traffic had started to pick up as they walked toward the town center.

"He's—happy?" Beth's voice faltered a bit, like she wasn't sure she wanted to know the answer to that question.

"I guess. Sometimes it's hard to tell because of the dementia, but I think so. He seems to like having a place to call home. He seems to like the people who take care of him." Jordan looked over at Beth. "Are you thinking of it for your dad?"

She placed her hands in the pockets of her shorts and nodded.

After a moment, she sucked in a breath, like she was about to say something further, but then clamped her mouth shut and continued walking.

"What?" Jordan said.

Beth glanced up at him. "What, what?"

"What were you going to say?"

She sighed. "Ugh, I just hate all this." She shook her head slowly back and forth. "When it comes to caring for your aging parent, it's so easy to make the wrong decision and almost impossible to get it right."

They walked in silence for half a block, the homes now drawn closer together as small twins and clusters of row houses. Downtown was just a few blocks away.

"I had it easier," he said. "I was pretty confident my father's living situation would improve by moving him to Springtime versus living alone in a studio apartment with a failing memory." He shrugged. "It's weird, I thought I hated him. Or at least stopped caring about him. But I . . . wish I had been able to intervene sooner." A lump formed in his throat. "So obviously, you need to do what you think is best for your father, and also what's best for you."

"Oh, is that all?" she said with a dry laugh that he joined in on. "I can tell my dad just wants to get better. He wants a magic wand to instantly return him to his old self, his old life," she said. "I don't have a magic wand, but Springtime does have really good rehabilitation facilities. And it's way better than a nursing home."

Jordan got the sense that Beth was trying to talk herself into moving her dad into long-term care.

"I have a feeling, though, he won't be returning to his old life. And that's hard." She rubbed the back of her neck. "I'm glad it's been a good fit for your father. He deserves a nice place to call home."

Jordan had to admit he agreed.

After a quick dinner at Zeke's, the two walked back to the fields to retrieve their cars.

"I guess I'll see you next week," Beth said, turning toward him. She slipped her hand into his just as he leaned in, kissing her for the first time. Her lips were soft, and she smelled of sun and vanilla-scented shampoo.

"I've wanted to do that since junior year," he said when they parted. Beth blinked. "Really?"

"You didn't know?" He thought it was obvious—he'd behaved like a Labrador retriever puppy around her in high school.

She shook her head. "I assumed I scared everyone in high school, being so tall and playing on the boys' soccer team. Certainly didn't do much for my social game."

"I thought you were amazing. It's partly why I volunteered to assist the coach. That way I could watch you from the bench almost every day." He grinned. "You were so serious. So focused. I admired that."

Beth's cheeks reddened. "I was a lot less together than you're making it sound," she said. "Thanks for the advice about Springtime. I think my dad might just like it there."

Jordan pulled away. "Speaking of which, I promised I'd drop by the Center tonight and see my father. He's starting to forget who I am, so I'm finding ways to remind him." He shrugged. "Kind of a hopeless task. More for me than him, I guess."

After Beth drove off, Jordan wondered if there were ways to jog what was left of his dad's memory. He knew he didn't have much more time to find out.

CHAPTER 20

BETH

A week later, Beth—clad in a thin tank top and running shorts—waited for Ally after practice. The field was located near the head of the Rancocas Creek Trail, a favorite exercise spot for locals. But few were out and about this Wednesday afternoon. The East Coast was going through the first real heat spell of the season, and Beth wondered whether going for a run was a wise decision for her pregnant best friend. Today, Beth had given extra water breaks for her well-trained preteens, so she probably should have canceled her and Ally's run in the interest of safety. But Ally surely was on her way and didn't like breaking her routine—never had—so maybe Beth could talk her into a brisk walk as a compromise.

A few of the balls had gotten away from the girls and ended up in the bushes at the edges of the field. She needed to retrieve them before stowing away her soccer equipment in her car. Beth breathed in the scent of trees and pollen and cut grass. Outside was where she needed to be—right here, right now. What a day. What a *week*. When the Springtime Center, Mount Holly Hospital, the nursing home, and

Medicare had all signed off on her dad's application to relocate, Beth knew she had no time to lose.

After spending weeks in the ICU and then later being confined to the stroke-rehabilitation wing of the nursing home, her dad yearned to return to his real home—he'd expected it. As grateful as she was that the color had returned to his cheeks and that he'd started eating solids on his own again, he'd declined in ways she'd never imagined. He wasn't going home.

He needed help getting to and from the bathroom. He ingested a shocking number of medications, timed in careful increments throughout the day. He used a wheelchair and walker with assistance to get around.

Beth could handle all that. Or she thought she could get used to it. He'd been on the older side when she'd been born—he in his forties, her mom in her thirties—and as a motherless only child, she'd vaguely anticipated having to figure out how to care for her aging parent before her peers would. Someday. But she now knew she had a lot to learn.

The stroke had robbed Ralph Snyder of the one activity he loved most in life—talking. Right now simply communicating with her dad was a painful and tedious affair that tested their patience. It broke her heart watching him struggle to form the words that populated his mind. She could see when he tried to talk that there was some broken connection between his brain and his mouth, as if one was controlled by the hare and the other by the tortoise. Who would he be if he couldn't talk to people and swap stories? Beth didn't know, but she could see the darkness of depression descend on him the longer he stayed in the nursing home. He couldn't go home—now out of the question—but he could live someplace where he'd enjoy a little more freedom and be surrounded by his things. A middle ground, of sorts. So after wading through her dad's finances—renting for now with possibly buying in after selling the house—the Springtime Center it was.

Her signature on the paperwork hadn't even been dry by the time Beth had rented a U-Haul and hired a kid off Craigslist to help her move her dad's stuff to his new one-bedroom unit and set it up. When he moved in yesterday, he'd had access to much of his old life—his TV, bed, tables, plates, silverware, clothes, toothbrush, and books. Feeling a little self-conscious, Beth had brought in and carefully set up the soccer shelf exactly the way her dad had it at home. She'd also retrieved the corkboard from the station, which she'd hung on the bedroom wall. It was all a little hard to look at now that she was retired from the NWSL—a development her dad didn't need to know about. When the boxes were cleared away and the linoleum floor swept, the place had looked as close to home as possible in a senior community.

Beth hoped her dad would eventually think so too.

Beth looked up and saw Ally's SUV make a left turn into the parking lot. Ally stepped out, pausing to unzip her hoodie and throw it onto the passenger seat. She waved as she approached. Ally's baby bump was visible under her yoga capris and loose-fitting tank top.

"Sorry I'm late," she said. She fanned her face. "It's warm today. I've been in the air-conditioning all day and hadn't even noticed that it'd gotten so hot."

"You sure you want to run?" The logical side of Beth knew exercising while pregnant was safe—encouraged, even—but the last thing she wanted was Ally to collapse from heat stroke on her watch.

"It's fine," Ally said, waving her off. "I'll walk if it gets uncomfortable. How did the move go?"

"It went as smoothly as it could, I think. We got most everything he needs. Broke a glass and a picture frame—that was me—but nothing that can't be replaced. We even got that TV in there."

Ally grasped her ankle and stretched her quad. "He must love being out of that nursing home. And into his new place—how's he doing? Does he like it?"

He hates it.

Beth's certainty crushed her. She would have paid anything to see his depression lift the instant he was wheeled into the apartment yesterday. She would have loved to watch his eyes light up, to see him work to twist his mouth into something that resembled a smile. She didn't need a thank-you, just a hint of joy.

Or at least not disdain.

Instead, she'd waited a painful thirty seconds for him to spit out, "What's this?"

"It's your new apartment, Dad," she'd said through a tight-lipped smile. She glanced up; the attendant's hands still gripped the handles of the wheelchair as if it were the steering wheel to a getaway car. As if the aide were ready to back up and peel out—he just needed to say the word. "I brought all your things, so you'd feel right at home."

His face did not come to life at the sight. "Not. Home."

Beth couldn't decide whether to scream or cry. She wanted to do both. After all this—the phone calls and paperwork and working with the insurance company—couldn't he at least just fake that he liked it one teeny-tiny bit? Couldn't he recognize how much effort it had taken for her to clear out his things and arrange them in this space so that he could feel at home?

The attendant—perhaps reacting to the look of anguish on Beth's face—straightened. "How about we go take a look?" Her voice was cheery as she pushed the chair through the doorway. "Wow, that's quite a TV."

The three took the short tour through the apartment. Beth's dad's face remained expressionless. This certainly wasn't the first time she'd disappointed him, but to strike out on this scale when she'd swung for the fences felt like she didn't even know him well enough anymore to provide him what he needed and wanted. She'd failed him precisely when he needed her the most. Though what success might have looked like, Beth didn't know.

Leaving him there yesterday afternoon—after kissing his cheek and assuring him she'd be back soon and then closing the door behind her— just about knocked her out. She didn't even make it to her car before she was sobbing into her hands. What had she done?

Even thinking about it now brought tears to her eyes.

"He's—" Beth paused to compose herself. "Getting used to it."

Ally's eyebrows pushed together. "Aw, Beth. He will." She stopped stretching, placed both hands on Beth's shoulders, and looked right in her eyes. "He *will*. This is a big transition for him. He's got a long road ahead. And I'm sure that setting up his new apartment like you did with so much care will help ease that transition. And he's got *you*. You're the most important person in his life. Thank goodness you're able to be here, you know?" Ally gave her shoulders a quick squeeze and let go.

Remorse weighed on Beth. Not only had she failed her dad, she also didn't want to be in Fillmore any longer than necessary. She'd already spent more consecutive time in town this spring and summer than she had her entire adult life. Setting up her dad at Springtime was part of her escape plan. The next step would be selling the house so he could afford to stay there permanently. But first, he had to want to be there. She couldn't just leave him someplace that made him unhappy. Alone.

Ally looked down at the bag of soccer balls. "Want to pass?" she said, a slow grin spreading across her face.

They hadn't kicked a soccer ball around together since high school, Beth realized. While most girls their age had bonded over long afternoons at the coffee shop or strolling downtown, Beth and Ally had spent endless hours gabbing while passing the ball back and forth. Or taking shots on one another. Or practicing foot technique.

"Sure," she said, feeling like a teenager again.

Beth took out a ball from the bag and jogged several yards from Ally, pushing the ball in front of herself with her feet. When she was far enough away, she kicked it to Ally, a clean, crisp pass, right to her feet. Just the kind of pass she'd been teaching the girls earlier at practice.

They passed back and forth in silence for a little while as Beth let the moment sink in. She had her friend back. She'd never realized how much she'd missed this, their friendship.

The late-afternoon sun beat down on them, and Beth was sweating despite the relatively little effort of kicking the ball.

"You OK?" Beth said. "This heat is no joke."

Ally gave her a look. "You worry too much." She kicked the ball to Beth.

Beth shrugged. "It's hot, just sayin'."

"Hey—so, summer. Fourth of July is behind us. We've got a lot of girls playing next year. It's our biggest year yet."

"That's awesome, Ally."

"With so many new girls added to the mix, I thought the travel teams would benefit from morning clinics over the rest of the summer. Like, eight to eleven or noon for training. Maybe fun team-building stuff in the afternoon. I'm even thinking of summer tournaments. What do you think?"

"Sounds great." Beth wiped the sweat off her lip with her shirtsleeve and came under the ball with her instep, giving it a little lift. "Who'd run it? You?"

"*You*, dummy," Ally said, laughing and trapping the ball at her feet. "I know you've been training the U13s, but that's just a couple afternoons a week. Besides, you'd be perfect."

Beth doubted she'd be "perfect" for this job, but she'd surprised herself with how much she'd enjoyed coaching over the last couple of months. It certainly hadn't been easy—can anything involving twelve-year-olds be considered easy?—but coaching scratched some itch in her she didn't know she had. Maybe it had something to do with imparting the experience she'd accumulated over the decades to players who were just starting out. Or maybe it wasn't about her at all. Maybe that's what she liked. For once, she didn't have to think about herself or her level of fitness or her health or even what she'd eaten for breakfast. All she needed to do was turn her focus to those girls and help them succeed.

"I don't know," she said. "What if I decide to try out for the Australian league?"

Ally stepped on the ball. "Give me a break."

Beth frowned. "What?"

"You are not trying out for the Australian league."

"Who says?"

"I think the universe says."

Ally's condescending tone irked her. Beth had known the likelihood of her playing for the Australian professional league was a bit of a long shot, but she didn't need Ally, of all people, telling her so.

"How do you know?" Beth had kept the unwelcome news from her neurologist to herself. She hadn't even told her dad yet. She wasn't sure she'd ever tell her dad.

"I know you're not 'on leave,' OK? You're not on the roster anymore. I looked it up."

"So I'm not playing this season—that's not exactly news."

"You shouldn't be playing at all." Ally passed the ball. "Come on. Three bad concussions over the course of a career in sports would knock out anyone. And those are just the ones that have been diagnosed. You don't want to do permanent damage."

Beth had thought quite a bit about how quitting soccer would feel. Soccer had allowed her to escape Fillmore without abandoning her father. During pro soccer season, or the World Cup, or the Olympics, she could be there for him on his giant flat-screen television doing what made him most proud—playing the greatest sport in the world.

"Just"—Beth rested her hands on her hips and looked up to the cloudless sky, as if searching for answers in the heavens—"don't tell Dad."

"You haven't said anything?"

"I don't know, Ally." Beth glared at her. "Maybe after suffering from a debilitating stroke, being in the hospital and nursing home for months, and now relocating to a brand-new living situation, my dad just couldn't take having his heart broken again."

Ally raised her hands in surrender. "Fine, fine. I get it."

The two kicked the ball between themselves in silence, and Beth's thoughts returned to the previous evening.

Before Beth arrived home after leaving her father at Springtime, she hadn't given much thought to how she'd feel living in a space with so much missing. When she opened the front door to her father's house, half-empty and devoid of the things her dad loved the most—the things that made the house a home—she hardly knew what to do with herself. She'd cleared out almost entire rooms.

Stepping into the living room, she could see all that remained behind were a reading chair, rug, ceiling fan, and nails in the walls. She wandered into the kitchen—the table and chairs were gone. His bed and dresser now resided at Springtime with him. The house was now defined by what was missing—including her father.

The interior of her dad's house appeared like she felt—empty. She couldn't possibly have prepared herself for any of it—her dad's deteriorating health, his new living situation—but least of all the idea of coming home to a space that didn't feel like the house she grew up in. She hardly slept that night and wondered how she would manage the rest of her stay in Fillmore. She needed something to do. Something worthwhile. And if she was quitting soccer for real, then she needed to fill out her résumé with experience showing she could perform tasks aside from blocking shots and punting a ball deep into the other half of the field.

"I can run those summer clinics." Beth pushed a sweaty chunk of hair that'd escaped her ponytail behind her ear.

Ally looked over and grinned. "I thought for a sec I'd have to beg you."

Beth smiled back. "I do love this league, you know. You've created something that we could only dream of when we were kids." She passed the ball to Ally. "This is a really good thing. You probably already know this, but you're making a difference."

Not everyone who raised families in Fillmore had grown up there, and Beth knew most parents probably just signed up their daughters for travel soccer because that's what girls played in the towns they'd been raised in—that they might take the league for granted, as if it had been there for decades. Ally didn't get the credit she deserved for creating this league from scratch in a place that until recently didn't encourage girls to play competitive soccer. Or soccer, period.

"Thanks," Ally said, her cheeks turning an even deeper shade of red. She kicked the ball back, a little hard and not quite to Beth's feet.

Beth leaped to trap the ball with her foot and winced. A twist of pain stabbed her temple. Unsure whether it was the heat or the sudden exertion or a phantom ache from her concussion, Beth pressed her palm to her head out of reflex. She'd tried to keep her headaches at bay with ibuprofen, but sometimes they flared out of nowhere—and too often than she liked to admit. Each one represented another nail in the coffin of her soccer career.

"Mind if we take a water break?" she said, lowering her hand and hoping Ally hadn't noticed.

"You OK?" Ally said.

Beth couldn't believe her pregnant friend was asking her—the pro—if *she* was OK after a few minutes of passing the ball around.

"Yeah, fine," she said, downplaying it.

Beth shuffled the ball to where they'd laid all their stuff down and picked up one of her water bottles. She drank in deep gulps.

Ally reached for her own bottle and unscrewed the cap.

"So have you slept with Jordan yet?"

Beth almost choked. She'd forgotten how blunt Ally could be. She straightened and wiped her mouth with the back of her hand. At least they weren't talking about her head.

"Jeez, Ally."

"Well?" Ally sipped her water.

Beth took a breath. "We're taking it slow."

In high school, Ally had always pressed Beth for details about her limited experience with boys. Kisses and more at parties and in cars, mostly. It hadn't bothered her. Ally wanted to know everything about everyone, especially Beth. But for some reason, her interest in Jordan felt different. Special, somehow. And she felt protective of whatever had blossomed between them.

He'd kissed her for the first time right in this parking lot. Jordan had leaned in to kiss her, placing his hand on the back of her neck and pulling her toward him. Her cheeks flushed just thinking about that kiss.

Ally lowered her water bottle. "'Taking it slow,' eh? You must like him."

"All right. Enough of that." Beth resisted rolling her eyes like she imagined Morgan would in moments like this. "You mind if we call it a day before we melt out here?"

Ally cocked her head. "Fine." She stuck her index finger toward Beth. "For now."

CHAPTER 21

ALLY

While Ally washed the last of the dishes, she eavesdropped on her ex-husband's conversation with Beth in the dining area. Although Ally and Rob got along just fine these days, he never stayed longer than necessary after school or committee meetings. Today, however, she knew as soon as he'd walked through the front door that he was excited to finally meet the famed Beth Snyder and find a way to pepper her with questions about being a professional athlete. God, she hoped he'd be on his way soon. The first planning meeting for the gym dedication in the fall had ended fifteen minutes ago. Beth had only stopped by to pick up new practice pinnies for the team and had caught the end of the meeting, which was exactly what Ally had intended.

"Ally said you have a new baby?" she heard Beth say, and marveled at her skill at deflecting a conversation away from herself.

"Not a baby anymore." Rob's voice was infused with pride. Ally remembered how he'd talked like that about Morgan and Emily when they were little. "He's two. Hard to believe how fast it's going."

"I'll bet he's super cute." Just the right thing to say.

"Yeah. We're now at the point where we need to make a decision about Jules returning to work or if we're going to try for another. She's taking her time. Kline and Deutsch will take her back whenever she's ready, and on her terms."

They'd met at work. He was already a manager at the accounting firm and she a newly minted MBA with a background in tax fraud. They'd started dating the moment Ally and Rob separated, and it was only since she and Noah had gotten serious that Ally didn't feel a slight pang in her gut when she thought about how ready he'd been to move on from her. "We're really lucky, but I'm not getting any younger, you know?"

He was nervous and impressed by Beth, Ally could tell. He always got too chatty and open when meeting someone who intimidated him. Now was a good time to get him out of there.

She emerged from the kitchen drying a Tupperware container.

"Tell Jules thanks for the cookies. They were a big hit." She handed him the container.

Rob glanced around the dining room, as if noticing it for the first time, an uneasy look on his face. He turned his focus on the credenza.

"Hey. Did you swap out the buffet?"

Ally looked over at it, a heavy wooden block of furniture she'd inherited from her parents—the one that had been there since the day they'd moved in. She'd always wanted to buy a new one—heck, trade in her old dining room set for something sleeker and more comfortable—but that had never seemed like a wise investment. More pressing expenses had always presented themselves first.

"No. Same one." Every time he came over, he seemed to think something was different that wasn't.

Rob shrugged. "Oh well." He turned back to Beth and stretched out his arms. "Really good to meet you. Sorry about your dad." He paused. "Ally told me."

"Good to meet you too," Beth said, accepting his offer of an awkward hug. She made eye contact with Ally. *Help me,* her eyes seemed to say.

"I keep forgetting to ask," Ally said. "Why did you buy those earrings for Emily?"

Rob pulled away from Beth, a quizzical look on his face. "What earrings?"

"Those little flower earrings. She said you bought them for her?"

"For what?"

"That's what I wanted to know. You have a pretty strict policy on buying stuff for the girls, and it just seemed a little weird that you'd buy these earrings for her out of the blue."

Rob looked down, a serious look on his face, like he was trying to concentrate. "Yeah, no, I don't remember buying her anything since her birthday."

"Did you give her money to buy them?"

He shook his head. "Come on, you know me."

She did know. "Cheap bastard."

He laughed. "But seriously, I have no idea where she got them. Maybe a friend or something?"

Ally couldn't figure it out, either, but Emily had said she'd received the earrings from her dad. Ally had had a nagging feeling that Emily wasn't being truthful with her. What if she'd stolen the money to go buy them? Ally hated to even entertain the idea, but no better theory presented itself to her. She rarely kept track of her cash and doubted Rob did. Could she be taking money without asking first? She made a mental note to check her wallet.

He tapped the Tupperware. "I gotta go. Jules has her hands full this weekend."

The girls were at Rob's. Between two surly teenagers and a two-year-old, Jules certainly did.

"Bye," Ally said as Rob let himself out.

Beth turned toward Ally. "I can't believe you're really taking this on."

"Don't start." She grabbed a sponge from the sink and then wiped down the kitchen table.

Beth sank into a chair. "Of course there'd have been no way to keep the thing simple, once the planning kicked in. But come on. Seems way over the top, just for dedicating a new building. Even for you."

Ally was glad Beth had kept her reservations to herself when she'd dropped in at the tail end of the meeting. But, in truth, she needed her friend on her side.

"You saw how excited the committee was. It's going to be *the* event this fall." She walked the sponge back to the sink and rinsed it, then turned and counted off on her fingers. "Chris is donating kegs from the distributor. Nicole's catering business is contributing food. I didn't even have to *ask*. People *want* this, Beth."

"Yeah, well, do *we*?"

"What do you mean?"

"Let's just turn an even brighter spotlight on that fire, why don't we?"

Ally had tried to gauge Beth's reaction to the idea of the dedication when she'd introduced her to the committee, but Beth had given nothing away. She thought there was a chance she'd be OK with the idea, but maybe she'd been overconfident. It wouldn't have been the first time.

"The opposite. I think it'll draw attention to the *new* gym. It's not a funeral for the old gym, but a celebration. It's like we're rewriting the narrative. We'll get to celebrate the new building and all the new programs and the ways the community will use it." Ally hoped Beth would get on board with this story. But Beth didn't look convinced. "I put the water on. Tea?"

"Sure," Beth said, uncertainty tingeing her voice.

Ally walked toward the sink. "I haven't forgotten about the pinnies."

The electric teakettle clicked, and Ally opened cabinets, picking out cups, spoons, and a basket of tea selections. She set out the spoons, milk, and teas, and poured two cups of hot water. She set one of the steaming cups in front of Beth and sat across from her at the kitchen table, her own cup in hand.

"I need your help with this. I think that's the only way I'll convince Noah."

Beth raised her eyebrows as she sifted through the choices and selected a tea bag. "So Noah doesn't think you should be doing this?"

Ally waved her off. "Oh, he's just worried because I'm pregnant. I don't think he really cares either way about a dedication per se."

"Oh my God, I didn't even think of that. You'll be about to burst by mid-October." She dipped the tea bag into the scalding water. "We'll be rolling you around by then."

Stirring milk into her cup, Ally gave her a look. "Which is *why* I'm asking for your support. I can't do it by myself."

"No," Beth said, shaking her head. "You can't. Ally—" A pained expression formed on Beth's face. Ally wondered if she was getting another one of her concussion headaches. "I don't think you should be planning this dedication. It seems dumb."

Even though the house was empty, Ally looked around to make sure the two were alone.

"It was my idea—or sort of. After Faith Chen suggested it. It's also an excuse to take a look at those old records from twenty years ago." She lowered her voice to a whisper. "See if Jordan found anything that could be pinned on us."

"What's the excuse you're using to get to the records?"

"You know, to copy all the old dance tickets, game flyers, report cards, and playbills from the spring musical. Stuff like that. If we're doing a 'Party Like It's 1999,' then maybe we should reproduce some of the items from the time?"

Beth folded her arms across her chest. "Hmm."

Ally took a sip from her tea and then returned her mug to the kitchen table. "Only, I already tried to look for those records."

"What?" Beth said, leaning in. "What do you mean?"

"I used Noah's keys to break in to the archives in May."

Beth's eyes grew large. "What? That's insane. You know that, right?" She took in an excited breath. "What did you find?"

"Nothing."

"Oh. Well. That's maybe not so surprising."

"No. I mean, seriously: all of the boxes with the relevant materials from our year are *gone*. All the other years have all kinds of stuff that are just missing from our year."

"What the hell?"

"I know."

Beth sat back and narrowed her eyes. "And you've just been sitting on this information for all this time?"

She'd had to. She couldn't burden Beth with the information until she knew what to do about it. And if Beth had seen anything when she'd been with Jordan, surely she would have said something, right? They'd been casually dating now for months, seeing each other when he was in town, and she hadn't mentioned anything about what he'd found other than Mr. Miller might not have been the last person at the gym the night of the fire.

Ally nodded. "I didn't want to worry you. Not when your dad's health was so . . . fragile."

Frowning, Beth rubbed her chin. "Do you think Jordan took them? He wasn't supposed to take records from the archive, right?"

"I thought he did at first." Ally took another sip. "But now I don't know."

"And you're sure they're gone?"

Once again, Ally nodded. *Whoa boy, here it comes.* "But I found one of the folders yesterday in the trunk of Noah's car."

Beth's eyebrows shot up. "No," she said, gripping her cup.

"Yes." Ally's stomach tightened thinking about it. She'd been helping him unload the car after food shopping, and when she removed two of the bags, there it was, lying in the back of the trunk among some work he'd brought home from school.

"What was in it?"

Ally peered into her mug, her tea a chalky yellow. "I don't know. I didn't touch it."

"You didn't even look at it?"

"I just saw our year on the label—1999 to 2000. The folders are all labeled by school year. I could see one of those manila envelopes peeking out from the top, but that's it." Her head felt light. "I think I froze when I saw it. I almost dropped the bags of groceries. And then Noah came out of the house to get the last of the stuff, so I just didn't have a chance to even take a quick look."

"I wonder why he has it?" Beth said, her voice low, as if she were talking to herself.

Ally looked up. "What do you think it means?"

"I don't know. I mean, you know Noah better than I do." Beth took a gulp from her cup.

"Maybe I don't know him as well as I thought I did." Dread stirred inside her.

"It's just weird, because Jordan's the one who wanted access for his research." Beth tapped her index finger on the table. "Why would Noah have it? It doesn't make any sense. Unless maybe it was meant for Jordan."

"Has Jordan mentioned anything?"

Beth shook her head. "Not a word."

"He doesn't talk about it with you?"

"Not really. Why would he?"

"I don't know." She guessed she'd just assumed Beth and Jordan would've reached the sharing stage by now. "I can't stop thinking about that dumb folder," she said. "If I knew what was in it, I'd at least have a clue why Noah thought to hang on to it."

"Noah's not even from around here, though," Beth said. "Why would he want it?"

"I know." Ally bit her lip. Noah had attended high school in northern Jersey. He didn't move to Fillmore until he got the job teaching at the high school.

"He doesn't know anything, really, about the fire, other than what's already out there."

"Then why keep the folder?" Ally closed her eyes and rubbed her forehead. Noah wouldn't turn on her, would he? A paranoid shadow fell over her: He'd behaved so uptight and worried lately. He seemed to question every decision she made. "What if he found something and kept it because he wants to protect me?"

Frowning, Beth reached across the table and placed her hand on Ally's. Ally looked up. "Hey. You have a lot to deal with right now. You're getting yourself all worked up."

Beth rose.

"You're leaving?" Ally said, feeling some alarm. Why was everyone dismissing her lately?

"I'm running your summer clinics, remember? I have an early call tomorrow and need to plan the day." She took her cup to the sink and then walked toward the entryway. She grabbed her bag from the foot of the staircase. Ally followed. "Is Morgan coming tomorrow?"

"I think so, why?"

"Nothing." She offered an apologetic smile. "Just thinking about numbers."

"Numbers? Are the girls not showing up?" Aside from normal interruptions such as family vacations and the occasional cold or sprained ankle, the travel-team girls were required to show up to practices and clinics they'd signed up for. And Morgan always showed up. Without question.

"It's nothing," Beth said. "The girls are coming to the clinics."

"Well, that's good." Then why bring up Morgan?

Beth paused as she gathered her keys and purse. "And think about taking a little you time—you need to take breaks sometimes."

"Ha," Ally said. "Good one."

After Beth left, Ally couldn't shake the feeling that Beth, Noah, Rob, even her girls seemed to question everything. Lately, she'd been feeling on the defensive, always painted into a corner. And that folder in Noah's trunk . . . fear crawled up her throat.

Now it wasn't just Jordan she needed to worry about, but Noah as well.

CHAPTER 22

JORDAN

"Thanks for agreeing to meet last minute," Jordan said. He placed his messenger bag on the floor beside him and sat across the desk of Pat O'Rourke, Fillmore's fire chief. The small office was relatively spare—the desk had a computer monitor and keyboard, a nameplate, several photographs featuring people who Jordan guessed were his family, and a small American flag on a tiny pedestal. A bookshelf crammed with binders, books, stacks of papers, and three fire helmets filled the wall behind him. "I know you mentioned you were heading out of town."

O'Rourke nodded and absentmindedly smoothed his thick mustache. "You're lucky you caught me. Driving the family up to Lake George in the morning." He leaned his portly frame back in his desk chair and took off his reading glasses. "So what's this about revisiting the old gym fire?"

Jordan knew that opening up his own investigation might ruffle a few feathers, especially those of Pat O'Rourke, who had helped run the original investigation almost twenty years ago. In fact, it was his testimony at the trial that sent Jordan's dad down his own destructive path.

Jordan straightened. "Yes, like I said over the phone, it's the twenty-year anniversary and I'm doing a little research on the fire." The anniversary was irrelevant for Jordan, but he found the line could be a way in to gain access to people and resources he wouldn't otherwise have.

"'Doing a little research.'" Chief O'Rourke folded his arms across his chest. "Sure."

O'Rourke clearly was in no mood to make this easy for Jordan.

"Look, I discovered a couple of things that might call into question some of the testimony. You know, that my father was solely responsible for the fire. I thought I'd run some of it by you and get your take."

The chief lowered his brow. "And why would I want to do that?"

Excellent question. Why the hell would he?

Jordan paused to collect his thoughts. "Maybe because there's a chance the story we were told at the time wasn't the whole story. Maybe the town needed to point the finger at someone, and that someone just happened to be my dad." He swallowed. "And if that's true, it's important to set the record straight. Don't you agree?"

O'Rourke looked like the last place he wanted to be in that moment was sitting across from Jordan Miller. He met Jordan's gaze.

"What have you got?" The fire chief's voice was resigned.

Grateful and a little surprised that O'Rourke seemed at least open to hearing him out, Jordan picked his messenger bag up from the floor and slipped a grainy photo out of a thin file and placed it between them.

"What's this?" O'Rourke slid his reading glasses back on.

Jordan pointed at the picture of the charred remains of the old high school gym. "See here? These are the doors that led out from the boys' locker room to the gym."

O'Rourke nodded. "I remember. This was one of the photos from the trial that showed the wreckage."

"Yeah, well. The doors here are unlocked and open."

The chief looked at Jordan and frowned. "So?"

"My dad wouldn't have left those doors open like that. Especially not on a Friday. No halfway-responsible janitor would do it on any day, much less before leaving for the weekend. And I'm not just saying this because he's my dad—you can ask anyone who knew him: he took his job very seriously." Jordan took another photo from the file. "From this angle, you can see the doors to the girls' locker room are closed. But the boys' were hanging open. There's no way he would have left them not only unlocked but wide open." Jordan remembered his father being meticulous about securing every door before leaving for the day. "I think these open doors cast serious doubt that my dad was the last person to leave the gym that night. There's a chance someone else was there. He'd never be that careless."

Pat leaned back and crossed his arms. "This doesn't prove anything. A strong enough blast could have blown those doors open. But I don't know that that was it. Just because you say your father never left the doors unlocked doesn't mean he didn't that night. Everyone makes a mistake sometimes."

Jordan's neck burned. His dad certainly had made mistakes, but not when it came to protecting school property.

Pat shrugged. "We found no evidence of anyone else being on the premises just before or at the time of the fire. I'm sorry. I don't think I can help you." He glanced at his watch. "And I need to shove off a bit early this afternoon. You understand."

Jordan raised his index finger. "Just one last thing." He flipped through the folder and selected one additional photo that Noah had pulled for him. "This was printed off an old CD-ROM of photos. I'm pretty certain they were taken by a student, probably for the newspaper or yearbook. Definitely not the county newspaper."

Weeks after going through the high school archives and finding every yellowed edition of the *Tiger Times* from 1999 to 2000 at his fingertips, Jordan realized there might have been even more photos available. The newspaper staff had used digital cameras back then. Was there a chance the photos that didn't make the weekly editions had been saved? He'd brought it up to Noah, who thought that there was a good chance those old photos had been saved digitally, transferred to CD-ROMs, and stored with the computer-and-camera equipment. Nobody bothered to weed out digital files; it was just easier to save everything. Noah had located and pulled that year's disk for him, and yesterday, Jordan had finally gotten his hands on it.

Jordan placed the picture onto the desk. It was a photo of the destroyed boys' locker room. The benches were ash and the metal lockers warped and twisted. In the midst of the mess, Jordan could clearly make out steel bolt cutters.

Pat squinted at the photo. "What am I supposed to see here?"

"These bolt cutters," Jordan said, pointing.

Pat gave Jordan a look of confusion. "Wouldn't a janitor have bolt cutters? Like, for students who forgot their locker combination or something?"

Jordan nodded. "Yeah, but these aren't my dad's."

"How do you know?"

"Because he didn't keep his in the gym. He needed to have them handy, so he kept them in the main school building with most of his supplies. For exactly the reason you noted—for students who forgot their combinations. Or sometimes so the principal could get into a locker for other reasons, like for drugs or a weapon or something."

Deep in thought, Pat ran his fingers over his mustache again. "And you're certain of this? He didn't keep an extra in the gym?"

Jordan shook his head. "He didn't have an extra of anything. He operated on a tight budget, and that would've been wasteful. In the event he needed to use them in the locker room, he'd absolutely have just grabbed the ones from the main building."

Pat met Jordan's eyes. "So what do you need from me?"

"I guess—" Jordan looked down at his hands and then back up at the fire chief. "I just need to know I'm not imagining things. That there's a chance that maybe my dad wasn't the last one to leave the gym that day."

Pat sighed. "I suppose it's possible that someone else could have been on the scene that day. Unlikely, but possible."

"OK," he said, nodding. He knew the chief thought they'd blamed the right guy, but he didn't *know* his dad like he did. Hope flooded his chest. "Thank you for your time."

Jordan gathered the photos and slipped them back into the folder. He stood and shook the fire chief's hand.

"Good luck," Pat said and showed Jordan out of his office.

When Jordan settled into the driver's seat of his car, he took out his phone. It was close to 5:00. He thought about texting Beth to see if she'd made plans for the night. He'd told her earlier in the week he wasn't coming into town, but since he was able to schedule the last-minute appointment with the fire chief, he'd made the run down.

He liked her. A lot. She was no longer just an old, hopeless crush. She was a knockout, for sure, and in some ways she awed him. But she was also so . . . *real*, somehow. They had a lot more in common than he would've imagined. They were both raised—at least for a time—by single parents who didn't have it easy making ends meet. They shared an ambitious drive that had led them to delay or sacrifice traditional life choices—like marriage and kids and stability—for professional advancement. They each could alienate a lot of folks, which made them both lonely at their core. But Beth was warm and funny, and despite her sometimes borderline-intimidating intensity, was at the very least already a really good friend.

The pull to call her was strong—but it had some stiff competition tonight. His dad had gotten a new roommate a few weeks ago, which had proved to be a hurdle for him. The Center wasn't sure if this arrangement was going to work out, so Jordan had thought to keep a close eye on the situation and try to do his part in easing this transition. Not just because it would be nice for his dad to have some company. The fact was, he *needed* a roommate. Medicare wouldn't cover a one-bedroom unit just for him.

Sighing, Jordan started the car and set himself into motion away from Beth. He'd grab some takeout and check in on his father.

And next time he saw her, he'd take her out someplace nice.

CHAPTER 23

BETH

In the week since she'd moved her dad into the apartment at Springtime, he'd invented a reason for her to visit every day. He'd found some problem with the Wi-Fi connection, or the cable box wouldn't turn on, or the air-conditioning unit blew too cold, or his computer password didn't work, or the toilet wouldn't stop running. Always something. And he didn't like letting in "strangers"—meaning the well-qualified and caring support staff—*so could she please come and take a look?*

Today, Beth arrived at his apartment in the late afternoon—worn out after running the all-day summer clinic—to check out a leak under the kitchen sink. Her plumbing skills were nonexistent, and she knew if the solution wasn't something simple, she'd have to call a professional.

So she made a quick stop at the house to pick up her dad's toolbox and headed over to Springtime. It felt strange being at his beck and call after a lifetime of him supporting her, like she was being thrust into adulthood for the first time at the ripe old age of thirty-seven. After spending her whole life focusing solely on her own needs, her wants, her goals, it now occurred to her that her singular focus—soccer—had placed everything else important to her—her father, friends, boyfriends—as a distant second. She found herself facing the question: Had she really been this self-absorbed her entire life?

She knocked on his door to let him know she'd arrived before she let herself in with the key.

"Beth?" she heard him say through the door. "Is that you?"

His voice had grown stronger over the past weeks. His speech was still slower than before the stroke and slurred when he grew tired, but he'd been working with a speech therapist, and to Beth's delight, he'd improved.

"It's me, Dad." Her hand hovered over the door handle. "Are you decent?" *Ha.* How many times had he asked her that question growing up?

"Of course I am." His voice was slow but clear, impatience sharpening his tone.

Beth hoped he wasn't in a mood today. She pressed down on the lever and let herself into the apartment.

Her father sat in his wheelchair facing the TV, which was on, but silent. A commercial for energy drinks animated the screen.

Beth set the toolbox down onto the dining table and walked over to him, planting a kiss on his cheek, which was grizzled with white scruff. She made a mental note to call about having someone help him shave in the next day or two.

"You're here," he said, his speech measured and slow, but not slurred. "Stay for a while." His old line, which he'd say every time she visited, not only recently, but for the two decades since she'd moved away to college.

He gestured toward the couch. She could hang out. She'd coached earlier, and Jordan was back in Baltimore, so she didn't have anywhere to be.

"I'm here to look at the sink, remember, Dad?" She glanced over at the TV again, which now featured an ad for prescription medicine, judging by the sun-dappled images and the paragraph in tiny print at the bottom of the screen. "What are you watching?"

"The game," he said. "It's halftime, so I put it on mute."

She folded her arms. "What game?"

He gave her a look. "Your team is playing Phoenix."

Longing tugged at her chest.

"Really? How are we doing?" Beth sat on the sofa. Three glossy-looking former soccer players appeared on screen—two of whom she'd played with on the US Women's National Team—sitting behind a large desk and waxing on about the highlights of the match so far.

"Chicago's trailing, 2–1."

"Oh no." From what she knew about Phoenix this season, Chicago should not have been behind. But her interest was reflexive, she realized. The fact was, she hadn't followed her team—ex-team—at all since returning to Fillmore. She'd even had her apartment cleared and her things shipped to her dad's place. It wasn't much, just a few boxes. The Chicago apartment had been furnished and rented month to month because she never knew when she might be traded.

Or unceremoniously dropped from the roster.

Beth wasn't avoiding watching the games exactly, but she hadn't felt the urge to follow their season either. She hadn't pined to see what she was missing. But sitting here now with her dad, it felt like it used to—before the stroke, before injuries forced her off the field. It felt *normal*.

Beth turned toward her father. "Who do they have in goal? Kristen?"

Kristen Eder had served as the backup goalkeeper for the last two years. After Beth's latest concussion, however, she'd most likely moved into the first-string lineup. Beth liked her. Kristen wasn't as tall as Beth, who always used her length to her advantage, but she had such power in her legs and core, and with her lightning-quick reflexes, forwards would have a hard time getting anything past her.

Her dad nodded. "Yep. She's no Beth Snyder, I can tell you that." Lips pressed tight, he gave her a brief look and turned away.

Beth felt his disappointment like a weight in her gut and wished she'd had the chance to come clean about her nonfuture in the sport before his stroke. She hadn't had one honest discussion with him about her soccer career since she'd arrived in town. She'd told herself it was to protect him, but wasn't she really just protecting herself?

She got up from the couch, grabbed the toolbox off the dining table, and walked over to the kitchen. She opened the cabinet under the sink, where someone had placed a bucket under the pipe. The bucket had about two inches of water in it.

"Dad, how long's this bucket been here?"

"The whole time," he said. "I can hear it drip when I eat."

The whole time? Her stomach twisted. This leak was officially the Center's responsibility, not hers. She wished her dad would loosen up about having "strangers" in his apartment.

She opened the toolbox and inspected the contents. Outside of cars, her dad would never be considered the handy sort, which was well indicated by the meager selection of items presented to her. He cleaned the gutters once in a while and could spackle and paint over a small hole in the wall, but otherwise, he hired out. Or—more likely—he'd trade favors with his electrician, contractor, and plumber friends. She took out a wrench and adjusted it to fit the pipe.

"Did you try calling Fred?" she asked, crouching down at the sink. She removed the bucket and tried the wrench. "He's much more qualified for this sort of thing than I am."

"He retired," he said from the living room, his back to her. "Lives in Sarasota year round now."

Beth twisted the wrench around the coupling and pulled. Like a miracle, it tightened. She replaced the bucket, stood, and turned on the faucet.

"Florida." She shook her head. She'd hated playing in Florida. The summer heat and humidity slowed everything down, including her. It felt like playing in hot soup. Not to mention the bugs. No thanks. Her dad, though. He'd started to watch his social circle begin to migrate south over the course of the last few years. Would he be happier there than in Fillmore? She hadn't thought about that before.

"He and Mary can take the grandkids to Disney now," he said.

Beth crouched again, scanning for drips. Nothing so far.

"Livin' the dream," she said, almost to herself.

"Game's on."

She rose and walked back to the sofa, leaving the water running. She needed to wait on the leak anyway, so she might as well spend a little time with her dad. Watch the second half. Pretend it was five, ten years ago and the team they were watching lose hadn't just fired her.

Beth sank down onto the couch and focused on the game, settling in to the comfortable silence she'd always shared with her dad. In high school, before the professional women's soccer league had formed, she'd loved watching the US Women's National Team play in the Olympics and the World Cup with him. The summer before her senior year, he'd thrown a viewing party for the epic final game. The US beat China in penalty kicks after two hours of play in the brutal Pasadena sun. Everyone she knew remembered Brandi Chastain peeling her jersey off in triumph after scoring the winning goal, but Beth zeroed in on goalkeeper Briana Scurry's calm-under-pressure demeanor. Beth idolized Briana. She wanted to play just like her. She wanted to *be* her. Ally, of course, wanted to be Mia Hamm, the team's all-time top scorer. The two dreamed of one day playing in the World Cup. And Beth had. Twice.

Her dad grumbled. Chicago's center forward had dribbled the ball one too many times and lost it at the top of the box.

"She should shoot when she has the chance," he said. "We could have tied the game."

Of course he was right, though offering opinions from one's living room was a lot easier than making those split-second decisions on the field. However, after decades of watching from the sideline, he knew the game as well as anyone.

Beth wondered what it would have been like if he had stepped up to coach an all-girls team when she and Ally were learning the game. Instead of sending her off to learn from the "experts," he'd have participated and learned right alongside her. Maybe he'd have become more understanding of her play, of her injuries, of her vulnerabilities on the field and off. She glanced over at him, his gaze glued to the game. Who was she to question how he'd supported her? He loved the game of soccer and lived to watch her play. He believed in her. That should be enough.

Her focus returned to the game. Phoenix had made their way onto the Chicago side of the field, and after a defender interrupted a pass from a midfielder up the side of the field, she passed it to Kristen, who kicked it to the defender on the opposite side. Beth knew she was trying to mix it up a bit. Give the girls on the right side of the field a breather and let them battle it out on the left for a little while. But when their defender attempted to send the ball down the line, Phoenix's right midfielder shot up and headed it dead center toward their forward, who happened to be open. The ball landed at the forward's feet, and seizing the opportunity, she reared back and kicked it hard and low to the outside corner. Kristen pounced a moment too late and landed hard on her right side just as the ball shot to the back of the net. Three to one, Phoenix. This game was getting away from them.

Her dad thumped the arm of his chair. "That shot would not have gotten past my Elizabeth."

"Not true, Dad." *Well, maybe.* Her long arms would have helped in that moment, but she didn't have Kristen's powerful and responsive quads either.

He turned toward her. "When are you cleared to go back? Seems like they've sidelined you long enough."

A sock right to the gut. The question put a halt to any suspension of reality she'd enjoyed since she arrived at his apartment. Should she put him off about it again? Suggest the idea of playing outside the US?

Or should she just come clean? How ready was she to break his heart in this moment?

She sucked in a breath, deciding he needed her honesty.

"What if I didn't go back, Dad?"

Utter confusion clouded his face. "Not go back." His speech was thick and slow, but his tone dismissive. "You'll go back. They need you." He gestured toward the TV. "They're *losing* without you."

As much as part of her itched to return to the field, an even bigger part of her recalled with horror that the last time she'd played, she'd gotten knocked out by a knee to her head. If something like that ever happened again, her neurologist warned she could be facing CTE by the time she hit middle age—which, at thirty-seven, wasn't that far off. Australian tryouts were in a month, and she wasn't even close to ready.

She now wished she'd been a little more forthcoming about the seriousness of her injuries with her father. Maybe he wouldn't be so dismissive of her now.

"I'm getting older, and after the third concussion, well," she said, considering how to frame the news, "the league takes it seriously."

He looked over at her and frowned. "What are you talking about? You're young. You're healthy. Show them you belong out there."

Her dad made it sound so simple, his logic unquestionable. To him, her talent, ability, and work ethic equated to minutes on the field. Every moment off the field when she could have played meant her unique skills were being squandered in some significant way—by her coaches? The team owners? Herself?

Beth understood it wasn't true. Her brain couldn't take any more blows. She was still dealing with residual headaches. She didn't know if they'd ever fully disappear.

Beth realized she couldn't be upset about it anymore. She wasn't going to try out for the Australian league. She wasn't heading to Europe. She was done.

Her dad switched his focus back to the game.

"Dad," she said. "I'm serious. I think my playing days are over."

He didn't turn around. Didn't acknowledge that he'd even heard her. He just sat there, looking small in his wheelchair, like a child who wasn't getting his way. Was this his brain on stroke? Her "new" dad? Or was this always him, a man who could only see her as his elite-level soccer star?

Beth rose from the couch and checked the sink. No leak. At least by some miracle, she'd fixed something today. Done one thing right. She washed the bucket and set it out to dry on the dish rack.

"I'm going, Dad," she said while drying her hands. "I've got some stuff to do at home."

He sat with his back to her, watching the game.

She walked over, gave him a quick peck on his scratchy cheek, and then grabbed the toolbox and her bag from the table.

"Love you," she said. "I'll see you tomorrow."

When she closed the door behind her, she placed her hand on her chest, as if feeling for the tense knot that had been building over the course of her visit. Or maybe it had been building the entire time she'd been back in Fillmore, like a growth, a malignant tumor.

She'd expected her dad to improve in this place, to thrive, even. In some ways he already had—he'd made gains with his speech and recovered some mobility. But she'd been wrong about almost everything. It disturbed her that her previously happy and proud father couldn't shake the depression and anger that had developed since the day of his stroke. And she couldn't make it right.

Beth sniffed. She didn't have anything to do tonight. Jordan, back in Baltimore, had mentioned having to catch up on some work. She'd head to her dad's house. And as soon as she walked in through the front door, she'd log on to her computer and continue the job of researching the local real estate agents. Beth knew she wasn't moving anywhere while her dad was in this state, but the act of adding names to her growing list of potential agents gave her some degree of control.

False control.

She didn't want to think about how she'd failed her father. Or her team. Or her body.

Instead of turning left toward the check-in desk and out the front door to the parking lot, Beth made a right down the hall and headed toward the dementia wing, despite her fear of facing the man who'd clung to the devastation and resentment she imagined he'd felt since the high school fired him for a crime he didn't commit all those years ago. Beth had resisted this detour since her dad had moved in. What if she found Mr. Miller upset and depressed? She didn't want to cause him any pain. But what if he'd moved on? What if he'd found peace? Her heart swelled at the thought. Jordan hadn't mentioned much about his dad, other than that he lived at Springtime and that their relationship, though improving, had been estranged since he'd left the family.

Beth decided she needed to find out for herself. She turned the corner and searched the nameplates under the small whiteboards next to each doorframe. Some of the whiteboards were blank, and some had notes printed in erasable marker that said stuff like *Patio*, *Dining Hall*, *Worship*, signaling, she imagined, the occupants' current locations. One of the first things she'd noticed about her dad when he moved in was that he'd been outfitted with a GPS tracker that he wore on a chain around his neck. Anyone in the memory-care units needed to be tracked, but Beth imagined dementia patients took tracking to another level. They needed watching around the clock, and those whiteboards likely served as an additional precaution.

She'd walked almost to the end of the wing before spotting a nameplate with **MILLER** printed on it. There was nothing written on the whiteboard, a sign that maybe he would be in his room. Beth checked the time: 5:48. Her own dad would be wheeled to dinner at 6:00, which the Center did in waves every fifteen minutes. She had time. She could say hi, make it brief. The soonest anyone would swing by would be in more than ten minutes, which gave her plenty of time to reintroduce herself and ascertain whether or not he was a well-adjusted, happy person, right? No harm in giving it a try.

Beth knocked on the door.

She heard nothing. No movement, no voices. She knocked again, wondering if she was breaking some protocol by knocking and waiting, like she would for someone without Alzheimer's. Most people probably just let themselves in with a key. Beth was glad her dad wasn't in that position. Yet.

"Yes?" a voice said from the other side of the door.

Beth looked around. The hallway was empty.

"Mr. Miller?" she said. "Can I come in?"

She heard fumbling and then something crashing to the floor.

"Mr. Miller?" she asked, concern edging into her voice. Maybe this was a bad idea. "Are you OK in there?"

The handle turned, and the door opened. Beth found herself staring into the face of Jordan's father. Mr. Miller was a good ten years younger than her father, but Alzheimer's seemed to have sped up time for him. Everything sagged—his face, his posture, even his ears.

He wore flip-flops, cargo pants, and a grimy white undershirt. His hands were also dirty, as if he'd just been digging in the garden. Beth hadn't stood in such close proximity to him in twenty years, and an uneasiness settled into her entire body.

"I'm sorry—" she said, starting to turn away.

"No, please," Mr. Miller said, his tone welcoming. "Come in."

He opened the door and ushered her in, as if he'd been expecting her.

Beth could see right away that Mr. Miller's apartment had a different setup from her dad's, and the living room furniture—all in gray stain-resistant fabric—appeared plain and impersonal, as if provided by Springtime. And unlike her dad's place, Mr. Miller's apartment didn't have a full kitchen with an oven or stove. But the kitchenette did have a refrigerator, a toaster oven, and a small round table and four chairs. This left more room for living space, which housed a sectional sofa, two side tables, a coffee table, a flat-screen television, and two plush lounge chairs, complete with footrests. Beth's eyes located what might have been the source of the crash—a planter of geraniums lay in pieces at the foot of the coffee table. A plate and a fork rested among a dusting of planting soil on the table's surface. She glanced back as he closed the door behind her.

His face crinkled into a lopsided grin. "Boy, am I glad to see *you*."

Beth raised her eyebrows. "I'm not—"

I'm not . . . what? Who does he think I am? Maybe he did know. Maybe he saw right through her. Or maybe he just needed help cleaning up this mess.

She decided to let Mr. Miller take the lead. "What happened?"

He stroked his chin, leaving behind speckles of potting soil on his face. "Can you tell me where you left it?"

Beth shook her head. "Mr. Miller, I don't know what you're talking about."

"It was right here." He gestured toward the kitchen. "It's missing and I need it."

She scanned the kitchen. Aside from an old *Home & Gardens* plant book lying face down on the countertop, the kitchen was spotless.

"What's missing?" Beth picked up the guide. "Is it this book?"

His smile faded. He didn't seem so happy to see her now. He shook his head and placed a hand over his right ear, as if he'd heard something that bothered him.

She put the book down and decided maybe she should be the one to take the lead. Clean up the plant and get out of there. Checking in on Mr. Miller had turned out to be a big mistake.

"Why don't I help clean up?" She opened what proved to be the broom closet and removed a broom and dustpan, and then marched over to the living room.

When he saw her crouch down beside the broken planter, readying to scoop up the mess, his eyes grew large.

"Stop!" he said. "Don't touch that."

Beth rose, dustpan in hand, her cheeks hot. This was getting ridiculous. She should have left when she had the chance.

"I don't want you to cut yourself, Mr. Miller."

"Leave it," he said, his tone sharp. "It needs watering."

He raised his hand again to his ear and squeezed his eyes shut. Beth set the dustpan on the table.

"OK," she said. "Let's just sit for a second, all right?"

She led him to the sectional and had him sit down. He opened his eyes again and, with caution, removed his hand from his ear.

"Feel better?" she asked. She hoped so. In just the last hour, she'd upset both her dad and Jordan's father, two men who deserved better.

Mr. Miller bent his head and peered over at her as if seeing her for the first time today. "You look familiar."

"I don't think you'd remember me, but I remember you."

His face lit up. "You do?"

Beth gave him a little smile. "You were the janitor at the high school."

"I remember you," he said, pointing his index finger at her. "You were a student there, weren't you?"

Her heart stopped. She knew how unlikely it was that he'd remember her, especially after twenty years. Surely literally thousands of kids had come and gone during his tenure as Fillmore High School's custodian. Even someone who didn't suffer from dementia would have forgotten the vast majority of those kids. But it unsettled her how certain he appeared right then.

With caution, she played along.

Beth nodded. "I was a student there."

He took in a breath and looked up at the ceiling, as if trying to recall something. She wondered what was going on in that brain of his.

Mr. Miller lowered his chin and looked straight at her with clear eyes. "Beth Snyder."

Beth almost fell off the couch. He knew who she was. What else did he know?

A knock at the door startled her, and then, helpless, she watched as the handle turned and Jordan stepped through the door carrying a paper bag. His face contorted from relaxed to surprised to confused in a matter of seconds.

"What are you doing in my father's apartment?" he said, frowning.

It felt more like an accusation than a question. Like she'd violated his trust. But what was *he* doing in Fillmore? Had he lied about having to go back to Baltimore? Or had his plans changed? She decided to table that one for now.

"Hey," she said, trying to gather her thoughts.

She rose from the sofa but didn't move beyond that, as if her feet were encased in cement. Jordan raised a good question—what *was* she doing? Initially, she'd just wanted to check in on him and make sure he was, what, OK? Happy? That he appeared like he belonged in the Springtime Center brochure?

"What's going on?" he said, setting the bag on the kitchen counter.

Beth followed his gaze from the dustpan on the coffee table to the broken potted plant on the floor. "Just trying to clean up a minor accident," she said. She grabbed the dustpan again.

Jordan folded his arms. "Dad, you can't take the plants inside. It's not allowed."

Mr. Miller clenched his jaw. "Gardening is *not* a crime."

Beth pressed her eyebrows together. "I was trying to help. I heard a crash from outside the door, recognized his name on the nameplate, and knocked on the door."

The details were right but out of order, which turned her statement into a lie. Her stomach clenched. Not a great way to grow a romantic relationship.

Jordan's face relaxed a little. "Thanks for thinking quickly."

Beth swept the potting soil from the table into the dustpan and then started picking up the large pieces from the shattered pot. She kept her gaze on the task at hand.

"I thought you weren't in town," she said, carefully placing the shards into the dustpan. "Aren't you supposed to be in Baltimore this week?"

Jordan frowned as he unfastened the stapled paper bag. After two months of seeing each other, she knew he valued his independence as much as she did. It was something they shared. Neither enjoyed being grilled regarding their whereabouts.

"I"—he glanced over at his father, who'd begun to maneuver from the sofa—"missed you. I came back early hoping we might spend some time together this weekend."

Her heart jumped.

"Oh?" Beth's cheeks burned. She'd missed him too.

Mr. Miller stood and wandered to the kitchen, where Jordan had taken out two plates from the cupboard.

"Isn't your dad in, like, another wing?"

She stood and walked over to the garbage can, where she dumped the remains of the planter into the trash. "I got a little—turned around after visiting my dad," she said. "I'm still getting to know the place and sometimes get a little lost on the way out."

Two lies. And counting.

"Well," she said, watching Jordan spoon portions of Chinese noodles and vegetables onto the plates. She wiped her hands on her leggings. His dad lowered himself into one of the dining chairs.

"You going to join us?" Mr. Miller said, winking at her. "I don't think your husband will mind."

"My husband?" Beth said, raising an eyebrow at Jordan.

"Who's her husband, Dad?" Jordan said, sliding over a plate of food.

Mr. Miller raised a fork. "Artie, of course."

"Who's Artie?" Beth said. The whole memory-care side of the Springtime Center left her in a state of confusion.

"His new roommate," Jordan said. He sat next to his dad. "Want to stay? We have plenty. My dad clearly likes you."

Warmth spread across her chest, but she'd stayed long enough.

Beth reached for her bag and toolbox. "I've got to go, but text me later." She turned toward Mr. Miller, who was focused on spearing a carrot slice with his fork. "Thanks for talking to me, Mr. Miller."

Jordan's dad looked up. "So long, Beth Snyder."

CHAPTER 24

ALLY

Ally was feeling grumpy as she and Noah shopped for paint. Four cans in the color "early dawn" seemed excessive. The guest room wasn't *that* big. Two cans would do it. If they needed more, they could always return to the hardware store, though these places the size of warehouses overwhelmed her, and the closest one was a thirty-minute drive outside Fillmore. Long way to go for paint. Noah was fully aware of her attitude toward hardware stores and had probably overbought, knowing neither one of them wanted the headache of returning for more paint.

Early dawn. Couldn't just be light yellow.

She and Noah would decorate the room in a gender-neutral scheme, as advised by parenting magazines and blogs everywhere. So different from when she'd been pregnant with the girls, especially with Morgan. She and Rob had gone over-the-top "girl" everything. Lavender for her room—walls, curtains, furniture, the rug. Even the toys looked like they'd been spray-painted in light purple. Ally had thought the room looked perfect and couldn't wait to welcome her new girl into this decidedly girly sphere. But as soon as Morgan was able to express an opinion, she'd let her parents know she loathed purple and wanted her room painted blue. So they did.

Emily, on the other hand, emerged from the womb fixated on dinosaurs, so her room's walls had soon been made over from light rose to wallpaper covered in T-Rexes and brontosauruses.

Even now, their rooms continued to evolve and express each girl's obsessions and identity as they grew older—soccer for Morgan, fashion and art for Emily. Ally learned to like it that way.

This go-around, she and Noah decided to wait on learning the sex of the baby. In truth, Noah wanted to wait—and Ally was ambivalent. Sure, find out the sex when the baby's born—why not? The baby's sex certainly wouldn't make a difference when choosing a paint color for the guest room. A color that would most likely change every few years until the kid left for college.

Ally figured she should stop calling it the guest room now anyway. *Baby room, baby room, baby room,* she reminded herself.

She fed her credit card into the card reader at the automatic checkout while Noah loaded the cans of paint back into the shopping cart.

"I still don't understand why we need to give up the guest room," Ally said as Noah pushed the cart toward the exit. "The baby can sleep in our room. It probably will, in a bassinet, for the first few months anyway."

"And then what?" Noah said. "Morgan's not moving away for college until next August at the earliest. And where would she stay during her breaks?"

Ally handed the receipt to a woman in a red apron at the store's exit, who swiped a bright-orange slash across it with her highlighter pen.

"Have a nice day," she said as they wheeled past.

Ally glanced up at Noah. "We'd figure it out. It's just so nice having that space. I like knowing I can put up my family or your parents or Beth or whoever at the drop of a hat."

"When was the last time you used it?" Noah navigated the cart toward the parking lot. "It's been at least a year. Sure, sometimes you work in there, but no one's stayed in it since I moved in."

True, Ally didn't say. *But I want it.* She knew she was being irrational. Ally loved having a guest room. It was one of those items, like a dishwasher and a washer and dryer, that made her feel like she'd arrived. That she was a grown-up.

But having a guest room and no room for her baby didn't make sense. Being a grown-up meant making a space for this kid that was going to arrive in just a few months.

"Fine," she said. "You made your point." She glanced at the cart again. "And we bought all of this *paint.* Guess we have to use it. Good grief." She held out her hand. "Gimme your keys, and I'll pop the trunk."

Noah tossed her his car keys, and Ally walked ahead to his car. She unlocked the trunk, ready to move items around, including, she remembered with a flush of nervous energy, the folder from the high school. She'd been desperate for another chance to take a peek at the contents, but hadn't had a moment to herself.

And now, when she peered inside, the trunk was empty. She blinked, hoping she was just seeing things. Or *not* seeing things.

"Hey, scooch," Noah said, taking a can out of the cart. He touched her back to move her to one side. "What are you staring at, kid? We gotta unload."

Frowning, Ally stepped aside. "Did you clean out your car?"

Noah ducked to place the paint inside the trunk. "Not really. I needed to clear out a few work things from the trunk to make room for paint. And any other baby-related items we might run across this weekend." He looked at her and grinned. "Aren't you excited? We're setting up the *nursery.*" His eyes dazzled. "I can't believe I just said 'nursery.' It's like it's getting more real every day, you know?"

Ally did know. This reality seemed to make Noah increasingly giddy with each passing day. As the due date drew closer and her belly grew bigger, Noah behaved like a helium balloon that yearned to soar. And her balloon was full of lead.

What had compelled him to pull that folder? She still couldn't make sense of it. He had zero ties to the area at that time. He hadn't even moved to Fillmore until he accepted the teaching position at the high school ten years ago. Had Jordan's investigation inspired Noah to start snooping around? All the buzz around the new gym? The twenty-year anniversary? And that led to the question: What had he found? And had he shared it with anyone else—like Jordan Miller? Ally mentally kicked herself for failing to take five seconds to check the inside of that folder.

Noah placed the last can of paint in the trunk and slammed it shut. Their next stop was shopping for a crib, but Ally's stomach grumbled in protest. She was hungry all the time these days. She glanced at her watch: 10:37. Not even 11:00. She placed her hand on his arm. He looked over at her, concern clouding his eyes. She weighed whether it'd be worth it to mention anything. He could go from giddy to worried to irritated in a matter of moments. Her fun, sexy, spontaneous boyfriend had all but disappeared.

"Early lunch?" she said. "I'm famished all of a sudden."

"Seriously?" Noah reached for his key fob. His voice was not unkind, just surprised. Ally pressed the key into his hand. "We just had breakfast. Can it wait until after Baby Mart?"

Ally's stomach, in its firmest voice, growled "no."

Her phone vibrated in her purse. She pulled it out, and Morgan's name flashed on the screen. Wasn't Morgan at a clinic this morning? Why would she call now?

"Morgan," she said, holding the phone up to her ear. "What's up?"

"Mom." She sounded breathless. "Emily called. She's at the mall. She got caught shoplifting, and they're holding her at the store. They say you need to come down."

"Wait, what? Slow down." Her stomach had dropped. Ally cupped the phone to her ear. "What mall? Which store?"

"Cherry Hill. Gloss. It's a makeup store," Morgan said. "She said she tried to call you, but you didn't pick up. And Dad's on a business trip."

"We've been shopping for the baby's room, and I didn't have the sound on." Ally closed her eyes. *Emily, shoplifting?* "We're on our way."

Ally's hunger was replaced by a rage that roiled in the pit of her stomach. She had *not* raised her daughters to steal. Yet here she stood in the back office of a Gloss at the Cherry-Fucking-Hill Mall. Ally and Noah had crossed through the sleek showroom, which looked like a combination of *Star Trek* and the inside of a Virgin airlines plane. The women who worked there all wore the same polished black dress, many of them brushing and blending powders and creams onto customers' waiting faces.

As they'd made their way toward the back office, Ally had thought the whole thing felt incongruous, like it couldn't have been possible for someone to pull off something as pedestrian as shoplifting in this futuristic store.

Emily sat in a chair beside a desk with a computer on it. Ally had imagined she'd witness remnants of crying—a guilty, tearstained face, maybe—but instead, Emily's face gave nothing away. If anything, she appeared angry, defiant. Cool.

"You're the parents?" a woman asked, wheeling away from the computer. She glanced over at Emily, sighed, and then stood. Ally guessed the woman was in her late twenties, but the heavy makeup made her look at least ten years older. The shiny name tag on the front of her black dress uniform read VICTORIA.

Ally nodded. "I am. Her father is out of town. This is Noah, my fiancé." She placed a protective hand on her stomach. "You're the manager?"

"The director," she said without a trace of humility or irony in her voice.

"What does that mean?" Ally asked, genuinely curious, not sure where this title fit at a store that sold beauty products.

"It's like a manager."

"Fine." Ally wanted to get to the bottom of this as quickly as possible so that she could take Emily home and ground her forever. The sooner the better. "What happened?"

"You daughter decided to take a few items without paying for them. One of our cast members watched her take an eye shadow off the shelf and place it into her bag. As soon as she left the store, we confronted her about the missing items. Your daughter denied it at first. Lied about it. And then when we pressed her about the eye shadow and said she'd been caught on camera, she fessed up. When we emptied her purse, we found a sealed lipstick and mascara in there too." Victoria paused, as though for effect. Or maybe it was Ally's turn—Ally's line, since they were really playing up the director/cast-member shtick.

Ally glared at Emily, who had so far found no reason to say a word. She just sat there in her black crewneck sweatshirt over black jeans, and her eyes rimmed with black eyeliner. In Ally's uneducated opinion, her daughter certainly looked the part of a criminal today, though Ally could detect her sweet, funny baby face underneath all of it.

"What do you have to say for yourself?" Ally said.

Emily crossed her legs, cocked her head, and glared. How had her Emily—at fourteen she was half-girl, half-woman—found herself in this mess? Ally realized she had no idea how her daughter had even gotten herself to the mall. Public transportation was not a system Emily navigated on a regular basis, and it would have taken an hour or more. Uber? Had she come with a friend?

"Well?" Ally said, her patience already at her breaking point. "How did you even get here?"

Silence. Ally vowed to herself that she'd get to the bottom of *that*.

She turned back to Victoria. "So what happens now? You have your items back. No real harm was done." Ally shot the woman her best "thank God" look. Her hand rose to her chest. "On behalf of my daughter, I am sorry. Emily will certainly be punished, and I assure you, this will never happen again."

Victoria sat down and leaned back in her desk chair. "It's actually not that simple. Gloss is a national corporation, and we have certain policies in place when it comes to theft."

Theft.

"Oh?" Ally's hand now moved up to her neck. She didn't like the sound of "certain policies." Noah squeezed her shoulder.

"All our locations are equipped with monitoring equipment that can view the store from all angles and vantage points, and we're prepared to hand over all evidence to police."

"Have you?" Noah asked. Ally looked up at him, grateful to have him by her side today. "I mean, did you call the police already?"

Victoria nodded. "We always call the police and the parents—if we can reach them—at the same time." She glanced at the time on her computer monitor. "The police are taking their time today—usually they're here by now. Must be a busy day." She paused and looked from Noah to Ally. "Look, Emily is a minor, and it's the first time she's been detained at a Gloss location. We don't know her broader track record, though, so we always involve the local police in the process in case this has been an ongoing problem."

No matter how guilty Emily was in this moment, Ally couldn't imagine her younger daughter sitting in some jail cell in an orange jumpsuit.

"Where do we go from here?" Ally said. "Do we need to hire a lawyer?"

"Every time this happens, that's what the officer advises."

Ally's heart raced. All her rage, worry, embarrassment, pregnancy hormones, and low blood sugar threatened to take over every molecule of good sense she had left. She simultaneously wanted to throttle Emily and ached to smack the smug corporate look off Victoria's overly made-up face.

She took a calming breath, inhaling a floral powdery scent that wasn't unpleasant. Noah took her hand in his.

When the officer finally arrived, he escorted Emily out of the mall while Noah and Ally followed close behind, her heart breaking for her daughter and at the same time believing she deserved the humiliation. Maybe she wouldn't shoplift again. Ally hoped the justice system would scare Emily straight. But as she witnessed the surreal scene of the officer placing her Emily in the back seat of the police cruiser, complete with the cop-show touch of cupping the back of her head as she entered the vehicle, it took every amount of restraint to stop herself from leaping to her daughter's rescue.

On the way to the station, Noah located the number of a friend he'd gone to graduate school with, who'd been in the law program. He'd landed a job as a criminal-defense attorney, and both Ally and Noah hoped the guy would give his high school principal buddy a break.

What a disgrace.

Ally kept a hand on her belly as she drove. How could she possibly bring another child into the world when she didn't even know what was going on under her own roof?

CHAPTER 25

BETH

As the hotel door closed behind them, Beth practically leaped onto Jordan. She yanked off her jacket and stepped out of her shoes, while keeping her lips locked on his. He'd started unbuttoning his shirt. She pulled him toward the king-size bed, the sheets already turned down by hotel staff earlier in the day.

Part of her noted with a certain amount of delight that she was in yet another hotel room. Because she'd spent so much of her adult life traveling, chain hotels had become a sort of home. She'd grown accustomed to the sameness of the percale sheets, the bland color scheme, and the predictable array of shampoo, conditioner, and body lotion left on the bathroom counter. Even the smell—the light, clean scent—awakened something inside her that she found comforting and familiar.

At her dad's house and even in her own apartments over the years, Beth sometimes felt like a visitor, a stranger in someone else's space. As Jordan kissed her ear and her neck on those clean sheets, she felt a sense of belonging, a feeling she hadn't had in a very long time.

She could never have predicted that today would conclude with her and Jordan finally ending up in bed together.

Something within her had clicked the day before. Over the spring and summer, Beth had felt a sense of renewed purpose in coaching those girls, and it occurred to her—why couldn't she put some of that energy toward making life better for Jordan's dad? It could never make up for the fact that she'd allowed him to take the blame for the fire, but there was no reason why she shouldn't at least try to make his life even a little more like the Springtime brochure. And watching how Jordan had opened himself up to his dad—a man who had abandoned him, his mom, and his sister—she decided she could make the most of her numbered days in Fillmore and do better, *be* better.

"How about we pick up your dad and bring him over to the house?" she'd said over the phone that morning. "I just got back from the nursery with a ton of bulbs and flowers."

Cleaning up the remnants of the plant in Mr. Miller's living room had clued Beth in to the fact that he loved nothing more than working in the garden. She knew that Springtime indulged residents with small potting projects here and there, but Beth thought that if he wanted to dig in the dirt, maybe she could offer for him to do it at her dad's house. The backyard had become overgrown and weedy over the last couple of months and needed several caring hands to get it under control. And if she was going to get the place ready to sell eventually, then wouldn't it make sense to make Mr. Miller's day and get the garden looking better?

"Great," Jordan said. "Let's meet him after lunch and spend the afternoon. Dad will love it."

For someone who some days didn't remember what he ate for breakfast that morning, Mr. Miller proved an expert in the garden. The three cleared the weeds and prepared the soil. By the end of the afternoon, they'd planted and watered all the new plants Beth had bought that morning.

She and Jordan cleaned up, dropped off his dad, and grabbed a bite to eat at Zeke's.

When the waitress set their drinks down, Jordan raised his pint of beer.

"To a great idea," he said, clinking glasses with hers. "I don't think my dad wiped that smile off his face all day. He was so in his element."

Beth felt her cheeks warm.

"I'd planned to take you someplace nice, though," he said. "Someplace that wasn't the same old Zeke's."

Beth had shrugged. She liked Zeke's. And she really liked Jordan. She wouldn't have minded if the day could go on forever, so when he'd asked her if she wanted to spend the night, she hadn't hesitated.

◆ ◆ ◆

Beth curled into Jordan, resting her arm over his bare chest, and closed her eyes. It was late on a Sunday night, and she didn't want to think about how she should probably leave soon so she could get up early enough to lead the middle and high school girls' soccer clinics on Monday morning. She just wanted more time to lie in this hotel bed with Jordan with nothing more to think about than how they could make each other feel.

Jordan rose, propping his head in his hand.

"Do you mind if I take a shower?"

Beth gave him a kiss. "Just hang for a little bit. I'll have to get going pretty soon. I've got an early call tomorrow."

"Soccer camp?"

She nodded and nestled into the crook of his arm.

"Me too."

Beth scowled. "Soccer camp?"

He laughed. "No. Early meeting."

Her stomach clenched. "Oh?" she asked, her voice meek and sounding far away. "Work related?"

Jordan raised an eyebrow. "No, actually. Gym-fire related."

"Ha ha," she said weakly. All of a sudden, her calm comfort evaporated. Beth felt suspended and ready to plummet, like the bottom had fallen out from under her, as if someone had removed a trapdoor she didn't know she'd been lying on.

He leaned in and kissed her shoulder. "I'll make it quick," he said. "Don't go anywhere." She nodded.

He stood and walked to the bathroom, closing the door behind him.

Beth wouldn't stay long. She'd find an excuse to leave once Jordan finished his shower. The hotel no longer suggested a kind of home to her, but instead a space that potentially housed evidence that could be used to expose her and Ally. Spending time with Jordan, possibly improving his dad's well-being, couldn't erase what she'd done. And Jordan still wanted answers. He'd been quietly working on his own investigation for months. She couldn't ignore that. He wasn't in Fillmore for her. He was here to find answers. He wanted to expose the truth.

She began pulling on her clothes as she heard the spray of water turn on and the crinkle of the shower curtain closing.

If he had a meeting about the fire tomorrow, maybe he'd brought evidence with him. Could it be somewhere in this room? If there ever was a time to hunt for it, now was that time.

Beth didn't want to let herself second-guess this. So seizing her opportunity, she started to comb through his hotel room, being as quiet and quick as possible. Those folders Ally had been obsessing over had to be around here someplace, right? Beth wondered what he would find useful in them—photos, perhaps, of the wreckage? Old articles chronicling the fire? Perhaps it was his own father's testimony that just didn't square with the facts of the fire investigation.

She scoured the hotel room, which only took about a minute. Everything in the room that Jordan owned he'd brought in carry-on luggage, which didn't leave a lot for her to find. She found no sign of any manila folders that Ally had been so worried about. Beth paused at the desk, where Jordan's laptop sat alongside an unlabeled CD in a plain white sleeve; a well-worn messenger bag was propped up against the back of the desk chair. In spite of herself, she smiled listening to Jordan's singing over the sound of the shower—a mangled version of "Sweet Caroline." He had no idea she was snooping on him. She tried to shake off her guilt as she unfastened the clasp and opened the bag.

The bag revealed an empty manila envelope and several pads of yellow lined paper among a tangle of cords. So far, no smoking guns, and Beth couldn't decide whether to be relieved or terrified. She pulled out the pads and saw most were blank; but one, on the top page, featured a few barely legible scribbles. She squinted at the lines on the page, but most were just one word or short-phrased questions.

> *1999 conclusions?*
> *Subsequent findings?*
> *Gas valve*
> *Spark?*
> *Bolt cutters*
> *Open doors*

Oh God, he must know about the bolt cutters that Ally had left behind. How had Jordan found out about that? After the fire, Beth had scoured every article written about it, looking for any clue that could have been traced back to her or Ally, especially those bolt cutters. Nothing. All the attention had been focused on building a case against Mr. Miller, which virtually erased all evidence that might have cleared him.

The last phrase, "Open doors," was circled. Heat rushed to her face. This was new. *Open doors?* What did he mean by that? What was the significance? Was this what Jordan's meeting could be about?

The shower switched off, and Beth's heart made a little leap as she crammed the notepads back into the bag. For an agonizing few seconds, the cords made the pads' entry into the bag impossible. Beth took the cords out, slid in the notepads, and then stuffed the cords back in. As the bathroom door clicked open, Beth refastened the clasp.

Jordan, with one towel around his waist and rubbing another on his wet hair, emerged along with a plume of steam.

"How'd you like my Neil Diamond impression?" he said, smiling broadly. He stopped and frowned. "Hey, you look like you're ready to leave."

Beth nodded. He had no idea just *how* ready.

"I'm sorry," she said. She grabbed her discarded purse from the floor. "Like I said, early morning. And this—was kind of an unplanned activity."

She walked to him and kissed his cheek, avoiding his eyes.

He tilted her chin up, forcing her to look at him.

"Are we OK? Seems like I go in the shower and you're one person, and another when I get out."

Beth nodded. She'd realized that she'd been falling for someone who was dead set on exposing her secret. She couldn't betray Ally like that, but just the thought that she'd made the decision to nose around in his things made the bile churn in her stomach.

"I'm OK. Just have a lot on my mind."

She kissed him on the lips this time, feeling herself fall into him again. They parted, and she let herself out.

Beth didn't know what to do about Jordan, but she was certain she needed to talk to Ally about what those notes could mean.

CHAPTER 26

ALLY

"Thank you for your time," Ally said and then hung up the phone. She had a feeling that might be the last time she'd speak to Stephen Meier, Esq.; a.k.a. Noah's graduate school buddy; a.k.a. Emily's defense attorney. Well, no, not *really*.

Ally had felt lucky for the free consultation about Emily's predicament, but there was really nothing he could do about it other than clarify exactly how Emily would pay for her crime of shoplifting. She wasn't going to jail—thank God. She'd pay restitution by volunteering for the local animal shelter for community service all summer, and her record would be clean by the time she went to college.

So, then, what was the problem?

Ally would never condone stealing. Of course she wouldn't. She wasn't a monster. She was a good mother. Ask anyone. Everyone in town would go on record to say that Ally was a good mom. She volunteered for everything. She fundraised. She'd donated school supplies and reams of copy paper at the start of every school year to her daughters' schools since they'd started kindergarten. She started a travel soccer team just for girls in part so her talented daughter could play and be challenged, but mostly to fill in a giant blank in their small town. Who did that? Good mothers, that's who.

But this shoplifting thing was humiliating. For one, the items were so small—makeup, for God's sake. Emily had been caught on camera shoving makeup into her pockets. It was so . . . juvenile, like stealing gummy worms from a candy store. Petty and dumb.

And second, Ally suspected this wasn't Emily's first and only attempt. This was merely the first time she'd been *caught*. So after the three of them returned home from the police station, Emily was summarily grounded for life—her remaining summer days would now be spent helping out at the soccer camps in addition to fulfilling her community service hours.

Ally decided she'd overrated the sanctity of her daughter's privacy and would now make it her mission to keep tabs on any new items that may have landed in her closet. Was this a one-time thing or something requiring therapy to resolve? Whatever it was, it needed to be dealt with, and now, before it became a problem.

Before it became a problem for *Ally*: if word got around her daughter was shoplifting, she'd be forced to endure the silent judgment of all the soccer parents that she'd raised a thief. Not that anyone expected perfection from their kids, but stealing indicated that Ally had failed one of the most basic lessons parents impart to their children. At the very least, it would be embarrassing. And worst case? It meant there was something more serious going on with her younger daughter.

Heart hammering, Ally was reliving the moment the cop folded Emily into the back of his cruiser. Just then, the doorbell rang. She glanced at the clock—almost four. *Oh, right. Beth.* She'd forgotten that Beth would swing by after camp to pick up extra uniform jerseys for the guest players playing in this weekend's tournament.

"I almost forgot," Ally said as she opened the door. "I'll need to dig around to find the shirts. Any idea of size?"

"I don't know, medium, maybe?" Beth didn't appear too concerned. Her eyes darted around the room. "Are you by yourself?"

Ally nodded. "Noah's picking up the furniture we ordered for the nursery, Morgan's out with her friends, and this is Emily's first day at the shelter."

Beth raised her eyebrows. "Wonder how that's going?"

"At least there's nothing to steal, except maybe a stray dog or cat." Ally waved off the thought. "I can't think about that anymore. God, between Emily and the baby and the league and a wedding looming over my head, I need a vacation."

Beth bit her lip. "I need to tell you something."

Ally braced herself. "What?"

"I found some of Jordan's notes about the investigation last night."

Ally's mouth went dry. "In a folder? Did you find any of the folders?"

Beth shook her head. "His laptop and a CD with no label were on the desk. I don't know his password or anything, so I wasn't able to check either." She swallowed. "But I got a look at one of the notepads."

"What'd it say?" *Two angry teenage girls burned down the gym and blamed my father.* She tried to will the truth away from her mind.

"I know he had a meeting this morning. He didn't say with who. A couple topics he wanted to cover, I'm guessing, like what sparked the fire, what they found at the time, and if they'd discovered anything new." Beth touched the tips of her fingers to her forehead. "But I think he knows about the bolt cutters."

Ally crossed her arms over her chest. "What makes you think that?"

"It was a bullet point in his notes." Beth shook her head slowly from side to side. "I just don't remember any of the school newspapers mentioning it. Do you?"

"No," Ally said. "But wouldn't custodians have bolt cutters? Like, to cut the locks off of lockers from students who forgot their combinations and stuff? Or forgot to get their things before summer?"

"True. But if it was on that list, it must mean something, right?"

Ally shrugged. She was the one who'd left those bolt cutters behind. She'd almost forgotten about it. Her dad never mentioned they were missing either. "I don't know. But there's no way to prove who they belong to. Wouldn't they just assume they were Mr. Miller's?"

Beth didn't look convinced. "He also wrote down something about 'open doors' and circled it. Like it's important."

"Is it?" Ally blinked. This was no revelation.

Beth's face scrunched with worry. "I mean, why would it be *circled?*"

"I don't know. Maybe it's just a question about the layout of the gym? Or something he saw in a photo?" For once, Ally realized with a flash of pride, for once she wasn't the paranoid one. "Or maybe it has nothing to do with the fire? Jeez, Beth. How did you get access to Jordan's notes, anyway?" She took a beat. "You slept with him, didn't you? Way to bury the lede."

"So what if I did?"

Ally saw the familiar return of defiance cross Beth's face and raised her hands in defeat. "I know I can't tell you who to see and not to see. And, objectively, Jordan seems like a good one." This softened Beth's demeanor a bit. "You seem to really like him."

She nodded. "I *do* like him. I haven't felt this way about a guy in a long time."

A twinge of jealousy seeped inside Ally. Why was everything in her life falling apart while Beth's was looking up? She wanted to be the type of person who could share in her best friend's slice of newfound joy after a mentally and physically challenging few months—returning home to deal with her sick father, recovering from a third serious concussion, being forced into retirement from a career she loved and had devoted a lifetime to. Ally had to remind herself she wasn't the only one challenged by mounting stresses.

"I'm happy for you," she lied, ending the conversation. "Let me get those uniforms."

CHAPTER 27

BETH

Over the last few weeks of August, Beth had started including Mr. Miller along with her dad in her near daily visits to Springtime. Her visits varied depending on time of day and whether they included an activity, such as going for a walk or to the grocery store, or were just to relax and watch a game or make dinner. But she'd made a habit of stopping by Mr. Miller's room to check in and say hello.

On most days, she would characterize Jordan's dad as confused, but happy. His face always lit up when he saw her. He might not have known who she was, but he seemed to understand on some level that she was someone he could trust, which, on one hand, made her feel honored. Always, though, doubt crept in at the edges. She knew she didn't wholly deserve Mr. Miller's trust. Or Jordan's.

On the last practice before their big Labor Day tournament, Beth held a scrimmage between her team and a neighboring town's team. She decided to bring her dad to see the game and watch her coach from the sidelines. He'd enjoyed the outing, but by the time she returned him to his apartment, he was beat and getting a little punchy. She arranged for the Center to deliver his dinner to his apartment, kissed his cheek, and said her goodbyes.

She checked her phone—it was only 5:00—and decided to swing by Mr. Miller's room.

She knocked on the door and pushed it partway open. He smiled when he saw her and waved her inside the apartment. Beth always wondered what went through his mind. Did he recognize her as someone from the past? Or someone related to Jordan? Did he realize that she and Jordan had been seeing each other? Or perhaps he thought she was simply someone who'd offered him a bit of kindness today? Beth suspected it could have been any of these, or all.

"Sit, sit," he said, motioning her toward the sofa. "I have something to show you."

Beth was struck by how lucid he seemed, and his speech was so clear. Lately, she'd seen enough to know that he might leave a sentence unfinished or even fall into gibberish. Jordan had mentioned he thought his father was getting worse at a more rapid pace than he'd noticed before. He tried to hide how much it bothered him, but Beth could see witnessing his father's decline was deeply unsettling.

"Yeah?" Beth walked over to the couch and took a seat. On the coffee table was a yellowed copy of Fillmore High School's *Tiger Times* open to a page that featured the team photo of that year's high school soccer team. They'd just won the state championship, and the paper included a short article about the game. Seventeen-year-old pony-tailed versions of Beth and Ally in their team uniforms and with pasted smiles knelt in the front row, surrounded by boys. Beth almost couldn't believe her eyes. An actual copy of the school paper? From their senior year?

"Where'd you get this?" she asked, but she knew the answer—Jordan.

Mr. Miller shook his head, as if he wasn't prepared to be interrogated today.

"It's OK," Beth said, placing her hand on his arm. She didn't want him to get distracted and possibly lost in a fog of dementia. "Thank you for showing me this."

He grinned at her, his eyes sparkling.

"I remember you. You and that girl were the only girls on the team." His smile faded suddenly, and Beth worried she might have lost him. "But the boys weren't nice to you."

Beth shook her head—no, they weren't nice.

He remembers.

Mr. Miller looked up toward the ceiling and then closed his eyes, as if conjuring an image. "They locked you in that broom closet in the gym. You were in there for hours. I found you." He opened his eyes and met Beth's. "And I let you out."

Beth's eyes rimmed with tears. She nodded. "You did."

He nodded again but didn't say anything further. She wondered what was going through his head.

"I'm grateful to you for finding us. You were so kind that day." She wiped her eyes with the back of her hand. "You were always kind."

"And then the fire." Mr. Miller had raised his index finger, as if making a point, but Beth could see a flicker of pain cross his face. "That whole gym burned to the ground. Remember?"

Of course Beth remembered. It was the day she could never run from. The memory followed her wherever she went, all over the world.

"I remember," she said.

Mr. Miller stared at the page. "I saw a lot at that school," he said, his voice quiet. "I was invisible. Nobody paid me any mind." He turned toward Beth. "Which was fine by me. I liked it. I liked my work. I felt I was doing my part for the kids, just like the teachers and the staff."

Beth sat up. "You did. I didn't realize it at the time, but I do now."

He allowed a little smile. "Most of the time, the kids are all right. But the way you and that other girl were treated that year? It wasn't right." He shook his head. "I wish I had said something to the coach. He was clueless."

Beth chuckled a little. "Clueless" was the perfect description. She gave his arm a squeeze.

"It wasn't your fault." *Nothing was your fault.*

She turned the pages of the paper, just to see if anything other than the team photo looked familiar. She saw reminders for midterms, homecoming, and a choir performance. She paged through old ads bought by local businesses. At the end, her dad had taken out a half page advertising his service station. He and Bill in their coveralls stood proudly in front of the office, the sign in full view. His chest puffed out, her father appeared robust, healthy. He still had most of his hair, which hadn't yet turned fully gray. This was twenty years ago. What was the date of this issue? Beth frowned and closed the paper, flipping to the front page.

The headline pasted on the front was in huge black letters, FIREFIGHTERS RESPOND TO FOUR-ALARM BLAZE AT FILLMORE HIGH SCHOOL—GYM, LOCKER ROOMS DESTROYED, and the page featured a photo of the aftermath underneath. That was the story that week.

The front page had caught his eye. He pointed to the picture.

"I should never have messed with that gas valve," he said. His voice shook. He looked as if he'd gone back twenty years in his mind.

A wave of guilt flooded through Beth. She ran a finger over her bottom lip.

"That wasn't your fault either," she said.

Doubt crossed his face. He didn't believe her. Or maybe she just wasn't clear. He wasn't hearing her.

Jordan was desperate for him to know the truth. That he wasn't to blame.

"The fire wasn't your fault." Beth repositioned herself and faced him. She started to say *Ally and I started that fire,* but she held back. What good could possibly come from throwing Ally under the bus? For twenty years, Ally had wanted none of this to be exposed. She had a life here. A home, an established business, kids, Noah—all that would go up in a puff of smoke if anyone found out she'd been involved. *Leave her out of it.*

Beth took a breath. "I started that fire. *I* was responsible, not you."

He dismissed her with a wave and stared at the coffee table in front of them. But he seemed to be present, listening. And he was, because then he said, without looking up from the table, "You don't know what you're talking about."

"I do, because I was *there*." She cleared her throat. "I waited until after everyone had left, including you. *Especially* you. I wanted to get back at those boys. I placed some homemade stink bombs in the boys' locker room, and when I removed the caps, it set off an explosion." The words unspooled out of her. She'd waited so long, the story flowed out of her mouth as easily as water from a faucet. "I ran out of there as fast as I could, through the gym, and when I finally got outside, I didn't have a scratch on me."

Mr. Miller didn't take his eyes off the table. She dared to hope he'd heard her, though she couldn't read whether he was stunned, upset, or angry, or even if he'd understood her.

"When I got to the sidewalk just off campus, I looked back. The locker room was all flames, and the fire had reached the gym."

"Old wood. Like kindling," he murmured. "No saving it."

He remembered.

Beth did too. She remembered just how scared she'd been, how she and Ally had raced back to her parents' house, how they'd been caught by Ally's younger brother, Drew, who'd stayed up late playing PlayStation and had watched them come in through the downstairs den window. Beth had been too stunned to say anything to him, but Ally thought of a lie on the spot—that they'd been to a house party and if he didn't tell on them, they wouldn't tell on him for sneaking video games after his bedtime. Deal.

Once Ally's bedroom door had closed behind them, they promised to keep this secret as long as they lived. No one needed to know they burned down the gym. No one needed to know their stupid prank had resulted in a catastrophic mistake. Thank goodness the casualties were buildings, not people. Still.

They had no idea that their accident would ruin Mr. Miller's life. That it would result in a trial that railroaded Mr. Miller and tore his family apart. But she and Ally were both off at college when all that happened, starting their lives, the fire long behind them.

But Mr. Miller remembered.

"I'm sorry I let you take the blame," she said. "I should have come forward." She felt sick. She deserved to feel sick. She deserved so much worse. "It's my fault you suffered."

Mr. Miller didn't say anything. He sat very still, his hands resting in his lap. Beth didn't know if ten seconds or ten minutes had gone by, but Mr. Miller looked over at her. His eyes were dark. He stood and walked to his bedroom, closing the door behind him.

Beth sat, stunned, waiting for the repercussions to come crashing down on her. Was her confession able to lodge in his brain, connect in some way to a permanent memory of that night? Or had it disappeared, lost in the mist of dementia? Beth squirmed, wishing Mr. Miller would snap out of his haze, charge back out of his bedroom, and bring down the wrath of God onto her. But the door remained closed.

Beth pressed her hand to her mouth and erupted into sobs.

PART III: FALL

CHAPTER 28

ALLY

"Hi, Judy," Ally said as she waltzed into the department office. The secretary was a Fillmore High School pillar, who'd been fielding calls from parents, dealing with students, and enduring the clerical and administrative needs of six successive principals over the course of more than three decades. Ally held up a bulging white paper bag. "He's free?"

Judy pushed her pale-blue plastic glasses up her nose and looked up from her computer. "He's expecting you, deary. No meetings until two." She lifted the office phone receiver to her ear. "Ally's here."

She'd brought lunch and a baby checklist. They still had so much to arrange before the little one arrived—yet, a nice diversion from planning the gym dedication.

"Thanks," Ally said. She flashed Judy a smile and let herself into Noah's office.

He rose when he saw her. Books, folders, papers, and a keyboard littered his desk. A desktop monitor stood in the corner. Ally wondered if maybe they should move to the cafeteria for lunch.

His gaze drifted to the bag. "I'm starving. Let me carve out a little space so we can eat and talk."

Noah cleared his desk, and the two set up a makeshift dining area. Ally pulled a folded printout from her purse and smoothed it out on the desk while Noah took out two sandwiches and napkins from the bag. She lowered herself into the chair across from him, her legs spread slightly to accommodate her girth.

"I still think keeping the larger items on the list would let people know what we still need," she began. "No one has to buy us a high chair or car seat. I'd be happy with hand-me-downs. A nice stroller is a nice stroller, you know?"

"We can't accept a hand-me-down car seat. You know that, right?" Noah bit into his sandwich. He swallowed and then patted his lips with a napkin. "Before we talk baby stuff, I need to discuss something with you that you're not going to like."

Ally immediately felt her defenses rise. She'd had enough unpleasant news lately.

"What do you mean?" She tried not to sound guarded.

"It's about Morgan."

Morgan. The one part of her life she didn't have to worry about so much.

"What, was she late to class or something?" Ally pulled an onion piece out from her sandwich. She hadn't been able to stomach onions since she'd gotten pregnant, and she kept forgetting to ask to leave them out.

"No, it's a little more than that." Noah's face was serious, and Ally could see that it gave him no pleasure to say whatever was coming.

"What, then?"

Noah set his sandwich down and rubbed his hands together, releasing the crumbs. "I've been told she's been bullying other girls."

Ally frowned and shook her head. "No way. That's not Morgan. She's not a bully." She took a bite and chewed. Reports like that smacked of overreaction or jealousy or maybe lack of a sense of humor.

Noah leaned in, fingers pressed together, looking more like a principal than her boyfriend. "Judging by what I've heard these past few weeks—from a few parents, a teacher, and now the girls' soccer coach—she's been pretty unpleasant to a few girls. So much so, one girl has been struggling with thoughts of harming herself since tangling with her. The girl has a previous history of anxiety and depression, but still. Morgan's been a trigger."

"Like what?" Ally said. On the one hand, she sympathized. Through running a league for ten years, she'd seen up close how mental illness could adversely affect teenagers, but anything could stand in as a "trigger." She failed to see how another girl's troubles could have anything to do with Morgan. "How has she been a 'trigger'?"

"Well, she's been particularly hard on a fellow soccer player, a freshman who's shown considerable talent." Noah looked down at his hands, as if avoiding meeting her eyes. "Like she's considered competition, possibly, so Morgan lashes out—makes nasty comments about her, works at turning the team against her. I've been told the other team members now leave the girl out of key plays on the field, and off the field, Morgan hid one of her cleats before practice, doused her uniform with water, stuff like that. The coach said they were 'pranks,' but it seems like they've gone too far."

Ally knew the difference between pranks and "pranks" from personal experience. She searched her mind for who this accuser might be. She was familiar with most of the high school team players, who were among the best on the travel teams. Morgan had always been at the very top—top scorer, top in assists. She'd always seemed to welcome the competition, insisting it made her play harder. Ally thought Morgan was a better version of her in some ways—an extrovert and a leader like Ally, but more confident and assertive. Less second guess-y. And Morgan *did* like to play jokes—on her sister, her friends, her teammates. Could this be a misunderstanding?

"Morgan's always joked around. Everyone knows that."

"If it were an isolated incident, I might chalk it up to the girl just being new and not knowing, but we're into October already, and Morgan isn't letting up. Stealing someone's shoe before a mandatory practice? Soaking someone's uniform? Sounds a little mean, in my opinion."

Mean? Heat rose from Ally's chest to her neck to her face, like mercury through a thermometer. Is that how Noah viewed her daughter? He was spinning Morgan's best qualities as an assertive leader into a mean bully. God, is that how he saw *her*? "Are you telling me as her principal or future stepdad?"

"Look." Noah's face was the picture of patience and kindness, which infuriated her. "I know Morgan's popular and well liked. She's a *good kid.* Maybe the stress of college applications is getting to her? Stiffer competition on the soccer field? Or that her mom's about to get married, with a new sibling on the way? She's facing a lot of change these days. Sometimes girls find ways to gain control, and in some, it takes the form of bullying. But it's gone on too long. You need to talk to her."

"If she's such a bully, why wouldn't someone tell you right away? They just let it happen? If it's so bad, why let her get away with it? Seems like it could be something other than Morgan bullying other girls."

He shook his head.

"You're not going to tell me who's saying these things about my daughter."

"I can't."

Ally wanted to scream.

"I could make a few phone calls to their parents, smooth things over." Smoothing things over was Ally's specialty.

"You really think Morgan is incapable of this 'mean girl' type of behavior?" Noah looked as if he was asking a sincere question.

"You don't know her like I do," she said. "It's all a misunderstanding. Her jokes maybe went a tad too far."

"Have you checked her phone, her social media lately?"

"No, have you?"

"No—she's not my kid. But maybe you should. Morgan's not perfect." Noah sighed. "I think you need to take your blinders off."

Ally flinched. Emily had just given her a wake-up call she'd never have expected, and now Morgan? No.

"And I think you need to not be so judgy."

She stood suddenly, feeling slightly wobbly and out of balance for a second, and placed a hand on the back of her chair to steady herself.

Concern washed over Noah's face, and he rose as if to catch her. "Be careful."

"Don't tell me what to do," Ally said. She turned her back on him, leaving her lunch and baby list splayed out on Noah's desk, opened the door, and walked out of the office.

"How you feeling, deary?" Judy asked as Ally emerged.

Ally paused in the doorway. She felt . . . horrible. Judy, like all school secretaries, knew everything, so it wouldn't surprise her if she'd been the first to learn about Morgan's alleged behavior.

Judy patted her own stomach to clarify.

"Oh," Ally said, relieved. She glanced down at her swollen belly. Her pregnancy seemed to be the only thing people wanted to talk about with her, thank goodness. She faked a smile and repeated her standard line. "Fine. Past the morning sickness phase. Now I just feel big."

"Isn't that nice?"

No one listened. They all asked, but no one really cared.

Ally hurried out. She wanted nothing more than to drive from that parking lot and straight out of town. It's like her family was all conspiring against her. She felt the baby shift positions and then the eerie sensation of it giving her a little kick.

Even her unborn child couldn't resist kicking her while she was down.

CHAPTER 29

JORDAN

"Are you calling to tell me your plans changed and you'll be in Fillmore for Columbus Day after all?" Beth said into the phone. Her voice sounded light, happy even.

The *Sun* had assigned Jordan a story covering an all-weekend concert in the Inner Harbor sponsored by none other than Questlove. He was halfway through the easy-enough gig. But he would have much rather been able to hang out with Beth. Or even better, convince her to make the trip down to Baltimore, enjoy the backstage perks together, and then stay with him at his apartment.

"No, unfortunately," he said. "And I'm guessing your team's tournament wasn't canceled either?"

"Not a chance. The weather's been perfect." She paused. "I miss you."

"Me too," he said. "I have news. Good news, I think."

"Really?" Beth said. "I do too. But you go."

For weeks, Jordan had been stalled on his investigation into the fire. He'd googled, combed through the files, scanned every photo on the CD-ROM Noah had given him, delved into all the databases the *Baltimore Sun* had made available to him. There was evidence—those bolt cutters and the open doors—that someone other than his father could have been in the gym and locker room that day and set off the fire. But he couldn't figure out *why* someone would want access to the space after hours. There wasn't anything of value to steal. Literally nothing other than cleaning supplies and basketball nets. Jordan was stuck.

This afternoon he'd gone over his father's testimony for what seemed like the umpteenth time. The gas valve. He'd left the gas valve open, which he admitted he shouldn't have done. Then Jordan turned his attention to the investigation report. Again. And a small detail that had escaped him now jumped out. The hydrogen sulfide residue found on some of the lockers. Hydrogen, he recalled from his long-ago chemistry class in high school, was flammable. Why would its residue be found on the lockers? And what was hydrogen sulfide used for, anyway? According to a quick conversation with the *Sun*'s science reporter, he learned it's used in oil refining, in food processing, and in creating . . . stink bombs.

"What if . . . ," he said, leaning back into his sofa and propping his feet on the coffee table, ". . . I told you that a kid might have set off that explosion?"

"What?" Beth's voice sounded strangled. "What did you say?"

He glanced at his phone—four bars, not a bad connection.

"I said, I think a kid may have sparked the fire." Jordan waited for a response. Nothing. "Hello? Beth?"

"I'm here," she said. Something about her tone sounded off. Like the air had been let out of a soccer ball.

"I'm not one hundred percent sure, but there are clues that point to flammable residue that could have come from a stink bomb combined with the open gas valve on the other side of the wall. That could set off an explosion." Jordan dropped his feet and sat forward. His heart thumped in his chest. "Could have easily been a kid from Eastampton." Fillmore High School's rival. "Or maybe it was an inside job. Can you imagine? We could have gone to school with the person who set off that explosion."

Silence.

"Beth? Are you there?"

"Sorry. Yes. I think it's my phone." She sighed. "Are you sure about this?"

"No. But it seems *plausible*, doesn't it? Who else would want access to that old gym other than some kid playing a prank?"

"Yeah," she said, sounding far away. "I guess that makes sense."

"God, I've been racking my brain going over the archival documents, the photos from Noah—"

"The what?" Jordan sensed alarm in Beth's voice.

"The photos—the photos from the *Tiger Times*. You know, the vast majority that didn't make it into the paper. The school stored them on CDs. Noah remembered they weren't in the archives in the library and pulled them for me."

Silence.

"Beth?"

Jordan wondered if Beth either wasn't interested in talking to him about this further or maybe just couldn't hear him well. He wished he could see her face.

"So what about you?" he said finally.

"Huh?"

"You said you had good news too. Tell me."

"Oh, right," she said. "I got a job. Just found out this morning."

"A job?" Jordan didn't know she'd been looking, but then, why wouldn't she be? Things seemed to be settling down for her in Fillmore. "That's great! What's the job?"

"Assistant coaching," she said, picking up steam. "UCLA wants to hire me as an assistant to the goalkeeper coach for the women's team. It's short notice—sort of came out of the blue. But it's salaried, with benefits. I'd get to travel, save for retirement. I get my life back, Jordan."

She'd get her life back. Beth might as well have punched him in the gut.

"I didn't know you were looking for a new position so soon." Jordan realized now he sounded flat. Not exactly the excited, "happy for her," "it's about time" tone she might have expected from him.

Instead, he felt like she'd knocked the wind out of him.

"I wasn't. Not really. My Chicago coach had heard murmurings about it and recommended me." She laughed feebly. "I think she felt sorry for me after making me retire. She knew I needed to be back in action as soon as possible."

"When's it start?"

"Fall season has begun already. But they know I have a lot of loose ends here. Once the contract is signed, I'll probably be ready to leave for good in about a month."

A month.

"Jordan? Are you still there?"

"I'm glad you're happy about it," he said, feeling petty. Would it kill him to say something nice?

"I *am* happy about it," she said.

His skin bristled.

"Have you told Ally yet? Or your dad?" Jordan let the mean-spirited impulse take over. "The teams you've been coaching? All those girls? What are you going to do about them?"

"I don't know, Jordan. I just received the offer. I'll figure it out."

He imagined the heat of her anger radiating through the phone.

"I don't get why you can't just be happy for me," she said.

"Really?" He couldn't believe she didn't get it.

Her voice quieted. "You knew I never wanted to stay in Fillmore. I've spent my whole life avoiding it. Now I can leave. I can go back to my soccer life."

Jordan sighed. "I guess I misread you, misread us. Maybe I'd hoped you were happy or at least working your way toward something like a life here."

"In Fillmore? *You* don't even live here, Jordan."

"You're right. And now I can quit thinking about how to spend more time there once this investigation is over." He cleared his throat. "Look, I'm glad you're happy. I hope it's worth it. I guess I'll see you next Saturday at the dedication."

CHAPTER 30

BETH

Beth sat in the driver's side seat of her car, her mind swirling with conflicting emotions. She stared at the email from the head coach of the UCLA women's team, her heart doing a mini dance just at the sight of it. She'd opened it before her team's first game Sunday morning.

They want me. Me!

The thrill of being picked never got old.

She had so much to think about and *do*, but she'd gotten her wish—she could finally leave Fillmore.

But then Jordan had called. And when she told him about the opportunity, he couldn't even pretend to be happy for her—she heard the disappointment in his voice. She hadn't told anyone else in the twenty-four hours since. Not that there'd been time to. She'd have to spell it out for her dad and do so in person. She had a lot of ducks to get in a row, and some of those ducks involved him. She wouldn't tell Ally yet. That was a conversation impossible to avoid—especially since it involved quitting her coaching gig—but she had to put it off until the time was . . . right. She had no idea when that would be because Ally was behaving even more extra lately. Beth hadn't even signed a contract yet, so she could at least wait until it was *official* official before letting Ally know in the gentlest way possible.

Even though Beth didn't think Jordan would be doing backflips over the possibility of her move to LA, she thought he would at least get it. As a reporter, he of all people would know the impulse to jump on an opportunity when it presented itself. Journalists leaped from job to job all the time. Instead of understanding, he'd judged her. It wasn't like him to lash out. Maybe—she swallowed the rock in her throat—she'd hurt him and now he was mad. Not only that, but she'd hoped to keep a window open for them to continue seeing each other, maybe stay in each other's lives more permanently. Who knew, perhaps there would come a moment when he could apply to the *LA Times*? Seemed like wishful thinking now.

But she also needed to be honest with herself: Right now, he was closer to discovering the truth about the fire than he realized. Beth should seize the opportunity to get out of Fillmore as soon as possible.

Talking to Jordan seemed like a mistake—she could hear the pain in his voice—but she had so much to do. Her next phone call would need to be to her Realtor. But first, she had to coach the girls for the final day of the holiday weekend tournament.

That evening, Beth arrived at Fargo's, Fillmore's lone pizza parlor. The team and their parents had arrived ahead of her, with the girls stationed at various video games and air hockey tables, and the grown-ups seated around a large table, hovering over menus and sipping cold drinks.

"There she is," Ella's mom said as Beth walked past the hostess station and salad bar. The parents turned to face her and started to clap as Beth made her way toward the table. She waved off the applause, but it only built. One by one, the parents stood for her.

Frank, Katie's dad, raised his fist in the air. "Here's to Coach Beth!"

Beth's throat felt thick. She certainly didn't deserve this attention, and as nice as it was, it felt like a blow, knowing she was about to abandon them for the West Coast.

Finally, the clapping died down, and everyone returned to their seats. Some of the girls wandered over to give Beth high fives, just like she'd given them all summer.

Beth's hands flew to her chest. "Oh my gosh, you guys."

She was truly touched, but the girls had worked hard and deserved most of the credit. She knew that up until this summer, the team had experienced a few challenging seasons, with coaching changes and some of the girls leaving reluctantly to play for more competitive teams. But over the last few months, they'd improved by a lot and had played in several tournaments together. This weekend, they won the Columbus Day Cup, their first. When Ally found out, she texted Beth that she was so proud, she'd spring to get their medals engraved with each girl's name and jersey number. Beth, who'd merely stepped in to help Ally fill in some coaching holes, hadn't expected to be embraced so immediately and wholly by the team, which now made her feel even worse for leaving.

Meg, Leah's mom and the parent manager, tapped Beth on the shoulder. She turned around.

"I'm glad you're here," Meg said, clutching a glass of white wine.

Beth noticed for the first time that Leah and her mother shared precisely the same broad nose and disarming smile. "Me too," she said. "The girls did amazing."

"Yes, well, that too," Meg said. "But I mean, I'm glad you're their coach. The girls look up to you so much. Leah's felt very fortunate."

Beth smiled back at her. "Well, it's been a treat for me. This is a great team, nice girls. They would have succeeded regardless."

"Leah has gained an enormous amount of confidence working with you over the summer." Meg took a sip from her glass. "She adores you."

Beth could feel her face redden. She wasn't used to praise for something she felt like such a novice in—coaching. "Leah has mad skills. She was the only one who didn't know it."

"Ally said you're planning to stick around for a while?" Meg said. "That's so great. Continuing this momentum would be such a plus for them. They've never had a regular coach that stuck it out for even a whole season."

Beth looked up at the paneled ceiling, avoiding the hope in Meg's eyes and attempting to process all the information the mom had just revealed. *Damn you, Ally.* Making promises for Beth when she should have just kept her mouth shut. Now Beth would look like the bad guy. Classic Ally.

Was now the time to reveal the UCLA offer? Should she just rip off the Band-Aid?

"I think Ally may have misspoken," Beth said. She rubbed her damp palms together. "Fact is, I'm moving in a few weeks to coach for UCLA."

Meg's smile faltered, but she remained composed. Beth could see this was more of the same kind of disappointment she and all the other parents and players had become accustomed to. How many other temporary coaches had given them similar stories?

"I'm sorry," Beth said. "I just found out." A lump formed in her throat. "It's an opportunity I just couldn't pass up."

Meg nodded. "I understand," she said, a forced pride resonant in her clipped tone. "Congratulations." A dim facsimile of her smile returned. "Well, I guess it's back to square one for us."

"I'll talk to Ally next week and help find a suitable coach. One that's able to stick around."

Meg's smile tightened. "Don't worry about it. You'll be busy with your new team. You'll want to make a good first impression and not have to worry about us."

The words stung because they were true.

Getting this new job and escaping Fillmore for good wasn't feeling as amazing as Beth had hoped.

CHAPTER 31

ALLY

Four days after the team's Columbus Day tournament triumph, the medals arrived from the engravers in a box via UPS. First place. So many things had gone brutally wrong over the summer, but asking Beth to coach for her had been nothing but a win. She'd taken this little ragtag team of seventh-grade girls to the Columbus Day Cup and won the whole thing.

Those soccer clinics had been a success, something that had eluded Ally when she'd attempted to run them herself. Which, she decided, was OK. Better than OK. Ally would love to make them permanent. And Beth had proved to be a natural coach. One more thing she excelled at. The girls looked up to her. She knew how to not only explain complicated plays and strategies in ways that they understood, but demonstrate them. She got those girls to work on and master the basic fundamentals— throw-ins, set plays, long balls. Every single player at the clinic knew how to head a ball properly. And Ally was grateful for Beth's help with the league. She'd become a true asset.

So instead of drifting toward the familiar feelings of jealousy, she made a deliberate attempt to turn toward grace. These awards would bring a smile to Beth's face; at the next practice, she would be able to hand them out to her players, each engraved with the girl's name and jersey number.

Ally loved their friendship. And, as a practical matter, she needed Beth on her side, especially since, from what she'd gathered from both Beth and Noah, Jordan's investigation was not only succeeding in casting doubt on his father having been solely responsible for the fire but on the process that had been in such a rush to punish him so severely. In fact, Noah was now so convinced of Mr. Miller's essential innocence that he'd set about drumming up a way to honor him at the dedication tomorrow.

And this was all as it should be—yes, the poor man had contributed to the explosion by tinkering with the furnace, but it had taken Ally and Beth's reckless contribution to set off the whole conflagration. But did that mean they should announce their involvement to the world? Hell no. They'd be fools not to sidestep that if it could be sidestepped without hurting anyone else, wouldn't they? And if it came to that, it would take the two of them working together to figure out and execute a strategy that would make it work.

Especially since Ally, at eight months pregnant, was all too aware that she was operating at nowhere near the top of her game. Her hormones were putting the screws to her mood. Her world seemed to be closing in on her. She just needed to have this baby. Maybe her anxiety would calm once the little bugger was out—and then maybe her daughters, boyfriend, and best friend would be able to tolerate her again. And maybe, so long as it didn't direct unwanted attention to herself or Beth, Jordan's investigation could end up quashing an untrue narrative about Mr. Miller that he didn't deserve. She looked forward to feeling a little lighter after this weekend. And, of course, after she had this baby.

The box of medals sat in the front seat, the seal intact. She thought she'd surprise Beth today. She knew Beth didn't have practice—she'd given the team the day off. There was always a chance she wouldn't be home—her dad, Jordan, or a shopping trip or a workout could have easily claimed her attention. If that was the case, she could wait to give them to her. These medals were too special to not hand over in person.

As she made the left turn onto Beth's dad's street, the first thing she noticed was a large red-and-white Realtor sign staked into the Snyders' lawn right at the sidewalk's edge.

Ally slowed to a stop, and her mouth went dry.

FOR SALE the sign read, above a phone number and the grinning headshot of the yearbook's Most Popular Scott Montague, who'd graduated their year.

Ally pulled the car to the curb and got out, not quite believing her eyes. Beside the sign stood a small box shaped like a tiny house with a clear pane in front. Flyers. Ally lifted the lid to the box and slid out one of the pieces of paper.

> *Schedule your appointment today to view this charming three-bedroom, two-bath bungalow just steps away from Fillmore's bustling downtown. A large front porch welcomes residents and visitors alike and is the perfect spot to sit and watch the world go by. Step into the spacious, light-filled living room, featuring large windows and high ceilings . . .*

Ally couldn't read any more. Seeing Scott's saccharine real estate language applied to her best friend's childhood home triggered the nausea that had remained dormant for months.

Why hadn't Beth said anything to her?

Oh right—maybe because Ally'd been hormonal as hell the last few weeks. Beth and everyone else in her life were walking on eggshells around her.

But still. Weren't they best friends?

Ally was trying to rise above all the craziness that had overtaken her the last few months. And—*and*—she had these medals to give her. To show her best friend that she wasn't jealous of her. That she was happy and grateful Beth could bring out the best in this team. That Ally *trusted* her.

But the house being for sale—what did that mean? Where would Beth live?

The penny dropped: *Elsewhere, you dummy.*

Beth had decided to move on.

How perfect. How just like her. How perfectly *Beth* to tee everything up and then just take off. Ally felt like a fool for having believed that she might decide to stay.

She ripped the flyer across the center of the page, tearing the photo of the outside of the house in two. She ripped it again, and again, and again, until it had been reduced to confetti. She let the pieces go, watching them spread over the manicured lawn.

But the simple act of littering wasn't enough.

Ally found herself in motion, driven by an irresistible need for . . . destruction, it turned out. With no one around to stop her, she succumbed to the urge. She grasped the little house-shaped box on either side and lifted. Surprised at how easily the metal post below it slid out of the grass, she flipped the post so that she could grip its damp, slightly soiled butt end with both hands and swing it like she would a bat at a pitched baseball. The little house's rooftop lid flew open, and all the flyers soared out of the box and into the air, where they hung, suspended for a few beautiful seconds, before fluttering to the lawn.

Still not satisfied, Ally tried smashing the box onto the ground, but she did little damage beyond bending the metal stake; the box remained intact. At least she wasn't a home-wrecker.

She dropped the box and turned her attention to the corrugated vinyl FOR SALE sign next to her. It dangled above her, attached via metal clips to a white post designed to look like wood, but with the weather resistance of plastic. She bent her knees, trying her best to keep her balance, gripped the post toward the bottom, and attempted to lift it out of the ground like she had the box of flyers. It didn't move—too heavy, especially for a pregnant woman. She tried pushing the sign, but it didn't budge. Then she kicked it.

"Ouch," Ally said, lowering herself onto the grass and rubbing her toe. She scowled up at the sign, which waved from above, taunting her.

Eyeing her vehicle parked in the street, Ally had another idea. She got up, dusted the grass off her pants, and walked toward her car. She glanced at the house. There had been no movement either inside or outside the house and no car parked in the driveway. She shut her driver's side door and turned on the ignition. The SUV purred as she tapped the gas pedal. She looked over at the box of medals on the seat beside her. So much for her mission of goodwill.

Ally placed the car into drive and slammed on the gas. The tires took a second to grip the asphalt, but once they took hold, the car careened over the curb and up the sidewalk. She drove into the vile FOR SALE sign with the front of her car and heard the crunch of her bumper as it rammed against the post, knocking it backward. The sign sagged, but it remained stubbornly upright. Like a boxer, Ally was looking for a knockout. She put the car in reverse and backed up. Then, she pressed on the gas again, crashing into the sign and, this time, uprooting it. When she backed up, it lay flat on the lawn, now marred by deep tire tracks.

She smiled to herself.

For the first time in a long while, Ally's rage had quieted.

CHAPTER 32

BETH

The next day, the Saturday afternoon before the dedication, Beth spotted Ally the second she stepped into the main gym. Ally was teetering on a ladder, almost stumbling as she tried to plug in a string of lights to an outlet just out of reach. Almost comical if she weren't so hugely pregnant.

Students, parents, teachers, and travel-league athletes of all ages buzzed around Ally with activity and purpose, yet no one noticed the pregnant woman about to fall off a ladder.

Ohmygod.

Beth jogged over. "Hey," she said. "Gimme that."

Ally looked down, frowning. "I've got it."

"No, you don't. I've got six inches on you. Let me try."

Ally reluctantly backed down the ladder and handed over the string of lights. Beth climbed up and plugged them in. They lit up in a dazzling white display around the perimeter of the gym.

"Thanks," Ally murmured.

Beth waited a beat to take in the sight of it. *Stunning.*

She descended the ladder. "What a great turnout," she said, glancing around the space and seeing dozens of volunteers. "I don't see Noah. Is he here?"

Ally placed her hands on her hips and rolled her shoulders, like she was working out a knot in her back. "He is not," she said, her voice flat.

"OK," Beth said, sensing tension in Ally's tone. *Maybe they had a fight? Leave it alone.* "What can I do?"

Ally shook her head. "I don't know, Beth. What *can* you do?"

Beth flinched at this swipe, which seemed to come out of nowhere. She looked down at Ally's swollen belly and took a breath. Patience seemed to be in order today. The dedication and party had taken so much planning and effort, not to mention how loaded the event was for both of them. And Ally appeared ready to have this baby anytime.

"Right, I'm late—sorry. And I'm sorry Noah isn't here. But it looks like you've still got a lot of help today. And I'm here now. Put me to work."

Ally crossed her arms. "Yeah. The community came out. Because they live here and are committed to Fillmore."

Another swipe.

"What's that about? I'm here to help, just like anyone else." Beth had kept the news about UCLA to herself since first telling Jordan and then blurting it out at the team's pizza party. His reaction had stung. He hadn't been angry. Worse than that, actually: she'd hurt him. She didn't want to do the same to Ally.

"I wondered when this day would come," Ally said. "I actually thought there was a shot you'd stick around for a little while. But I guess not." Ally leveled a flat stare at her. "I saw the sign in your yard yesterday."

Beth recognized the smug, self-satisfied look in Ally's eyes.

"That was *you*?" She'd thought maybe the mess in her yard was the result of a tipsy driver or something.

Ally placed her hands on her hips and tilted her head.

Beth leaned in. "You know, the lawn has deep tire tracks all over it. I'll have to get some of it resodded."

"Yeah, I bet that's gonna hurt the curb appeal."

Beth raised her hands in defeat. She didn't have the energy for a fight when they needed to set up for this party.

"The house needs to be sold, Ally. Scott already replaced the sign and the flyers. You can't do anything about it. Not now, anyway."

"You're ditching me." Ally's hard mask crumpled. "Leaving me totally in the lurch with my league. With my *life*. I'm about to have a baby, and I don't want to be alone. I thought we were friends."

So I should stay in a town I've never wanted to live in to help you with the business you started and the child you've chosen to have—and so you won't be lonely? Beth knew better than to say any of this—or simply scream, which was what she really wanted to do. Instead, she sucked in a deep breath, and then another.

"OK," she said. They could attempt this conversation tomorrow, when Ally was no longer out of her mind. "I'm going to get some of the party supplies for tonight out of my car."

Without waiting for a response, Beth walked away, through the gym, through the double doors, and made her way to the parking lot. She looked up. Dark clouds covered the sky, making the late afternoon feel more like early evening. She heard the doors behind her *ca-chunk* open and then thunk closed. Beth didn't turn around and kept walking in the direction of her car, but heard the sound of rapid footsteps on gravel marching behind her.

Ally.

"Don't you just walk away. I'm not done talking to you."

Maybe I'm done talking to you. She picked up her pace.

Beth reached her car and whirled around. "Fine. Get it off your chest. What do you want to say?"

Ally stuck out her chin. "You"—she pointed her finger at Beth—"run away when anything gets difficult."

"Really, Ally?" Beth laughed. "The last six months have been the most difficult in my life. And I *didn't* run away." She counted off on her fingers. "I got my dad situated in long-term care, I sold the business to Bill, I figured out the will, Medicare, cleaned out the house. Jesus, Ally. It's been nothing but difficult the whole time I've been here."

A gust of wind blew through the parking lot, sending Beth's hair flying.

Ally hugged her thin cardigan to herself. "You've spent the last six months counting the days until you can get up and leave. That's the truth. That's what you do. You came home, connected with the girls, got to be a friend for a little while, and now, poof—gone."

"That's part of my job. Soccer takes me all over the country—all over the world. I'm never in one place long."

"Well, that's not really an issue anymore, is it?"

Beth's cheeks burned. "I'm taking a break. I *had* to. My dad—"

"Stop lying. You're embarrassing yourself. I know you can't play. You're done with soccer." A horrible grin spread across Ally's face. "You're too old. You're too beaten up. You've had too many concussions. No one wants you on their team anymore. You're expensive and a liability. And again, *old*."

Beth felt each truth Ally had thrown at her like they were punches from a heavyweight fighter—a heavyweight fighter who needed to come off her high horse.

"You know what? Your jealousy is really ugly. It has been for a long time." Another wind gust ripped through the parking lot. The flag flapped at the top of the newly appointed flagpole. "It's made you mean. You're a bully. Just like Morgan. Now I know where she gets it."

Ally's nostrils flared. "Leave my kid out of it. You have no right."

Beth put up her hand. "Fine. But I don't think you get it. I don't even know who you are anymore. The Ally I used to know in high school was sweet and curious and cared about people other than herself. But since then, she's been glossed over, erased."

"I *get* that you'll find any excuse to take off," Ally said. "Even fake excuses, like a team on another continent you think you want to try out for even though you haven't even been cleared to play."

Another blow.

"You're right. I'm not playing anymore." She crossed her arms. "I've been asked to coach at UCLA. Found out a week ago."

Ally's eyes widened. "And when, exactly, were you going to tell me?"

"I don't know, Ally. After the dedication? Next week? Never? Maybe because I thought you might react exactly like this."

"You're a liar. A total fraud."

"At least I know who I am." Beth sniffed back tears as she stood straighter, taking advantage of her full, imposing height. "You've got the successful job, the new man, baby on the way. Maybe you didn't leave literally, but you abandoned your old self and bought a new one. You can't just erase the past. Or what we did. It happened, no matter how much fundraising you do or how popular you are right now or how big the league is. Or organizing this stupid dedication. No matter how big a deal you think you are, you're a fake."

That shut Ally up. Heavy drops of rain pelted the graveled parking lot.

Beth crossed her arms. "The only way I would stay is if I could be honest with Jordan and tell him that we were the ones who burned down the gym."

Ally reared back. "Are you *serious*? You would give that information to a reporter who could turn around and publish that in the next day's news? Or turn us in? Our lives would be *over*."

"I'd finally be honest with my boyfriend." *My boyfriend.* It was the first time she'd defined their relationship that way, and it felt . . . accurate. The thought of giving up on their relationship made her weak. "I want to apologize to him. We didn't come forward, and his whole family suffered because of it. I know it's not totally our fault, but I need to take ownership of what we did. I'm sick of feeling guilty about this. I've tried everything—moving away, following my dreams, and now coming back, giving back to the community. I even confessed to Mr. Miller. I told him everything, but of course, it doesn't matter."

"*What?*" Ally's eyes blazed.

Beth brushed off Ally's outrage. "It doesn't matter—he doesn't even remember me on a regular basis, let alone a fire that happened twenty years ago."

Ally slowly shook her head. "If you tell Jordan, I will never speak to you again."

Beth let out a mirthless laugh. "And that's exactly what I thought you'd say. You'd rather throw away our friendship than let Jordan finally learn the truth. He deserves to know. You'd prefer that I leave forever than be embarrassed by a twenty-year-old secret."

"You think this is about me being *embarrassed?*" Ally wiped away a raindrop that had fallen onto her cheek. "I think you're forgetting that I've *been here* this whole time. I'm the one who's going to be punished. I'm the one who's going to be crucified for what we did. My whole family will suffer—my girls, Noah, my parents, even Rob's going to get shit for it. You? You still have the option to escape the consequences. While you escape to California, I'm stuck here, whether I like it or not."

The rain was coming faster now, and Beth could feel her hair getting weighed down by it. Rain pelted Ally's sweater and T-shirt where her belly extended. Beth knew it would only be a few minutes before they were both totally soaked, but she didn't care. She knew what she had to do.

"But I don't want to escape," Beth said, her words catching in her throat. "That's what I'm saying. I want to confess because I want to give up that coaching position and *stay*. That's the problem. I think I might be in love with Jordan."

CHAPTER 33

ALLY

Rain-soaked and standing on her porch, Ally paused before inserting her key into the front door lock. After her showdown in the downpour with Beth, the last thing she wanted was another confrontation.

She could use a nap. It was all she could do not to sink to the welcome mat and rest her wet head on the wooden porch floor.

She could also use some dry clothes. Thank goodness Morgan and Emily were staying with Rob this weekend. She turned the key and walked through the door.

Ally stripped off her cardigan and hung it on the coatrack, where it dripped water onto the floor. She didn't care.

Noah descended the stairs.

"I thought I heard you," he said. He lifted his eyebrows. "Whoa, kid. Stay there. I'll get you a towel."

Noah sprinted up the stairs and came back down seconds later, folded bath towel in hand. Ally kicked off her shoes and, using the railing for balance, peeled off her socks.

"Thanks," she said as Noah gave her the towel. Ally squeezed her hair dry and then blotted her face, arms, neck, and legs.

Noah watched her, a puzzled look on his face. "Did you get stuck outside?"

Walking toward the living room, Ally wrapped the damp bath towel around herself and plopped down on the couch. "Sort of."

Noah followed. "What were you doing out in the rain?"

"Beth and I had a fight in the parking lot during the dedication setup." Said like that, it sounded *so* high school.

"Like a 'meet me in the parking lot after school' kind of fight?" Noah said. "What happened?"

"I saw the 'For Sale' sign on her front lawn yesterday, and it just set me off."

Noah nodded. "Oh, that."

Ally frowned. "You've seen it?"

"I've driven by. Her dad's house is downtown, so it's sort of hard not to see it." He sat in the recliner across from the sofa. "I saw the Realtor hammering it in the lawn two days ago on my way home from school."

Ally clenched her jaw.

"So tell me what happened." Noah searched her face. "You're still mad. I can see it."

"Well, she showed up to help out before the party tonight. I just thought, you know, she was done, right? Like, she already had one foot out the door." Ally shook her head. "I think she's had one foot out the door this entire time."

"But I thought that was just Beth's thing. She's got soccer or whatever pulling her in one direction or another. Wasn't the deal always that once she got her dad settled, she'd go? Ah, but now Jordan. I bet he's complicated things for her."

Ally's throat constricted. *If he only knew.* Her head swam.

"Oh God, Noah." She looked down at her hands, her fingers still puckered and white from all that time out in the rain. "I have to tell you something."

Noah sat straighter in his chair. "What do you mean?"

"You might not want to be with me anymore after you hear it." Tears dribbled down her cheeks. "But I have no choice at this point. I have to tell you."

"Let me know what?" Noah reached out and grabbed Ally's hands. He looked at her with intent. "There's nothing that would make me not love you. Nothing."

Ally's mouth twisted, and she couldn't stop the tears from streaming down her face. She knew this wasn't true. Noah would finally see her for who she was.

She released his hands and wiped her eyes, taking a big juddering breath. "Twenty years ago, Beth and I accidentally burned down the gym and the locker rooms."

Noah blinked at her. Blinked again.

"We were trying to get back at these boys who'd made our lives hell on the soccer team. They locked us up in a closet for hours, and they weren't punished. Or not punished enough."

Noah leaned back in the chair. "Wait. I thought it was a system malfunction in the boys' locker room. The pilot light was off, and the heater blew up. It sounds like Jordan thinks it was an accident. No one knows who or what provided the spark."

"Beth and I provided the spark." Ally swallowed. "That night, we broke in to the gym and put stink bombs in Evan's, Travis's, and Kyle's lockers. They were all next to each other, and that row of lockers was right in front of, apparently, the room containing the heating system, which we didn't know. We found out later that when we set those stink bombs to go off, they ignited the pilot light and blew everything up. We were lucky to escape without getting hurt."

Noah pinched his lower lip. Ally could see him processing this information.

"I had no idea," he said finally.

"No? What about that folder in the trunk of your car?"

Noah's eyebrows knit together. "Huh?"

"The folder?" Ally shook her head. "I for sure thought you were on to me."

Noah closed his eyes. "The CD. It had old photos on it. From the newspaper staff. I'd remembered we had kept those old photos saved on CDs and pulled it for Jordan." He opened and narrowed his eyes at her. "No, I was never 'on to' you. I was just trying to help out Jordan."

Ally looked down at her feet, even further shamed for thinking Noah could be anything other than on her side.

"Why didn't you say anything?" he said. "It was an accident."

She put her hands over her mouth. They shook. "We were afraid. We were kids. And we both could only think of the immediate consequences. And there were some: Beth had so much to lose—college and scholarships and playing at a Division 1 school. I was looking at college, too, and knew it could fuck up my future. Neither of us wanted our parents to find out, or anybody at school. For all we knew, we could've gone to jail. We were so scared."

Noah's pensive expression changed, and a look of understanding came over his face. This was the moment Ally dreaded.

"And Jordan's dad took the fall." Ally could tell he was trying to remain neutral, but the combination of disgust and disappointment was almost too much for her to bear. "You let Jordan's dad take the blame for what you did."

Ally's chin trembled. She nodded and buried her face in her hands. She wept.

After letting her cry for a while, Noah let out a breath. "So why tell me all this now?" His voice was measured and in control. Ally didn't like that.

"Beth's confessing to Jordan tonight. She's telling him everything."

"A double confession. How nice."

Ally had never wanted anything more than to disappear right here, right now. She wished the couch cushions could be removed to reveal a portal to another world, like Narnia or Hogwarts or Wonderland.

Beth was right—Ally *was* jealous, but not of what Beth thought she was jealous of. Sure, Ally longed for her friend's talent and ballsiness, but even more, she'd always envied Beth's ability to escape to far-off places that had no knowledge about or interest in her past. For Beth, that had meant regularly relocating and immersing herself in cities like Chicago, Seattle, with games all over the US. Soccer transported her to China, all over Europe, Australia, Africa, South America. And now, maybe, Los Angeles. That would be far enough too.

Ally didn't have that ability to disappear. Essentially, she'd built her own prison when she got pregnant the first time at nineteen and then again at twenty-two. She loved her girls and wasn't sorry she'd had them, but she was stuck. If she wanted to survive here, the first step had been burying the old Ally. Declaring her dead.

And now, thanks to Beth, the old Ally was being resurrected.

"She says she loves him and wants to be honest with him." Her own voice sounded weak and far away. It was like someone else had taken over her mouth and formed the words for her.

"That's rich. Honesty," Noah said. "Beth wants to finally be honest with Jordan, which forces you to be honest with me."

Ally nodded. Beth's honesty had required Ally to finally own up to Noah.

"I can't even look at you right now." He stood. "You're on your own tonight. I don't want to celebrate a new gym that had to be built because you burned the old one down." Noah crossed his arms. "A situation I'm learning about for the first time today."

She hugged the towel around herself and watched him begin to walk away from her.

"I'm sorry," she said to his back. She could think of nothing else to say.

Noah spun around. He looked on the verge of tears. "I'm sure you are," he said, his voice hoarse. He sighed and ran his fingers through his hair. "You know what hurts the most?"

Ally didn't want to know.

"That you didn't trust me enough just to tell me on your own. Burning down the gym? As stupid as it was for you and Beth to set off the fire and then allow Jordan's family to suffer because of your mistake, I'm not even mad about that. Or, it wouldn't have been enough for me to not want to be with you. You were teenagers, for Christ's sake."

Ally's brow creased, confused. "What do you mean? What *are* you mad at?"

"I mean, you didn't just share something about yourself with me because you trusted me or because you loved me." Noah rubbed the back of his neck. "You're not confessing to me right now because you want to get something off your chest. You're telling me because you're about to get caught. This is nothing but self-preservation, Ally."

Her breath caught in her throat. Well, yes. He was right about that. She was in survival mode.

"But who cares about the timing?" she said. "I'm telling you now."

He placed his hands on his hips. "Would you have confessed to me at all if Beth wasn't about to go to Jordan with her story? Jordan, the reporter who could turn around and write an article about it? If you ask me, Beth's taking a huge risk here, but at least her heart's in the right place. She's doing it because it's the right thing to do."

"You don't think I have anything to risk here?" Heat rose to Ally's cheeks. "This is my *life*. It's all here, it's all in Fillmore. When the truth comes out, I lose. You know what Beth can do? She has the option to just leave. I don't. I never have. You want to know why I don't just volunteer the fact that Beth and I burned down our school gym? Because *everything I've worked for vanishes*. You think I could have built an all-girls travel league from scratch if the town knew what I had done? You think they would have ever trusted me with any responsibility? Do you think you would have even considered asking me out for that coffee a year ago?"

Ally stood. She rubbed her belly and, through her skin, felt the baby shift positions. It was such an eerie, wonderful, intimate feeling, and the anger drained away from her.

She took a step toward him. "Would you have been so willing to fall in love with me so quickly? Join our family and want to have this baby with me?"

"I don't know," Noah said. His candor cut right through her. "But if you think that part of you now is not that seventeen-year-old girl, then you're wrong. You've let that one event rule every decision you've ever made, every action you've taken. You've let it define your whole life. And that"—Noah didn't seem to want to finish his sentence—"is sad. I'm sorry for you."

He turned and grabbed his raincoat and keys.

Panic rose in her chest. "Where are you going?"

"I'm going for a drive. I need to get away from you right now."

Ouch. "Are you coming back?"

"I don't know."

He didn't pause, didn't even look at her.

As the door closed behind him, Ally fought the desperate urge to chase after him and fling herself onto his back, tackle him to the ground, force him to stay with her and take back what he said.

But he was right to be angry. If the situation were flipped and he'd been the one to hide this secret from her until he had no choice but to share, she probably couldn't have stood to be around him either.

Instead, she retreated to the couch and curled up into as much of a ball as she was able. All she knew was that she was about to become a pariah in this town, and she'd have to endure it without Noah and without Beth too. Her daughters would suffer the consequences of her actions from twenty years ago. Would they turn against her? She couldn't bear it, but she'd understand. She'd understand if they wanted nothing to do with her.

Oh God, was Noah right? Had she been defining herself by this secret this entire time? Ally believed with all her being that she'd done the opposite. By ignoring it, burying it, she'd hoped it would eventually cease to exist.

In truth, at her rotten, hidden core, this secret finally seeing the light of day was forcing her to examine who she really was. How much of her was still that scared seventeen-year-old girl? The one who just wanted everyone to like her. The one who wanted nothing more than to play soccer as much as she could before turning into an adult. The one who was humiliated by those boys and never forgot that sick feeling of utter panic, complete loss of control, as she was forced into that closet. Ally hated that girl. But that girl was still Ally.

The baby moved again, and Ally placed her hand over her stomach, feeling the sharp angle of a knee or maybe an elbow.

This baby was about ready to meet the world. What would he or she think of this flawed woman called "Mom"? This woman who'd made so many mistakes and never owned up to them until it was too late? Who'd let her secrets create a wedge between her and this poor little one's father? Who'd driven their father away because she was so in denial of who she really was? She'd tried to escape her past just like Beth had, but she didn't have anywhere to go—so she'd denied it.

And Noah was right: instead of going away, it had defined everything that followed.

She couldn't run away from the truth, punt the blame away to Beth or anyone else. She'd have to face any consequences that were coming to her.

Ally rolled onto her back, covered her face with her hands, and let out a long, mournful moan that morphed into a wail. She heaved big guttural sobs that came from somewhere deep inside her, someplace she hadn't even known existed. She sobbed until she was nothing more than quaking shoulders and shudders and hiccups. Despite her big globe of a belly, Ally felt hollowed out.

She sat up and pressed the corners of the towel to her red, swollen face. She looked around her empty house and knew then that she was very much alone.

CHAPTER 34

JORDAN

"It was me." Beth intertwined her fingers with Jordan's, like she was clinging onto a life preserver.

The pounding afternoon rainstorm had given way to a majestic fall evening. The clouds had mostly cleared, revealing a pink sky. They sat out on the front-porch steps of her dad's house, in the cool dusk air, about to go pick up his dad from Springtime and take him to the gym dedication together. Jordan had dressed up for the occasion in a sport coat, slacks, and a button-down shirt. She wore a deep-navy cocktail dress that showed off her long legs, which he appreciated. But there was something about her tonight that seemed off. Maybe she was having second thoughts about moving to California? Maybe she'd already decided there was no point in trying to make a long-distance thing work and was breaking up with him?

"What?" he asked. "What was you?"

She squeezed his hand. "The boys' locker room doors were open because I slammed them open, running to the gym after the first explosion."

Jordan's mouth fell open. A sudden coldness hit at the center of his being.

"I'm sorry," he said, blinking. "Can you repeat that?"

Beth grimaced and looked down at her feet. "I was the spark. I started the fire. The gym burned down, and I let your father take the blame."

"What—" Jordan frowned and took back his hand. "What are you *talking* about?"

"I was getting back at some boys on the team. I created what turned out to be some too-potent homemade stink bombs. Those bolt cutters? They were used to cut the locks on their lockers and then, when I ran, left behind."

Jordan felt dizzy. He bent forward on the step, cradling his head in his hand. "After all this time during my investigation, you never said a word?"

"I am now. Too late, I know. But I am now."

He straightened and tilted his head toward her. Tears had pooled in her eyes.

"Why didn't you come forward?" he said. "Back then, I mean. You were—you were just a kid."

"Probably *because* I was a kid?" She wiped her cheek with her palm, but the tears kept coming. "I was so scared. I had a full scholarship. I mean, I had *dreams* that were about to come true. I'd worked so hard. My dad was so proud of me. I didn't want to—I *couldn't* screw it up. And that would definitely have screwed it all up."

He hardened his eyes at her. "And you just let *my* dad be the scapegoat."

She nodded slowly, the tears now streaming down her cheeks.

"I'm sorry," she said. "I'm so, so sorry. If I could go back in time, I would come forward. I'd take all the blame."

"Lot of good that does me. Lot of good that does my dad—my family."

Beth winced.

Good, he thought.

"I know. I wish there was something I could do. But I knew I couldn't hide it any longer. I had to tell you."

"Really?" Jordan couldn't keep his incredulity and anger out of his voice. In that moment, she repelled him. He descended the steps and swiveled to face her. "Why tell me? Why now?"

She covered her mouth with her hand and gave him a pained stare.

Beth took in a jagged gasp of breath. "Because I'm in love with you," she managed.

His lips twitched. He felt as if he was on the verge of being sick. "I want nothing to do with you. Nothing to do with *this.*"

"Please," Beth said. "I'm sorry."

He raised his hands. "I hope I never have to see you again." He wasn't sure he meant it, but he hoped he'd hurt her. Though there was no chance in hell he could hurt her anywhere near how she'd hurt him.

And before he could take back what he said, Jordan turned away and hurried to his car.

CHAPTER 35

BETH

Beth hesitated in the lobby before stepping inside the gym and joining the party in progress. Her chest ached. She knew she'd waited too long to tell Jordan the truth, and her heart couldn't lie to him any longer, not if they were going to give their relationship a real shot. She couldn't wrap her mind around how badly the blow his rejection, his absolute revulsion toward her, had demolished her.

But she needed to put that aside for now. Beth let herself into the gym and scanned the room. One of the current high school kids pumped music from his MacBook into strategically placed speakers while the adults danced, most with a drink in their hands. Many of the attendees clustered in groups to chat or seated themselves at tables to nibble on the usual party fare of cocktail shrimp, tiny spring rolls, and cut-up vegetables on small plates.

Beth searched the gym, desperate to find Ally or Noah.

As stunning as the Fillmore High School gym was by day, the space absolutely dazzled by night. Since she'd left so abruptly that afternoon following her spat with Ally, the gym-dedication planning committee had gone even further overboard with the decorations.

They'd completely transformed the gym from a sleek, functional space for a variety of indoor athletics to a lavish venue fit for a fancy party. Windows that lined the perimeter of the upper quarter of the gym revealed the star-filled night sky. And the twinkling lights hanging below the windows danced in reflections on the polished gym floor.

Along one wall, a bartender mixed drinks and poured wine at one table, and on another stood framed articles, documents, and photos chronicling the gym in use through the decades, close-ups of the mural, the aftermath of the fire, and the slow process of reconstruction.

Many of the attendees stood in line at the buffet. At the end of the gym, on a raised portable stage, stood a podium flanked by two tables. A glittering disco ball hung from the center light fixture.

Beth wasn't interested in any of it. She had to let Ally know that she hadn't ratted her out, that her secret was still safe, but that Jordan now had enough information to exonerate his dad and blame Beth alone for the fire. If he wanted to.

Whatever he decided, Beth was fine with it. Relieved, even.

She felt she could actually pass out from the relief that she didn't have to carry around that guilt anymore.

But her heart broke all over again thinking of Jordan and how his eyes had reflected his bewilderment, confusion, and betrayal when she'd confessed to him. He didn't understand she'd done it out of love—she couldn't love Jordan or let him love her without him knowing the truth. And now he wanted nothing to do with her. The pain she'd caused him took her breath away.

Beth paused in front of one of the tables and steadied herself on a chair.

"Are you OK?" a portly older man in a tux asked. He was seated across the table, with a bottle of Yuengling and an empty paper plate in front of him.

Beth nodded and, eyeing his beer bottle, decided now was the right time for a drink. Ally had to be around here somewhere. You'd think it wouldn't be so hard to spot such a heavily pregnant woman.

She walked toward the bar and joined the line. It seemed most of Fillmore had turned out for this farce of a party. They were all ready to eat and drink and celebrate this new gym that had to be paid for and rebuilt because of her. Sure, the whole town would know the culprit wasn't Mr. Miller. They'd believe the fire was an accident. But they wouldn't know the whole truth.

Out of the corner of her eye, she saw Noah approach the table with the DJ. Noah wore a white dress shirt tucked into dark trousers, his tie already loosened. She watched as he bent down to say something to the teenage boy, nod, and then give him a thumbs-up before backing off. To Beth's surprise, he spotted her and quickly made his way over to the bar line.

"I wasn't sure you'd be here," he said. His voice rose above the volume of the music. "Have you seen Ally?"

Beth frowned. "I was about to ask you the same thing. You didn't ride together?"

Noah shook his head. "No." He placed his hands on his hips and glanced worriedly around the room. "We didn't."

It seemed improbable that Ally and Noah wouldn't have bothered to show up together to the event Ally had spent the last three-plus months planning. That would have been the cherry on top of this sham celebration. The party couldn't really begin until the two of them—the high school principal and his pregnant fiancée—walked in, hand in hand, like they were prom king and queen.

"Ally's not here?" Beth said.

Maybe that was *good*. She could seek out Ally and talk to her in peace and quiet without having to compete with the music and the drinks and the entire town. But it didn't make sense. It was completely out of character for Ally to miss this dedication. Beth knew that no matter what, Ally would have made it her priority to put on her game face and attend this thing, even if her own dress was on fire.

"Look." Noah leaned in, and Beth caught a whiff of whiskey on his breath. "If you see her, will you tell her I'll be making my remarks in a few minutes?"

She nodded, understanding that soon, from the podium, Noah intended to give Ally credit for heading up the planning committee. It would look weird for him not to. But it would also look weird for Ally to not be there to receive it. She quickly scanned the room again. No sign of her.

"Is everything OK?" Beth said as she faced Noah. But the music blared, and he'd already turned his back and started making his way to the stage. Despite not getting a response, she knew the answer—everything was *not* OK.

Beth stepped out of the bar line. She didn't want or need a drink. What she wanted most was to go home, crawl into bed, and cry herself to sleep over Jordan, who'd taken the smart road and chosen to get as far away from her as he could. How could she have been so stupid to think he would have been able to forgive her and love her after what she'd done not only to his sweet father, but to his entire family? Did she really think he would trade his love for his family for his love of *her*? Beth's cheeks burned with shame for even considering she'd deserved him. At least in a month, she'd be far away.

The music stopped. Noah set his drink on a nearby table, stepped up to the podium, and switched on the microphone. He tapped it twice and then tilted it toward his lips. "Hello, everyone."

A hush fell over the crowd. Beth watched Noah straighten his tie and affix his "high school principal" face, knowing he'd probably put these remarks off as long as he could.

It suddenly occurred to Beth that Ally could be in labor at that moment. Maybe that's why Noah seemed so upset. Her throat went dry. What if Ally was holed up somewhere—at home, in a bathroom, in her car—alone, with no way to communicate . . . and in labor? As angry as she and Ally were at each other, Beth would never want Ally's health or her baby's health in danger. She felt for her phone in her back pocket, checked it, and saw she'd received no messages from her. She gave the crowd one last scan, willing Ally to make her presence known, but from where she stood, she saw no sign of her friend.

"Thank you for coming tonight to celebrate the Fillmore community's new sports complex." Noah's hands gripped each side of the lectern. "As you know, twenty years ago this month, the high school gym burned to the ground. Some of you were around then; some of you weren't even born yet. But we were *all* affected by its absence." He paused, and the crowd seemed to cock their heads to hear him continue. "For two decades, we've shared facilities with the middle school and made do with portable locker rooms. We dreamed of one day building a new, state-of-the-art facility. And after years of raising funds, some from the state but most from generous contributions from you, the community"—Noah gestured to the crowd and then raised his fists in triumph, which was met with enthusiastic applause—"we *did* it. We've made that dream into a reality."

Beth had been honest with Mr. Miller—though, granted, he most likely hadn't remembered even an hour later—and confessed her responsibility to Jordan, but to hear Noah pumping up this audience with self-congratulatory rhetoric felt false with her in the room. She didn't want to hear it. By bearing witness to this speech, she was implicitly claiming herself a party to its message—we're all healing from this loss and celebrating this new structure that we worked hard together to have built. But she was their enemy, not their comrade. Maybe this was why Ally had stayed away. Maybe she finally couldn't lie anymore.

Movement from an exit door far to the left of the stage attracted Beth's eye.

Her breath caught. Jordan was backing in with his father in a wheelchair.

Jordan wheeled his dad toward the stage and then stopped and faced Noah, an expectant look on his face.

Noah leaned toward the mic. "I also want, on behalf of the entire town of Fillmore, to formally apologize to Mr. Miller. I know it's nowhere near enough to pay for the nightmare you endured, starting twenty years ago with that fire." Noah sucked in a breath and appeared to fight back emotion. "We know now, thanks to your son's investigation, that you were not at fault and suffered greatly. We honor you tonight and are pledging to set aside funds for the rest of your stay at Springtime."

What sounded like most of the crowd responded to this with warm applause that lifted the hairs on the back of Beth's neck.

Beth wondered if Mr. Miller understood anything that was going on. She expected he'd find the event at least confusing and possibly upsetting, but instead she watched a grin spread across his face. He reached for Jordan's hand.

She couldn't take it—this entire spectacle was incomplete. She'd confessed to both Jordan and his father, but she hadn't taken full responsibility. The only way that would happen would be to lay it bare for everyone. What did she possibly have to lose? She'd lost Jordan, probably Ally too. In a month, she wouldn't even live in Fillmore anymore. This would be her way to come clean and say goodbye.

She pushed her way through the crowd.

She needed to get to that stage.

CHAPTER 36

ALLY

Just outside the entry to the gym, Ally heard Noah speaking into the microphone. He always could rise to the occasion. No matter how hurt and betrayed he might have felt, he made sure no one knew it. But Ally could tell. Just from the sound of his voice. She heard the effort it took for him to rise above the flat inflection. He needed to rouse the crowd and project a sense of earnestness and excitement that he knew the event required. He understood his role, and he wasn't going to let anyone down. Ally needed some of that same resolve to get out there, show her face, and then leave.

Before Beth had dropped the bomb this afternoon that she would confess everything to Jordan, Ally had felt no reluctance to attend this dedication. She'd planned it, for God's sake, and she'd been looking forward to it. This occasion would mark her refusal to stagger under the weight of responsibility for that fire. She'd had enough. After all, she'd given back to the community, worked tirelessly to raise funds for the new—better, shinier—gym, which was an achievement to celebrate. What more could she possibly do? She was done.

And now here she stood, showered and changed into her floor-length, off-the-shoulder maternity number, wondering if she could even set one foot inside that new gym.

She wasn't who anyone on the other side of that door thought she was. Unlike Noah, who'd chosen to play a role for just this one night, she'd been playing one for twenty years. Probably longer than that.

She took a breath and slipped inside the door. The gym was packed with probably everyone she knew, the whole town dressed in their best to celebrate this new chapter in the book of Fillmore. The gym had been transformed by the night sky and the twinkling lights. She had to hand it to herself and the planning committee—they'd done a spectacular job.

Noah stopped talking and raised his fists in victory.

The whole gym erupted in applause. No one appeared to notice her among all the hubbub, and she relaxed slightly. OK, she could wait out the speeches, go up and say a quick thank-you if called upon, circle the room, and then make a quick exit. Fifteen, twenty minutes, tops.

And that's when she spotted Jordan wheeling in a man who only could have been his father.

Mr. Miller.

Ally hadn't seen him in person since high school, and the twenty years since had aged him, but she'd never forgotten the kindness he'd shown her all those years ago. And sure enough, she recognized that same light in his eyes today.

To anyone else, Noah might have appeared solely moved by the circumstances that had afflicted this poor man's life. Only Ally knew of the additional layer of awfulness he'd been made aware of—that not only had Mr. Miller been wrongfully accused of accidentally setting that fire, but that his own fiancée was to blame, and had never come forward. He wasn't just shaken—Ally would have bet money he was feeling shady for knowing the whole truth and not just the slice he'd presented.

She watched as Noah soldiered on, promising the township would take care of Mr. Miller for his remaining days. Once again, the community clapped their approval.

To Ally's surprise, Beth appeared from within the crowd at this moment and headed for the stage. After their argument this afternoon, Ally hadn't expected her to attend the event at all, yet here she was, marching up the ramp toward the podium.

Ally wasn't alone in her surprise. Standing beside his dad, Jordan stared, wide eyed, as Beth approached, and confusion clouded Noah's face.

As Beth tried to step past Jordan, he grabbed her wrist, stopping her before she reached the podium. She attempted to shake him off, but he held on, whispering something to her. Judging by the look on her face, Beth would not be thwarted. She shook her head, and Jordan let go, but his face betrayed his disapproval.

Beth approached the podium, and Noah raised his hands in defeat and stepped aside. Clearly, the event had gotten away from him, and he had given up.

Silence came over the room. Beth leaned into the microphone. She appeared calm and relaxed, poised, even.

"I'm going to make this short and sweet. My name is Beth Snyder, and I was part of the graduating class of 2000." Beth looked over at Jordan and then his dad, who smiled up at her. She smiled back. There were tears in her eyes. "Mr. Miller was wrongfully accused of setting the fire that burned the gym to the ground twenty years ago. He was fined, lost his job, and served probation. During this time, his community turned its back on him. He and his whole family suffered due to something that wasn't his fault."

Ally placed a protective hand on her belly.

Oh, no no no no no. She'd better not.

"We all know he wasn't there. He was home that night with his wife and children. And Jordan's investigation"—Beth faced him, a look of pride on her face—"uncovered some facts that the fire investigation didn't, namely that the doors from the locker room to the gym were unlocked and open, something the custodian, Mr. Miller, never would have done. As someone who was very good at his job, he *always* secured the building from the inside out when he left for the day."

Ally wanted to escape, but her legs wouldn't let her. She stood powerless and frozen in the back of the gym, watching as Beth prepared to reveal their terrible secret.

For twenty years, Ally had done all she could to keep it buried. Knowing how this would affect her, Morgan, Emily, her unborn baby, Noah—even her parents and Rob . . . Ally now had no choice but to prepare to own it. Own who she was at the time—a person who'd been willing to let an innocent man take the fall while she flourished. That's who she was then—and who she was now.

"No one knows who left those doors open," Beth said. "And Jordan was careful to explain that it didn't mean his father didn't make mistakes by taking it upon himself to adjust that furnace valve, and by misrepresenting his qualifications to perform that work. But from the very beginning, we missed a clear seed of doubt about his guilt, and he should never have lost his job or spent any time being grilled in a courtroom." Beth drew in a breath and steadied herself on the lectern. "I know for a fact he didn't leave the doors open. I know, because it was me. I was the one who left those doors open, because I'm the one who started the fire."

A collective gasp escaped the crowd.

"It was an accident," she said. "But I did it."

Ally's breath caught in her throat. She almost didn't think she'd heard right. Beth had said "*I* did it," not "*we* did it." Just her. Alone.

Was she letting Ally off the hook?

The flood of relief that Ally had expected to feel—the release that she'd waited a *lifetime* to feel, at no longer having to worry for herself, her livelihood, her family, her standing in the community—didn't come. Instead, she felt nothing, empty.

"It was a prank that went terribly wrong," Beth went on. "An accident. But I didn't come forward, and I let our custodian take all the blame."

Still frozen in place, Ally watched the scene continue to unfold. Noah's expression was both horrible and fascinating: a combination of shock, confusion, disbelief, and resignation. Jordan looked like he wanted to disappear. So did Beth.

The initial shocked silence from the crowd was deafening. And then Ally could make out hushed whispers.

"What the hell?"

"What did she say? Set the fire?"

"She burned it down?"

Ally watched as they all gaped at Beth, making a spectacle of her. Several whipped out their phones and began recording as if she were a crime or car accident in progress. Ally expected Beth to run from the stage. But she just stood there and took it, absorbing what they said about her. Accepted their confusion, their judgment. And she took it alone. Like always.

Ally was just going to allow this to happen? Was that what friends did to one another?

Oh, for fuck's sake.

Ally pushed her way from the back of the gym through the crowd. She walked up the ramp to the stage, and that's when Beth seemed to wake up. Her eyes widened, then narrowed.

"Get off the stage," she said through gritted teeth as Ally approached. Ally shook her head.

Beth's face twisted into anguish. "Now, Ally. I mean it!"

Ally attempted to get to the microphone, but Beth blocked her and then made a grab for her wrists.

"Stop it, Beth," Ally said above the chatter on the gym floor below her. She broke free and took the mic. "I was there too. I was there too! We both did it."

Everyone strained to listen.

Beth frowned and mouthed the word *no* to her as a last-ditch effort to put an end to this, but there was no stopping Ally now.

Ally leaned in close to the mic and spoke quickly. "We were seventeen. It was an accident. A stupid prank. I know it doesn't excuse what we did, but it might help explain—"

"Both of you can fuck off!" Jen Burford blurted from the crowd. She was the mother of Amanda, one of the girls on Morgan's travel team.

"You two should probably leave," called a concerned-looking older woman in the front.

Ally felt dizzy and off balance all of a sudden. Her cheeks grew hot. Was she going to *faint*?

Beth took her arm and peered into her eyes. "You OK?"

She wasn't, but she nodded anyway.

Noah appeared by her side, and the three of them walked off the stage together and made their way to the nearest exit.

Once outside, Ally cupped her hand over her mouth and looked up into the night sky. What had she done? In a matter of seconds, she'd destroyed everything she'd so carefully built. A whole life.

A whole *fake* life.

Noah touched her shoulder. "You should go home," he said. "I have to stay. But I think this party is pretty much over," he said with a weak laugh. "Clearing out of here as soon as possible is best for you both."

"Are you coming home?" Ally didn't bother to mask the desperate hope in her voice.

He paused, seeming to give Ally's question some thought. "Yeah," he said finally. "I'll be late, though. Don't wait up."

Well, at least it was a start.

Noah turned and walked back toward the gym.

"I wish you hadn't said anything," Beth said. Her tone was not unkind.

"I had to," Ally said. "I couldn't just let you stand up there all alone. Besides, it's the truth." She shrugged. "I know I'm going to pay for it, but I didn't have a choice. Or maybe"—she stopped, considering—"I realized I *did* have a choice, and that was to finally own up to it."

"You're a good friend," Beth said. She gave a feeble laugh. "And we are in deep shit."

"At least we're in it together." Ally reached over and hugged Beth to her.

CHAPTER 37

ALLY

"I'm Claudia. Please," the therapist said, "have a seat." She gestured toward the love seat.

Ally gingerly lowered herself onto the couch, cradling her immense stomach. It took so much time to get herself in and out of seats. This therapist better be worth it.

Claudia was tall and fortyish, with curly blonde hair that fell in waves to her broad shoulders. She adjusted her glasses and asked, "When are you due?"

Ally squinted at her. "Aren't you not supposed to ask that anymore? Isn't that an invasive question?"

The therapist lowered her eyes and offered a conciliatory smile. "You're right," she said, nodding. "A reflex. Sorry." She sat in the reading chair opposite the love seat and clasped her hands together. "What brings you to my office today?"

Ally sighed. Of course the woman had asked. Her girth couldn't have made her condition more obvious. She was just being friendly, and Ally was on the defensive. "I'm due any second," she said. "I could have this baby on this couch."

She looked up and thought she sensed a flicker of worry cross the therapist's face. "Don't worry. I'll try not to."

Claudia let out a nervous laugh.

Ally scanned the office. It was simple, almost homey, with well-worn furniture, wall-to-wall carpeting, a bookcase full of psychology books, and a coffee table in front of her with a box of Kleenex. The window looked out onto a small parking lot. She could see her car below and Beth's dad's service station off in the distance.

"My fiancé wanted me to talk with someone." She sucked in a breath. "About the fire."

Claudia nodded. "Yes, you mentioned on your intake form the circumstances around the fire at the high school."

"He said if we were going to go through with the wedding and be together—raise this baby together—that I needed to see a therapist." Ally's cheeks burned.

"And do you agree?" Claudia slid a pad of paper and a pen from the small table adjacent to her chair.

Ally looked down at her hands. Noah hadn't asked out of anger. He'd asked out of kindness. He'd asked because he said he loved her. But when they talked the morning after the dedication, Noah said he thought she was in deep denial. He wanted her to start being honest with herself, which may have been the scariest thing she'd ever been asked to do.

"Probably," she said. She tried smiling, playing it off like it was a little joke between her and the therapist. Claudia didn't smile back.

The therapist glanced down at her notes. "So it's been almost two weeks since the gym dedication, is that right?"

Is that all?

It seemed a lifetime.

"Yeah."

"Do you feel comfortable sharing what's happened over the last couple of weeks?"

Where do I begin?

"Well." Ally eyed the Kleenex, vowing not to cry within the first ten minutes of her inaugural therapy appointment. She harbored no expectations of sympathy from this woman. From anyone. "I lost almost everything."

"OK," Claudia prodded. "What do you mean by 'everything'?"

"My business, for one." Ally's stomach clenched thinking about how, one by one, mothers and fathers had removed their girls—and their yearly fees—from her beloved travel league. Not everyone, but those who wanted to pull their players and place them into neighboring townships' soccer programs did—leagues that had followed her lead and developed girls' programs of their own once they saw her league flourish. With dwindling funds, Ally was swiftly losing all the nonrefundable expenses for tournaments, leagues, practice space, and field rentals for the entire year. There was an increasing chance she'd have to file for bankruptcy and shut down the league. Or maybe she could hand it off to someone else to run. The thought made her chest ache. "I'm toxic now, and no one wants their daughter playing in the league I built from the ground up."

"That must be hard," Claudia said, writing on the pad. "To lose something you created on your own."

Ally nodded and reached for a tissue.

Just in case.

"I get it, though," Ally said. She did. If she were in their shoes, she might have pulled Morgan and Emily too. "Parents refuse to support my business, so they move their daughters to other leagues run by people who didn't burn down a high school gym and destroy a family and a decent man. And then lie about it."

"What else have you lost?" Claudia asked, pen poised on the notepad.

Ally clutched at the tissue.

"My friends are keeping their distance. No one can stand to make eye contact with me. Not even at the grocery store." Her lips twisted. "I don't blame them, but it's hard when you're a people person and no one wants anything to do with you anymore."

Ally knew the community didn't owe her a thing. Up until two weeks ago, she'd never taken responsibility for the fire, when in fact she'd benefited from the lie, essentially hiding in plain sight.

"And your family?"

This was the question Ally dreaded. She took in a deep breath.

"They're all mad at me. My parents are deeply disappointed, but at least they'll talk to me. My teenagers are another story." Ally felt the emotion welling up in her. She swallowed. "They're furious with me—understandable. I wouldn't want to be related to me right now, let alone be my kid. I think it's really sucked to be them, thanks to me, their mom."

"How are things at home?"

"The girls have—" Ally wasn't sure she could utter the words. "They're living with their dad now."

The therapist nodded in a way Ally could only describe as nonjudgmental.

Her lips quivered. "It might be permanent."

The tears flowed, and Ally dabbed her eyes and nose with the Kleenex.

"The worst part is, I understand all of it," Ally said, sniffing. She tried to regain her composure. "But it also feels like punishment. Or *more* punishment. But my heart hurts for my kids. I'm in literal pain thinking about how much time may go by before they'll talk to me again."

"Do you feel like you're being punished by coming here?"

Ally shook her head. "Noah's not trying to punish me." He loved her for who she was, flaws and all. It was almost more than she could bear. She was luckier than she probably deserved to be. "He's in my corner. *Our* corner." She patted her belly.

Claudia scribbled on the notepad.

"My younger daughter, Emily—she was caught stealing last summer. Turns out she'd been at it for a while." Ally swallowed. "I was at least able to convince her dad to encourage Emily to start talking to someone about it. So I'm not the only one in therapy these days." A tiny smile formed on her lips as she looked down at her hands. "It's been hard to be any sort of parent from the outside. But I'll take this small win. I hope she's sorting out her feelings about me too."

"You've talked a bit about your losses. And those are real losses. You're allowed to be sad about those." Claudia put the pen and notepad on the side table and sat back in her chair. "What about your friend—the soccer player?"

"*Retired* soccer player," Ally said, nodding. She grabbed a second tissue from the box on the coffee table. "Beth lost a lot, too—her boyfriend broke up with her, UCLA rescinded their offer for her to coach. She had to take her dad's house off the market. She just wanted to escape, but, ironically, the scandal forced her to stay because she had nowhere else to go."

"How has that been for you?"

Ally's cheeks reddened. "It's—how do I say?" She paused. *Wonderful* seemed not quite right and frankly insensitive to Beth's experience. But it wasn't far from the truth. She didn't know how she would have been able to stand on her own two feet without Beth. "She's like my family. She *is* family. And now neither one of us has to go through this alone. We have each other."

Beth and Noah buffered the chill the vast majority of the community offered her these days. But not everyone had turned their back. There was the generous loyalty from the families who decided to stick with Ally's travel league. The neighbors and community members who didn't drop their eyes or turn their carts around when they saw her at the grocery store or picking up dry cleaning. Even her monthly book group hadn't kicked her to the curb.

Susan Diorio, one of her parents' longtime friends, called Ally the day after the dedication to tell her that as a teenager, she'd driven drunk late one night coming home from a party and had lost control of the car and slammed into a utility pole, killing her best friend, who'd been riding in the passenger seat.

"The accident haunted me. For years after the wreck, I was looking for others to forgive me, when all that time, I needed to work on forgiving myself," Susan had said, her voice strong. "It doesn't excuse what happened. We all make mistakes. That's part of life. But it's how we *learn* from them, you know?"

Ally did know. Which was why she'd agreed to Noah's demand that she talk to a therapist. As much as it pained her to put herself out there to be picked apart, analyzed, and then put back together like a psychologically damaged humpty-dumpty, she needed to do it. She had a lot of work to do, and it needed to start from within. She'd spent far too much time seeking approval from others.

After the appointment, Ally waddled out to the parking lot. She thought about that long road she and Beth would have to navigate over the coming months, maybe years. The only way out of the mess they'd created was through. And soon, she'd welcome this child into the world, a child who needed support and guidance from day one.

Ally decided Beth would make a pretty good godmother.

CHAPTER 38

ALLY

One Year Later

Leo fussed as Ally tugged his shirt over his shock of blond—almost white—hair. At birth, his hair had been dark brown, but after a couple of months, it was slowly replaced with this spiky, light glow, like a baby version of an early-1970s David Bowie.

"There you are," Ally cooed as his face emerged from the neck of the T-shirt. His eyes widened in delight when he saw her, and when he grinned, a long string of drool escaped, dripping down his clean shirt.

"Whoops." Ally reached for a baby wipe and patted his chest. He needed to look as clean as possible, at least until company arrived.

She picked him up from the changing table and made her way to the living room to check on Beth's progress with the decorations.

Brightly colored balloons and rainbow streamers were hung behind the couch and on the walls. In the dining room, Ally noted the **HAPPY FIRST BIRTHDAY** banner now hanging over the buffet, on which stood an Elmo-themed cake with a candle in the shape of a one. Sitting on a chair at the table, Beth secured a balloon over the nozzle, released the helium, and tied it with the deftness of someone who'd done this task dozens of times before.

"What do you think? Enough balloons?" Beth asked. Leo soaked in the whole scene, a look of wonder filling his face. "Maybe I should be asking Leo that question."

Ally laughed as she watched him take in the view. "It's juuuuuust right."

She'd learned to lean in to these moments of joy this past year. And she knew how fortunate she was that she had Leo to help shine a light on those moments for her. Today was a day to celebrate with the people she loved and who loved her back.

In more ways than she could count, it had been a year of abandonment for Ally. With some notable, cherished exceptions, many of her friends, members of the community, her league parents, even Morgan and Emily had decided they could do without her.

Ally turned to the sound of the front door opening and then shutting, followed by the rustling of plastic bags.

Noah appeared in the doorway and held up multiple dripping bags of ice in triumph. Noah, too, didn't come away unscathed—for months after the dedication, some in his faculty had treated him like he was guilty by association. There were murmurs of having him replaced. But he'd stuck it out. After summer break, it had been business as usual.

"Had to hit four different places," he said, breathless. "Got the last three bags at a 7-Eleven in Wrightstown. I guess this is what we get for having his birthday party during an Eagles game."

Ally walked over and kissed Noah on the cheek. "Leo couldn't help the day he was born, could you, Leo?" She nuzzled Leo's neck, which made him squeal.

"Here, I'll take him." Noah reached for Leo. He held him up and sniffed his bottom. "I think this little man could use a change."

Ally could only smile. "Thanks." She grabbed the ice and made her way into the kitchen as Noah took Leo back to his bedroom.

"That little boy works fast," Beth said.

"I know, right? It's like clockwork: as soon as I get him changed and in his cute outfit, he decides it's time for a dump."

Ally poured the ice into the ice chest and started taking cans of soda and beer out of the refrigerator and placing them in the cooler. The entire kitchen counter was crowded with snacks and dips and salads.

"I think we're ready," Beth said, rolling the tank into the coat closet and closing the door. "Decorations are up, cake is out, snacks are out, giant hoagie is on the way—I just got a text from the deli—and Leo's awake. Now we just need guests."

Ally went through the guest list in her head. Her parents, Noah's parents, her brother and his family, one of Noah's sisters and her kids, and with Beth, Noah, Leo, and her, that was it. The sum total of all the people who wanted to spend important birthdays and holidays with her.

The league, while still little more than a shadow of its former self, was at least up and running. She could almost always go to the grocery store, the library, the gas station, and not feel a force field of stink eye anymore. But it had taken time. Claudia was helping her to be grateful to those who chose to stand by her and to give everyone else space to take their time to come around. Ally also worked on accepting that some would never come around.

Ally was thankful every day she got to wake up with Noah by her side. He'd always be Leo's father, but he had the *choice* to be Ally's husband. As a start, he'd asked for her to see a therapist, but he'd also wanted complete honesty. And no groveling. It took a while for her to find that balance. She was grateful to him. And she was sorry. But they both needed equality and balance in their relationship; otherwise they'd each become resentful of the other.

No, Ally was quite aware of how lucky she was. But she missed her girls with every fiber of her being. Every day that Morgan and Emily didn't wake up in their beds in their rooms and didn't make their lunches in her kitchen was a day that was already lacking in Ally's mind.

Sure, Rob and Jules were making do with taking over, but it wasn't easy for any of them. And it was her fault.

Beth touched Ally's shoulder. "Are Rob and the girls coming?" From the tone of her voice, it sounded like she'd been holding on to that question all day.

"I don't know." She'd invited them through Rob. But Morgan and Emily had skipped the wedding. Skipped Thanksgiving, Christmas. Morgan had asked Ally to stay away during her high school gradua- tion. So Ally did. Morgan was far angrier at her than Emily was, maybe because Emily had made a whopper of a mistake of her own by shop- lifting and owning up to it, and with the help of her therapist last year, possibly understood the visceral shame that went along with it. Ally held out small hope that maybe she would come around first, and then, after enough time, Morgan too. She desperately missed them both. Her chest tightened thinking about all that she had missed. College tours. Emily's first real girlfriend. And then three months later, their reported breakup.

In February, Morgan had announced to everyone on the planet but Ally that she intended to go to Temple on a full athletic scholarship. Ally learned from Rob, naturally, that she'd been banned from dropping Morgan off at her new dorm and attending any of her games. Not only had Morgan, for the first time in her soccer career, been placed in the humbling position of a sub, the coach didn't give her many minutes of play during games, and no time during crucial matches. Rob marveled at how this enforced humility had not only not shattered or enraged their daughter, but softened some of her sharp edges in the best way— she was finally learning, at this late date, how to be a team player. She couldn't take for granted she'd always serve as a starter. At every practice, she worked hard to earn her place on the field and be ready to make the most of those rare moments in the sun. It hurt Ally's heart to think she wasn't there to witness this remarkable shift in Morgan's maturity. Both her girls could surprise Ally in the best ways, and she hated missing out.

Every single one of these seminal moments in her daughters' lives felt like a stab wound. Sometimes she hadn't known if she'd wanted to go on. Except.

Beth.

Noah.

And, most of all, Leo.

"I'll be one of those moms who, when asked about their children, will have to say, 'I'm estranged from my daughters.' *Estranged.* I always felt sorry for those people. Now I'm one of them." Ally looked down at her hands, which a year ago were so swollen, she couldn't wear her engagement ring. "Leo is my little ray of sunshine right now." She turned toward Beth and gave a sad smile. "Third time's the charm, right?"

"They'll come around," Beth said. "They just need time."

Ally hoped she was right.

"Hellloooo!" Ally's mom called from the front door. She always just let herself in.

"Mom." Ally stood and met her mother and father in the dining room. Her dad kissed her on the cheek and handed her a large professionally wrapped box.

"Where's the birthday boy?" her mother asked, glancing around like an addict looking for her fix. Ally placed the present on the console in the living room.

"Right here," Noah said, appearing from the hallway. He walked gingerly behind Leo, who, holding the tips of Noah's fingers, was, one foot at a time, walking unsteadily toward them. Ally watched as Leo recognized his grandma and grandpa, let go of Noah's fingers, bent down onto his hands and knees on the floor, and power crawled over to them.

Ally's mother picked Leo up and hugged him to herself.

"He's not the most patient thing," Ally said as her son giggled in her mother's arms.

"Gee, I wonder where he got that trait," her dad said.

Ally forced a laugh. She needed to be on today to show her family that she was fine. But a fire smoldered in the pit of her stomach. Both Emily and Morgan were bananas over Leo, which was why she held out hope they'd make it for his first birthday today. But the ground rules had always been crystal clear: whenever they came to see him, Ally had to leave. She'd never been in a room together with Noah, Leo, Morgan, and Emily—at least, not since Leo had left the hospital. She'd spent a year respecting their space, and she thought maybe it was becoming too much to manage.

The doorbell rang, and Ally's heart leaped inside her chest. Noah opened the door to let in two delivery guys from the deli, carefully balancing an eight-foot hoagie. Noah led them to the dining room.

Beth gave Ally a look. Yeah, she may have gone a bit overboard. All this food would feed them for a week.

Noah's family and then Ally's brother and his wife and kids arrived, and everyone got drinks and munched on snacks and talked and oohed and aahed over Leo. The kids played in Ally's backyard. And Ally played her role. A part of her was enjoying herself.

Ally felt a squeeze on her shoulder. Beth. Beth, more than anyone, knew how Ally was really feeling. She knew all the complexity going on under Ally's sunny exterior.

By late afternoon, Leo had already had one meltdown. He needed his nap. They cleared a space and spread out a large plastic tablecloth on the living room floor. Ally led Leo out to the tablecloth, and Noah set down a slice of Elmo cake. He looked confused and slightly upset when they erupted into the "Happy Birthday" song, but was soon consumed with delight as they urged him to try the cake. Which he did with gusto. In seconds, he was covered with red and green and orange icing.

"Whoa, he's going to need a bath," Noah's five-year-old nephew said, to good-natured laughter. "Can I take a picture and post it on social?"

◆ ◆ ◆

The party started to wind down around five o'clock, and after hugs and kisses goodbye, Ally retreated to the kitchen and kept herself busy wrapping up hoagie leftovers and pieces of cake. Noah had wiped as much cake off Leo as he could and put him down for an overdue nap in his crib. He then took the cooler to the backyard to drain and clean.

Beth wandered in to help consolidate packages of salads and chips. They worked together quietly.

Beth spoke up first. "Good job today, Mom."

Ally looked over. "Thanks." She sniffed. "Thanks for being here."

"I'm here to stay."

"I know you are."

Headlights shone briefly through the kitchen window as a car turned into the driveway and stopped. Ally looked out to see Emily emerge from the back seat of Rob's Volvo, followed by Morgan. Each carried gift bags. She held her breath and thought her heart might burst at the sight of them.

Ally turned to her friend and draped her arm across her shoulders, watching the girls make their way across the lawn.

"They made it." Tears poured down her cheeks.

In that moment, Ally's voice was filled with optimism and hope. And she believed it.

CHAPTER 39

BETH

The next day, Beth spied Jordan before he saw her. She'd been shopping for brightly colored container plants to replace the ones that had died under her care over the summer. Although she enjoyed working in her dad's garden, she discovered there was a steep and unfortunately lethal learning curve for someone with as little experience as she had. She'd committed to keeping up the outside of the house to the best of her ability. Turned out her ability was lacking.

Jordan's attention seemed focused on the containers of mums. Beth wondered if the mums were for him or for his dad, who she knew still obsessed over his potted gardening at Springtime. Even with his decline over the year—Mr. Miller spent most of his time in the wheelchair and had lost his ability to speak—he still got such joy out of digging in the dirt.

Beth had never stopped feeling strongly pulled toward Jordan, never stopped wishing she could reconnect. Just seeing him after all this time took her breath away. She'd had such a lonely year, and she'd missed him, but she knew to squash the impulse to run to him.

Since the dedication, Beth had learned early on not to approach anyone she knew. After her public confession, most of the community understandably kept their distance. But what she hadn't predicted was how, after some time, the rejection would continue, even when simply running into an acquaintance at the grocery store or the hardware store or at Springtime. She learned to resist making eye contact and never smiled or greeted anyone first. A simple hello could elicit narrowed eyes or a turned back. She knew Jordan wouldn't say anything vicious or mean, but she also was pretty sure he wouldn't go out of his way to be gracious to the woman who'd ruined his father's life.

More and more, though, neighbors, team parents, her dad's friends started offering her a little kindness. She wasn't raking in invitations to dinner parties or anything, but occasionally, someone would ask about how her dad was getting on, how she was faring with the house, how she was holding up. Those little slices of goodwill could almost bring tears to her eyes. She hadn't asked for forgiveness—she couldn't—but some people gave it to her anyway. The constants who'd stayed by her side were her dad and Ally. And for that she felt quite lucky.

Beth decided to save Jordan the discomfort of seeing her by escaping the nursery. She could always return another time. But when she looked up again, he was no longer standing by the mums. Keeping her head down, she made a beeline toward the cash register on the way out of the store. A hand reached out and grabbed her shoulder. She spun around and was face to face with her ex-boyfriend.

"I thought that was you." Jordan's curls were cropped short. He looked fit, a flannel shirt tucked into blue jeans, and smelled like soap and potting soil. He held a small plant with sturdy green leaves.

Beth's chest, neck, and then face warmed at the sight of him. She'd avoided running into Jordan for good reason. Just taking him in now was breaking her heart all over again.

"It's me," she said, past the lump in her throat. She needed to get out of there.

"Scuse me," said a balding man who was trying to get to the cash registers. He frowned at both of them. Beth couldn't help but wonder if he was just annoyed they were in his way or if he recognized her as the Town Villain.

Jordan led Beth to the empty edge of the nursery, where there was no traffic.

"I knew sooner or later we'd run into each other," he said. He didn't sound mad, but he didn't sound like he was all that happy to see her either. "I just—" Jordan paused and looked out toward the entrance. The glass doors reflected in his brown eyes. "I don't want it to be awkward. I don't want you to avoid me. I'm still making the trek almost every week to see my dad. I assume you're just living your life. Visiting your dad at Springtime too."

Little did he know.

"I started working there," she said.

"Really?" He shook his head in disbelief, but his voice registered a note of respect. "You've really gone out of your way to lie low there, then. I haven't seen you there in a year."

"I have to." Beth shrugged. How could she tell him it was too painful to see him? That just talking to him now made her eyes water? "I think it was burning down the gym, letting someone else take the blame, and then hiding it."

Beth looked around. They were still alone in the corner of the nursery. No one paid them any attention.

Jordan looked down at his shoes. "Yeah, well, there's that."

"Other than my dad, I hardly see anyone at Springtime," she said. "I'm not working with patients. I'm on the cleaning staff, nights, while I go back to school."

He raised his head and looked at her. "You're back in school?"

"For physical therapy." A smile formed on her lips. It was the one thing she was proud of this year.

Jordan smiled back. "That's great, Beth. Truly." He glanced at the plant. "I . . . better go. My dad's waiting."

Her heart thumped. She didn't want him to go away so soon. He'd *smiled* at her, and she wanted to linger in the small, warm ray of the moment. On impulse, she reached out and grabbed his arm. He looked at her curiously.

"Can I—?" She wanted to ask if they could start over, go have that first drink together at Zeke's, get to know each other all over again. She wanted to hear about his new life in Washington now and writing for the *Post*. She wanted to tell him that she'd read every article he'd written this year and was so proud of his work. She wanted to tell him that her dad was doing well, that she'd started rebuilding her life from scratch. She wanted to tell him she still loved him.

Instead, Beth pulled her hand away and folded her arms tight across her chest. She had no right to ask him anything, let alone ask to see him.

Concern clouded his face. "What?" he said. "Can you what?"

She took a shallow breath, her hand reaching for her throat. "I'm glad to run into you. And I'm"—her voice cracked—"still so, so sorry."

Jordan's face softened, and he set the mum down onto a nearby shelf display. He took her into his arms. She practically collapsed into his chest.

"I know you're sorry, Beth," he said. "It's OK."

Beth looked up at him. "Really?"

He glanced at the ceiling as if collecting his thoughts and then gazed at her.

"Yeah. I think it's been OK for a long time." He sighed. "In fact, after letting myself be angry and hurt for a little while, I realized I missed you."

It was almost too much. He hadn't the slightest idea how much she'd missed him. Or maybe he did.

Beth couldn't weep out in the open in the garden department, so she buried her face in his flannel shirt. Jordan gathered her in his arms and kissed the top of her head. For the first time in a year, she felt safe.

She looked up at him.

"I miss holding you like this," he said. "I miss the smell of your shampoo. Our long walks and talks."

She laughed. She missed their marathon conversations too.

"I miss *us*," he said. He glanced over at the plant. "Let's drop off this mum to my dad's and grab a drink at Zeke's."

Beth wiped her eyes and nodded.

"Yes. Let's catch up."

THE END

ACKNOWLEDGMENTS

When I was a kid, soccer was everything to me. All through grade and high school, I played for fun with my friends, on travel teams, and for school. I continued to dabble in the sport through college but eventually let it go as other interests—athletic and otherwise—took its place. It wasn't until I had my daughter ten years later that I returned to soccer and joined the first of many teams of fabulous, fierce women. Playing again as a grown-up and new mom was one of the greatest gifts I gave myself. I knew it was only a matter of time before I'd write a story about a friendship born from that love of soccer and bonding with a team.

This book would never have come together without its own team. First, I must thank my awesome agent, Tina Schwartz, who championed this book and found its perfect home. She's a true literary partner, and I feel incredibly lucky to work with her. Her assistant, Joel Brigham, is an astute editor and helped me get the manuscript in shape before we pitched to publishers.

Major thanks, of course, go to the editors at Lake Union Publishing. I'm especially grateful to Melissa Valentine for seeing something special in this story and whose keen eye for character made this book into the friendship story it was always meant to be. I was also incredibly fortunate to work with genius developmental editor David Downing, who was instrumental in helping me take the book to the next level. Thanks to copyeditors Alicia and Iris, who made the prose sing, and Elyse, my proofreader, who zeroed in and helped me correct my stupid language mistakes.

I'm forever grateful to book coach Dawn Ius, who served as the manuscript's first reader and collaborator. There is no one better at coaching than Dawn. When I started writing and publishing novels, most of my progress was a direct result of her guidance. She's an extraordinary book coach and an even better friend. I'm so lucky to have her in my life.

In the novel's early stages, I worked with Elizabeth Brown and Kathryn Craft, and critique partners Jennifer Klepper and Barbara Conrey. I sent the draft to my beta readers and dear friends Kaela Parkhouse, Anne Pomerantz, Heidi Siegel, and Amy Weber. All these women generously lent their feedback to the manuscript when it was in (very) rough form.

Shout-out to former US Women's National Team member Catherine Whitehill, who shared with me a glimpse into the world of professional women's soccer and the life of a professional athlete. If anything about the professional soccer world in the book rings true, it's thanks to Catherine.

Many thanks to the academic and writing communities that ensure writers are never really alone, especially the Department of Language and Literature at Bucks County Community College and the Women's Fiction Writers Association.

I'm deeply grateful to my family. My dad planted a love of soccer in me at a young age—he was my first soccer coach. And finally, my husband, Josh, and daughter, Virginia—I don't know how I could possibly manage to do All the Things without their support and encouragement. Go Team Bruck!

ABOUT THE AUTHOR

Sarahlyn Bruck is the award-winning author of three contemporary novels: *Light of the Fire* (2024), *Daytime Drama* (2021), and *Designer You* (2018). When she's not writing, Sarahlyn moonlights as a full-time writing and literature professor at a local community college. From Northern California, she now lives in Philadelphia with her family.

For the latest book news, events, and announcements, check out her website: https://sarahlynbruck.com. Follow her on Facebook, Instagram, and Twitter: @sarahlynbruck.